Praise for The Merch:

"*THE MERCH* has a cast of magnetic characters who range from a scary socio-path to a saintly jazz drummer. Their stage is the dark underside of Charleston, the city weighed down by racial conflict and its long and bittersweet history. The time of this fascinating mystery is at the beginning of the civil rights revolution in the South. The characters talk a talk that is sizzling in its craft and intensity, sometimes in low country Gullah and sometimes in hip musician smart talk. Eldridge's entertaining dialogue carries the people and the mystery to a surprising conclusion. Robert B. Parker would have loved this book."

– Dr. Charles Israel, Professor Of English, Columbia College.

Lifetime Board Member South Carolina Academy of Authors.

"*The Merch* presents fascinating characters enmeshed in the nightlife of historic Charleston. An unsolved murder echoes through the fast paced plot, and the narrator draws the reader into arcane corners of the cityscape. Eldridge knows his subject and tells it well."

– Dr. John M. Bryan Professor of Art History, University of South Carolina

"Just completed the initial read...blew me away...the separate but connected "worlds" totally work with the strong characters...so much that I felt I personally knew a few...encompasses many genres of a novel (no 1 trick theme here)...thanks for the "edgy"cation, Jimmy...& yes, "the truth is whatever you believe it is..."

–Pat Woods

"An intriguing, suspenseful novel set in Old Charleston, SC. The local color, streets and locations, are accurate and memorable to me. This novel would make a good movie because it has a lot of action and character movement throughout the entire book. Things were mentioned that I had totally forgotten existed when living my childhood there. This creative novel is so far from the historical tourist scene presented to outsiders. The dialect is written with actual sounds heard from the native Charlestonians."

– Kathy Johnson

"Jimmy captures a Charleston known to but a few Charlestonians and virtually none of the thousands of visitors who grace her every year. He has created characters that beg to live on in future stories. I was there when the early parts of the book occurred, and heard whispers. NOW, I know. If you love REAL characters, and a good story well-told, you'll LOVE *The Merch*!"

– Skip Baker

"Having been born just before the author and living in Charleston, the people and places named are very familiar to me. The book has great characters, many twists and turns, and a surprise ending to whet the appetite of any reader who appreciates thrillers and mysteries. Having frequented The Merch around the time of the story, my interest was kept strong from beginning to end. Being familiar with the "real" characters named in the book, I kept wondering if I knew who the fictional ones were."

– William E. Stevens

This novel grabs your attention from the first words and pulls you into the dark side of Charleston—and human nature. Eldridge's narrative and dialogue are almost poetry. As the protagonist is a sax player, the reader is treated to a trip into the world of jazz, its music spilling off the page and mixing with a stew of voodoo and malice. Wonderful read.

– Jamie Hendricks, retired high school English teacher.

There is nothing like a good southern writer combined with a brilliant "who dunnit." You can smell the air and hear the wind. He takes you on a trip up and down a flute and around the marsh. Have you heard the quiet of a town after a rain? You can in this book. Miss Marple, get out of the way, there's a new boy on the block. The weaving of the layers of the social strata in the city is amazing. The descriptions take you places that you have forgotten about. NPR should have him read it. I can't wait for the next one.

– L. L. Dunbar

Eldridge writes a true image of the Charleston scene interwoven with similarities of real persons from that time. I lived there and walked the same streets as he expertly describes. What a time machine's wild ride!!!!

– Kay Howerton

What a good book "The Merch" is. I found it to be a very interesting read. It's hard to put down as it keeps you continually on the edge of your seat. Great Job!

– John Sullivan

Other Books by J. Nelson Eldridge

The Faux Finish Artist:
Decorative Paint Secrets for Aspiring Painters and Artists
By J. Nelson Eldridge

Red Tail
By J. Nelson Eldridge and Michael Easler

THE MERCH

Poking the Bear Collaborative

ISBN-13: 978-1499784480

ISBN-10: 1499784480

eBook Edition: ISBN 978-0-692-23127-2

Hard Cover Edition: 978-1-4951-3502-6

For Further Information please contact:

J. Nelson Eldridge via email: j.nelsoneldridge@gmail.com

Cover Design by Carl Miller

Colonial Lake Photograph by David Archer

Page Layout and Typesetting by Eileen Easler

This is for:

Joanne

Your love and patience make my life literally possible.

My Inspiration

Bobbie Storm, Les McEwen, Barry Clarke and Marvin Lanier

Without you four there would be no story.

My Children and Grandchildren

Jon, Elizabeth, Micah,

Tracy, Buck, Tivis, Josh, Jake, Meghan,

Jamie and Caleb

For My Family Who Have Crossed Over

My father James O. "Jim" Eldridge, 82nd Airborne, 504th PIR

My first born child Micah

My mother Thelma Nelson Eldridge

My Charleston Family

Tim, Maria, Andrew, and Patrick Hager. Tricia and David Ford

Acknowledgements

I couldn't have finished this book without the selfless enthusiastic encouragement of the following people: These retired educators have a combined total exceeding one hundred years of experience teaching thousands of students. My heartfelt thanks go to Dr. John M. Bryan, retired professor of Art History at The University of South Carolina and author of ten books on the history of art and architecture, including Princeton University, the Biltmore House and Coastal Cottages of Maine. Dr. Bryan came up with the idea of starting our fiction writers' group. Thanks to John we meet every week in the library on the USC Columbia Campus and burn through two hours like they are fifteen minutes. This group is the real deal.

Dr. Charles Israel, at whose feet I could sit for days listening like a student of Socrates, as you explain the subtleties of nuance, tone, theme and language most writers starting out spend years learning. Is, I literally hang on every word.

Jamie Hendricks, whose lifetime of dedication to his thousands of high school students gives him an insight into the creative process, and a depth of understanding which makes him, in my eyes at least, the literary equivalent of a word surgeon.

Mike Copeland, your vast knowledge of the way the world works technically, socially and biologically is a gift beyond measure, thank you for your encouragement, enlightenment, and guidance in getting the eBook formatted and uploaded. Each of these four men took my manuscript and graded it like a senior thesis. You can't put a price on that level of encouragement.

And finally, with regards to the writers group, thank you to Janette Turner Hospital, our first guest author, your insight into the world of the mechanics of writing and publishing gave me the last piece of the puzzle which enabled me to finish this novel and prepare for the next one. I took notes and not a word you shared with us went to waste.

Carl Miller, my lifelong friend, brother and fellow soul traveler, I can't thank you enough for your unselfish labor of love, in designing the cover, taking time to read the rough draft, make meticulous notes, ask the hard questions, and keeping your foot in my seat, until I got this novel finished.

To my adopted soul brother Wayne Corbett, who walked me through all things computer, and though we haven't laid eyes on each other for over forty years, we are always joined in spirit, thank you Wayne for always being there.

To my writing partner over the last four years, Michael Easler, who may be the one person on earth who knows me, better than my wife. God put us together for a reason my friend, and I live for the day we can share with the world the story we're crafting at this very moment.

And saving the best for last, my sincerest love, admiration, appreciation and deepest respect to Mary Thiedke Grady. Were it not for your firsthand spot on accurate knowledge of the subtleties details of the time period, your attention to the minute details concerning everything from which streets flooded, to the world of difference between how the county and city police operated back in the day, and the details in military protocol, not to mention your years of writing police reports, I'd still be in the research phase. Your tireless contribution to proofing the first and second draft gives this work the historical continuity the time period covered deserves. I could not have done this without you.

To each and every one of my closest friends who took the time to give me feedback on the beta versions of the manuscript.

And finally, my deepest and sincerest thank you to the African American Communities of Charleston, Columbia, Charlotte and Atlanta during those turbulent years and the ones which followed. I would not be the blessed man I am today were it not for all those hot sweat soaked years we worked, performed, protested, and lived side by side, shoulder to shoulder, and soul to soul. Your friendship, loyalty, trust, and training taught me the true meaning of honor and respect, and instilled in me a value system I wouldn't trade for all the money in the world. Thank you my dear brothers and sisters for accepting me, on so many, many levels and occasions as one of your own.

". . . with evil things God cannot be tried nor does he himself try anyone. But each one is tried by being drawn out and enticed by his own desire. Then the desire, when it has become fertile, gives birth to sin; in turn, sin, when it has been accomplished, brings forth death."

– James 1:14-15

"If you know the enemy and know yourself, you need not fear the result of a hundred battles. If you know yourself but not the enemy, for every victory gained you will also suffer a defeat. If you know neither the enemy nor yourself, you will succumb in every battle."

– Sun Tzu, The Art of War

Nothing I see in this room means anything. I have given everything I see in this room all the meaning it has for me. I do not understand anything I see in this room. These thoughts do not mean anything; they are like the things I see in this room. I am never upset for the reason I think. I am upset because I see something that is not there. I see only the past. My mind is preoccupied with past thoughts. I see nothing as it is now. My thoughts do not mean anything.

– A Course In Miracles. Lessons 1-10.

"The primary thing when you take a sword in your hands is your intention to cut the enemy, whatever the means. Whenever you parry, hit, spring, strike or touch the enemy's cutting sword, you must cut the enemy in the same movement. It is essential to attain this. If you think only of hitting, springing, striking or touching the enemy, you will not be able actually to cut him."

– Miyamoto Mushashi, The Book of Five Rings

Table of Contents

PROLOGUE

3 a.m. June 2, 1969, Columbia, South Carolina

Headlights flickered along rows of scrub pine tracing a concrete ridge cap, which topped the hill behind the parking lot. The lights flashed twice, then went out. I climbed the thirty feet of muddy bank, pulling myself up the incline one sapling at a time until I reached the edge of the pavement. The black car, next to the black wall, was all but invisible save the orange ebb and glow of two cigarettes in the front seat. I climbed in back.

"What've we got?" I said.

"Two dead soldiers," said the driver.

"OD'ed on smack cut with strychnine. We think they were targeted."

"Why?" I said.

"Both black," said the driver.

"Back in Nam they had 6% habits before coming home," said the other.

"Found both of 'em in the same gas station restroom," said the driver.

"Anything else they have in common?"

"Yeah," said the driver. "Both from Charleston. Got families involved in the hospital strike."

"That why you called me? Because I'm from Charleston?"

"We think the dealers are posing as either SDS or Weather Underground," said the driver.

"One of our UC agents needs an intro. We want you to set up a meet."

"Your guy white or black?' I said.

"White."

"He from around here?'

"Charlotte," said the driver.

"By way of Boston," said the other.

"Well, that sucks," I said.

Laughter from the front seat. "Never heard it put that way," said the driver.

"Heard 'sucks hind tit,'" said the other.

"Give it a year or two, everybody will be saying it," I said.

"Well, that sucks," laughed the driver.

Six Months Later. Same Time. Same Place.

"Your boy blew my cover," I said.

"We heard," said the driver.

"We got them anyway, thanks to you," said the other.

"My drummer told the others. They kicked me out of the band," I said.

"How'd he find out?" said the driver.

"Your dip-shit with his Boston accent showed up right before rehearsal demanding I talk to him. The drummer walked in, I told your boy I was busy; he flashed his badge."

"That was it?" said the other.

"As if it wasn't enough, when the drummer wanted to know what was going on, your idiot threatened to lock him up. Then he chewed my ass because I didn't give him top billing on the smack dealers."

"I'm... That is, we're sorry," said the driver.

"I'm kicked out of a band I spent five years building, and you're sorry? That's it? That's all you've got?"

"At least take some pride in knowing several good soldiers, granted, with problems, were spared."

"Don't confuse me with those soldiers. There's no comparison, OK? We had a deal. I did what I did to cover my own ass. So spare me the patriotic bullshit. I do what I have to do to survive." I got out of the car.

"Here," said the driver, handing me an envelope. "It's a thousand dollars. A token of our appreciation."

"Donate it to the USO," I said. "I don't want your money. I have my own fucking money." I walked around to the driver's window. "One more thing. Tell your Boston boy, he better not show his face in Charleston."

"He's no longer with the agency," said the other.

"He comes to Charleston, he'll no longer be with the human race," I said. "Tell him."

"I'll tell him," said the driver.

PART ONE

"The important thing in strategy is to suppress the enemy's useful actions, but allow his useless actions."
— Miyamoto Musashi, The Book of Five Rings

CHAPTER ONE

Present Day

We'd parked across the street, a block up from Calhoun on the right side of East Bay, as you're heading north toward the Ravenel Bridge. Jack and I sat up front; Sinclair hung out the back window tweaking a pair of binoculars.

"Jesus, Skinny, they're only twenty yards out, thirty tops," Jack said.

"My eyes ain't what they used to be," Sinclair countered. "I think I remember the big fella. We played ball in college before he got picked up by the Hawks."

"NBA to a demolition crew, quite a spread for one life," I said.

"Vietnam made Paul a long-shot. Not sure it's him, though." Sinclair leaned farther out the window. "This guy is way younger, might be his son."

"Lose the shades," Jack said. "You're about as subtle as a film crew."

"Thing is, he looks familiar, just not a hundred percent he's who I think he is. Paul was thin, played point guard forty years ago. My man right here is built like a fullback."

"Things change, people gain weight," I said.

"Speak for yourself. I'm still wearing belts I wore in high school," Sinclair squinted through the glasses.

From 8 a.m. until 10:30 the three of us watched the demolition crew gut The Merch. Six hardened black men in white, sweat-soaked T-shirts, hauled tables, chairs, bar stools, even the water-ringed desk from Roy's office, out to the parking lot where they handed them off to a guy in an Anointed Bateau Mission stake body truck. The built in fixtures would be next; followed by the walls, ceiling, duct work, wires and plumbing. My best guess was an hour before they started ripping up the floor. And fifteen minutes later they'd find Bootsy and life as I'd known it would change forever.

"Anybody talked to Barry lately?" Jack said.

"Les told me Barry's livin' large, he's a rich hermit," I said. "Been remodeling his house for twenty years. Stays home except for temple."

"How's he run a strip club from his house?"

"Everything's computers. Got his third floor studio set up like a Vegas casino security center. Cameras all over the joint feed info 24/7 to monitors all over his crib. He keeps tabs on the bar, the door, the young ladies and watches HBO and ESPN from his Lazy Boy."

"Does he still start his car by remote control?" Jack said.

"Some things will never change," I said.

During the early 60s through the mid-70s, The Merchant Seaman's Club was the best kept secret south of Virginia Beach and north of Jacksonville. Barry ran the only legitimate blackjack game in town. By legitimate, I mean Barry didn't cheat. I fronted a blue-eyed soul band called The Magnificent Seven. Between the music, gambling and women, everybody who was anybody "Perched at The Merch."

Sinclair said, "He's wearing the Yankees cap. Fifty says he's less than 13% body fat."

"How're you gonna prove a thing like that?" Jack said.

"Here," Sinclair dropped the glasses in Jack's lap. "Not a wrinkle on his face."

"I don't need Nikon's help to see twenty yards. But if it will shut you up..." Jack focused in. "He's the boss. Says superintendent on his shirt."

Sinclair retrieved the binoculars. "Yeah, you right. Can't be Paul, but I've seen him somewhere. I think he's the preacher at the church on John's Island I went to about twenty years ago. Funny, he ain't aged a bit."

"Blacks don't age like whites, because they don't worry like white people," Jack said.

"Best mind your mouth," Sinclair said.

"Josie knows black people don't stress out like white people."

"You something else. You know that? Ain't he something else, Josie?"

"You're both something else," I said. "I'm just not sure what."

"Take Skinny and me, for instance," Jack continued, "he's two years older than me; I've got four times the wrinkles."

"Because you're four times the asshole I am," Sinclair said. "Worry got nothin' to do with it. Your face feels sorry for your poor old asshole, always being left out of the conversation. Exactly like your mind. So, your face's secretly tryin' to copy your ass. Dr. Su says imitation is the sincerest form of flattery," Sinclair nudged my shoulder. "Tell 'im I'm right, Josie."

"One thing I know for sure; neither of you is *right*," I said, still focused on the crew.

"I'm right about this," Sinclair said. "Explains why when people meet old Jackie-boy here, first thing out they mouth is 'that guy looks like an asshole.'" Sinclair leaned back, lit a cigarette. "I study this stuff, you know. Shantel runs a segment on her show called 'Psychoschizmatic Sympathy Disorders.'"

"You mean psychosomatic," Jack said.

Sinclair paused, "You a doctor now?"

"Psychosomatic means talking yourself into getting sick by believing you're sick. Psychoschizmatic isn't even a word."

"You wanna bet? I recorded the show. Fifty says I'm right."

"OK, you want a piece o' me? I've got a fifty says the bar will be the first fixture they tear apart." Jack reached for his wallet.

"Anyhow, when Shantel said, that over time the way you think starts affectin' the way various body parts age, an' if your head jumps time it'll show up all over you. Then I remembered how your pitiful face is gettin' all wrinkled up like an asshole. And I started thinking 'this explains what's happenin' to Jack,' and now here you are a confrontational bias. My girl Shantel stood the truth straight up."

"Put your mouth where your money is." Jack popped the fifty between his thumb and finger.

"I'll take the stage." Sinclair peeled a bill off a roll he kept in his pocket. "The bar's made of mahogany. Nice piece of furniture. One of 'em probably wants it."

"All the more reason to take it first," Jack said.

"Watch and learn, Pucker Face."

———

No uniformed Merchant Seamen ever set foot in The Merch. In fact, no uniformed service personnel got through the front door. The only military allowed inside were Navy Jazz Band horn players in civilian clothes, who came and went with the frequency of their deployment. The name stuck because of the club's paradoxical location, next to the Longshoreman's Union Hall.

Roy Vincent was a good man, a proud former Merchant Marine, an old school, sharp dresser, who loved women, R&B and J&B Scotch. He could've named the club Roy's or Vincent's or 525 East Bay. But he wanted to placate his vanity without drawing attention to himself. Since he'd been a Merchant Seaman, he called it The Merchant Seaman's Club. He always treated me right. Himself, not so much. Night after night glasses of scotch left the water rings on his desk and put Roy in his grave.

After the truck had pulled out, four of the crew heaved the stage, still covered in filthy royal red carpet over the side of a blue dumpster. Jack held the fifty up between two fingers.

"Thank you." Sinclair snatched the note. "Shows how much you know about black people."

"What's being black got to do with anything?"

"Well, Jackie my boy, if you'd paid attention during our formative years together, been more of a student and less of an adversary, I could've shaved a full decade off your basic knowledge of the human nature learning curve. Now you're runnin' about ten years late. Still got that flip phone, don't you?"

"Wonder what they'll do with the kitchen appliances?" Jack said.

"Been gone for years," I said.

"Here's your lesson for today, what time is it?" Sinclair said.

"10:30," Jack said.

"It took two and half hours to clear everything they could carry, right? Last chair went up at break time. Back me on this, Josie. Tell him I'm right." Sinclair poked my shoulder.

Jack shook his head. "Was he always like this? Or has he gotten worse over the years?"

"You've known him longer than I have," I said.

"So, now the real work is about to start," Sinclair said. "The hammers, crowbars, all the hard-down-back-breaking, shit labor and it's an hour and a half to lunch time."

"God almighty. Josie say something before he starts explaining shit."

"What most white folks don't understand about us Brothers is, unlike you, we know how to pace ourselves. Josie understands this, don't you, Josie?"

"But then you aren't in actuality a black-black, Skinny. On the inside, I mean," Jack said.

"How you say I ain't black? My skin is black, my hair is black. My momma and daddy? Both black! My wife's black, and my kids're black, my grand babies are black, 'cept Teletha's boy, and he's more black than white."

Jack turned toward Sinclair then flipped open the front of his cell phone.

"What did I say, Josie? See that? Flip phone," Sinclair said.

Jack punched in a number. ABBA's "Dancing Queen" floated up from Sinclair's pocket. "Hear that? He's only black when he's manipulating people, inside he's actually white."

"Liking disco don't make me white," Sinclair said. "I love the Bee Gees, too. They sing like David Ruffin. Even dig me some Skynyrd now and then."

"Call me back," Jack said.

"Call you back? You're sittin' right here."

"Humor me."

Sinclair tapped his iPhone, and Jack's ring tone played "Giant Steps."

"I bet you don't even know who's playing sax," Jack said.

"Of course I know," Sinclair said.

"No, you don't. I can tell by your voice." Jack turned back around.

The foreman started walking toward us, got a call on his cell, and then changed his mind.

"It's Kenny G," Sinclair said.

"On that point! I rest my case," Jack said. "That's John Coltrane. Every black man worthy of his heritage knows Coltrane. Who's JJ Johnson?"

"JJ? Everybody knows JJ raps for Fiddy's label." Sinclair shot back.

"You're a disgrace to your race," Jack said. "I'm blacker'n you, and I'm an old white guy."

"Ring tone don't prove nothin'," Sinclair said. "My sister Clarissa's husband's got 'Dixie' for a ring tone. He rolls up in his Hummer, struts into Club Climax, gets a phone call, data-dot-dot data da-dah dot dot da-duh, everybody shuts up. When he answers, the whole place falls out."

"That is funny, you have to give him that one," I said. Jack laughed.

"Here's what I'm talking about, Cracker-Jack. Guess. Like a white dude'd guess if you was a white dude guessin'," Sinclair said. "If you were loading the furniture, how would you axe for the chairs different from a brother?"

"I'd say 'hand me another chair.'"

"Close, but no cigar. More likely you'd say, "Hey! Asshole! Don't stand there with one thumb in your mouth and one up your ass 'til somebody hollers 'Switch;' gimme another chair."

Sinclair dropped his sunglasses; he winked at me in the mirror.

"You asked me. I told you. Should've known you were setting me up." Jack smirked.

"Right!" Sinclair said. "Can't help myself. For the sake of argument ..."

Jack's eyes went to heaven. "I'm not debating with you."

"Now, since you're so black, tell me, what would a brother say?" Jack mimicked banging his head on the dash. "A brother's gonna nod once to his brother on the ground and say '*NEXT* one.' You still don't understand, do you?" Sinclair poked me. "Josie, the boy truly doesn't get it."

"It's a chair, for the love of Christ," Jack said.

"See, your condescendual attitude stifles your intellectual grasp of reality. I can't teach you nothin' without you gettin' pissed off. If you'd stop bein' such a high strung asshole and listen you might learn something from a people expert like me. Tell 'im Josie," Sinclair said.

"It's like trying to reason with a buzz saw," Jack said.

"I wish I had my voice recorder. I could sell this conversation," I said.

"One," Sinclair continued, "brothers use more mental telepathy, less bullshit. Our eyes cover ninety percent of the message in less than a second. And B, '*another*' is different from '*next*.'"

"Please. Kill me now," Jack said. "I've got a .38 in my pocket, just do me right here."

"Lemme break it down for you. *Another*, takes a tone of finality. *Another*, anticipates the end of the process with every chair, like the current chair could be the last one, unless there's *another* one. While *next*, on the other hand, means the work continues way beyond the chairs, to the next work, forever.

"White guys live to quit, they work to retire. For brothers, work never stops."

"This work will stop at the end of this day," Jack poked forward. "Even for these guys."

"Wrong! In his mind, only a white guy expects all his work to stop at some point. Then he sits on his ass or plays with toys. A brother is workin' even if he's not gettin' paid, his mind's always workin'. White guys can zone out, their minds can go blank; but us brothers'll be working' til we drop dead."

"That's the craziest line of bullshit I ever heard," Jack said. "You don't even have a job."

"Don't mean I ain't workin'. Those brothers gutting The Merch know work never stops. There'll always be a *next one* and a next one after that. Might be different, but there's always a *next*."

"It's like Dr. Phil and Al Sharpton had a baby; and hired Nancy Grace to raise it," Jack said.

"Here's a for instance," Sinclair said. "Say you come home to find some motherfucka' in bed wit your old lady, and you shoot him, but he don't die, so you gotta shoot him again. Are you going to put *another* bullet in his miserable ass or are you gonna put the *next* bullet in him?"

"I'll put another one in him, and another after that if I have too."

"My point exactly. *Another* is a white folk's term which implies finality."

"If I'm putting another bullet in him, where does *next* figure into your little scenario?" Jack said.

"Oh, *next* got nothing to do with this motherfucka', 'cause he's deader than a hammer after you put another bullet in him. Mission accomplice. *Next* pertains to the next motherfucka'. Cause your wife's so hot. Long as you're alive, there's always going to be a *next motherfucka'*." Sinclair rolled in the seat holding his sides.

"Susan is sixty-three years old."

"Josie, how old's Kela?" Sinclair said.

"She's sixty-five."

"Thank you, there's my point. You seen Christy Brinkley lately? Helen Mirren? Susan Sarandon? You guys got hot wives." Sinclair sat back in a huff. "Y'all's hand is full and you don't even know it."

"I know exactly how full my hand is, do either of you?" I said.

"You're aware he's totally mind whacked, aren't you?" Jack said to me.

"Stupid people," Sinclair said, "are so gloriously oblivious to how stupid they are. Ricky Rabbit said that."

"Did he really quote a cartoon?" Jack said.

"None so blind, huh Josie? Can't realize what he won't acknowledge."

"You used to quote Rocky and Bullwinkle," I said.

"Yeah, but that was a cartoon made for adults," Jack said.

"Truth is everywhere. Truth is whatever you believe it is." Sinclair sat up. "Change your perception of things, and the things you perceive will change. I learned that from a white cat on NPR."

"You mean ETV," Jack said.

"Same difference," Sinclair said.

"But without the pictures," I said.

"If you say so, Josie," Sinclair said. "Both owned by the same company."

Jack inhaled deeply and exhaled, blubbering his lips like a horse.

"Oh, lighten up, Cracker Jack. I ain't hung with your sorry ass in six months of Sundays. I'm just playing catch-up. I miss you, brother, you mortify easier than any human on the planet."

"Explain how your line of reasoning cost me fifty bucks."

"You think it's a coincidence? You think it was luck? He thinks it's all luck, Josie," Sinclair said.

"It is, unless you can explain it," I said.

"The stage wasn't nothin' to tear out." Sinclair plopped back against the seat. "Four pieces of three-quarter plywood nailed to some two-by-fours; fastened to the wall by a few deck screws."

"I kicked it back against the wall every Saturday," Jack said. "Should've bolted it to the floor."

Sinclair winked at me. "Monk probably tore it loose. Wallowed out the screw holes jumping up and down behind the Hammond? Remember, Josie? How Monk used to get all jacked to Jesus on acid?"

"He was one crazy son-of-a-bitch," I said.

"And his hairy arms, reminded me of a bald headed, organ playin' orangutan," Sinclair said.

"Monk could play a B3 to death," Jack said.

"Wind him up a tab or two, plunk his ass behind a set of keys then watch him go off like the crazy red Muppet drummer. What's his name?"

"Animal," Jack said.

"Yeah, An-na-mul! An-na-mul" Sinclair said. "I love that Muppet. He the one with the chain around his neck?"

"That's him." Jack rubbed his face in his hands.

"I spent those same seven years watching all y'all. Josie was more fun to watch than your sorrowful ass, but neither of y'all could hold a candle to Monk on acid."

"Bite me. Explain the fifty," Jack said.

"I'll try, but you gotta know your limits. Think he knows his limits, Josie?"

"I'll admit I don't understand Oreos like you," Jack said.

Sinclair slid over behind Jack. "Oh, my, I've offended your delicate sensibilities. You're pissed off because I was right? Again. Maybe you better call somebody, to help calm you down."

"I am not pissed off. I merely want to know how you knew," Jack said.

"You wanna phone a friend? Maybe poll the audience? Josie's sittin' right here. Maybe he can help you relax." Sinclair slid across the seat. "You think he's open to learnin' something, Josie, or is he still pissed because he lost a bet? You've been awful quiet today, brother. Something bothering you?"

The superintendent carried himself like a drill sergeant. He nodded again and I acknowledged him.

"The odds were against you because you never win bettin' against me, but you did it anyway," Sinclair said.

"Fifty bucks is nothing if it'll shut you up for a while," Jack said.

"Judge Sally says, makin' the same mistakes over and over while expecting different results is the definition of insanity.' You never learn, do you, son? You're right, I shouldn't take unfair advantage of a re-re. Now I feel bad." Sinclair laid the bill on Jack's shoulder. "Here, take your money back."

"I don't want your fucking money," Jack said. "I want you to shut the fuck up. Please."

"Come on," I said, and we got out of the truck.

CHAPTER TWO

The midday heat ricocheted off the asphalt like a fire hose blasting a driveway. We crossed East Bay Street. Laughter echoed from inside the building. When we approached the man in charge, he ignored us, yelling at his men, "Enough o' that foolishness!" A brief silence preceded another rollicking outburst; he bit his lip grinning.

"I got this," Sinclair whispered.

"Can I help you gentlemen?" The foreman said.

"Hey, Sir, how you doin'," Sinclair extended his hand. "Me and my two friends here used to work this joint years ago, and we were wonderin' if it'd be OK to take one last look around for old times' sake, maybe pick up a little memento from back in the day."

"The furniture was donated," he said, reluctantly reciprocating Sinclair's handshake, "might still be a couple chairs in the back room."

"Are you and your men from Charleston?" I said.

"Born and raised two blocks over on America Street," he said. "But I grew up in The City." I turned toward the historic district. "Not this city; New York City."

Beads of sweat glistened on his forehead. He removed his Yankees cap and wiped his face with a railroad bandana. He snapped on his gloves and started gathering scraps of splintered, nail spiked wood; tossing them into the dumpster. Sinclair walked toward the entrance, and the foreman cupped his hands around his mouth. "You got company!" He yelled. "Stop ackin' fool."

"Sounds like they're having fun," Jack said.

"All these other guys have lived on the East Side their entire lives. This is a historic day for them. You can help yourself to the chairs. Be careful. Lot of stuff flying around."

We surveyed the wreckage. The red door with the two-way porthole mirror was off its hinges and propped against the jamb. The walls were ripped and shredded, shards of paneling, wires, a few copper pipes and pieces of broken plaster clung to the lathe work.

"Hard to believe it's been forty years since you sold this place," Jack said.

Trying not to look obvious, I scanned the center of the floor for seams, but the debris was too thick. I looked at the ceiling. The electrical socket and brackets, which had supported the long gone disco ball, were still screwed to a rafter. I deliberately dropped my keys, and when I stooped down, sunlight cascading through the back door revealed my worst fear. The faint pencil thin rectangular shape was clearly visible; the parquet tiles hadn't been disturbed in forty-four years.

Sinclair traced his fingertips along the scarred back stage door, pausing over the indentations left by two patched bullet holes. Tiny blade marks, still visible under successive coats of paint, peppered the wood veneer. I stepped into our old band room, then out the side door into the entrance of the Regions Bank parking garage. When we were working, the lot next door was overgrown with weeds.

There were actually seven chairs. Three inside the dressing room and four others stacked outside on the concrete stoop. I brought the four in and repositioned them. Three on the left, three on the right, one against the end wall; the way we used to sit before we went on stage.

After a few minutes, the supervisor's orbit brought him back around to us. He was grinning this time, glancing back toward the laughter of the men inside the main room.

"Lot of history in this old building," I said.

"If you mean obscure, shadowy, dark history, then you'd be right," he said. "In fact, my uncle used to tell me stories about this place. He'd say, 'Boy, you ain't gonna believe this shit.' Montague was his name, Montague Bonneau, cooked in this establishment for twenty years. Fine upstanding gentleman; did you ever meet him, Mister…? Sorry, I didn't quite catch your name. Isaiah Bonneau is mine."

"Well, that explains everything," Sinclair said. Jack elbowed him, and the two of them looked back toward what was left of the kitchen.

Isaiah removed his gloves, and I offered my best dead fish handshake. I tried to make the greeting quick, but Isaiah Bonneau, nephew of Montague, refused to let go. In the old days, the line between civility and accountability was less defined.

"I'm sorry," I said. "I'm old school, this new politically correct environment makes me nervous. We're only here for one last visit. Thanks for your time."

Isaiah cocked his head slowly. He held the steady gaze of a black granny who knew how to manage time, motion and quiet to bring a conversation to a full halt.

"Not a problem," he said, still gripping my hand.

"I guess some consider not immediately surrendering one's name is a *non démarreur*."

"Non-starter, I get it." He looked around at the chairs, then released his grip.

"So, how far is this renovation going?" I said. "What's next?"

"I heard your first question," he said. "So, that's the question I'm going to answer first. Then I may answer the second one. Unlike some people, I do aim to be politically correct."

"I apologize, my name is Joseph. I meant no offense," I said, still holding out on my last name.

Isaiah stuffed his gloves into his hip pocket and pointed out the roof and walls. "Once all the loose stuff is out, we'll gut it. We'll rip the plaster off the concrete block, strip the ceiling down to the rafters and take the floor down to dirt." My stomach lurched. "Next . . .," he paused when a worker laughed.

Sinclair whispered to Jack, "See? What'd I tell you?"

"Oh shut up," Jack snapped.

"...we'll dig down deep into the dirt," Isaiah continued. "I take it you're familiar with dirt, Mr. Joseph?"

"Yes," I said, "I do know a thing or two about dirt."

"I figured you did." He nodded to Sinclair and Jack as they walked around behind me. "After we finish the tear out, we'll lay down a sub-base, tie in some rebar, then pour a six inch concrete slab." Isaiah put his gloves back on. "Dino's Pizza on the left, City Dry Cleaners on the right."

"Going from a nightclub to a dry cleaner," Sinclair said. "Got your work cut out for you."

"Not just a nightclub," Isaiah said. "A whites-only nightclub," Isaiah's voice gained strength with each word. "And not just a dry cleaner, but a dry cleaner for all God's children."

"Well, now, I might have to buy me some dry cleanable shirts so I, also one of God's own children, can be all emancipated and politically co-rectified." Sinclair didn't bat an eye.

"So, you're going to pour this slab right over the dirt?" Jack said.

"I get that question a lot. People ask me why a concrete slab needs a sub-base or even rebar—isn't a poured slab strong enough to support itself and the loads placed on it? The answer is yes and no."

"I understand," I said, motioning Jack and Sinclair toward the chairs.

"I believe you're beginning to," Isaiah answered.

"Grab these chairs," I told them, "this man has work to do."

They stared at the seven chairs for a few seconds, took one in each hand, and made their way toward the side door. I grabbed the last three chairs as two chainsaws fired up by the old kitchen door. The chop crew quartered the bar while four others hauled the mahogany rubble to the dumpster.

"So much for your fine piece of furniture," Jack said.

"I said they'd take stage first because the bar would take longer. Your fifty proved me right. Again."

"Still a shame for a beautiful bar to be torn apart like that," Jack said.

Before Roy converted the forty by sixty concrete block structure into a nightclub, the building had housed Baker Brothers Meat Market. The Baker family sold out to Dosher's Red & White, and the company immediately shut down the business to eliminate competition for their growing grocery store chain. I might've been the only person in Charleston who recognized the irony in this little known historical fact. Roy Vincent had converted one meat market into another.

A worker with a flat blade started scraping off the parquet tiles. Once those tiles came out, they'd have to pull up a layer of plywood nailed to 5/4 heart pine sub-flooring. I wanted to leave before the shovel clipped one of the cut marks, but Isaiah walked toward me, his head again cocked to one side. In his eyes, undisguised suspicion replaced insult.

"Joseph, man, you sure are edgy for a guy only indulging himself in a dose of nostalgia. What's your real interest in this building?"

"Just reliving some old memories," I said.

The chainsaws gave way to the screeching squawk of crowbars prying old two by fours embedded with case hardened nails from the cement block walls. Two workers donned surgical masks and climbed step ladders to pull down the suspended ceiling. Black acoustical tiles varnished by decades of nicotine crumbled, followed by a cascade of rat pellets. With each snip of a suspension strap dust and insulation swirled around buckling sections of moldy duct work.

Shovelfuls of six-inch parquet squares were tossed into a wheelbarrow and hauled to the dumpster. Each pass of the scraper erased another row of tiles, taking the scuff marks left by thousands of dancing shoes with them. At the rate they were clearing the floor, I estimated five minutes before the leading edge of the scraper snagged one side of the rectangle.

"Too dusty to stay in here without a mask." Isaiah grabbed a chair and walked out.

When the inevitable finally happened, the worker jimmied up the edges of the saw cuts. Screaming nails yanked out of the flooring gave up the ghost in creaking, moaning rips. I exited the side door so I could be out front when the last nails in the wooden rectangle finally gave way.

Jack had backed the truck up beside the dumpster and Sinclair waited by the tailgate. I hoisted my two chairs into the bed as the construction noise escalated into excited shouts.

"Ga'cious Gawd in heaven, da bun a dead skeleton up in underneath dea's board, idn't!"

"An' lookey heah!" Yelled another, "Scrong Man got him, too. See 'e got rooster claw hangin' 'round 'e throat, an' 'e gold cap tooth done fell off on 'e chest."

Isaiah dropped the chair and rushed into the building. Sinclair traded looks with Jack, I loaded the chair while both of them stared, first toward The Merch then back at me.

"What?" I barked.

Both men shook their heads. "Nothin'," they said, in unison.

We climbed into the truck, and slowly pulled away without looking back.

CHAPTER THREE

We drove to Waterfront Park, where I bought three Notorious Pigs from The Cast Iron Food Truck.

"Well, the monkey is out of the sack," Jack said.

"What kinda bullshit 'a y'all talkin' about, now?" Sinclair said between bites.

"Didn't you hear the guy screaming?" Jack said. "They found a body."

"You mean a human body?" Sinclair said.

"Hell yes! The dude was yelling something about a skeleton and 'Strong Man' and 'a rooster claw.' Made no sense to me," Jack said.

"Fool was prolly workin' without gloves. One of 'em might'a got his hand caught between a piece a floor and a joist or something, needed a saw man to cut him loose," Sinclair said. "Prolly got spooked by a cat skeleton from when one crawled underneat' the bull'din and died."

Apparently neither of them knew. All I needed to do was keep my mouth shut.

"OK. Lunch is over; it's now 12:30. Can I finish makin' my point?" Sinclair said.

"Give me a second," Jack said, screwing the cap off a flask. He took a pull on the whiskey and offered me a drink. I shook my head, and he handed it back to Sinclair.

"What's this?" Sinclair asked, sniffing the opening.

"It's bourbon."

"I'm not stupid, I know it's bourbon. What kind of bourbon?"

"Well, huh, let me check…" Jack searched under his seat, in the floor board, the glove compartment, "…best I can tell, it's the only goddamn whiskey in the truck at the moment! What the hell do you mean 'what kind is it?' Do you want a drink or not?"

"I'm just messing with you, man," Sinclair giggled, "you're easier to fool than an eighteen-year-old white chick." He poured a shot of whiskey in his cup, took a swig and passed the flask back across the seat. "The stage was simple. The bar should've been a good two hour project if anybody'd wanted it. You don't start a two hour job ninety minutes before lunch. You can bet they paced themselves with every table and chair, then tore up the stage like the DEA probing a sofa. Timed it so they could stop for lunch ten minutes early."

"Are you saying because they're black, they'd already predetermined how much work they were going to do, even before they started?"

"Basically. But them bitches work too fast," Sinclair said. "Must be working by the job instead of the hour."

"Well, it's all over now. Here's to our last 'Perch at The Merch.'" Jack lifted his flask in a toast.

"Purchased at the Merchant's." Sinclair sipped his drink.

Jack took another hit off his flask. "I knew the joint was haunted."

"Dead bodies don't haunt," Sinclair said. "Especially dead cats."

"How you figure?" Jack said.

Sinclair said. "Ghosts and spirits have different agendas. Same basic material, similar MO, but spirits have an attitude, ghosts don't give a shit. They're just lost souls wandering around like they're sleepwalking. You can't piss off a ghost, but if you start screwing around, playing games with a spirit, you better have some angelic backup from the other side."

"I found a cold spot one time, directly in front of the stage," Jack insisted. "I'd gotten a beer and was walking back to the band room, and I felt like I passed through a meat locker. Probably twenty degrees colder right where I bet they found that body."

"Celebrity Ghost Adventure," Sinclair said. "You forget this is Charleston? Every house has a haunt, cold spots, strange things rattlin' around, footsteps on the stairs, lights in the hallway, body imprints in the feather mattress. Most of these downtown churchgoers got more faith in haunts and hags than they do in Jesus. Ain't that right, Josie?" He fired up a joint, then passed it to Jack. "Josie understands all this shit, some people don't think so, but he knows. Right, Josie? Tell him about…"

"I'm telling you the place is haunted. I walked through a cold spot," Jack said.

"Jackie the spirit realm guitar picker. Gives 'Crossover Artist' a new meaning." Sinclair cackled.

"At least I'm not a Cross Dressing Artist," Jack said.

"It's called the height of fashion," Sinclair said, snapping the lapel of his sport coat. "Remember the time we all went to the Jewel Lounge, and Cleo came by our table. You remember Cleo?"

"I introduced you to Cleo."

"I still remember how red your face got when that tranny tried to tweak this fat little cheek right here," Sinclair tickled Jack's ear. "'My, my… What do we have here?' Sinclair ran his finger down Jack's face, laughed, slapped my shoulder, "Josie, your boy Jack here sunk so far down in his chair if his ass'd had teeth he would've gnawed a hole through the seat." Sinclair laughed so hard he could barely speak. "'I… I'm with him,' he stutters to Cleo and points at me."

"It was your idea to go," Jack said.

"Maybe so, didn't stop you from gettin' off watching Cleo work her mojo." Sinclair leaned over my shoulder. "'Put a spell on him, he tells Cleo. Make Skinny do some monkey tricks.' With me sittin' right there! Jack tells Cleo to put the hoodoo on me. What kind of friend'd do such a thing?"

"Those were the days," Jack said.

"Nobody'd believe us even if we tried to tell 'em," Sinclair said.

"My wife worked with the guy, selling furniture," Jack said. "His real name was Herk."

"And she didn't tell you Herky-Jerky the sofa salesman by day, was Cleo the hoodoo Queen come sundown?" Sinclair said.

"She called him a cross dressing magician. I didn't know about hoodoo like I do now."

"You got a mind like a steel trap, don't you boy?" Sinclair said. "Only yours has been left out in the rain so long it's rusted shut."

"I know what I felt," Jack said.

Sinclair shifted gears. "Listen, man, you don't want me going off on cold spots and ghosts tryin' to tell me about hoodoo, hags and haunts be like tellin' Alex about Jeopardy."

"Speaking of which, you ever conjured up an original thought?" Jack said.

"I'm tellin' you ghosts don't act like you white people think they do. And spirits ain't ghosts." Sinclair blew a smoke ring out of the window. "Ghosts hang out like this little wisp of smoke. You get the idea? They can't hurt anything or anybody. Most of 'em don't even realize they're dead. It's like they're humans trapped in some terrible cold dream with all the blankets off the bed. Sort of like you, Jack. When you're fucked up, I mean. Correct me if I'm wrong here, Josie."

Jack paused to light his own cigarette. "It was the dead of winter," he said, "besides, I'm sure the heat was on because I turned up the thermostat."

"Spirits don't haunt, they inhabit. And every spirit has a different personality, different tastes, and fetishes. Some prefer hot weather and some cold. Some like girls, others like boys, 'cause, unlike a ghost, spirits don't come in male and female. They're gen … gen … what's the word I'm looking for?"

"Gender neutral," Jack said.

"Yeah, generally neutral," Sinclair said. "Anyway, cold spots don't mean a place is haunted. You prolly caught a downdraft from the vent when the A/C kicked in. Cracks in old floorboards pull the air straight down. That's what you felt." Sinclair leaned forward. "Josie, when you were watching those guys tear out the duct work didn't you see the vent hanging over the middle of the dance floor?"

"Nooooo! I did not turn on the A/C," Jack said. "I remember pushing the thermostat up."

"You accidentally flipped the switch to cool instead of heat," Sinclair said. "Ghost-inspired cold spots ain't entirely cold, temperature wise. They're moist, clammy, like walking through one of those garden center misting machines during the summertime. Only there's always some static electricity in a ghost. Makes your arm hairs tingle and gives you wet goose bumps."

"Cutis Anserina," Jack said.

"Cute anus? What are you babbling about?" Sinclair said.

"They're called Cutis Anserina, goose bumps, it's the medical name for a reflex, which is also responsible for most fight-or-flight responses."

"Man, where you get all this medical stuff? You been living in a paramedical cosmos?"

"My father was a doctor. You couldn't ask him a simple question without getting a biology lesson. Die hard atheist, didn't believe in God, the Devil, spooks, haunts, hags, spirits, none of it. Until he came face-to-face with the Devil," Jack said.

"You're referrin' to a fiend. Satan don't make house calls. He prolly run up on an imaginary demon." Sinclair hit the joint. "Your old man drink moonshine liquor? Mix pills and wine? You can see some freaky shit, you start blendin' your poisons."

"Nope, a teetotaler. He said he saw the Devil, then he traded in his lab coat for a preacher's frock, pretty convincing, he has his own following. I'll tell you about it sometime."

"Yeah, I'd sure 'nough like to hear that story." Sinclair chuckled.

"He had a Come-to-Jesus meeting with my brother and me. We thought he'd lost his mind. Dad's conversion is why I became a guitar player. Rather be a musician than stuck in my old man's church."

"And y'all think I'm the crazy one?" Sinclair said.

"Again, all I'm saying is the body they found in The Merch proves I'm right." "You ever axe your daddy why a man's dick get hard just looking at a woman?" Sinclair roared laughing. "Bein' a doctor and a preacher who likes to talk—you prolly get one hell of a esplainational behind that question. Huh, Josie? 'At's what' I'm talking about."

"His head's definitely jumped time, you do get that. Right?" Jack said to me, "You think you know somebody."

"Yeah," I said.

Sinclair started singing a blues song. "How come you feel so right when your baby wanna go downtown?" He poked Jack in the back. "Must be da selfsame thang what makes a pastor lay his Bible down."

"Will you please stop touching me with your long, bony ass fingernail?"

"Hey, this is like old times. Minus the acid, of course. Can't find no decent acid no more, they must be too cost prohivital what with X, coke and crack everywhere. Man, I miss me some good acid. Owsley, Stanford Labs, Green Barrels; y'all remember that shit? That was some serious shit."

"You forgot weed," Jack said.

"You right, and weed. But weed is a joke. Weed is the new normal. Weed ain't dope."

"You're right. Weed ain't dope. It's an illegal Schedule 1 narcotic," Jack snapped back.

"Maybe they're tryin' to figure it out in some paralegal universe, but not here, not in the old Chuck, everybody in this town gets high on somethin'."

We all took a deep breath. Jack and Sinclair sipped their whiskey, finished off the joint and stared out the window.

"The Merchant has been gutted like a fish," Jack took another drag off his flask. "And here we sit drinking and smoking dope while the best years of our lives end up in shards, splinters, and scrap metal. The death of yet another era sinking into the quiet morass of Charleston history."

"And I'm your humidified entertainment narrator on the soul of your train."

"I've had enough for today," Jack said. "How about drop me by my car."

"Me too. I got joints to screw and bitches to smoke," Sinclair said. "Drop me by my crib, Josie?"

I drove Jack to the parking garage on Cumberland Street.

"I'll catch up later about the chairs," he said, and disappeared into the maze of cars.

Sinclair lived in his family home, passed down through five generations. The two-story, Shaker-style house sat across from Hampton Park. After I'd dropped him off, I drove around to the gazebo to think. This idea lasted all of three minutes before I did something stupid. I drove back to The Merch.

Given the circumstances, walking up on the site made more sense than drawing attention to my truck. I parked behind Wholesale Electronics, next to the

Union Hall, then jogged across the street. Two CPD cruisers, a coroner's SUV, an EMS van, blocked my view of the front entrance. A crew of HAZMAT guys were rifling through the dumpster. Isaiah Bonneau was sitting in one of the patrol cars talking to a uniform. I couldn't get a better viewing angle without being obvious, so I walked up the street toward the post office and came down the opposite sidewalk. About a hundred feet from the parking lot I froze. EMS techs were wheeling a gurney with a body bag into their van. Nobody puts a cat carcass on a stretcher.

Back in my truck I spread my files on the seat. In spite the humidity, the hot, salty offshore breeze was refreshing. I needed to clear the air of cigarette and reefer smoke. But when I rolled down the windows, a gust of wind whipped through the cab. I had to grab my notes to keep them from blowing into the street. I'd done my due diligence, by all accounts I should've been flush. I leafed through the files, replaying the events of the day; nothing jumped out at me.

Ownership of the lease had changed at least half a dozen times since I sold it. With the floor ripped up, there was no way to tell when the hole had been cut. Still, I couldn't shake the feeling something didn't add up. I needed to stay calm. Then discuss the whole situation with Kela when she got home from our beach house. I sat for five minutes racking my brain for anything I might've missed. As a precaution, I decided to call Les.

"Hel-lo, this is Les," he said.

"Hey man, this is Josie, you got a minute?"

"Josie, long see no time. What's going on, man?"

"I want to ask your advice on a hypothetical situation."

"Shoot."

"Hypothetically speaking, if some bullshit got dredged up from a past we'd all rather stayed forgotten, and a friend could be linked back to it, what would you suggest I tell him?"

"Well, speaking hypothetically, how long ago did this situation exist?"

"Forty-four years give or take."

"Any money involved?"

"No."

"Possible jail time? For your friend, I mean."

"Don't know for sure."

Thirty seconds elapsed. "Kind of late in the game for this shit, don't you agree?"

"Absolutely," I said.

"A lot of Ashley and Cooper River have flowed into the harbor."

"Enough to form the Atlantic Ocean."

"I'd tell him 'Tucker's Rules.' In order."

Tucker's Rules: If confronted deny everything. Get your story straight. Stick to your story.

"My thoughts exactly, but running it by an unbiased third party never hurts."

"Second opinions are a must these days."

"Thanks, Les."

"Anytime."

I rolled the window up, turned on the air conditioner, a cold blast hit me and a chill ran up my spine. For forty-four years I'd believed only Montague and I knew Bootsy was buried under the floor. The ceiling tear-out exposed the entire ventilation system in The Merch. Ten gauge electrical wiring ran from the breaker box to the mounting bracket supporting the mirror ball; which would have blocked any air flow from a vent. No vent ever existed in that spot. So why did Sinclair ask me if I saw an A/C vent over the "middle of the dance floor." He wasn't in the building when the workers discovered the body. How could he know the cold spot Jack walked through was centered under the light bracket?

I was pulling out of the parking lot when I saw Isaiah Bonneau in the rear-view mirror. He'd stepped out from behind the Union Hall and was copying my license plate number. I cut out across the traffic running a red light on the corner of Calhoun Street while motorists, making their way through town, slammed on brakes, waved their fists, shot me the bird, honked their horns and cursed me for a son-of-a-bitch. My palms were sweaty, I hooked a left on Alexander Street and pulled in between the Oleander bushes and the loading dock at the stage entrance of the Galliard Auditorium, to catch my breath.

I sat there with my eyes closed for about ten minutes, my heart pounding, remembering something Roy told me he'd learned while touring Japan after the war. "When conflict is inevitable, there's no dishonor in throwing the first punch," he'd said. "The samurai took it a little further, they believed you never ever draw the sword unless you draw blood. Even if you have to cut yourself as a reminder." He told me when the Irish mob machine-gunned their Italian rivals, they'd called it "preemptive self-defense by proxy."

Thirty minutes later, I was scrambling around my home office clearing off my desk. Our housekeeper, Estelle, who'd heard me rush up the back stairs, checked in on me.

"Mr. Chapman, are you alright? You look frazzled. Is something wrong?" She eyed the papers, books and legal folders I'd dumped on the floor.

"No, I mean yes, what I mean is yes and no. I mean yes, I'm alright and no, nothing's wrong."

"May I bring you something to drink before I leave?" She said.

"Sure," I replied, "a bottle of scotch from the pantry."

"Ice? A pitcher of water? Fresh glass?"

"Yes, yes, of course," I said.

I opened a new pack of legal pads and grabbed a pen before she came back carrying a tray.

"Are you sure you're OK? Do you want me to stay over until Ms. Chapman gets in?"

"No need," I said. "I'm going to be right here catching up on my writing."

"What sort of writing?" She set the tray on the coffee table. "If you don't mind my asking?"

"Not at all," I said. "I'm going to write a book."

"Oh, that's wonderful. Do you have a title? You can tell a lot about a book by its title."

"Don't have a formal title yet, but the working title is Preemptive Self Defense by Proxy."

"Lot of busy words." She put ice in a glass and measured two jiggers of scotch.

Estelle was right, my story needed a simpler title.

"How about Strike Before You're Struck? I said.

"Much better." Estelle smiled, and set the crystal glass on a crystal coaster.

PART TWO

"Go alone to places frightening to the common brand of men. Become a criminal of purpose. Be put in jail, and extricate yourself by your own wisdom."
— *Miyamoto Musashi, The Book of Five Rings*

CHAPTER FOUR

September 11, 1970

Here's what happened. The skeleton's story started forty-four years ago, on a September Friday the color of smoke. Roy Vincent called asking me to stop by The Merch after lunch to review a few budget items. I knew what that meant. The numbers were off and Freddie May, the club manager, was blaming the band. I'd a signed contract with Roy which included my salary as sax player plus a ten percent bump for managing, which was none of Freddie's business and, therefore, not open for discussion. He still thought everybody in the group was overpaid, especially me. After lunch was fine, I wouldn't have shared a bag of chips with Freddie because I don't eat with people I don't like.

They'd tracked me to Jack's house out at Folly Beach. The small cedar siding cottage sat on eight-foot pilings nestled in a grove of live oaks. Wax myrtles, wild azaleas, and bay bushes hid the underside from the street, giving it the look of a tree house. Jack's small cabinet shop occupied half the footprint while the other side served as a carport. His family had owned it since the late forties. The crust side of the pie-shaped lot backed up to a deep-water creek that snaked through the marsh grass from the Folly River, which skirts the backside of Folly Island. Jack played guitar in the band.

I'd parked my Caspian Blue 1965 Thunderbird under the house to avoid a flock of black birds screaming in the trees. The driver's side window, which had been working intermittently because of a short in the switch, was stuck open halfway up, which was bad enough. And I sure as hell didn't want to add bird poop all over my car to my maintenance list.

Jack and I were taking a beer break from working out the horn parts for "Sticks and Stones" off the *Mad Dogs and Englishmen* album. The tide was changing from low to high as we walked out on the porch to watch a pair of bottle-nosed dolphins cruise the tidal currents. They were porpoising around the floating dock searching for minnows.

Low-lying fog hugged the surface of the creek and brown pelicans sailed overhead in a silent V-formation while river turtles sat motionless on a dead tree trunk half-submerged in the creek. Except for the dock, the view was so ancient and primeval a feeding brontosaurus wouldn't have looked out of place. When we walked back inside, a flock of seagulls landed at the far end of the dock rail and immediately shit all over it.

"Sky rats," Jack yelled from the screen porch. But, the seagulls, to quote a Gullah story, 'just laughed at him and went on about their business.' "Seagulls are nature's assholes," he said. "They've got the entire marsh, plus the whole Atlantic Ocean they could shit on, and they pick my dock."

"They must like you." I said, "Take it as a compliment."

"That why you parked under the house? To keep the blackbirds from complimenting your car?"

I paid Jack thirty bucks, out of my pocket, for each finished arrangement; he furnished the beer and scenery. It was one way we shared the wealth. When the phone rang, Jack's wife, Susan, took the call.

"That was Roy," she said. "He didn't want to interrupt you guys while you were working. He wants Josie to stop by The Merch after lunch, he wants to discuss budget items with him and Freddie May."

I thought it odd for Roy to relay a message through Susan, especially one about money, when he knew I was right there. Roy was cool, though. I figured if he left the message with Susan rather than asking to speak to me, then Freddie was probably standing right beside him. We never discussed money over the phone, especially with Jack and Susan close enough to listen in. Leaving a message with the word "budget" in it, instead of interrupting work in progress, was unusual but not completely out of character. It would be a way to buy time and give me a heads up without causing suspicion.

"Freddie complaining about how much y'all are making again?" Susan said.

"Dumb ass can't see how much you save the club. Doing all that paper work and tax stuff. Hell, managing a seven piece band takes time," Jack said.

"Wish Roy would stand up to him." Susan walked back inside.

"Roy thinks Freddie's muscles are impressive," I said. "That's all Freddie is to him. Besides, my deal is with Roy. I know it, he knows it and soon, Freddie is going to know it. But for right now, I have to play along."

"There's a lot of speculation as to exactly what that deal entails," Jack said.

"What do you mean'?" I asked, "Nobody knows but you, Roy, Montague and me."

Jack looked toward the kitchen, scratched his neck and lowered his voice.

"Well, not exactly. I kind of slipped up and said something to Susan."

"You told Susan?" I asked, lowering my voice as well.

"Hell's bells, Josie. I couldn't keep something like that from my wife, man. It's that job security thing; women worry about that shit." When I didn't say anything, he looked toward the kitchen then back at me.

"Who else?" I said.

"You, of all people, ought to understand about job security."

"Who else knows about my deal with Roy?"

"Just Monk."

"Monk knows?"

"Yeah, and Sinclair, but that's all, man, I swear."

"How the hell did they find out? For God's sake Jack, I trusted you, man. If Freddie finds out I'm trying to buy the club, the shit is going to hit the fan." I was trying to keep my voice low so Susan wouldn't hear me getting on Jack's ass.

"Sinclair overheard Montague and me talking and said something to Monk."

I took another sip of my beer and shook my head. There was nothing I could do about it now except hope Monk and Sinclair had sense enough to keep their mouths shut.

"Well, you know what they say, Jackie, my boy," I said, picking up his guitar and strumming it, "speculation's good for the soul."

By the time I left Jack's house, it was almost three o'clock. The moisture permeating the air all morning had settled into a fine mist that rolled off the salt marsh on the tidal breeze and floated over Folly Road like a smoke machine at a rock concert. For three weeks, low hanging clouds had drenched the Lowcountry when not actually raining on it. This intense saturation, on the heels of an unusually hot summer, gave the marsh grass a surreal iridescent hue that Jack called Electric Kelly Green. Daytime highs in the low seventies followed by near freezing temperatures at night, wreaked havoc on the crocus, pansies and rose bushes in the yards lining either side of the road. I was listening to the local AM jazz program on WPAL when the DJ on the radio interrupted with a weather update.

"Ahhhhhh, I can see you out there, you're lookin' GOOD. Shake hands with an extended hurricane season, brothers and sisters," he said, "this is High Cotton, your local weather guru and turnip patch prevaricator, here to tell y'all that a tropical depression, betwixt here and Bermuda has organized herself into a tropical storm named Sub-Tropical Storm Three by the National Weather Service, but we gone call her Eunice after my main squeeze, cause she PO-WER FULL and she'll sho' nuff blow a man down Ahh Sookey Sookey. And dat ain't all, little chil'rin, they's another low pressure system stalled out over the southeast, producing one hundred percent humidity, as if somebody have to tell us, cause I know y'all all wet, jus' like me, so watch out fo' shallow coastal flooding right on through this evenin' and steer clear of that gully wash near the bus stop at the foot of Calhoun Screet. We don't need no mo' o' y'all washed out to sea, we done had enough o' that foolishness. If...you catch my drift."

The lights at the intersection of Folly Road and Maybank Highway were flashing red, signaling the drawbridge was about to go up. I put the Thunderbird in park and couldn't help wondering if Roy's phone call had anything to do with Jack spilling the beans about our deal. Even if Freddie got suspicious, he couldn't stop a deal that had been seven years in the making. Raising and lowering the bridge was a ten-minute wait at best. I turned the engine off and thought about everything that'd happened since the day Roy and I met.

———

The year was 1963, I was sixteen, it was Labor Day weekend and the legal age for drinking was eighteen. With Monday being a holiday the beach music crowd was unusually large and unusually drunk. Six of us from the St. Andrews High School Marching Band had formed a top 40 rock & roll group called The Vistas. We played the Folly Beach Ocean Plaza Pier every Sunday afternoon to an admiring sea of young girls in bikinis. Life was good.

We'd learned from gigs at the NCO Club, The Enlisted Men's Club and The Am Vets to keep our eyes peeled for any unusual activity in the audience. I'd noticed this older man standing alone in the back corner and wondered why he was so interested in a band playing Wooly Bully for a bunch of screaming teenagers. When The Vistas took a break, Roy walked over to the edge of stage, calling me down to eye level with his big grin.

"Boy, you need some hands-on, professional experience if you're going to learn to play that horn right," he said. "You should drop by my club sometime and sit in with a real band." As I listened, he painted a full color picture of the house band at The Merch.

"All the horn players are Navy jazz band musicians," he said. "They'll think it's cool having a kid on stage. They play Stax-Volt, Chess and Atlantic soul music, you know, Sam and Dave, Otis Redding, Isley Brothers, Solomon Burke. I call it dirty Motown, black music for white people with plenty of room for horns. You'll dig it; it'll be great training for you working with cats who can really play."

I immediately wanted to accept Roy's offer but a crowd of young girls fooling around by the corner of the stage, distracted me.

"I'm not offering you a job kid, just an opportunity to see the real world of music." Roy said. "You think these little girls like you now, wait until they grow up a little and you really learn how to play, that's all I'm saying."

I couldn't think of anything cool to say, so I said, "OK."

After The Vistas packed up, Roy drove me to Robinson's Cafeteria and treated me to the best fried seafood platter in Charleston. Over shrimp, scallops, oysters, crab cakes and flounder, we discussed everything from tone, technique, and stage presence, to the differences in the musical styles of Be-Bop and Hard Bop players like Charlie Parker, John Coltrane and Roy's all time personal favorite, Ike Quebec.

From Robinson's, we went directly to The Merch where I spent the rest of the night playing beside the best musicians in Charleston. From then on, Roy was at the beach every Sunday. Wearing one of his many Hawaiian shirts, elbows on the sill of the outside wall, breeze blowing his silver hair, beer in one hand, pipe in the other, he watched and listened. Every Sunday, after Robinson's, I was back in school at The Merch learning the ins and outs of the private club business. At the end of the night, after the other musicians were gone, Roy would slip me a twenty and ask, "What's Rule Number One?"

"Nothing is free," I'd answer.

Roy's wife died somewhere along the way, and while The Merch gave him something to do, it obviously wasn't enough. He had no children and he knew I had no father, so he took me under his wing determined to help me become a seasoned professional.

By my eithteen birthday, I was playing at The Merch six nights a week, and Roy was drinking a fifth of scotch a night. He usually stayed in his office for the first three sets, only coming out after midnight when the crowd had thinned. From the stage, I watched him move through the smoky haze to the same back corner booth where he sat alone, alternating between his pipe and a glass of J&B on the rocks. His wrinkled smile glowing in the light of a green webbed bar candle. Whenever I took a solo, he'd lift his glass in a toast.

Roy had impeccable taste. Every night he arrived at the club wearing a different pastel Gant shirt, rep tie, khaki slacks and spit-shined Weejuns; his navy blue blazer slung over one shoulder, the top of a madras breast pocket bi-fold extended just above the lip of his left hip pocket. One night, I asked him why he stayed so dressed up.

"It's about respect, Josie," he said. "Any man worth his salt owes it to the women in his life to look as good as he possibly can at all times."

I thought that was a strange thing to say. To my knowledge, there hadn't been a woman in Roy's life since his wife died. Two years passed, then one night during a break he called me into his office.

"I've been listening to you progress as a player for a little over two years now," he said. "I think you're ready for the next level."

"What's that supposed to mean?"

"The Tams are looking for a sax player to take on the road."

"The Tams are all-black. I'm a white boy. Why would they want me?"

"Their manager is white; he's been in here to hear you play. He called me to see if you might be interested in the job. They play nothing but white nightclubs and fraternity parties. A white boy in the band will ease some of the tension in these turbulent times. I think it's a good idea; you'd learn a lot. Besides, a few years on the road with a real soul band will be good preparation," he said.

"Preparation for what?"

Roy came out from behind his desk and closed the door. Back in his seat, he removed two glasses and a bottle of J&B from the lower desk drawer.

"How'd you like to own this place someday?" He poured us both a drink.

"By someday, I mean in several years, when you're ready to settle down."

"There's nothing I'd rather do," I said.

"The Merch will cost you fifty-five thousand dollars."

"I'll never make that kind of money going out on the road."

"You'll make the money; the group pays for your meals and lodging. You'll have no expenses except incidentals like tooth paste, shaving cream and dry-cleaning.

But trust me, and this is from God's mouth to your ears, if you have a weakness, the road will find it." He threw back the scotch in two gulps. "And the weakness will take the money. Do you understand what I'm saying?" I nodded and downed my own glass.

"If you can handle money on the road, you can handle owning this club."

"You're serious," I said.

"Dead serious."

"I don't know what to say."

"Just say, OK."

"OK."

He clinked his glass against mine.

"You leave in a month so start getting your affairs in order."

"So, this is the end?" I used the bottom of the wet glass to add my own water rings to the collection already on the desk.

"The end? What the hell are you talking about?" He poured another for each of us. "Boy, this is just the beginning, if you're careful, if you keep your chops up, don't practice drunk or high, save every dime you can, and stay in touch. I might cut you an even better deal if I decide to retire early."

That night somebody stole my horn. I suspected a junkie trumpet player who was sitting in with us, but I could never prove it. The next day Roy took me to Carolina Instrument Service and paid Kooky Dave Collis $750 dollars cash for a brand new Selmer Mark VI tenor sax.

"Forget about that piece of crap you've been playing," he said, handing me the new horn. "I ordered this for you a month ago. Just my way of paying you back for all those twenty-dollar nights back in the early days. Besides, you can't go on the road with a student line Conn, they'll laugh you off the stage."

"The horn doesn't make the player," I said.

"True, but show up with an axe like this and respect is instantaneous."

"I'm speechless, Roy," I mumbled, tracing my fingers over the elaborate scroll-work orchid etched in the honey gold lacquered bell. "It's beautiful."

"You don't have to say anything. Life is too short to worry about the things money can buy. Those things can be replaced easily," he said. "If you've got to worry, worry about holding onto the things money can't buy. This is America, son, you can always find a way to get more money. Getting money is easy; keeping it's the hard part." Then Roy did something he had never done. He hugged me.

"Play the music, son," he whispered, "the money will come."

CHAPTER FIVE

When the drawbridge locked down, the light turned green. I started the car, toggled the driver's side window switch, but the glass still wouldn't move. A southwest breeze blew down the Wappoo Cut from the harbor, filling the Thunderbird's interior with the tart, greasy petroleum stench from the bilge backwash of the merchant vessels, warships and tugboats. Ships had prowled Charleston's waterways for hundreds of years, but it took diesel fumes to anoint the salt air with the aroma of progress. From atop the bridge I glanced across the harbor toward the mansions lining the Battery. No matter which route I took downtown, driving through flooded streets was inevitable.

Viewed from that height and distance, Charleston appeared diminutive and cordial, a thin line of structural design tracing the water's edge. Church steeples, situated deeper in the landscape, punctuated a skyline which stretched inland from the harbor across the peninsula toward the Cooper River conferring solemnity on the illusion, concealing a big city cold streak packed beneath a layer of genteel snobbery.

Whenever rain accompanied a mid-afternoon high tide, I tried to avoid Calhoun Street, much of which would be under water. Most people (even the locals) couldn't find their way from the Ashley River Bridge to East Bay if they had to stay off Calhoun. My original plan was Cannon Street to King, left on King, right on Columbus and straight across America to East Bay. But a line of cars, backed up almost to the bridge, made me change my mind.

I hooked a right on Lockwood Boulevard, hung a right on Chisolm, another on Tradd, figuring Murray Drive along the Battery would be a safer route, since it never floods. The gated mansions displayed their elegant French, Spanish and English architecture. Huge columns supported metal roofs painted red, green and silver, interspersed with verdigris copper and terracotta tile. Front elevations of plantation brick, brightly colored stucco and wood siding back dropped waterlogged shrubbery. Three-hundred-year old live oaks dripped with Spanish moss so soggy clumps of the stuff had formed gray puddles at the base of the tree trunks. Half the formal gardens were ankle deep in standing water with rye grass so high some lawns looked more like rice paddies than courtyards. It was par for the course in Charleston, where nothing, least of all the weather, was predictable.

At Battery Point, I doubled back to East Bay.

Further up, huge cranes unloaded cargo containers from freighters moored at the State Ports Authority. Like giant metallic wasps building a steel nest, they loaded the freighters oblivious to the weather. A Paradise Food Service truck plowed through the water soaking every car within ten feet of its wake, including mine. Even driving slowly, with the sun visor blocking most of the open window, the spray drenched the left side of my face and hair, leaving muddy spots on the upholstery and my clothes. The driver of the truck looked right into my eyes and laughed with the glee of an idiot child in a bumper car.

Thunderheads hung over the harbor, where Montague alleged Strong Man has resided since the early 1700s. Strong Man is the Gullah nickname given a West African snake god formerly known as Python to his original Senegambia subjects. Legend holds this spirit is no ordinary demon, but one of an elite class of fallen angels who operate independently of celestial law, aligned neither with Christ nor Satan.

These arguments between Montague and Sinclair went on for hours, often toe to toe, screaming at each other in some unknown tongue, each one thoroughly convinced of the most ludicrous absurdity.

"Jest like dat Royal Prince of Persia, He gotcha," Montague had wailed. "Scrong Man done put 'e personal hag' on yo' slave drivin' ass, das why yo' Lordin' over da brethren."

"All I said was clean up da dam' kitchin, an' you have t' go startin' all dat fool-ishness!" Sinclair retaliated, pointing his finger in the old man's face.

According to Montague, Strong Man manipulated the actions of certain humans to exercise his control over each of Charleston's four major divisive groups:

racism, politics, poverty and harlotry. Montague was convinced that Sinclair, in particular, was one of them. This, Montague said, explained Sinclair's callous disregard for his fellow black employees in general and Montague himself in particular.

The way I understood it back then, Strong Man's historical role was protecting certain black ivory successors and their benefactors. Black Ivory refers to slaves. In particular those brought up from the sugar plantations of the West Indian Islands, specifically Barbados, who were relocated by Spanish merchants, to the rice fields of Charleston. From the time slaves began working the plantations, through the opening volleys of the Civil War, right up to the present day, Strong Man has periodically revealed himself to a select group of humans who form a spiritual pecking order. This hierarchy's sole purpose, is keeping Holy City sinners in balance. Any humans seeking to upset this balance are divided against themselves by the actions of the faithful until would be usurpers get the punishment they deserve. I understand it differently now. The unspoken rule is simple: Disrespect the spirits in Charleston at your own risk.

I didn't buy into all that Sea Island mumbo-jumbo. To me, the massive black cloud hanging over the harbor simply meant more bad weather blowing in off the ocean. A flash of red sheet lightning fired up the inside a cloud as thunder rolled over the harbor and reverberated through my car. The fresh, clean smell of ozone wafted over the city, washing away the industrial stink.

I wanted to watch the light show, but I had to pay attention. Trucks and cars were stalling out up and down East Bay Street. '65 Thunderbirds have a ground clearance of eight inches, at best, and though mine displaced the water with the tenacity of a tank, I knew the engine was getting wet. My brakes were slipping, water was gurgling over the bumper up to the headlights, the beams illuminating the waves; giving the water a sickening aura of olive drab and puke yellow light. Some weird red substance, probably dye leaking from a container sitting somewhere on the docks, gave the illusion of blood in the water. The Merch was still a quarter mile up on the right. The last thing I needed was to stall out. Seawater would flood the interior, ruin the engine and destroy the seals in the transmission.

Because I'd traveled East Bay Street since I was a kid on a bicycle, negotiating the peaks and valleys in the pavement helped me avoid the deepest areas. My parking space was next to the side door, beneath the burned out street light, between the pay phone and the beat-up, motor-less, mustard yellow '54 Studebaker. Before liquor by the drink was legal, South Carolina Law Enforcement agents raided The Merch on a regular basis. During a raid, the bartenders hid their liquor reserves in the Studebaker's trunk. I maneuvered the T-Bird into its slot, trying to avoid potholes while getting as close to the yellow car as possible without scratching my own. I walked around to the front door and looked up at the metal sign fabricated to resemble half a ship's wheel. The words "MSC Club" arched under the handles. Neon lights around the border would add a nice touch, I thought, as I mentally geared up for the meeting.

Going over the budget with Roy was no big deal; we did it all the time behind Freddie's back. Lately, Freddie May had mistakenly come to view The Merch as his private domain. He realized live entertainment distracted customers from thinking about the money they were spending and since he had a stake in making sure the clientele stayed cash-happy, very little got past him. Along with a percentage of the net profit, Barry paid him a cut of the "the vig." That's short for "the vigorish," which is Russian Yiddish slang for the house take on the blackjack game. Barry took most of the vig; with a healthy bump for Roy. The more vigorous the game, the larger Freddie's cut. Lately his main concern was increasing the net profit and, by extension, his percentage.

I'd assumed band money was the subject up for discussion, because it was the one area of the club's finances out of Freddie's control. The expenses associated with the band were strictly between Roy and me.

Giving Freddie any say over my money would require renegotiating my agreement with Roy, which was on file in a lawyer's office. That required a level of creativity Freddie had yet to achieve. Word had it Freddie was connected, but none of Freddie's bullshit concerned me. Connected or not my relationship with Roy was off limits. He knew it, I knew it, and it drove him nuts.

CHAPTER SIX

Nukes and Beep, two bus boys, leaned against the trunk of a maroon Camaro taking a smoke break. They wore yellow hooded raincoats and a steel mop bucket sat on the pavement between them. "Sweet Soul Music" blared from the Camaro's stereo system. We high five'd each other as they started laughing.

"Don't ask," I said.

"I can fix that mess on yo' head. Jest stick it in this bucket," Beep said, doubling up.

"Yeah, you give new meanin' to all washed up," Nuke said, slapping Beep's hand.

Sinclair opened the front door and shot them both a look. When he saw my hair he started laughing. His competition Afro rivaled any I'd ever seen on Jimi Hendricks, Larry Graham or Angela Davis. The huge, purple Afro pick protruding from the top looked more like a handle attached to his scalp than a specialized comb. He pulled it out and tossed it to me. "Here, boy," he said. "I think you need this more'n I do."

I dragged the comb through my tangles, handed it back.

"Buckin' for a gig with the Black Panthers, Sinclair?" I slapped his outstretched palm.

"What's the word?" He returned the slap.

"Thunderbird."

"What's the price?"

"Thirty twice."

"What's the reason?" We touched elbows.

"Grapes in season." We bumped hips.

Sinclair and I went through the cheap wine soliloquy as a token of mutual respect, acknowledgement and acceptance of our relative stations in the grand scheme of Charleston's nightclub scene.

"Who's on the hit parade tonight?" I said.

"Stacy, Nancy and Kim called to make sure everything was cool."

"With those three working the room, it should be a star-studded evening."

The girls were part of a group of pros who worked the various night spots when they weren't hooking convention twisters at the Francis Marion Hotel. Their ticket to "Perch at The Merch" was a snapshot of themselves, which they gave Sinclair at the front door. On the back of each picture was a price. Sinclair wrote another number beside it indicating the minimum drink order required by the bar before the john could leave with the girl. Stacy, Nancy and Kim were $200 + 5, each.

Sinclair passed this information to Freddie who collected the fees and enforced the drink quota before handing the picture to the john. With picture in hand, the mark hooked up with the girl and they left. When the trick was turned, she brought her picture back, and Freddie paid her. This tight little arrangement solidified Freddie's vig, the club's drink quota and insured the girls got paid without a hassle. If the girl wasn't back within three hours, Nukes and Beep went looking for her. If she'd been mistreated or beaten, or forced to service other men, then the john was tracked down and beaten within an inch of his life. It didn't happen often, but when it did, the results gave brutal a new meaning. Disfigured for life is putting it mildly.

One girl, cute little redhead named Darla, was found beaten to death in a ditch along Maybank highway. This happened shortly after I got back into town. Roy was crushed and Freddie went berserk because the john was a Citadel cadet and the son of an out of state senator. It took a while to track the guy down because he left halfway through his junior year and joined the army.

The letter said he died in the Mekong Delta after being ambushed by the Viet Cong. His parents and the paper called him a hero who died in service to his country. A few weeks later, his old man dropped dead of a heart attack when a box of his son's personal items was delivered. What took him out weren't his son's wallet, watch and rings, but the guy's severed head with a picture of Darla's dead body nailed between its eyes.

Word got around the FBI was involved, but I never saw them around The Merch. What I did hear, from some of the brothers who had family working in the Citadel, was the hole between the eyes, where the nail went, wasn't made by a nail. It had been drilled.

After the Darla incident I wasn't thrilled about playing music in a Lowcountry whorehouse, but the system was in place when I came back, so there was little I could do about it. At least knowing which girls were working helped me keep an eye on them. From the stage, I could see every corner of the room. We all stayed on our toes in case a situation got out of hand.

The Merch was closed during the day and the front door stayed locked until we opened for business. Friday was a major clean-up day so Sinclair was on hand to make sure Nukes and Beep could come and go, as needed. As I entered the tiny foyer, I pretended The Merch was already mine and reflected on the history I had with the building. During the five years, I was on the road, nothing had changed. The ship's wheel sign outside, the model of a World War II freighter mounted in a glass case on the wall behind the counter and the two way porthole mirror in the red door leading to the club's interior were the only maritime objects in the place. Every other aspect was straight out of the roaring twenties.

Nukes and Beep followed me inside, on their way to mop the kitchen floor. Sinclair locked the door, then grabbed a bar towel and started wiping down the table tops near the door to Roy's office. Montague was behind the bar restocking the shelves with freshly washed glasses. He poured a shot of Wild Turkey, set the drink on the bar and said, "You see them dark cloud out de' ova da harbor? Scrong Man in 'em."

I looked across the room; the door to Roy's office was closed.

"You know I can't listen to that Sea Island mumbo jumbo." I tossed back the whiskey. "Is Roy here yet? We're supposed to be having a budget meeting."

"You bes' be careful in there. Montague indicated the office with his eyes. "Somethin' ain't right."

"Be careful with who? Roy or Freddie?" I said.

"I ain't seen no Mr. Roy for a couple days now, just Mr. Freddie in there right now an' some other white boy 's in the bathroom, that's been meetin' with him since noon." Montague's eyes locked onto mine. He didn't say a word, but I knew what he was thinking.

"When this place is mine all this roaring twenties shit is coming down," I said. "I'm going to decorate the walls with all my memorabilia from the road."

"You know I can't listen to all that countin' chickens befo' they hatch mumbo-jumbo." He rinsed my empty glass in the sink.

Sinclair, the master eavesdropper, shook his head and snickered. And as I moved away from the bar toward Roy's office a dark haired wisp of a guy blew out of the restroom, past Sinclair and bumped into me. His face drained, almost skeletal, with frightened eyes ringed by dark purple circles. When I paused to let him pass, we made eye contact. I saw the face of a man aged well beyond his actual years. The word "junkie" sprang to mind, and I wondered immediately why he was in my club. When I stepped aside to let him pass, he stopped abruptly and put his hand on my arm.

"Josie, is that you?" His exhausted expression flashed with the cautious optimism of someone who thought they recognized an old friend. "It's me, man. Tommy, Tommy Bennett. Don't you remember? We went to St. Andrew's High together."

For a full fifteen seconds I couldn't place the name or the face. Stalling, I pretended to recognize him.

"Hey man, how long's it been?" I still wasn't sure who I was talking to.

"I don't know, man, five years at least." He looked me up and down. "Did you get splashed or something? Your head's all wet and there's mud on your shirt."

A light went on in my memory, and recognizing his voice. Immediately I backed off the old friend routine. This was the junkie suspected of stealing my horn. True, I got a new Mark VI to replace it, but it's the principle of the thing. You don't steal a man's tools.

Something had gone very wrong for Tommy Bennett. The whites of his eyes were yellowed and bloodshot and his skin was jaundiced. Karma is a bitch, I thought.

"Window's broken in my car, truck sprayed me," I said.

"Man, he got you good. Long see. No time."

Reversing clichés in a feeble attempt at humor was an old Charleston cliché in itself. I don't recall the idle chit chat we engaged in, the Wild Turkey on a beer lunch and a half-empty stomach was kicking in, but I do remember him asking for my phone number. When I said I didn't have a phone, he insisted I take his number.

I remember thinking how ghostly Tommy looked as he scribbled the number on a matchbook cover. The blue veins in his hands, obvious as tattoos, were visible through the surface of his transparent skin, fingernails chewed down to the quick. He smelled like a hospital room medicine cabinet. Even with the heat duct blowing warm air right over our heads, he trembled like a man suffering from chills and fever. With shaking hands, he passed the matchbook to me, then gave me a good-natured punch on the arm.

"I've heard about how The Mag Seven is coming together. Freddie thinks he can get me a pretty good gig, when his money loosens up a little. I want to hear you guys."

"So, are you working, Tommy? With a band, I mean."

He shifted his weight from one foot to the other and scratched the back of his head while I stood there, looking at him.

"No, but, I've been practicing again," he said. "I can still hit a double high C when my lip is right. It ain't always in tune, but it's gettin' there. Trumpet's all about the chops you know," he rubbed his chin. "Freddie and I've been talking about going into business together, booking bands. He has the contacts, and I'll do the legwork. I could use the extra money."

"Hey, that's great." I punched his arm as he had mine. There was nothing there. He had the arm of an eighty-year-old woman; frail and thin like a bird's leg. I wanted to break it.

"Life sure isn't like high school, is it, Josie? I mean, who would've thought we'd end up like this." He was having a hard time controlling the quiver in his voice.

"End up like what?"

"What I mean to say is, not that there's anything wrong with this, the gig I mean, you know, I mean really wrong, it's just I never thought I'd, we'd be… doing, you know what I'm trying to say?" He searched my face for the help he needed to climb out of the Freudian hole he'd dug.

"You mean playing music for a living?"

"Yeah, it ain't like playing music is really work-work," he said, relieved. "Too much fun to be a real job, but, I guess a job is a job; right? Everybody got to make a living somehow. Having one beats looking for one, right?"

I hated Tommy's kind of thinking. It reminded me of my experience with a bank manager I'd dealt with when I applied for a loan to buy band equipment. He asked me what I did for a living. When I told him I was a player, he stated, "Oh, you don't work?" Roy ended up cosigning the note because I didn't have a "real job."

Tommy Bennett couldn't find a gig because he couldn't play, simple as that. I smiled again, nodded and looked at my watch.

"Speaking of work, I'm keeping the boss man waiting," I moved toward Roy's office.

"Oh, I'm sorry, man," he said. "I'll let you go. I didn't intend to hold you up."

"No problem," I said. "It's good to see you. Good luck with your job search." He burped out a half-hearted laugh, I interpreted to mean, "Yeah, right, and if you believe that…."

He gave my hand a cold, soft pat, nodded toward the inside of the club and whispered, "The stage looks real nice." Then he raised his eyebrows, shrugged his shoulders and said, "Catch you later." I immediately figured he was after my job. Paranoia will do that to you.

Sinclair followed Tommy to the door to let him out. He skulked through the foyer, surveyed the parking lot, making sure the coast was clear before he ducked, Dracula-like, behind the building and disappeared.

"Wonder why he didn't want anyone to see him leaving," I said.

"Junkies and drama," Sinclair said, "go hand in hand, they deserve each other."

An adrenaline spike shot through my chest.

"Why was this guy in my club looking for work?" I said.

"You got me."

"If he wanted to play in my band or even book it for that matter, why didn't he come to me instead of going to Freddie? He knew I was running this show, he so much as said it."

"Like I said Cap'n, I don't know the dude; this the first time I seen 'em."

Every hair from my arms to my scalp stood at attention as both Montague and Sinclair continued their chores without looking at me. As I stood in the middle of the room wondering what to do next I looked at the stage. A black wrought iron handrail outlined a stage floor covered in royal red carpet. Double-stacked, black Marshall amps flanked a beautiful set of Rogers Silver Pearl drums highlighted by brass cymbals. Gary, the drummer had a towel draped over his snare.

The mighty Hammond B3, with its twin Leslie speakers still spinning was the essence and soul of the band's sound. Since every major hit song from Booker T and the MG's "Green Onions" to Deep Purple's "Hush" featured a Hammond organ solo, its importance to the overall sound of the band was unquestioned. Montague found this B3 in an all-black Pentecostal Holiness Church on the Upper East Side. The pastor passed away, leaving the organ to the choir director. A B3 weighs upwards of four hundred pounds and the Leslies were over a hundred pounds each. The lady had no room for the beast. I offered her a thousand dollars for the whole rig and she took it.

The slowly spinning Leslie speakers made me shake my head. With all the bad weather we were experiencing, I was pissed that Monk Moon, my organ player, had left the B3 on again. One good power surge would fry every tube in the rig. I'd asked him a dozen times to make sure the organ was turned off and unplugged before he left. But when Monk finished a night of wailing, with his bald head bouncing behind his black Ray Bans, the last thing on his mind was maintenance. I walked across the parquet tiles and stepped on the stage, turned off the organ and adjusted the three microphones for the horn players that stood in a row to the left of the B3. A gold banner with dark navy blue letters made a simple statement: The Magnificent Seven. Glowing in a wash of green, blue and yellow lights, the whole stage was state of the art Rhythm and Blues and reminded me of how far I'd come and why I was back in Charleston.

I'd been in the music business too long and seen too much to worry about job security. My real ace in the hole, what kept me going night after night, was my relationship with Roy. We were more like family than business partners. I knew I could weather any storm as long as he and I were tight.

Standing on stage, I looked out over the low ladder-back chairs painted black with black Naugahyde cushions, grouped in fours around standard pedestal bar tables. Sinclair wiped each table, then spread a clean, white tablecloth over each one. The swinging door to the kitchen was propped open with a cardboard box marked Paradise Food Service and the floor was still wet from being mopped. It had been my idea to cut a pass-through window so food orders could go straight from the kitchen to the servers station without opening the kitchen door.

Moving the stage to the end wall right next to the ladies room was also my idea. Every girl who came to the club eventually had to walk past the band. It was yet another way of sharing the wealth. By moving the blackjack table to the alcove left of the stage, Barry had more time to clear the table if we had a raid.

To this day, people don't realize the critical role this one nightclub played in determining not only past history in Charleston, but the current political mood. Back then the Baptists were the whipping boys taking the heat for pushing the draconian legislation known as the South Carolina Blue Laws. In reality, those laws, like every other law governing the state during the 50s, 60s and 70s served the interests of bootleggers in bed with corrupt politicians who had a no-holds-barred, venture capitalist interest in masking themselves as the saviors of civilized Christian society, so they could control every illegal activity in town. Nobody worried that you could buy toothpaste on Sunday, but not a toothbrush, or hair rollers but not hairpins. What mattered were liquor laws, gambling laws, the courts or lack thereof, which fueled the private nightclub business and, by extension, the veritable river of money, from a variety of illegal sources, flowing through them.

Many of the members who loved to "Perch at the Merch" where affluent residents of Charleston's historic district, belonging to the upper echelon of downtown society. More than a few doctors, lawyers and politicians used the club as a base of operations. Filtering tax-free cash through the blackjack games, crap tables and simple under the table payoffs, established The Merch as the borderland between downtown Charleston's high society and the poverty stricken East Side. From my vantage point on the stage, I could study every face in the room.

I was proud of the changes Roy had allowed me to make during the brief period since I'd returned and I was looking forward to making more changes when I owned the club. During those first few months, his trust in me had reinforced my self-confidence. But now, Freddie May seemed determined to make me look like a two-bit horn player who should be blowing "Night Train" behind the strippers on Reynolds Avenue.

Power tripping was one thing, but I shouldn't have had to remind him of what I brought to the table. I was becoming increasingly concerned not only by the liberties he was taking as manager, but by Roy's obvious reluctance to dial him back. Roy's frequent absences from the club were also becoming more conspicuous. Not attending a meeting he had called was even more unsettling.

Freddie, a short, barrel-chested lefty from Brooklyn in his early forties, didn't look up when I opened the office door without knocking. Writing upside down, hunched over Roy's desk, he was transferring a list of numbers from a sheet of spiral-bound notebook paper to a ledger book. The light from a single-bulb banker's lamp cast his apelike shadow on the back wall of the dark room. I pulled up a seat opposite the desk.

The temperature outside could drop below freezing and Freddie would still wear a blousy, short-sleeved, silk shirt to work. The top three buttons opened to reveal a forest of black hair on his chest. His biceps stretched the limits of his shirt sleeves down to stubby fingers with each hand sporting its own two-carat diamond ring. His pants fit him like a coat of paint. The shoes were stiletto-toed black leather lace-ups made in France. Each had a steel cap riveted to the tip with a tiny blade on each side of the point. His intimidating continental style stood out in stark contrast to that of the Charleston bubbas who frequented The Merch. Oddly enough, his capacity for violence didn't scare me. There was something else; something reptilian about him made the hair on my neck stand up every time he got near me. After I stopped carrying a gun, my stand on violence became simple: If it's not worth killing over, it's not worth fighting about. If it is worth killing over, sub it out. Freddie May had me rethinking my position.

Over the course of several months, I'd learned to appreciate his capacity for all kinds of surprises. I never learned to predict what would set him off, nothing got him going but money. Even though Freddie had yet to figure out he needed me more than I needed him, he still made me nervous and not because of his shoes. My major worry was that he'd obviously gained more control over Roy than I'd realized.

"You get your head lodged in a toilet, Elvis?" Freddie said, without looking up from the ledger. I wondered how he knew my head was wet when he hadn't even looked at me.

"How'd you know I got splashed?"

"I know every fuckin' thing, when you gonna realize that?"

"I passed Tommy Bennett as he was leaving," I said.

"I know. The guy nickel and dimes me to death." He shook his head without looking up and heaved a sigh. "He's got to get off the junk before he gets any help from me. What did he tell you?"

"Well, he didn't tell me how you knew I got splashed."

Freddie leaned over the desk and pointed his pencil past me toward a box of frozen T-bones, marked Paradise Food Service, holding the door open to the kitchen. I recalled the truck driver's face when he splashed me.

"I've got eyes all over this city, Chapman. And while I might've been born at night, I wasn't born last night. So I ask you again, what'd scum bag Bennett say to you?"

"Nothing," I said. "Other than you were going to help him find a gig. Maybe book some bands on the side."

"What else did he say? You got a father confessor look, Elvis. People confide shit in you because you're so fuckin' trustworthy." I recalled Sinclair's warning.

"Where's Roy?" I said. "I thought all three of us were meeting."

He ignored my question, slammed his ledger shut, came around the front of the desk and sat on the edge with his feet within striking distance of my face.

"He had some unexpected business, so I'm handling the meeting." He looked me up and down with his hand on his chin. Then he slapped his hands on his legs and said, "I want you to check something out for me."

"Sure Freddie, I'm always anxious to drop what I'm doing so I can step and fetch for you." He ignored me.

"There's a new girl singer working over at The Apartment Club. She got in town a couple weeks ago from somewhere in Florida, some Navy town, Pensacola, maybe. Anyway, word has it she's hot. Her name is Betty or Barbie Smith or something like that; I want you to check her out. If she's good, I wanna hire her."

"How do you propose to pay her?"

"How the hell should I know? Maybe we'll drop somebody and add her; maybe we'll add a cover charge. That's not the point. The point is we're off by 30 percent since she hit town." He slipped off the desk and walked out the door, across the dance floor and stared at the stage, then turned back to face me. "The parking lot at the Apartment Club has been full every night this week. If you don't want a pay cut, I'd suggest you find a way to talk to this broad and convince her ass to get over here. You can do it, Elvis. Chicks love that fag charm of yours. But only if she's any good, dig?"

"You know you're talking an extra three hundred a week," I said. Freddie put his hands in his pockets and rocked back and forth on his heels. "Two-fifty for her and fifty for me."

"Josie, Josie, Josie…man, don't start this crap with me again." He pursed his lips and stared back at the floor shaking his head, and then he looked up at the ceiling and started whistling. I knew when the meeting was called Freddie and I would eventually square off on the subject of my money, even if I had to bring it up. Roy's absence didn't stop me, though; I was ready for the discussion.

"If you don't wanna pay me to manage the band, Freddie, get somebody else to manage it. Maybe, hire Tommy Bennett." I was as surprised by the tone of my voice as he was. "You can buy out my contract, I'll sell you all my equipment—the lights, the PA, even the B3 – and you can give him twenty bucks a week and a place to sleep."

"This isn't right, Josie. You're already knocking down twice what these other clowns are getting. Plus, you get a cut off the door on weekends. No other player in this township is fixing that sort of dough. You're starting to price yourself out of the market."

"I bought all that equipment out of my own pocket," I said, pointing at the stage. "That's a substantial investment and I'm still making the payments. I do most of the arranging. What songs I don't arrange, I pay Jack to arrange, OK? I take out the taxes, I match the social security, pay unemployment, keep the books straight and I make sure the bar tabs get paid. I do all that out of my pocket, Freddie. These other guys simply show up and play. Monk won't turn off the organ unless I remind him, even when there's a thunder storm outside. I'm the only legitimate musician in this whole damned town, don't try to make it sound like I'm selling protection."

"It ain't like you're Quincy Fuckin' Jones, either."

It was all I could do to hold back from biting my tongue in half. Where was Roy when I needed him? Freddie took his hands out of his pockets so he could pace, preach and point with more emphasis. I'd been through this before, with other club managers who'd tried to play hard ball. Tension was building to the point where the threat of firing me was crossing his mind. Outright confrontation challenged his management skills. He preferred intimidation to negotiation, and didn't like it when anyone stood up to his tough guy persona; especially me.

"You've got my ass in a sling right now, Elvis, and I hate feeling trapped. You and I both know, without The Merchant, you got no place to play. You got burnt bridges all over. Name one other club in town supporting an eight-piece band." He was puffing.

"Seven," I said.

"What…?"

"The Magnificent Seven. We're a seven-piece band. You said eight-piece band."

"You add the chick, it's eight."

"You don't pay for the chick, the chick won't come, then it's seven," I said.

"And another thing I don't like…" he started up again. "Is you taking all the fuckin' credit for our relative success here, I've done as much as you to make this place go."

"You take money out of The Merch, Freddie, but you put no money in."

He didn't miss a beat. "And I'll tell you something else – some weeks your check is bigger than mine, and I run the damn place." He stuffed his hands back in his pockets and once again, rocked back on his heels.

Freddie's self-righteous complaints were making me sick. In addition to his cut of the vig, he was skimming off the bar for three to five hundred a week. He also got free steaks from the Paradise guy and sold, for cash, the liquor we stocked as "club members' liquor" out the back door of the kitchen. Montague had watched him and showed me how he did it. He had no clue either of us knew, and I couldn't say a thing about it. Not yet. Partly because, I didn't want to implicate Montague, and partly because I was waiting until Roy and I closed the deal to confront him. After that, as far as I was concerned Freddie May could kiss my ass.

"Listen Freddie," I said. "I don't give nothing away for free. Never have, never will. It's all there in my contract. If I have to manage an eighth member, then I want the money that goes with the job." I put my own hands in my pockets and rocked on my heels mocking him. "You can pay me or you can buy me out."

"Man, your rice ain't done or you got a hold of some bad oysters or…" He paused and searched the ceiling for the right words, "I've got it. You're a few cred-its short of a music degree, Brother Chapman." He grinned and shook his head, a sneer molding his face. He knew I hadn't studied music, that I had no formal education. This was the closest he'd come yet at attempting an intellectual cut. Realizing he'd scored a hit, he continued to lecture.

"When I let your unemployed ass come to work here," he said, "you'd just lost your gig at The Apartment Club. Before that, you lost your gig with the biggest act in the southeast. Nobody out there in the cold, cruel world wanted you, and I took you in. Now you treat me like a bad stepmother. Sometimes, I don't even think I know you. Money's all you think about money, money, money. Where's that love of the music your artistic ass is so famous for?"

His audacity knew no limits. Freddie believed spouting bullshit out loud somehow made it true.

"I quit The Apartment Club gig because my position at The Merch finally opened up. The only reason I took the job in the first place was because I'd finished my last tour with Freeway three months before Roy's bandleader was due to be transferred. You know all this," I said.

Bill Reed, the owner of the Apartment Club, knew I was waiting for my gig at The Merch to open up. He asked me to play in his house band until then. It was simple, uncomplicated.

I was there to build a legitimate band and turn The Merch into a legitimate private club. People don't believe this, but The Merch didn't make enough money off the gambling to justify the risk. Freddie brought in the games so more customers would come in and drink. The Merch made money on reserve liquor and set ups, not cards, dice or hookers. Freddie was the one who made money on the games and the girls, not Roy. The gambling had been his idea. Then came the girls, what was next I wondered, hit men? Then I remembered Darla and calmed down.

I understood, Roy was tired, he had needed a manager. The fact that some chick singer at The Apartment Club could take business away from The Merch proved the point. Freddie showed up suddenly, six months before I did, and started acting like he owned the joint.

Freddie was right about me when it came to money, though. I'll give him that. Being paid more than any other musician in town was my way of keeping score. During those "You are what you own" days, I soon discovered how many of the below-Broad crowd, living in those inherited old mansions, went without heat and lived on Hamburger Helper in order to pay property taxes. I didn't intend to end up like them.

Of course, I couldn't say what I was thinking. At this point, my money had become a secondary issue to being hammered by a guy who had no right sticking his nose in my business.

"You're breakin' my heart, Freddie," I said, and turned toward the door.

When he yelled, "I mean it Chapman! I'll fire your ass!"

Something inside of me snapped. The muscles in the right side of my neck cinched up, causing a tic in my face. My left eye started to spasm uncontrollably, and I stopped, turned, and started walking back toward him. He was back on his feet with his arms at his side like a gunslinger preparing for a shootout.

By then, I didn't give a damn about his pointed-toed shoes or his negotiating skills. What Freddie May needed was a reminder that he wasn't dealing with a rookie.

"You want as much as you can get, don't you, Freddie?" I hissed, rubbing my eye with the heel of my hand. "The amount, isn't nearly as important as knowing you got all there was to get. Not getting a piece of me drives you crazy. I know it, and you know it. But, what you don't seem to understand is you're stuck with me, whether you like it or not. There's nobody else in town who can handle this job."

I stopped short of telling him I knew he was skimming. I didn't want to involve Montague.

"And what, if I might ask, makes you so fuckin' sure of that?" He uncrossed his arms.

"Number one: I own all the band equipment and no other musician can afford to set up the stage like it's set up now. Number two: I have a signed contract with the club owner which stipulates, in detail, how much and how often I get paid. Number three: Your name is nowhere on my signed contract, Freddie. Translation: I don't fucking answer to you, man, about anything. I'm only standing here, right now, out of courtesy. In fact, I'd have been well within my rights to walk out of here the moment I realized Roy wasn't going to make the meeting. I don't work for you Freddie. I work for Roy. Are we clear on that? And last, but certainly not least, number four: Nobody but me has a reason to marry a job like this, knowing that putting up with an asshole like you is currently part of the deal." The split second the word "currently" passed my lips he stopped glaring at me, stopped hating that he couldn't touch me. As soon as I said the word, his face softened into a knowing grin. You could've tightrope walked the tension between us. He had pushed my buttons until I played the song he wanted to hear. My deal with Roy had given me an inordinate sense of self-worth. Freddie May knew I would've never stood up to him without serious backup.

In the nightclub business, when a member of the band lets his alligator mouth overload his hummingbird ass, the other members usually pay for it; unless, of course, the band member has an alligator's ass to match his mouth, which is rare. Normally, in situations like this, the boss has the last word. Freddie said nothing. He just grinned the grin of a poker player about to rake in the chips, then casually walked past me toward the bar, grabbed the box of steaks off the floor while the swinging door to the kitchen swished back and forth on its hinges.

I looked around for Montague and Sinclair but they were nowhere in sight. A minute later, Freddie reappeared through the kitchen door.

"You're right Elvis, you don't work for me; I got a little carried away. No hard feelings, OK?" Freddie said.

"OK," I said.

"It's just a suggestion," he said, still smiling, "If you can find the time to check out the girl, I think it would be in both our interests. If not, don't worry about it. Nightclub people are fickle as hell in this town. Soon as the newness wears off, our numbers will even back out."

"I'll put her on my 'to do' list," I said. "Maybe I can slide by The Apartment Club before I come in tonight."

Freddie nodded and walked back into Roy's office and shut the door. I wiped my face with both hands trying to massage the muscles, but the twitch in my left eye wouldn't stop completely. Walking through the porthole door I bumped into Montague, who was in the foyer emptying the trash cans into black plastic bags. Sinclair was wiping down the counter.

"What's up?" Sinclair said.

"He wants me to run an errand for him," I answered.

"Why you put up with his shit?"

"Give it time, brother, give it time." I walked through the front door into the parking lot, still deeply concerned about Roy skipping out on the meeting.I wouldn't have telegraphed my emotions if he'd been there, but he wasn't. I was pissed about that.

Even so, walking out to my car, I felt proud of myself for standing up to Freddie. I thought maybe now he would realize I was his meal ticket, his edge against the competition, not the other way around. Maybe, just maybe, he'd get off my case and let me do my job in peace.

When I got in my car, rain blowing in through the partially opened window had soaked the seats. My pants got wet when I sat down and I squirmed around to warm up the moisture between my butt and the leather. Someone had tossed a copy of *The Eternal Truth* through the window. The cover showed a thunderstorm with menacing green eyes bearing down on some poor slob running down the beach, his hands over his ears. The cover title was a question: "If You Died Tonight, Would You Go To Heaven Or Hell?"

"What a stupid question," I said to myself.

What did catch my attention was how much the shade of green in the eyes of the storm matched the iridescent green of the marsh. If I could get Freddie May dumped in the marsh grass behind Middleton Plantation, I wondered, would it get me into heaven? The address was rubber stamped in black ink. The ink was running, but the address was legible: The Apostolic Prophetic Redemption by The Holy Ghost Tabernacle & Center for Deleverage. A revival on "Overcoming Temptations of the Flesh" was in progress for the next seven days. Somebody'd slogged in the rain, through all that water to put a religious magazine in my car. They must've figured anybody who starts nightclubbing at 3:30 in the rain, when they can't even get their car window fixed, must have a serious, sin-of-the-flesh problem.

The inside front cover showed the thundercloud spawning four tornadoes, each with its own set of green eyes and lightning bolts closing in on various groups of unsuspecting sinners. The pictures were artist illustrations. One depicted a bar scene showing a man fondling a woman, dressed in fishnet stockings drinking, while another woman leaned against the wall, talking to a man offering her money. A picture of a hungry child begging for food was next to that of a protest march populated by picketing, black militants being taunted by members of the KKK. Below the pictures was an article with another question for title "Whose Hands is Your Life In?" I tossed the tract on the seat and started the car.

I was about to back out, when Montague tapped on my passenger side window. He was carrying a bag of trash and had a plastic trash can liner tied over his head. I lowered the window, and he looked inside, eyeing me carefully, rain water dripping from the plastic onto his face.

"Let me look at you, boy." He reached across the seat, taking my chin in his hands so he could examine my face. "What's wrong wit yo' eye?"

"Just a nervous twitch, I get it sometimes. It's nothing."

"Nothin' huh? De lef' eye bun de truthful eye. You wanna know the truth 'bout somebody you look in 'e lef' eye." He still held my chin in his hand, examining me curiously. "Hmm. Yo' skin crawlin' anywhere?"

"As a matter of fact it is, Dr. Montague," I said, twisting my face from his grip, "My ass is wet from the seat, my scalp itches because my hair is dirty from being splashed by bilge water, and my clothes are soaked from sitting here in the rain with my window down talking to you."

"I b'lieve somebody tryin' tell you som'thin, boy." He nodded toward the tract on the seat beside me. "You bes be careful, I b'lieve, Scrong Man is heah, walkin' round 'mongst us, and he watchin' e'breything 'cause he got a plan for all of us, includin' you."

"Could've saved himself the trouble," I said.

"You bes' mind what I'm tellin' you, boy. . ."

"I know I need to get my window fixed, Montague."

". . .or you gonna find yo'sef in a world o' hurt."

"Thanks," I said. "I appreciate your concern. Now if you don't mind, I'd like to go home and take a shower."

He walked around to my window, leaned forward placing his fingertips over the top edge of the half open glass. Stooping down to eye level with me, his face came close to the opening.

"You bes' mind," he whispered. Then he looked up toward the sky. The storm cloud had moved off the harbor and stationed itself over the city. Pink sheet lightening flashed, and the low rumble of thunder pealed from the black sky over The Merch. "Scrong Man be watchin' you."

CHAPTER SEVEN

The last high water was receding, leaving pods of trash on the higher protrusions of asphalt. Clumps of paper, cigarette butts, beer cans and harbor silt littered the streets with enough man-made garbage and salt marsh hay to keep two street sweepers busy all night. My hair was matted, and my butt still itched as I squirmed on the soaked leather of the car seat. The tic in my left eye had settled down, but the muscles in my neck and face had knotted into a dull headache. I needed a shower, clean clothes, three Bayer aspirin, a stiff drink and a better attitude if I was going to brighten up in time to see this Betty or Barbara or whoever she was.

During my road days, a manipulating club manager like Freddie would have never gotten to me. I felt stupid, dirty and disgusted with myself for allowing him to push all the right buttons until I played the song he wanted to hear. I remembered something else Roy had taught me. "People treat you the way you teach them to treat you." I felt like a fool.

Why wasn't Roy at the meeting since he was the one who called it? Or did he? Did Roy even know Freddie was thinking of expanding the band? Here's a perfect example of the difference between real paranoia and a heightened sense of awareness.

Jack's wife, Susan, had delivered the message. So I'm thinking if Roy knew I was there, why didn't he ask to speak to me? Right away. "Hi Susan, this is Roy, may I speak to Josie?" That's all he had to say. Nothing to it, but to do it. The question had been nagging me since the phone call. To my knowledge, Susan had never met Roy or even set foot in The Merch. In fact, Susan hated the nightclub business. She tolerated Jack's gig because it allowed them to stay home together during the day. Since Jack seldom talked to Roy, even at The Merch, it was doubtful Susan would have recognized Roy's voice over the phone. Was it possible that Freddie had impersonated Roy when Susan answered the phone? Getting her to pass along the message; calling me down to the club so he could grill me alone? The more I thought about it, the more convinced I became this was exactly what had happened.

Freddie's sudden change in personality meant something was up. Maybe he was testing me, trying to see how far he could push me. Still, strange as it was, by the time I pulled up in front of my apartment, I'd tried to put the whole Freddie and Tommy incident on the back burner.

Mr. Rigney, J. Reynolds, III, to be exact, jet spray garden hose ever at the ready, was herding clumps of high-water debris off the sidewalk with the meticulous precision of a child torching ants with a magnifying glass. The sidewalk ran adjacent to "the family property" as he affectionately referred to the small, subdivided house at 3 Savage Street. He owned the house and lived on the first floor. I rented the upstairs efficiency.

We had an amicable arrangement: I was quiet, paid the rent on time and he didn't meddle. Mr. Rigney's "don't know, don't want to" attitude was refreshing, given the gossip whores I'd worked with. He liked to chide me with subtle quips designed to denigrate my musical expertise. His refined snobbery and self-aggrandizement always lifted my spirits, because he never took himself too seriously.

"Well, well, if it's not the alleged musician come dragging up soaked as a dead wharf rat in the mouth of an ailing alley cat," he taunted.

"Don't knock my car, J. R," I said.

"That's Mr. Rigney, to you."

"Oh, I'm sorry. Did I assume an undue level of familiarity?" I grinned.

"Rough rehearsal? Or did your saxophone solo trip the sprinkler system?" Another butt filled crevice in the concrete fell victim to the deadly jet spray. "For the life of me, I can't understand how anyone makes a living blowing such an incestuous instrument."

"Incestuous? Do you mean like cousins hooking up?"

"You know precisely what I mean. The saxophone is nothing more than the retarded offspring of a clarinet crossed with a trumpet."

"I'll try to remember that the next time I wrap my lips around my mouthpiece."

"Please don't tease me, I'm old enough to be your dirty uncle."

J. Reynolds believed only classical music was legitimate. He favored Puccini operas by day with the occasional atonal dirge thrown after sundown; his homage to the slighted dead. A touch of Edgar: Prelude to Act III wafting through my apartment added a measure of civility to my otherwise bohemian existence. I didn't even mind him rattling pots and pans whenever he felt compelled to burst into song during an aria. I slipped downstairs one evening while he twirled in his kitchen like a wood nymph at a Bacchanalian feast. Bottle of wine in one hand, wooden spatula in the other, he spun around with his apron flaring until a plate crashed on the hardwood floor, jerking him back to reality. I laughed so hard, I laid down in the grass holding my sides.

However much he liked me, the proprietor in him insisted on maintaining a respectable distance. "Due to the implied business nature of the guest/host relationship," he'd said, when I signed the lease, "socializing, at all hours of the night, or day for that matter, on a regular basis, with members of the opposite sex, would probably not be conducive, as it were, to maintaining long-term residency." I loved his hypocrisy because, like most native Charlestonians, he was so easily appalled.

"J. Reynolds, my good man," I said, stepping onto the curb, "I got splashed by a delivery truck, would it be possible to use that exquisite hose of yours to wash the salt water off my car?"

"You call that thing…" he said, tossing a quick squirt at the T-Bird, "a car? I rather think it resembles a lead sled. Moreover, to my knowledge lead does not rust. So why waste the water?"

"You're right, of course, as always. I should give up on it, just let it sit right here in front of your house until it corrodes into a rusty pile of bolts and bad taste."

"Oh, have it your way," he said, handing me the nozzle, "but please be so kind as to wrap up the hose when you're finished. You know my fetish for keeping up neat appearances. An uncoiled garden hose in the yard is so unbearably tacky."

He smiled, wiped his hands on his garden apron and turned back toward the gated walkway leading to his front door. "And Joseph," he added, "by all means, please attempt some modicum of respect for the water meter, will you? Your personal showers are long enough, God knows, but it would be a sin of a most singular nature, to waste too much city water on that wretched…" he paused, "thing." J. Reynolds did not like American cars, especially the "superficial, two-door sport variety." He once remarked, "Ford must've used a dead catfish for a model during the Thunder-turd's design process."

J. Reynolds Rigney, III, was unimpressed, never worried or flustered. Nothing fazed him except the "obvious stupidity inherent in the oblivious masses," which he pointed out on a regular basis to anyone within earshot. I liked him because he called it like he saw it, which was usually like it was. Charleston could've used more men like J. Reynolds Rigney, III. I often wondered what the Jr. and Sr. versions were like.

Our light-hearted exchange helped ease the tension I'd built up during my meeting with Freddie. While I hosed off the Thunderbird's tires, rims and hubcaps, I remember thinking "To hell with Freddie May. What can he do to me? Fire me? Please don't throw me in the briar patch," I said to myself. Since I was already damp and dirty, I lay down on the street beside the Thunderbird and rinsed the undercarriage, brake rotors, transmission and exhaust system. During this process, the jet spray dislodged a single black wire hanging loose with a frayed bare end. I figured the wire must have snagged a piece of floating debris during my cruise down East Bay Street. When I tried to stuff it up under the car to get it out of the way, I heard a crackle, saw sparks and realized it was hot.

"Damn it," I said. "What's next?"

Back on my feet, I noticed the driver's side window had dropped another inch. The loose wire was the problem. At least the electric window motor wasn't bad. I rolled up Rigney's hose, went upstairs, making a mental note to get the T-Bird on a rack as soon as possible to reattach the wire.

Stepping into the old shower felt great. I indulged myself for twenty minutes, long enough to drain the hot water tank. J.R. must've felt sorry for me because he didn't bang on the ceiling after I passed the ten-minute mark. As I dried off, I noticed two Darvon capsules lying next to a pack of Juicy Fruit gum on the nightstand by my bed. By the time I was dressed, it was six o'clock.

I still felt anxious. I needed to calm down or I'd be exhausted before midnight. Looking back at the pills, I remember thinking it was better to have them and not need them than to need them and not have them. So, I popped a piece of gum in my mouth, wrapped the pills in the tin foil, slipped the foil into the pack and put the pack in my shirt pocket. With two hours to kill before the band started at The Apartment Club and four hours before my own gig, I decided against taking the Darvon. I was already too jacked up for my own good. If anything, I needed to calm down. If I crashed before midnight, I'd take it then.

I decided to kill a couple hours over a few drinks at The Swamp Fox Room in The Francis Marion Hotel. Grabbing a fifth of Wild Turkey (with my name on it, of course), from the cabinet over the refrigerator, I shoved it in a brown paper bag, grabbed a dish towel and headed down stairs. Crossing the lawn, I looked back over my shoulder. J. Reynolds eyed the bottle in my hand from his kitchen window and shook his head, eyes going to Heaven. I acknowledged his mortification, wiped down the seats, then hopped in the Thunderbird, thinking how nice his ordered life must be.

It took me thirty minutes to go a mile and a half because I got behind a street cleaning crew. By the time I got to The Francis Marion, all of the flood tide water was gone. The street sweepers were herding the debris to the curb, with the Charleston Sanitation Department employees right behind them, piling the muck into heaps with push brooms. A front-end loader scooped up the mess and transferred it to a dump truck. I waited another five minutes for the crew to pass before pulling into the parking lot to the right of the hotel.

The Francis Marion Hotel was a sleeper. Located on the corner of King and Calhoun in Charleston's historic district, it had an almost utilitarian look. Taking a cursory view it could have been any red brick building in downtown Manhattan, Chicago or Detroit. Behind its pedestrian façade, however, was an elegant interior replete with large, tightly woven velvet, pleated drapes cascading over elegantly tall windows and heavy wooden furniture. The tables and end tables were all big. The lamps and chandeliers were big, the lobby was big, the rugs were big and the sofas and chairs had broad blue, red and yellow brocade rolled out over what looked more like parapet walls than arms rests. For all of us from the west side of the river, The Francis Marion Hotel was the epitome of class.

The Swamp Fox Room was a small, quiet piano bar located on the second floor to the left of the lobby. I liked going there Monday night, my night off; because the room was usually empty and I could drink without actually being alone. But this was a Friday. All ten tables had customers enjoying good conversation over happy hour cocktails. The black baby grand piano pointed out from the corner eight feet from the bar. An end table with an emerald green glass ginger jar lamp was positioned left of the piano. An empty wine glass sat next to the lamp. Marcus, the bartender, glanced at his watch when I took a seat at the bar. He wasn't expecting to see me this early on a Friday. I handed him my paper bag and ordered a Wild Turkey Manhattan on the rocks.

The decision to go out for a drink was more impulsive than planned. I needed to relax and whiskey at The Swamp Fox Room relaxed me. A guy, in a suit, two stools down tried to get my attention, but I ignored him. Back then I had a thick rule book, especially when I was drinking alone. I never discussed my personal life with strangers, never talked about business, never discussed anything concerning mutual acquaintances, politics or religion and never, ever, sat in with other musicians when I wasn't sober. There were exceptions, of course, but not many. It was a throwback to two of Roy's admonitions. "Don't practice drunk or high," and "if you have a weakness the road will find it." I'd fine-tuned those basic guidelines into hard and fast rules.

Marcus set me up again and as I stared into the glass, the lamp light refracted through the green glass of the ginger jar, sparkling into the ice cubes. For a second the iridescent green eyes from the funnel cloud in the religious tract flashed in my glass. A cold chill ran through my whole body as Montague's voice overrode my thoughts. "You bes be careful, I b'lieve, Scrong Man got plans for you."

The feeling was definitely not whiskey thinking, and not paranoia, I was well-acquainted with both. This was more of a heightened sense of awareness, similar to the moment you know the acid is kicking in. The lights looked brighter, the cubes went 3D on me, inside the glass, looking like little mirrors with my face and those green eyes where mine should've been. The second Wild Turkey Manhattan went down fast, and when I set the glass on the bar, there were trailers. I thought I was having a flashback, then clarity arrived like a vision. In an instant, I knew; Freddie knew. Somehow I had to contain Freddie.

"You OK?" Marcus said.

"Yeah, it's been an eventful day," I said.

Marcus set up my third drink in twenty minutes.

"Heyyyy there brother man, I know yoooou." It was the suit, he was drunk. He'd closed the gap between us. "You're tha' guuuuyyy, that horn player down at The Merchants. Man, fug, you arrrrre one mean muthafuggain' horn honker, I could lissen t'you play all fuggin night. Randall is my name, Richard Randall. I'm a sinnnator, get it? Sin-a-tor. Ha ha ha ha ha ha. I like cue, boy, you somethin else. Hey, I wanna ast you a quest'un."

For me, personally, alcohol and drugs were not therapy, they were tools of the trade. If I was social drinking, I could nurse a glass of bourbon for an hour. But if I was firing for effect, the way I was this particular night, the last thing I wanted was a conversation with a political lush.

"There's a panana o'per there," he burped, "why'cu play som'thin, man, show all these utter muthafugga's how fuggin good you are."

I tried to smile. I tried to think of something witty, something innocuous to say, something that would let a sleazy foul-mouthed drunk as shit politician down easy. Nothing came to mind, except this, "You look like a well-educated man." He bobbed his head in agreement. "Do you know what William Faulkner said when an interviewer asked if he ever read the work of other writers?"

"Noooo'pe," burp, "Whaaaa...whaaaaa'd......what'd he fuggin' say?"

"He said, 'Have you ever heard of a whore sleeping with men for free?'"

"Whaaaa. . . Whaaaa. . . Wha'd d'fug's at s'pose ta mean?"

"It means sir, I'm not a whore."

Bewildered doesn't come close to describing the look on his face. His eyes glazed over, he looked at Marcus, rolled them around the room, back at me, up at the ceiling, then he spun around in his seat, passed out and fell to the floor. Two bellhops carried him out.

I looked at Marcus, who never missed a beat cleaning the glasses. He looked at me, and for the moment, at least, I'd forgotten all about my Freddie May fueled acid flashback.

I'd picked up my bottle bag to leave when a young woman sat down at the piano and started quietly playing "Lonely Summer Wind." She spent a full minute on the introduction before she started to sing.

Clearly an accomplished musician, she had a low, silky, voice which she modulated to drop between the musical patterns her hands arranged. Playing like a cross between Liz Story and Don Cherry, her musical symmetry perfectly complimented her looks.

She dressed like a model straight out of Vogue, wearing a tailored man's black silk tuxedo jacket with well-cut jeans. Her white, ribbed turtleneck tucked in at the waist, was held tight by a thin gold chain belt. Black and white paisley socks and charcoal gray suede low-cut loafers polished off the image of a Radcliff girl who'd done time in Greenwich Village.

Her warm, dark hair appeared jet-black until the lamplight hit it. Then the color glowed a rich dark brown. She'd pulled it straight back and clamped at the base of her neck with an Art Nouveau clasp fashioned from tortoise shell, with small blue stones arranged in the shape of a scarab. Her wide forehead was smooth and round. The thick eyebrows were shiny and slightly lighter than her hair tapering to a point just beyond the ends of her eyes. And the eyes themselves had an open, powerful gaze made even more dramatic by their hazel color. She had a classic, almost patrician nose and high cheekbones. Her mouth had a wide, clear, distinct shape, like a small pyramid, closely resembling Brigitte Bardot; the full lips sloped up at the corners. The whole picture ended with a closely curved chin. It was the face of a woman born for black and white film, a twenty foot canvas or both. Her timeless beauty extended down from her face and voice, through her arms, hands and fingertips, then flowed across the piano keys in a performance blending in perfect harmony with her appearance.

While she played, all conversation in The Swamp Fox Room ceased. Obviously used to performing solo, her music took total control of the atmosphere in the room. As her eyes opened and closed during each phrase, her chin listed slightly to the right making the lyrics sound more like soaring contemplation than simple, melodic narrative.

The fingers of her left hand floated over the piano keys like the wings of a opsrey riding an ocean breeze, her right hand made countless small variations in position complimenting the tonal quality of her voice. She used ghost notes to weave subtle inflections of her personality into the bass line, which haunted the melody. Her mind wasn't on the music, it was the music. I felt both inspired and intimidated.

For the moment, alone at the bar on a messy Friday afternoon, she put me at ease so naturally, I felt I'd known her all my life. Her ability to convey serenity to her audience with such effortless mastery was astounding. She was talented, beautiful, relaxed; comfortable with her environment. I envied her.

When she finished, a gentle applause rippled through the audience. She signaled Marcus to refill her wine glass and smiled while jotting something down in a spiral notebook placed on the piano's music stand. I told him to put her drink on my tab. He glanced at her and she tipped her empty wine glass in my direction.

"From one player to another," I said, returning the gesture, "the gods have smiled on you; you have the thing that can't be taught."

"Thank you, kind sir, but the wine list here is limited so, like you, I bring my own bottle." She shifted slightly, mimicking a curtsey.

"Well, it's the thought that counts," I said, "it's been a while since I've heard 'Lonely Summer Wind' played by a master. Where'd you go to school? Berklee? North Texas State?"

Marcus sat two glasses of wine on the coasters while I mentally kicked myself for name-dropping the only two colleges I knew with reputations for turning out excellent jazz musicians. Generally, I made a point of never revealing anything about my music education, especially around other players. Being self-taught didn't embarrass me, so why was I trying to impress her? If I'd had an ounce of sense, I would've realized I was over-compensating for the wave of self-doubt arguing with Freddie had resurrected. His cut about my lack of a formal education juxtaposed to this obviously accomplished musician, gave me second thoughts. I might really be just a "fake artist." Not a bad artist or false artist, not even a hypocrite, but more like an artist at faking art by parodying legitimate players' licks, then passing them off as his own. I was all show-biz hype in Freddie's book, selling the sizzle not the steak. Listening to this girl play only reinforced my growing lack of self-confidence. That's not how good music should work. I sipped the wine.

"No jazz for me," she said. "I studied at Julliard."

I almost sneezed my drink. She was a trained classical pianist playing in a cock-tail lounge. Probably some doctor's daughter, I thought, down here in Charleston paying soft dues instead of doing hard time in New York. Maybe she was a fake artist, too, only better at it. There was one way to find out.

I moved to the stool next to the piano so I could see the sheet music. A spiral bound copy of Great Jazz Standards was open to "Lonely Summer Wind." She's a reader, I thought, she doesn't play by ear. Not that there was anything wrong with reading, it's just none of the people I worked with ever used charts on stage. Even the horn arrangements Jack and I put together were memorized, not set on a music stand, like fucking Lawrence Welk.

"My name is Josie Chapman, I play flute." I felt more comfortable telling her I played flute since it was a classical instrument.

"Bobbie Storm," she said. "Anything special you'd like to hear? Mr. Chapman?"

In those days, if you wanted to make money, playing music in Charleston, there were certain songs you had to know. "Misty," "Stormy Monday," "Ebb Tide," "Summertime," "I Left My Heart in San Francisco" and "Georgia on My Mind," could get you a gig almost anywhere. They were as predictable as a Greek tragedy. She leafed through the titles in her book.

"How about 'Summertime?'" I said, leaning forward, trying to keep from grinning. I knew I was invading her space, but I wanted to see if she needed her fake book for the song. Sure enough, she started flipping the pages, found the cheat sheet and started playing.

Half way into the intro she looked up from the fake book, signaling Marcus with her eyes. "Summertime" wasn't a song she knew very well, but she never lost her place. Marcus came toward the end of the bar and while still looking up she said, "Marcus, be a dear and serve Mr. Chapman a glass of the Bordeaux I brought in. He appears to possess a discerning palate."

"I don't mix wine and bourbon in equal amounts," I said. "Gives me a headache."

"But you're a flutist!" she said.

"I didn't realize being a wino was a prerequisite." I held her gaze until she had to either look back at the music, get lost or play the tune by ear.

Here's a fact for you. When the piano player can carry on a conversation with two different people, while looking both in the eyes, without missing a note, they don't need the book.

"But you have barbaric taste," she said warmly, never missing a note.

"All my ancestors were barbarians," I said. "Non-Greek, non-Roman, non-Christian, they moved to Charleston when they discovered all their friends were here. We all drank bourbon with our grits while growing up."

"Really? Why, that's appalling," she feighned a dramatic sigh. "My husband is an American barbarian. He is a Captain in the Navy. We were transferred here last month."

Well, that was the buzz kill for me. No sooner had I recovered from Freddie May's bullshit session, a green-eyed acid flashback, a drunk politician, than here I was, once more fearlessly flying into the mouth of oblivion. More often than not, husbands and boyfriends of female musicians are jealous as hell.

They hate the attention drawn to the performer. I could've slapped myself for not checking her out with Marcus first. Since she wasn't wearing a ring, I'd assumed she wasn't married, especially after the way she let me get close to her. Once again, I'd proven to myself, I was the stupidest son of a bitch on the planet. I should've known she either had a boyfriend or was married.

"You're a great player, Bobbie, great hands, great voice, really." I looked quickly at my watch and finished off the wine as Marcus sat another glass of the Bordeaux on the table.

"What's the rush?" she said.

"Bad timing. I've got to hear a girl singer across town, before my own gig."

"My husband's in England. He won't be back until next week."

"It's not that." I lied. Because it was. "Sorry, I'm already running late."

She cut "Summertime" short and slipped her hands under her seat.

"I'll be off in thirty minutes," she said. "I haven't met many musicians here."

"What about your husband? Won't it bother him if he finds out you're hanging out with the non-classical riff raff?"

"Really, I think you know by now that I'm not really, as the saying goes, with my husband. We share an address, but little else."

"I'm afraid you don't understand."

"What's to understand?"

"Understand what I do. Where I play," I was sliding across the bench.

"Where do you play?" She coaxed in a whisper, sliding with me.

"Well, I'm the sax player at The Merch."

"Is that a bar?"

"Yes. The Merchant Seaman's Club. It's a nightclub on East Bay Street."

I made another attempt to slide off the piano bench.

"Wait a minute, don't leave yet," she put her hand on my forearm. "I only want to ask you two more questions. Then you can go." I sagged back onto the bench and looked down at the floor. "Tell me why you said you were a flute player, if you're a sax player."

"Flute is my secondary instrument. I should've said I was a sax player. I made a mistake." I started to get up again, but she continued to hold my arm. "OK," I said, "There's something about the way you play that touched me. You play like you feel it, like the music flows through you. I wanted to sit in with you and … I never want to sit in with anybody, ever."

"Do you read music at all?"

"Nothing much past running eighth notes and a few old jazz standards."

"Name one," she said.

"Misty."

"What key?"

"It doesn't matter," I said, "I play by ear."

"And this Merchant Seaman's Club is your only job right now?"

"That's right," I said.

"No happy hour, no private parties, no students?"

"Nope."

"Well, you've really hit the big time, haven't you?" She said it like a tease.

"No offense, dear, but you can't make fun of me this early in the game. You wanted me to come over, even before you knew I was a musician."

"Don't kid yourself; I knew you were a musician. I've been watching you since you walked in."

Technically, she could play circles around me, even without using her fake book, and I knew it, but we were onto something bigger than music. Some kind of spark arced between us, like we knew each other, though we'd never met. We were instantly attracted to each other, but didn't know how to handle it.

"So who's this girl singer you're going to hear tonight?"

"Betty or Barbara Smith or something like that?"

"Rock? Blues? Jazz?"

"No," I said. "Classical."

"Don't lie. Tell me."

"I don't know her. Word is she's good. She works for the competition."

"Oh really, and what do you intend to do, once you hear her?"

"If she's really any good, I'll offer her a job, what else?"

"A real romantic," she said.

"You're right," I whispered. "I'm a real romantic, especially when it comes to listening to somebody who has all the training in the world, take shots at those who don't. Playing by ear is still playing, improvisation is musical mental telepathy. Bet they didn't teach you that."

"Yes, but," she bit her bottom lip, "If you learned to read, you'd have access to all the music ever written. Reading gives you the best of both worlds."

"Maybe," I said, "but if you can break free from the fake book, let the music play you instead of the other way around, you'll comprehend."

"Comprehend what?"

"That playing from the heart is as close as to the truth as you'll get."

"Close to what truth?"

"Everything," I said. "*The truth about everything.*"

"How much have you had to drink?"

"Too much, apparently."

She smiled. "I didn't say I couldn't play by ear. You assumed I couldn't because of the book." She closed the catalog.

Maybe it was the whiskey. Or the whiskey mixed with the wine. But I felt defensive. She talked a good game and seemed sincere, but for some reason I got the feeling she was putting me on. I wanted her to know I was good at what I did; I wanted her to know I had the juice, but there, in that moment in The Swamp Fox Room I knew I was in over my head. The last person I needed in my life was another man's wife, especially the wife of a Captain in the Navy.

CHAPTER EIGHT

Some guys enjoy living dangerously; Bill Reed was one of them. When he bought The Apartment Club on Highway 61, next door to Cross Seed, it was supposed to be a legitimate business. He hadn't planned to use it as a base of operations for his illegal activities, but his economics dictated otherwise.

My first encounter with Reed came right after he announced he was renovating the old Five O'clock Club. Nicknamed The Five, it was a sorry excuse for a supper club down at the end of Cumberland Street. He renamed the club The Caravan and booked my band, Freeway, to christen the place. We blew every club in town out of the water from the first week on. People lined up all the way back to East Bay Street and around the corner. When the owner of The Folly Beach Pier saw what was happening, he made an offer and Reed immediately sold the club for a nice profit.

Later on I learned that before moving to Charleston, Reed had been a building contractor in North Myrtle Beach specializing in timeshare condominiums. Thanks to a bank officer in the loan department of First Coastal Carolina Trust who owed him money from gambling, Reed was able to over draw on several major construction loans without an inspection. When he made his last draw on The Sea Oats Luxury Suites, the only thing standing on the site was a concrete shell. This fraud ruined the bank and the loan officer shot himself. Bill Reed, on the other hand, moved to Charleston, bought a house on the river, a boat and still had a half million dollars he'd laundered through a dummy corporation set up in Florence. He used part of his little nut to buy and remodel The Caravan then rolled the money into The Apartment Club.

When The Apartment Club opened, he made a big splash by telling everyone how far out the place was going to be and loudly putting down his competition in the other bars. Hiring me to play in his house band was a big deal to him. Even though I was only signed on for three months, he had the crazy notion I'd give up my new gig at The Merch and stay on with him.

When I arrived that Friday night The Reed, as he often referred to himself, was back in his office hunched over a spiral bound note book with a bottle of Jim Beam bourbon, a shot glass and a nickel-plated .45 lying next to an open bag of potato chips spilled out on the desk. He was copying numbers from a small stack of invoices into the notebook.

Another sharp dresser, he wore a custom, gray herringbone tweed sport coat, a starched white snap-tab collar shirt open at the neck, black slacks and cordovan Johnson and Murphy tassel loafers with no socks. His tie, draped over the doorknob, lay across a monogrammed white silk scarf. He had short black hair sprinkled with flecks of silver cut close with high sideburns and a square face that reminded me of a young Michael Douglas, only slightly better looking. Milky white skin only showed on his wrists, hands and from the neck up. The black hair on the back of the hands themselves stood in stark contrast to the gold watch, bracelet and diamond ring on the right. A single, initialed pinky ring was on the left. Miniature dice cufflinks rolling snake eyes had a tiny diamond centered on each cube. At five feet six, what he lacked in stature was offset by flamboyance, arrogance and a lack of taste usually reserved for the cadre of good old boy politicians he was always trying to impress. In the brief time we'd known each other, I learned, The Reed didn't like surprises, so I tapped on the door casing to get his attention. He glanced up from his accounting work and snorted.

"Well, well, if it ain't the fuckin' prodigal himself, come draggin' home to daddy. What the hell do you want, Deacon?"

Deacon was Bill Reed's nickname for me because he knew I didn't have any interest in making a name for myself via his illegal activities. To Bill's way of thinking, if you're not playing the game to win, you might as well go to church and if you're going to go to church, you might as well be a deacon, because while there can be many deacons, there can only be one preacher and he's playing to win.

"I just stopped in to say hello, any harm in that?" I said.

"Like shit. You're here to see my new girl."

"So, what's wrong with coming to hear a good singer?"

"A hell of a lot, if you're the pimp for the competition. Imagine me dropping by The Merch to hear your guitar player," Bill said. "Tell me you wouldn't wonder what the fuck was up?"

He shoved a handful of chips in his mouth and chased it with a shot of bourbon. He had a point. I'd done the same thing to Tommy Bennett earlier in the afternoon.

"So, other than that, Mrs. Lincoln, how'd you like the play?" I said, attempting to lighten his mood.

"Always the wise guy, ain't you, Josie? Is there anything specific I can do for you at the moment? I'm busy here." He went back to transferring the numbers from the invoices into the notebook. Interesting, I thought, Freddie had also been transferring numbers into an accounting ledger when I met with him; only his were from pages ripped from a spiral notebook; like the one on Reed's desk.

"Not really," I said, continuing to watch Bill work. "I was just in the neighborhood; thought I'd stick my head in the door and say hello."

"Right," barked The Reed, "and I'm a nigga' jet pilot."

After he finished recording each invoice, he wadded it up and tossed it into a small brass wastepaper basket by the file cabinet. The basket was full of those crumpled invoices. Again, I wondered why a businessman, especially one as corrupt as Bill Reed, would throw away an original invoice. Roy kept all the original invoices for The Merch. He showed them to me when he was teaching me his filing system. "You have to take care of your front," Roy had told me, "if you're going to cover your back." In other words you had to run at least one legitimate operation, if you were going to make money under the table. What Reed was doing didn't make sense to me, because I figured the club, like every other club in town, would be his front for under the table cash. But it was none of my business. After tossing the last wadded up invoice, he closed the ledger quickly, grabbed the .45, shoved it into the waistband of his trousers, then snatched the handkerchief and tie off the doorknob.

"Let's go up front. I'll buy you a drink so you'll know there's no hard feelin's about the way you left me hangin'." He stuffed the handkerchief in the breast pocket of his jacket. Without so much as a glance in a mirror, he flipped his shirt collar up, looped the tie around his neck and manicured a perfect half Windsor knot complete with a strategically centered dimple, then snapped the tab under the knot so quickly it all looked like a magic trick. The tie was perfect. He shot his cuffs and strolled toward the bar.

"I didn't leave you hanging and you know it," I said. "You asked me to play in your club until my gig at The Merch opened up. That's what I did. You even wished me luck when I left."

"Don't get so emotional, kid. I'm just razzin' you." He put his hand on my shoulder and wagged his finger in my face like he was sending me off to kindergarten. "Just make sure to keep your hands off my new star. Business is good lately and I wanna keep it that way. Now, what're you drinking? Never mind, I know what you drink."

When we reached the bar, The Reed licked his thumb and peeled a twenty off a roll of bills secured by a rubber band. It was too thick for either a wallet or a money clip, and he held it creased in his fist on the counter. The bartender was an exotic black female wearing a half unbuttoned yellow silk blouse tied at her waist. Big brass loops dangled from each ear. Her almond shaped eyes never blinked, giving her face a supernatural look, somewhere between a genie and those Abyssinian cats worshiped by the ancient Egyptians. She glanced at the bankroll, looked at Bill and smiled, showing off her perfect white teeth.

"Cricket, my love," Reed cooed, "pull a bottle of Wild Turkey from my personal stock and pencil Mr. Chapman's name on the label, will you, Honey?" He winked. "And pour him one on the rocks and put it on my tab."

"You buy drinks at your own bar?" I said.

"Inventory, my man, inventory; I run a legitimate business here."

As soon as he said it, I thought about the wastepaper basket full of crumpled invoices. Cricket passed the cocktail to Reed, which he then handed to me.

She tried to take the twenty out of his fist, but he held it tight, pulling her toward him. When he finally loosened his grip, she jerked the bill out of his hand, stuck out her tongue, rang up a three-dollar sale and stuffed the change into the front pocket of her white skin-tight short shorts. She bent over to take orange juice out of the cooler, The Reed couldn't take his eyes off her ass. How's he get away with being so brazen with this black chick, I thought, when everybody knew how jealous, Janet Collins, his girlfriend, could get?

"Thanks," I said, as if I hadn't noticed a thing.

"Enjoy it in good health. Anything else you want, tell Miss Cricket." He snapped back from his reverie. "I gotta go. And remember what I said; hands off my girl."

He gave me a good-natured slap on the back and started to walk away, then stopped to look back at me. "Of course, you're welcome here anytime, kid, you know that, don't you?"

"Thanks," I said, toasting him with the glass.

Reed shot me with his thumb and index finger pistol, then spun on his heels and strutted out the door like a banty rooster. I turned around just in time to see a busboy leaving his office carrying the waste paper basket and dump it in a thirty-gallon trash can.

"When do I get to see this girl singer I've heard so much about?" I said.

"She tends to run a little late, depending on the crowd, but you can hang out right here, with me, baby." Cricket leaned over the bar causing her blouse to open up and flash one of her breasts. "Oops!" she giggled and filled my glass.

I took a dark booth in the back as the band started warming up. There was no sign of the singer. A dozen white roses, a bottle of red wine and a tulip shaped wine glass sat on a card table off to the side of a partition behind the stage. While the guitar player tested the vocal mics, a waiter uncorked the wine, poured a glass and carried it behind the partition. The silhouette of a tall, slim woman wearing low-slung bell-bottoms and a halter-top took the wine and downed it. The wine bottle looked familiar. Then it dawned on me. That was the same Bordeaux Bobbie had Marcus serve me in The Swamp Fox Room. But, I didn't know anything about wine. I drank bourbon. Everybody could be drinking the stuff, for all I knew.

The drummer came out looking tired and distracted. He could've been stoned, but I sensed the pressure of gigging six nights a week was getting to him, probably the others as well. Drummers are the hardest working members of the band. Both arms, both legs, each doing something totally different, full body involvement, like flying a helicopter. Taking a week off, to see who else was in town, would probably do him some good. There's nothing like checking out the competition to give your own gig a renewed sense of purpose.

Instead of interrupting them during the sound check, like most idiots who start drinking early, I decided to wait a few minutes. The new voice I'd heard so much about, that was due to start in less than five minutes, still hadn't appeared on stage. Not a good sign.

When the band finished tuning, I went back to the bar and ordered another drink. The Abyssinian stood on tiptoe to run a bar towel across the counter top before she set the bourbon down on a napkin. The gesture, calculated to expose the nipples of her breasts, worked.

"You need anything else, Mr. Chapman? Anything at all?"

"Sure," I said, as I watched her pour every possible ounce of sexuality she could muster into writing my name on the napkin that served as my tab.

"Do you have a cherry?"

She batted her eyes and stuck her tongue out at me. The Apartment Club must be going through a few changes, I thought. I walked back across the the club, toward the back edge of the dance floor. The guitar player had finished tuning as I passed to the right of the stage; I decided to speak to him.

"So, what time do you guys crank up?" I said.

"As soon as Bobbie gets here," said the guitar player.

I thought I was hearing things, so I asked him to repeat the name.

"Did you say Barbie?"

"No," he said. "Her name is Bobbie, like in the socks."

I waited a couple beats and picked my chin up off the floor. There was no way it could be the same girl I'd just seen at The Swamp Fox Room. Bobbie Storm was a lounge act. This girl had a rock and roll reputation. I walked back to the bar shaking my head.

Cricket had implied the band only started at eight if there were enough people to justify it. I looked around and the room was about half-full. Not bad, I thought, for a club that, normally, didn't start jumping until well after ten. I said thanks and walked back to my seat in the back booth.

When the band kicked off with "Heat Wave," the singer still had not appeared. They vamped for a full minute then a girl stepped onto the back edge of the stage and picked up the wine glass. I watched her tilt the glass, draining it slowly. She wasn't out in the light yet but her features were similar to those of the girl from The Swamp Fox. Her dark hair was pulled back, covered by a baseball cap. For a minute, I thought the pianist had a twin.

Suddenly she stepped into the light, grabbed the microphone and all doubt vanished; it was Bobbie. But the person on that stage had nothing in common with the cocktail pianist I'd sat beside two hours earlier. All I could do was sit there mesmerized, watching and listening. The wine didn't appear to affect her ability to sing. And man, could the girl could sing. The rhythm and emotion she put into each lyric solid as granite.

They finished off "Heat Wave" and went right into "Respect." The energy level Bobbie projected was amazing. It wasn't hard to understand why The Apartment Club stayed packed every night. She was fun to watch, but her band wasn't able to sustain the same intensity she was projecting. It was obvious, to me at least, that she was holding back to keep them from sounding painfully inferior to her. She reminded me of a falcon on a leash.

Technically, the other musicians played OK. They were in tune, the guitar player never missed a note, the drummer was never late on the beat and the bass player was steady but not very strong. There was no spontaneity and no matter how she tried, she couldn't drag the band up to her level. So she held back. As a result the band never really took off. Bobbie took off, but as soon as the leash ran out, she was stuck straining at the end of it.

If I didn't know anything else about music, I knew how to project hard driving, climb the walls, get your rocks off, blow the doors off rock and roll. Because not only did I understand how the spirit of music used the performer as a channel; I'd also learned from Roy to surround myself with the best musicians. Unlike Bobbie, I had a tendency to gravitate musically to the level of the other musicians in the band. That's why I didn't sit in with mediocre players. I knew I didn't have what it takes to pull them up to my level, and I couldn't afford to be dragged down to theirs, especially not in public. As my brother Jackson Woods used to say, "Hearing notes and liking them is not the same as hearing notes and under-standing their relation to the melody. It's like throwing out your anchor and not knowing where the ship is."

In this band, Bobbie was the anchor, but the chain was too short. I couldn't help wondering how she'd sound if she was singing in front of The Magnificent Seven. It would be a humbling experience for all concerned, I knew that much.

I wasn't about to approach her during her performance, but for the first time in years I allowed myself to entertain the idea of getting my horn and sitting in with another band after I'd been drinking. If she was the real thing, standing next to her on stage would give me some idea of our potential together. This line of reasoning was the noble side of my bullshitting myself. I snapped back to reality when the voice inside my head said simply "You need to get up there and play with her."

Bobbie ended the first set by delivering a soulful rendition of "Try A Little Tenderness." The room exploded in a roar of screaming applause. I was on my feet the instant the last chorus sounded, clapping and whistling along with everyone else. Bobbie walked off the stage to a group of admiring fans, all eagerly trying to talk to her. I stood in the back watching with a smile so big it hurt. She scanned the room looking right past me, then her eyes darted back to mine in recognition. After politely excusing herself, she walked straight to my booth and hugged me.

"Well, what'd you think?" she said.

"Anything you can't do? Like yodel or gymnastics? You were great!" I gushed like a teenager.

"For the last two years of my life, this is all I've wanted to do," Bobbie said, as we slipped into the booth opposite each other. "I'd almost given up hope of ever playing full time. When we moved here, Mark stayed gone a lot, and I had all this time on my hands."

I told her she'd made the right decision to stick it out. She asked me to get my horn and sit in during the second set. I flew out to the T-Bird, grabbed the Mark VI out of the trunk and raced back inside.

"Ever seen one of these?" I took the horn out of its case. "All this scroll work on the bell is done by hand. The brass is recycled artillery shells left in France after World War II. There'll never be another horn exactly it."

She reached over, gently touching the bell with her fingers. "It's beautiful. Where did you get it?"

"My best friend bought it for me when my other horn was stolen," I said.

"Out of the darkness comes light."

"Yeah, silver linings and all that stuff. So, what are we going to play?"

"I don't know, what do you wanna play? The band is pretty weird about people sitting in. They're... how should I put this? Too structured. I don't think they adapt to change very well."

At that moment, Cricket walked up.

"Excuse me," she said, leaning over, like only Cricket could lean over. "I hate to interrupt you two lovebirds, but Bobbie, honey, someone would like to meet you. Could you take a moment?"

Bobbie put her hand on my arm, smiled and said, "Sure."

As if on cue, Tommy Bennett walked over. He acknowledged me with a polite nod, introduced himself to Bobbie, then proceeded to give her his card while going into detail about how wonderful he thought she was.

"I'm starting a new booking agency here in town," he explained. "We'll be doing a lot of private parties, club gigs and concerts. I'm hoping I can call you, if a suitable venue came open?"

I stared down at the table, amazed; Freddie had double teamed this girl. If I didn't get her then he wanted to make sure Tommy did. And if I didn't get her, chances were good Freddie would do everything possible to cut my throat at The Merch, especially if he'd figured out the details about my deal with Roy. Freddie was trying to set me up for a fall, I was sure of it, paranoia or no paranoia. Bobbie noticed my apprehension immediately.

"Thanks," she said. "But I handle my own booking, cuts out the middle man, I'm sure you understand." Bennett's jaw tightened. "This is my friend Josie Chapman," she said kindly, "he has a band, maybe he'd be interested."

"We're old friends," Bennett blurted. "How's it going, Josie? Nice horn."

"Great man," I said, intuitively tightening my grip on the Selmer. "I don't see you for five years, then you show up twice in the same day."

Tommy Bennett turned his bloodshot attention back to Bobbie. "Josie plays at The Merch, but I guess you already know that." She smiled, glanced across her wine at me and said nothing. An awkward silence ensued.

"Well, I just wanted to introduce myself and leave you my card. If you change your mind, give me a call. See you around, Josie." I nodded, Bobbie smiled, and Bennett walked, quickly, out the front door.

I was thinking how odd that Tommy, who four hours earlier was so strung out he had to write his number on a matchbook cover, shows up out of nowhere looking like he stepped out of Esquire with a fist full of business cards. The band was on stage for the second set.

Bobbie looked at me. "You ready?"

"Ready as I'll ever be." I got up with my horn in my right hand, carrying it like a rifle. It was a gimmick to make me look like a badass musician. I'd learned it from watching rock guitar players. You have to be careful where you grab the horn though, or you'll bend a rod, which would throw the action off, and you'd suck. Bobbie took my left hand and pretended to pull me to the stage. "Don't introduce me to the audience," I said. "I'll stand over to the side and play through the bass players mic when he's not singing."

"He sings one song," Bobbie answered, "and it's not until the next set."

Her smile was so infectious I battled to keep my feelings in check and concentrate on the music. I had to keep telling myself, over and over, that she was married.

The band kicked off with a 12-bar blues riff in C minor. I took a decent solo, but the other musicians were too inflexible. I couldn't play outside the chords without throwing them completely off. The whole experience was frustrating. Bobbie was right; the other musicians were too structured. There was no room to move around; the music was claustrophobic.

Bobbie Storm ended our first set together with a pumped-up version of "Knock on Wood." Determined to make my trip worthwhile, she hadn't let me out of the corner of her eye the whole set. Nothing could stop her for giving the last chord a fist-in-the-air, screaming, cut-off.

The cacophony of cheers, hoots and whistles was deafening, and then suddenly, she took off on her own without the band. Confidence and a need to fly drove her into a studied, a cappella crescendo. I understood instinctively what she was doing and followed her note-for-note, riff-for-riff without thinking about the notes. Together we became a channel for something larger than two individuals. She'd call and I'd answer; an act of raw emotion for both of us that went way past impressed.

When that second set ended, The Apartment Club erupted in yet another thunder of cheers, applause and whistling. My heart was pounding so hard my chest ached, but I kept my cool.

The other musicians slouched off the stage, I pretended to check the springs on my horn and adjusted the reed. After about thirty seconds of this fooling around,

I looked straight into her eyes without blinking and smiled. Bobbie Storm was glowing. I looked at my watch, knowing I had to go.

"I've never experienced anything like that," she said.

"There's a first time for everything," I winked.

"When can we do it again?"

"When can you sit in with my band?"

"Soon?" she said.

"The sooner, the better."

Bobbie walked me back to the booth where I'd left my horn case and stood beside me while I packed up. I explained that I hadn't meant to tip my hand about offering her a job while we were in The Swamp Fox Room. Besides, I couldn't offer her a gig at The Merch while standing right there in The Apartment Club. She understood.

She suggested she could come by one night during the following week, hear my band and maybe sing a song or two with us. I nodded in agreement then she grinned and I grinned. We understood each other completely and decided to have another drink together, before I had to go.

While Bobbie went backstage to get her wine glass, I walked to the bar and ordered bourbon on ice. Cricket held back on the nipple flash.

Over that last drink, Bobbie's excitement gave our conversation a definitely pensive atmosphere, but we were careful to never let long silences develop. We sipped our drinks, and she insisted on putting them on her tab. She leaned across the table pondering the chances of a full-time future in the music business. She told me she'd wanted to be a singer ever since she was a little girl growing up in rural Alabama. An old, black delta blues man played guitar on the front porch of the general store in her hometown of Hamilton. Her face went blank; her mind drifting back to some place far away from The Apartment Club. When she snapped back, she took a sip of her wine, looking down into the glass with her shoulders bunched. In a muted voice, she contradicted herself by saying she wasn't sure she could get used to working so much. The hours were already getting to her.

"Don't you have a gig to play?" she said.

"I don't have to start until ten," I said warmly, knowing it was already a quarter to ten.

"Will you come back and sit in with us again?"

"Of course," I said. "The owner told me I could play here anytime."

"There's something about that man," she said, then caught herself.

"You don't have to explain Bill Reed," I said. "I know all about him."

Bobbie slid out of the booth and looked back at the bandstand. I heard the drummer tap his snare and high hat and then the sound of her guitar player returning.

We'd shared something she was having difficulty understanding. I sensed that not understanding was a feeling she knew firsthand. Uncertainty both excited and depressed her. She didn't know it, but that was one reason she was so good at the blues. In the end, the good ones have the blues in their blood, it enables them to empathize with the human condition and kick ass at the same time without developing a serious conflict of interest.

I walked toward the front door, past the cigarette machine and pool tables, dazed by the exhilarating set with Bobbie. I thought I was going soft in my old age, although twenty-three didn't exactly make me a candidate for a retirement village. To be honest, though, the disappointment of going back to the small time club routine was real. Even though I was working toward owning The Merch, I'd never been as on fire about it as I was playing beside a natural like Bobbie. I hadn't even worked up a sweat yet, but I felt very tired.

On my way to my car, the side door of The Apartment Club opened up. The bus boy who'd gathered the trash from Bill's office came out dragging the big trash can. When he heaved it over the edge of the dumpster several balls of paper spilled onto the pavement. They looked like the invoices Bill had wadded up and tossed in his wastepaper basket. The kid didn't appear to notice them. So after he went back inside, I picked them up.

CHAPTER NINE

There were three invoices from The Sea Oats Corporation; the same company Bill owned when he remodeled the Five O'clock Club. Two were for $7500 each, and one was for $5000. All three description lines contained serial numbers indicating tools and equipment for a dead president: George Washington, Abraham Lincoln and Thomas Jefferson. I thought it was very bizarre until I saw United States Navy Supply Depot, Charleston, SC, typed into the billing address. Reed was supplying the U.S. Navy with parts for nuclear submarines.

Another series of numbers, typed along the top of each invoice, ended with the letters "NS" in boldface type. I remembered the Navy jazz musicians from my early days at The Merch joking about NS. If one of them made a mistake, he'd say "Hey, it's only music, not NS." When I asked them what NS meant, they laughed and said "National Security." How, I wondered, could Bill Reed be doing any business at all with the Navy base? Stranger still was trying to imagine him supplying parts for nuclear submarines. I stuffed the invoices in my pocket, got in my car and drove back downtown.

My stomach fluttered when I walked back into The Merch that evening. Over yet another straight bourbon, I listened to Montague and Sinclair argue over a recipe for deer meat. Freddie May had arranged a catering job for Wednesday of the following week. The job would involve cooking wild game for the members of the James Island Hunt Club out at Mosquito Beach. Sinclair had asked about a marinade for venison, and Montague responded only a wall-eyed fool could be so stupid. After about fifteen seconds of mindless chatter over whether or not to use cloves, I went backstage to warm up. I folded the three invoices, and carefully hid two in a zippered microphone pouch I kept in my horn case. The other one went in my wallet.

Since returning to Charleston, I hadn't been particularly careful about warming up before the show. My ritual, including relaxing into the horn, making sure keys didn't stick, the reed fit right, the mouthpiece was clean, was more of a carryover from my days on the road. When I was new to the music business I was deadly serious about being on time and completely ready to play at a moment's notice. I'd practiced constantly, studied chord changes, breathing exercises and listened tirelessly to the Coltrane solos. Brand names of the instruments the side men used on all the records taught me who made the best saxophones, mouthpieces, gig bags, reeds. Like an athlete training himself for a shot at the Olympics wants to be the best, I became a perfectionist. Nothing prepared me for the sick feeling I had that night.

Each of us had a chair in the dressing room, mine was back against the wall. That evening I began to think, for the first time, that maybe moving back had all been a big mistake. Even though I knew I wasn't star material, I used to fill every minute of my day with some activity centered on the all-important goal of becoming a star. Better to shoot for the moon and hit an eagle, than shoot for an eagle and hit a rock, right? But, what was I starring in? My bedroom was a testament to my obsession. Littered with records, music books and posters from the gigs I'd played, there were backstage ID tags stuck in the edges of the mirror frame. Autographed pictures pinned all over the wall, traced the history of my career from the time I was eighteen: The Temptations, The Four Tops, The Miracles, Janis Joplin, Chicago, Jimi Hendrix. Press passes, road maps, booking agency fliers, motel reservation guides, block-booking convention security passes, and rock festival posters were still in packing boxes.

I'd made myself knowledgeable in every area of the business, but none of it really touched me. Living out of suitcase was a drag. I didn't even know if I'd ever enjoyed traveling, or particularly cared about being famous, either. I was sitting in a chair cradling my horn staring down at the floor, about as confused as I'd ever been, when Bill Reed stuck his head through the back door of the dressing room.

"Josie, you sweet thang. I heard how you killed 'em tonight." His country, redneck, twangy voice reminded me of a Jew's harp. "I hate to pop in unexpected, but I need a favor."

I couldn't believe Bill Reed was skulking around the back door of The Merch, and I didn't exactly jump at the chance of doing any favors for him. Especially, since I'd just been sent to steal his star performer.

"I've got this bag of money I need to stash for a few hours, and I can't find Strawberry," he said. "He's with some bitch from Charlotte."

"Man, I can't do that, Bill," I said. "I've got a gig to play."

"Deacon, this is a one-hour job. You don't even have to go anywhere. I'll be back in forty-five minutes, just hold the bag for me, that's all."

"Please don't ask me to do this, man," I said. "I can't be responsible for your money, what if something happens while you're gone?"

"Hey, this is The Reed talking. I ain't setting you up for no Mafia hit. Five Franklins to sit on this bag for fifty minutes. It's more than you make in a week at this joint." That wasn't true but I let him believe it.

Although everything told me to turn him down, he was desperate and I didn't want him mad at me. It had been something of a public humiliation for Reed when I left The Apartment Club. He'd taken it personally when I finished my obligation to him, and then went to work for Roy, but for some reason I didn't understand, he still trusted me. So, rather than telling him I wouldn't hold the money, stupid me asked for a thousand dollars.

"That's bullshit, man! You think I'm in the charity business?"

"Look, Bill, if you keep this shit up you're going to get us both killed. You'd do better going back to scamming banks out of construction loans."

"Do this for me, Deacon," he whispered. When he was desperate, Bill smiled like a wolf with its ears back. "I don't have time to hassle with you over this. Man, why you doing this shit to me? You know there ain't a bag in this town worth a G, just to hold."

"Sorry, Bill."

"You're sorry?" he said. "That's all you can fuckin' say? You don't know from fuckin' sorry, by God. You don't remember when you come to me? You didn't have two nickels to rub together. I made all my people jump when I said frog, except you." He was pacing back and forth outside, between the side door and the Thunderbird.

"Deacon, you wanted to put together a crew, make a name for yourself. You don't remember what I did for you? I built you a stage with nothing but top-notch equipment, lights, sound, the works. Man, I dug you. I made you a household word in this town. You owe me."

"Judas Priest, Bill, I played in your house band for six weeks over a year ago and bagged for you three times for nothing. Now you talk like you taught me everything I know. I don't want the responsibility, OK? If something happens to your money while I'm holding it, you'll kill me, or worse. It isn't the money and you damn well know it. I don't need your money."

"Oh, man, don't talk that shit. Oh, Josie, brother, don't ever let me hear you say you don't want my money. You don't turn down cash money. Nobody'll trust you if you start turning down free money. That's a bad sign, sign of a man going straight. I've seen too many good players get to thinking they're God's gift. If you start thinking that shit, you might as well go to church and if…"

"I know, I know, you sound like Freddie."

"Listen to him. He knows what's going down."

"If I listened to him, Bill, I would've offered your new singer a job right there in your own club." I thought this might make him believe my refusal wasn't personal.

"That's cold, real cold. Take seven hundred. I'll call later and tell you where to deliver it."

"Deliver it? Motherfuck! I'm not delivering shit," I said. "Call back; tell Sinclair what time Strawberry'll be by to pick it up. I'll keep it in my sax case."

"I'll be in touch," he said and tossed me a small zippered bank bag.

The money in the bag usually represented payoffs for bets placed in a numbers game. I'd heard about it, but up until then I'd thought the game was controlled by black domestic help who worked in the hospitals. Reed along with a few others had apparently pooled their money in an effort to buy in. I'd carried money bags for him a few times during my first weeks back in Charleston, but it made me nervous to be in the same room with so much of his cash. That nickel-plated .45 Bill carried had a reputation. Like a lot of rich rednecks, his excuse was that he needed it for protection from the "spooks."

Oddly enough, during the entire time I worked in Charleston's nightclub business, I never once heard of a racially motivated incident among the musicians or the gamblers in town. So, part of Bill's justification for the piece, I felt, was more to project his bad guy "you don't wanna cross me" image. Word on the street was he'd pistol-whipped two men in two weeks.

I'll tell you something about the Charleston I knew back then. Everybody knew his place; everybody knew his own business. When violence did flare up, it got handled quickly, without disrupting the natural ebb and flow of the money. But when a man like Bill Reed came to town unraveling his mouth and slapping people with his pistol, one of two scenarios quickly played out. Either the man left town of his own free will or the man died. If he was bad enough, sometimes even leaving town wouldn't save him. Whether or not this street justice involved the legendary Strong Man depended on who you talked to. But things got settled quickly, regardless.

A few seconds after Bill left, there was a tap on the dressing room door. I opened it and found Montague waiting outside the dressing room.

"He heh', ya' know? Rite cha' 'mongest us," he whispered. "You needs to know, dat."

"Who's here?"

"Scrong Man."

"Montague," I said. "Man, I don't need this right now. Could we talk about it later?"

Montague became indignant, raising himself up. I'd hurt his feelings. "Don' hab t' talk 'bout it. I jes' lettin' y'know so's you ain't caught unawares."

"I appreciate your concern, I really do, but…"

"Ain't no but. An' don't hab t' 'preciate nuttin', jes lettin' ya know. Here yo' keep dis."

Montague handed me a three-inch wooden crucifix, stained dark with a thin leather cord.

"What's this?" I said.

"'Carve outta slave pews cast out by de' First Scot Prezbyterium Chu'ch. It'll protek yo'."

"You think I need protection? Protection from what?"

"You bes' be 'ware's 'en hab yo' wits 'bout you's all I'm sayin'. Scrong man's he'ah, 'mongst'us, walkin' 'roun'." He started backing up, then paused, "an' he be lookin' fo' you."

I tossed the tiny cross into the accessory compartment in my sax case, then covered it with the money pouch.

CHAPTER TEN

Holding dirty money was a bad idea. I knew it the moment I agreed to it. But when he sprang the part about delivering it to God knows where, that was fucked up. Bill Reed had caught me in a weak moment, before I had a chance to think the deal through. But a thousand dollars would cover this drop and make up for the freebies. At least that's how I justified my decision. During the first set, I was kicking myself so hard for getting suckered, I couldn't concentrate. My missed cues, wrong notes, and general lack of focus didn't go unnoticed by the band. During the break, Jack and Monk cornered me by the men's room door. Jack went first.

"What's wrong with you, man?"

"I had a meeting with Freddie this afternoon," I said, looking around the room to see if Roy had showed up.

"What's on Twinkle Toes' mind these days?" Monk said.

"He wants to hire a girl singer to front the band."

"Oh, really?" Jack looked at Monk, who was running his hand over his bald head, then back at me. They understood the money issue immediately.

"What's Roy say about all this?" Monk rotated his sunglasses to the top of his head.

"I haven't had a chance to discuss it with him. All three of us were supposed to meet this afternoon, but according to Freddie, Roy, had an urgent business matter and couldn't make it."

"Well, he's back in his office, why don't you go talk to him?" Jack said.

"I think I'll do that." I walked back toward the office.

I tapped on the door. Roy opened it without speaking. The office was a dingy cream color with walls stained a light brown patina from years of nicotine. The brown shag carpet riddled with burn marks, and there was the desk, of course. Impeccably dressed in a navy blue suit; white shirt and rep tie, he sat down poured a shot of J&B into a highball glass. I pulled up a small leather chair.

"How you doin', Roy?"

"Not so good, Josie," he downed the Scotch. "Looks like our deal might go south on us."

My jaw tightened. "I don't understand. I've got a signed contract, not to mention your word as a gentleman."

"My health is not good. You want a drink?"

He looked exhausted. His hair had gone from wavy light gray to wispy white; tiny specks of dandruff lay on the shoulders of his suit coat. He pulled out a clean glass.

"What the fuck, one more can't hurt," I said.

"I'm going to have to get out of the business sooner than I thought. My liver is gone and the doctor has given me six months to get my affairs in order." He lifted his glass to toast me, "Here's to good health," our glasses clinked, then we threw back the shots.

"Does anyone else know about this?" I pushed my glass toward the bottle.

"My brother in Atlanta, that's where I'll be..." he poured two more shots, "staying, for lack of a more appropriate term."

"And you're sure about this, I mean the doctors, they're sure?"

"They're sure."

I sat there staring at him in stunned disbelief, my ears ringing static.

"Mind if I ask you a question off the record?" I said.

"Ask anything you want."

"Just between me and you?"

"Certainly."

"Did you call Jack's house today and set up a meeting between you, me and Freddie, to discuss hiring the girl singer at The Apartment Club, to front The Mag Seven?"

Roy and I'd been together long enough for him to surmise my posing the question meant the thing had happened. He leaned back in his chair, looked at the ceiling and let out a deep breath.

"He's out of control, isn't he?"

"Yep. That he is."

"Do you still want to buy this place?"

"Of course, that's why I came back to Charleston."

"You know, when you buy the business, that's all you buy. I mean, I don't own the property, I lease it."

All this time I'd taken it for granted the business included both building and property. Big lesson, that one: The thing you take for granted will nail you every time. I'd made this mistake before in a different context. It was the same mistake I'd made when I was with Freeway: Running a show doesn't always mean you own it. This new revelation threw a completely new light on the subject.

"So, who owns the property?" I said.

"I'm not at liberty to discuss it right now. I have a meeting with him here tomorrow at 2:30. Call me here at 2:45. I should know something."

I sat in the chair with my left hand wrapped around my alligator mouth and my right arm holding the glass across my stomach, trying to keep my humming-bird ass from throwing up. Roy had known me since I was a kid. He knew how heartbreaking the situation was, how much The Merch meant to me. I'd never imagined the club without his involvement. I figured he'd always be around even if it just meant coming down to hear the band occasionally. The break was over. I sucked it up, finished the scotch, and turned toward the door.

"When will you know something definite?" I said.

"Sometime early next week. I won't keep you hanging." Roy grinned, as only Roy could grin, then said, "Cheer up kid, it's not the end of the world. Might be the best thing that could've happened for both of us."

I found that hard to swallow, but Roy's courage in the face of his own bad news kept me from feeling too sorry for myself. At least I wasn't dying, which was something, which was better than nothing.

We played until three then called it a night. I lied to Jack and Monk about everything, told them the situation was under control and not to worry. I couldn't do anything until I heard what the property owner had to say. In a way, I was relieved the matter was, for the moment, out of my hands. Roy was gone by the time we quit.

Backstage, an envelope with my name on it lay on top of the bank bag. Inside, a note in Bill Reed's scribbled handwriting was wrapped around ten one-hundred dollar bills. The mark's name was Bootsy Williams. I was to go by the St. James Hotel and ask for a woman named Erlene Brown. She'd tell me where to find Williams to make the drop. The rest of the band was out the door by three-fifteen; I figured on having the drop done before sunrise.

The more I thought about it, the more bizarre the deal felt. For starters, there was an even twenty thousand dollars in the bank bag, half the amount in a normal drop. And the cash was all new bills, two bank wrapped ten thousand dollar straps of 100s, no wrinkled bills, in smaller denominations, wrapped with rubber bands, like those normally associated with an illegal operation. Making two stops also bothered me. Especially since one was a public building in an all-black neighborhood. Why wasn't I going straight to the mark? Paying a grand for a bag drop to a black man was strange enough. But to send a white boy into an all-black neighborhood, in the seamiest section of Charleston, in the middle of the night? Carrying that much cash? Just to get directions? It made no sense. But, like a fool I grabbed my jacket.

The Merch was empty except for Freddie, Barry and a couple die-hard blackjack players. I didn't hang around. My horn case went in the trunk of the T-bird, then I lifted the tray out of the console and slipped the bag down inside. Montague had left the other half of my sandwich in a paper bag on the seat. I set it inside the console.

By three-thirty, the rain had stopped, but a day's worth of moisture hung in the air, and the mercury vapor streetlights were haloed by concentric circles. There were a few cars parked at The Fork, an all-night restaurant across the street from the St. James Hotel, and one Blue Ribbon taxi idling at the curb. The late bus was empty, the destination sign read "Garage." I turned onto Hagood Street.

No signs of life emanated from inside the dark, dilapidated clapboard houses. A blanket of ground-hugging fog hovered over puddles on wet asphalt artificially illuminated by bounce back from the umbrellas of streetlights, creating a noxious glow in the shimmering gasoline rainbows.

I'd found a parking place on the corner of Hagood and Ashton Street, a block back from Spring Street. The car was off the pavement facing The Citadel and Hampton Park. The spot offered the best straight shot out of the neighborhood if I had to make a run for it. I locked the car and walked to the corner. The light at Spring and Hagood turned red.

A couple of shag-wags pulled up, a bright Pinehurst green twilight Coupe Deville with two suited-up fedoras maintaining perfect Philly lean posture, their brims close as possible without touching. They rolled up beside a red drop-top Buick Electra 225, driven by a man who could've passed for a preacher. Both cars were personalized with every bell, whistle, mirror, antenna, day-glow rhinestone studded mud flap and spring loaded curb feeler available from J.C. Whitney. The occupants exchanged a few words, then the Buick, mufflers gurgling, pulled ahead, dragged past the St. James and turned into the parking lot of The Fork. The Cadillac pulled in behind it.

Along the sidewalk, an all-night café called The Back Door Bar & Grill fed a steady stream of patrons coming out of the Club Ubangi. An odd assortment of wildly dressed night people made their moves in the muggy, dirty air. Pimps and their whores dressed like Sly and The Family Stone lounged in doorways leading to ramshackle second floor apartments.

There was an exotic foreign eroticism mixed with an almost Harlem or West Village energy which permeated the air of this wet, dreary night. Everywhere I looked, poverty and filth clashed with brightly colored fabric, oily hair, the flash of steel and fishnet hose.

The smell of fish fried in burnt oil floated over the sound of Sam Cook's "You Send Me" wafting out the windows of the St. James, down the narrow alleys between the buildings. In the distance, above the cellophane crackle of traffic splash, neon buzzing and music, I heard the jagged cough and muffled cries of an infant floating like a macabre refrain above the crashing and cursing of a man and woman fighting.

The scene in front of the St. James Hotel reminded me of something out of "Man-Child in the Promised Land" or "Sonny's Blues." The building, also covered by clapboard siding, sagged precariously to the left. Alligatoring white paint flaked onto a red brick skirt patched with gray stucco, cement, plastic wrap, anything they could find to keep the wind off the river from blowing under the floor. An orange neon sign read "St. James", written in script, but the "s" on the end of the sign wouldn't stay lit and sputtered from orange to black and back again against the dirty-white siding. The word "Hotel" was missing, but still understood. Broken shutters hung in place by bailing wire wrapped around hinge pins nailed to the window casings. I kept my hands in my pockets, my chin in my chest, and walked thru the front door.

In the lobby, an old black man with caramel-colored skin sat behind the reception desk. His line of sight was glued to an old black and white TV with a bent coat hanger flying a tin foil flag serving as an antenna. A halo of gray wool hair, the size and shape of a laurel wreath, wrapped around his small bald head. Black splotches the color of burnt motor oil dotted his skin. His reptilian eyes were yellow where they should've been white. He was frying fish in a skillet over a hot plate while a battle-scarred alley cat watched from under the front desk.

Ashley Ghastly's Super Horror Show, featuring Bella Lugosi, Lon Chaney and Boris Karloff reruns, usually fueled the late, late show. Creature from the Black Lagoon was the night's "Creature Feature." Growing up, I'd seen the movie a dozen times. The fish man had nothing on the turtle-looking guy I was staring at.

"I'm here to see Erlene Brown," I said.

"Ina kichin," he said, turning to face me. He stared at me and around me at the same time. I looked down the hall for a door that might resemble a kitchen entrance. All I saw was a naked, yellow light bulb hanging from a two strand drop cord and a grimy piece of pink plastic shower curtain nailed like a tent flap over a doorway adjacent to the hall. I looked back at his face and forced myself to focus on the one eye that appeared to be aimed in my direction. Before I could ask the obvious, he said, "Back dey," then turned back to his TV, and his plate of fish.

I turned down the hall toward the dingy entrance to the kitchen. The whole place smelled like burned grease, disinfectant and ashtrays. Cobwebs and nicotine hung on every surface, including the edges of peeling paint coming off the walls and ceiling in strips.

A scattered deck of Bicycle playing cards littered the buckled blue linoleum floor and climbed across busted wood grained Formica counter tops speckled with roach droppings and grease freckles. The bottom of the glass bowl of the overhead light fixture was half black with dead insects. The window over the kitchen sink opened onto an alley that must've led to Hagood Street. I could smell the garbage from inside the hallway.

Hushed voices drifted through the doorway to the pantry. I heard a black woman curse. "Muddafugga betta come across, I'll kill 'is honkey ass ib 'e fug wid me." Then an answer, a high-pitched black man's voice, "Easy, Mama, Billy ain' gone fug up, he's pro. Dis t'ang'll click like a nine ball scrate, ina side pocket." When I entered the kitchen, the talking stopped.

A skinny black woman wearing a stained white apron wrapped around a green, flowered print dress, stepped into the room with a cigarette dangling from her lips. She had a long face, a high-domed forehead and nostrils that flared like one of the four horses of the Apocalypse. Her skin was shiny, like polished leather. A nylon stocking, knotted at her hairline, gave her an unsettling look. Aunt Jemima from Hell popped into my mind. One brown and yellow eye, glazed over from a cataract, looked like a tiny crystal ball, and she smelled strongly of Spic 'n Span and bleach. She cocked her head to one side so the smoke curling up from the cigarette would miss her good eye.

"Well, well," she said, knuckles on hips, sizing me up like a cheap floor lamp in a garage sale, "I wonder wha' monkey's in dis' bag?"

"Excuse me?" I said.

"You Josie?" she had a wheeze in her voice.

"Yes."

"Well doan jus stan' nay, boy, git yo' thin-lipped, scrawny white ass on back heah."

She had hip trouble which caused her to shuffle along rather than walk. I followed her through the door, to the pantry. She pulled a rope hanging from the ceiling. Springs squeaking like warped tuning forks echoed through the hall as a disappearing stairway swung from the ceiling. The stairs led to an attic with another naked light bulb hanging from a drop cord.

She negotiated the steps with surprising ease. From the way she climbed, I gathered she wasn't in pain so much as something in her leg simply didn't work. The backside of the tin roof was spiked where the tips of several nails had missed the slats when the metal sheets were nailed down.

At the top of the stairs I heard her say, "Mind your head."

Dirt daubers and wasps nests all over the place; rat pellets and roach parts were sprinkled over the floor like spilled peppercorns. Reams of old newspapers were stuffed into the cracks along the side walls and an old wood burning stove was engineered so that the smoke stack vented through a hole in the wall. Another, much younger black man in a leather overcoat sat cross-legged on an overturned washtub watching me with an intense, carefully practiced glare. His dreadlocks framed a deeply pocked complexion, his large, thick-lidded eyes, measured me without moving.

Just looking at his hair, his nails, his coat, and jewelry I could tell he wasn't from Charleston. He had the high-priced, bad-ass look that only comes from illegal, out-of-state money. There were no jobs in the straight southern world where a black man, making an honest living, could afford to dress like this guy. I felt Erlene shuffling some papers behind me.

"I think someone made a mistake." I turned around. "I only work one on one."

"Das cool, Mon." He straightened up and motioned for me to sit on an upside down metal milk crate. When he lifted his arm his coat fell open and I saw the silver handle of an automatic sticking out of his belt.

"No thanks," I said and turned to speak to the woman. "Look, Bill said I was supposed…"

"No, no, you don't understand. He's just my son. Rashad. He's visiting." She wiped her forehead with a rag and then coughed into it. "He's cool."

"My pleasure, Rashad." I forced a smile. He pursed his lips, nodded and then yawned.

"But he stays with us." Erlene lit another cigarette.

"No problem," I said. "I'm just here for directions."

"He stays with us in the room." She coughed and wiped her lips again. "And when you go, he ridin' wid you. That, too."

If he was a pot smuggler, it didn't worry me so much since most of the ones I knew were basically nonviolent. That is, as long as you didn't cross them. I didn't like the gun, but half the people I knew carried guns either on them or in their cars. I sat on the edge of the milk crate, and pulled a pencil and slip of paper from my jacket. The pencil didn't have a point; the paper was soft and damp. Erlene took out her own pen and paper and pulled up a crate beside me. She smelled like sweet, jasmine scented perfume.

I didn't know how old she was—maybe in her early fifties, though her wrinkled eyes and chapped mouth made her look older. I slipped my pencil and paper back into my pocket as she started to slowly draw a map, like someone sketching a picture for a child.

I was vaguely aware of Rashad somewhere across from me as I leaned forward with my elbows on my knees trying to see what she was drawing. The rustle of his leather overcoat, the shift of his legs on the washtub all made me nervous. I spoke to his mother as if she were the only person in the room.

"Is this Bohicket Road?" I pointed to her diagram.

"No, this is River Road," she said, "you look at it upside backwards, this is Plow Ground, this one is Edenvale, Bohicket is here, Maybank is here."

I memorized my route from the St. James to the Wappoo Cut Bridge, right on Maybank Highway, past the Municipal Golf Course, past Buzzard's Roost Marina. I knew exactly where I was going without the map. Her hands closed round the paper and crushed it into a ball. She unrolled it and set it on fire with her lighter while whispering, "You know where you are so far? 'Cross Bohicket Road? You down by de old Davis farm on de road to Wadmalaw."

I didn't really want her to know that I'd hunted on the Davis farm since I was twelve. Frank O. Davis and I grew up together, and his grandfather had an arsenal of weapons from World War II out on the farm. That's where I learned to shoot. I wouldn't have told either of them this, but Grandpa Davis taught us how to handle everything from a .22 rifle to a Thompson sub-machine gun by the time we were fourteen years old. He was thoroughly convinced Eugene McCarthy was right about the Russians taking over the country. He taught us survival techniques, like how to field-strip an M1 rifle and an M14. He owned an Uzi ten years before anyone knew what they were. By the time I entered high school, I could unload a .357 Magnum into a target fifty feet away in less than eight seconds and the holes would all fit into a circle smaller than a paint can lid. It was fun. I didn't take it seriously. Guns didn't impress me once I understood how they worked.

Grandpa Davis, viewed guns as tools. His philosophy was simple: if it's not worth killing over, it's not worth fighting over and if it's not worth fighting over, it's not worth arguing about. I just didn't have any use for a gun in the music business. Again, there were always exceptions: Freddie May, for instance.

Erlene Brown reached down on the floor for another scrap of paper. She tore it into the shape of the Star of David.

"Take dis heah pen," she said, "and write down these three striptures: Psalm 23:6-7; Ecclesiastes 8:18; and James 1:26-28." When I finished, she delicately folded it into a triangle and ran her fingernails lightly along the folds to crease them.

"Carry dis in yo' lef' hand. It don't leave yo' hand, unless it goes in yo' mout' and yo' has to eat it."

"OK. Is that it?" I tried to appear calm. Tried to convey that I'd do what she wanted. The whole time my mind was screaming for me to get the hell out of there. I kept wondering why these secretive black people had chosen a white boy to run this particular drop. Was I some critical component in their plan? And whose plan was it? Her's or Bill Reed's?

"Now," she whispered. "When you get to de Davis place, parouse long de road ezackly fo' tents ob a mile. Dere you'll come on a dut road. On de right han' side, dere be a big oak tree has a limb dat hang like dis." She made a down and up, curving motion with her arm that could've been the shape of a ski jump or a sliding board. "Dat limb is so close down to de groun', de little chilrin sits on it to wait fo' de school bus. You turn down dat road, follow 'em til 'e end. Dey'll be a man down dey waitin' on you. Axe um if he's Mr. Boots an' when he crack'e teeph fo' smile, check'um fo' a gold one on de leff han' side, facin' um."

I'd had a long day and a longer night. Her voice was making my head spin. Her eyes made me feel like I was part of some ancient dark conspiracy hatched centuries ago. "Gib him de star an' de money. If he ain't crack'e teeph an' show dat gold toot, duck yo' skinny, white ass and run for yo' ca'."

I looked over at her son, his sleepy, vacant eyes held no response. She slipped the folded star into the palm of my hand and closed her fist around mine. The backs of her hands and fingers were ribbed with intricate welts and tattoos. I tried to pull my hand back from between the two of hers, but she held it locked in a super human grip completely out of proportion to her size and weight. She drew my hand up to her mouth and blew a cool breath across my knuckles while holding my eyes in an ice-cold gaze. I didn't know if she planned to kiss my hand or bite it off.

"You a horn player, idn't?" She whispered and I nodded.

She turned my hand over and holding it up to the light, took a full minute to study it. "Den you gone need deas." She hissed, indicating my fingers. "And we gon' need what's inside 'em to go scrate on down to de bosom of Abraham. Scrate to de bosom of Abraham..."

She repeated it like some sort of superstitious chant she had to recite before she could let go. I tried to pull my hand back by relaxing my arm, but she tightened her grip on me, steadily applying pressure with the strength of a man, at first, but then gradually increasing it until I was sure I was going to scream.

"Let' em go, Mama," Rashad said. "Let go da boy's hand." I didn't know what he was doing in the shadows across from me, and I didn't want to flinch. "I said, let him go. He don't know nothin', he just an errand boy."

Erlene's whirled on her son. "You don' tell me who is and who ain't," she hissed. "He's da one, he's a bridge. Ain't chu, my little, thin-lipped white boy?"

She started loosening her grip, but Rashad spoke again. "How you know that, Mama? He wasn't even the one supposed to come. Supposed to be some mutant-looking dude, named after a fruit, Pineapple or Raspberry, somethin' like that."

"Nothin' is s'posed to be but what is. . ." She gave me one last, quick squeeze and a tear ran down my cheek. She was smiling at me now and showing me her own gold tooth. I rubbed my hand lightly on the back to get the blood flowing again, and then sort of blew warm air into my fist. They were both staring at me.

I stood up, and she relaxed back into the lame woman who met me in the kitchen. I thought we were done when she motioned toward the stairs. I went back down first, and she turned slowly on her heel, forcing her legs to carry her, and limped down after me. When I looked back, I met Rashad's unblinking gaze. He was waiting for Erlene to the clear the steps before he came down taking the steps two at a time.

"Let's go," he said.

Erlene came over to us, her left hand in her apron pocket and her right hand open, as if offering a handshake, and I extended mine. We shook hands, and she angled her head so that I'd have a clear look at the wild cataract. "I knows you de man fo'dis job." She started humming. "I knows de good Lawd done send you to me." She made a melodious buzz by adding a whistle to the hum. I knew the trick. I used to make my saxophone growl.

As soon as the thought went through my head, she winked at me, "You know dat one, don' chu? I know you know, I see 'em go t'rough yo mind just now." She looked at her son. "He's one, he's a bridge. He don't know it yet his own self, but he gone learn, this boy chile got some education comin'."

She took my balled-up left hand into her right and led me down the hall, toward the plastic curtain separating the doorway from the lobby. Then turned to face me again and, still holding my hand, she said, "I knows de Lawd will watch ober you and gib you scrength. But jess in case He busy t'night…" and she jerked my hand out in front of her and with her left, raked the talons of a chicken's foot dipped in some dark red liquid across the back of my hand. The claws cut three, deep scratches between my wrist and knuckles.

I saw my own blood rise to the surface and mingle with the liquid. I jumped back, wiped the blood off on my pants, and bolted toward the front door. Torrents of adrenalin rushed through me. I felt myself growing dizzy, my ears ringing. I thought I was going crazy. Erlene Brown's hysterical laughing rose to a shrill shriek when I hit the edge of the clerk's desk. She was right on me, shaking that chicken foot at me and chanting in some archaic language. Just as I was about to pass out, she pulled away and positioned herself by the entrance to the hallway. In perfect English, she said, "Rashad, son, help Mr. Chapman up, it appears he's lost his balance."

I thought there was another woman in the room. My head was spinning; I was sick to my stomach. I couldn't get my legs to work and everything was out of focus. I was vaguely aware of Rashad's arms under mine, that he was lifting me off the floor. I got my elbows up on the desk and looked straight into the face of The Creature from the Black Lagoon.

He was behind the desk in an old coat, watching television. A wall-eyed, black man with spots on his face was forcing a girl over the side of a boat. She kicked and screamed until she fell overboard and sunk to the bottom of the lagoon, and the creature at the desk turned into the man on the TV.

I fainted but didn't fall down. I remember coming to while passing strange looking people on the sidewalk. Rashad, nervous and tense, helped me toward the car. He was clearly anxious for us to leave. Erlene stood in the doorway, hands on her hips, the chicken foot still in her hand. I was out on the street again, and nobody seemed to notice, like they didn't even see me, like I was a ghost. I felt like I'd stumbled through a hole in reality where nothing existed outside the nightmare I was going through.

Sitting behind the wheel waiting for my head to clear, the silence was suddenly broken by Rashad's voice through the open slot of window.

"Bitch's crazy! Got no bidness castin' spells on innocent unsuspectors!"

"What just happened? I feel like I got hold of some bad acid. Where the fuck am I, anyway?" I wasn't scared. Rather the opposite, I felt like I was floating, like I'd heard junkies describe heroin.

"She got no right, it ain't time yet, she's always pushin' ahead of de plan. She thinks it all funny, castin' spells on people. Trying to make believers outta non-believers. There's other ways, gentler ways, but she got this crazy notion in her head she can spot a bridge, even when the qualification process is just starting to get started."

"I don't understand any of this," I mumbled.

"You will understand, sooner than later, thanks to her. Did me the same way, pushed me before I was ready. She had no right."

Through the windshield the mercury vapor halos were refracting, I squinted and the spectrum splintered into tiny dancing needles of light.

"Pushed you off of what?" A warm glow flowed over me.

"I was only ten, when she made me do it."

"Hey, man, you ever done any acid?"

I heard a scuffling noise, the sound of a slap, a muffled female voice and Rashad's voice wheezing, "Stop! Stop it, Mama, stop it, now!" Rashad had his arms wrapped over his head, trying to protect himself. I thought she'd followed us out to the car. But when I raised my head, there was nobody there but him; alone, sitting on the ground, mumbling and crying. "I'll do it mama, I'll do it."

I hunched my shoulders over the wheel and started the car. When I put it in drive, the passenger door opened and a solemn-faced Rashad quickly popped into the seat beside me. I turned around and pulled out into the dank florescent haze descending over Spring Street. The pallid, dismal night sky seemed oppressively heavy, loaded with the poisons left by generations of people in pursuit of secrets. Lightning flashed in the distance. I silently counted to ten. The thunderhead was right over where we were headed.

"Di'ju hear my question? You ever dropp'ted any acit?"

"No."

"When I's over on 'a road, sometimes, I tooked LSD to stake me, I mean stay awake."

"Why are you telling me this?"

"How about MDE, I mean MEA, no, at's not it. MDA, thas it, ever take any off that?"

"When you know what I know, you don't need hard drugs."

"This shit feels a lot like acit, I mean acid. Looks like it, too."

"How you know what it looks like?"

"I mean the lights, the colors, the way it crawls around in my neck muscles."

"It's root work, she makes it herself, secret recipe."

"Why the chicken foot?"

"It ain't just any chicken foot. It's a rooster talon."

A voice different from my thinking voice whispered into my thought pattern. "You are the bridge." Cold chills raced down my backbone, through my legs to my feet, I shivered.

"I'm the bridge, huh? And who are you? Just another version of me I used to know'd, aren't you? We know how this game goes, don't we? We've been here before. I know this one, I know you. What're we going to do now, mutha fuckaa? Sit around until we figure out something profound, like feet go into shoes?"

Rashad looked at me. "Who are you talking too?"

"Myself. I'm talking to myself. This is nothing. I've done acid a whole lot more potent than whatever this shit is your momma cooked up."

"I don't know what you think you know, but whatever it is you're wrong."

"Yeah, sure," I said. "I got this shit all figured out, she put acid on a chicken foot, then scratched the shit out of my fucking hand. The drug went straight into my blood's stream and the next thing I'm knowin' is, I'm tripping. And drivin'. You see this? I'm fuckin' drivin' on acid, now how meeny minnie mo' mutha fuckers you ever see do that? Huh? Huh? How many? Not one, thas how many."

The electrified glare of Charleston's late night aura flared the night sky in my rearview mirror, an eerie ribbon reflection made the white dotted lines and yellow no passing lines appear to float on the surface of the sparkling wet, undulating asphalt. "Why go to all this trouble for one bag drop. Why'd she hav' to cut me? Motherfucker's gonna hurt like hell when this shit wears off."

"It ain't just any chicken foot; it's a rooster claw, and not just any rooster claw."

"Well, lemme tell you something, secret recipe or not, this is some piss poor acid."

I punched the gas. There was no traffic crossing the Ashley River. The Thunderbird leaped forward. The neon St. James sign still streaked spikes and bounced off the dotted ribbons trailing in the mirrors, like phosphorous in a boat wake. Time was bouncing too, like it does when you're tripping. I'd spent less than half an hour inside the hotel, but it felt like an eternity. I was ready to get my money and go home.

"It was a matador rooster claw," Rashad said. "It makes you feel invincible."

"So now I'm supposed to be afraid of some big bad boogie man living out here where I grew up. Niggah please don't throw me in dat dair briar patch! Lemme tell you somethin', I got this shit right here, I know this place we're going like the back of my scratched up hand. I ain't afraid of a fucking thing out here. Ain't nothin' gone fug wit me."

"You finished?"

"I's born and raised in a briar patch! I own this shit!"

Rashad leaned forward and touched the scratches. "Well, Bre Rabbit, for your sake, let's hope it keeps working," he said. "Where you're headed, you gonna damn sure need it."

CHAPTER ELEVEN

A crazy leer had plastered itself on my face as I aimed the headlights toward Wadmalaw Island and the dark cloud hovering above Davis Farm. The Thunderbird growled into the sanctuary called darkness, letting gravel fly as we blasted across the Ashley River Bridge toward Maybank Highway. The cold night air blowing in through my now half-open window wet and chilled the left side of my face. Rashad smelled like burned grilled cheese dipped in patchouli oil. He slumped down in the seat with his hands folded between his knees, staring at the floorboard.

Between pulses of passing streetlights accented by the magnolia trees lining the municipal golf course, I stole several quick glances at Rashad's face. Glossy tear tracks streaked his cheeks below his distant unblinking eyes. Tires whirred the grillwork of the little drawbridge over the Stono River by Buzzard's Roost Marina. The noise startled him, snatching his mind back to the surface. For a split second, I felt sorry for him, then I remembered who he was.

I was driving like a good drunk driver: both hands on the wheel, the left at ten grasping, the claw-marked right fist at two, for support, the fingers still frozen around the tiny piece of paper. We passed the curve on the right past the marina; I hit the brights and let the Thunderbird eat. With eyes bouncing back and forth between the dotted lines and the solid line on the road's edge, I concentrated solely on getting from point A to point B.

Rashad was transforming back into the cold, disinterested machine I'd met at the top of the attic stairs. I was still trying to figure out exactly what had happened to me back at the St. James. My hand burned from the scratches, my heart was pounding and my head was throbbing like I'd swallowed ice cream too fast.

Between landmarks, all I thought about was getting through this drop so I could dedicate the rest of my life to getting even with Bill Reed. Cold-blooded murder was out because murder in Charleston was reserved strictly for two classes of people: assholes who could no longer be publicly humiliated and assholes who had enough dirt on the entrenched power structure to threaten them with humiliation. Death before embarrassment is a Charleston code.

What Bill Reed deserved was to be broken the Charleston way. Slow death would be too quick, and he wouldn't suffer enough. In fact, death itself wasn't an option, not for me. Others might have felt differently. I wanted him to experience an everlasting torment, one I could watch. In other words, I wanted him to have to live so he wasn't only humiliated publicly, but also sure to make him grow old, miserable and frustrated. Lowered into the boiling oil by degrees, like people executed for witchcraft in 1400-1500s wouldn't be enough. He needed to rot slowly in inches, like someone dying from gangrene. I wanted him to suffer an agony so severe that dying and going to Hell would seem like a vacation in the Bahamas. What I wanted for Bill Reed was a fate worse than death. I wanted him to suffer the worst fate Charleston could offer. Embarrassment to the point he could never show his face downtown without everybody pointing and whispering.

So after giving the matter careful thought, I decided there were actually two courses of action I could take, two options that only the lowest of the Charleston low would ever sink to. I could turn him in to the I.R.S. or I could arrange for his girlfriend, Janet, to find out he was screwing Cricket. Or, I could do both.

In my mind's eye, I watched the cops padlock the door of The Apartment Club as Reed was hauled away in handcuffs. A crowd of people stood and stared as he twisted and turned, trying to free himself from the hands of the agents. I watched him lose his house on the river and his boat in the marina. They took his watches, his gun, his rings and jewelry. The safe in the backyard was uncovered and his half-million in cash confiscated. Everything in his closet, including his monogrammed silk boxer shorts and his Sea Island cotton dress shirts were boxed up, tagged and hauled out to a waiting Anointed Bateau Mission van. Inside the van were all his custom-made suits and sports coats with the little label sewn in that said "Tailored for Mr. Bill Reed" followed by names like Oxford Clothiers, Norman Hilton, and Hickey Freeman. Over a hundred pairs of shoes made out of everything from snakeskin to elephant skin were cataloged and crated. My leer turned into an open smile as I saw him sitting in a jail cell in stripes, his elbows on his knees and head hung low.

At this point in my reverie, the door to the cell opened and Janet Collins walked into the cell with a straight razor and a photograph of Bill with his face buried between Cricket's legs. Janet proceeded to shave his head, making sure she nicked him at every opportunity. When she finished his head, she shaved his arms and legs. Then the guards held him down as she rubbed him down with alcohol. When he screamed in my vision, I laughed out loud. Rashad looked over at me and grunted.

"What t' hell's so funny?" He said, wiping his face with his shirt sleeve.

"I hate to waste a trip, even one as bad as this," I said. "I was torturing a friend of mine."

"Betta get yo' mind on the bidness at hand, you got the money ready?"

"The money is ready." I lifted the lid on the armrest in the center console.

Inside was a brown paper bag splotched with grease stains. Rashad carefully picked it up.

"Looks more like yesterday's lunch."

"That is yesterday's lunch," I said. "Money's under the plastic liner."

He lifted the liner out of the console and felt down the side of the bulge over the drive shaft tunnel in the floorboard. I'd stuffed the leather bank bag into a corner, down near the bottom of the built-in ashtray. It's a great stash in a '65 Thunderbird. The only way you can see down in there is with a flashlight, even during the day. Most cops didn't know it existed.

The thundercloud closed in and the moon raced behind it as I crossed Bohicket Road. Delicate, translucent fingers of light and long stretches of silver streaks ripped through the rolling woolpack sky. The cloud's path across the moon indicated it came in off the ocean. As the moonlight broke into the car, I took another look at Rashad. In the eerie light, his head looked like it belonged on a puppet. His eyes were pitched down at the corners, his cheekbones stood out, his features reminded me of one of those African masks you see in National Geographic.

"Not a shabby hallucination," I said. "Maybe all is not lost."

He opened his coat and leaned back in the seat. His skin looked darker, his eyes clear and focused, his lean, muscular build reminded me of a man who chased antelope for a living.

"How African are you, Rashad? You don't look like a black with an American lineage."

"That's because you seeing my soul, not my body."

"What?!"

"She shouldn't a' hurt you, man." He touched my scratched hand with his finger. "She didn't had to do this, but she get crazy behind money."

In this relaxed position, his countenance had the timeless benign clarity of an ebony carving. When he spoke, only his lips moved, slightly parting in a straight line over his teeth, his eyes almost closed into thoughtful, compassionate slits like those of a man who only speaks after he has thought, long and hard, about what he's going to say.

I lifted my fist off the steering wheel of the car and tried to open it. The paralysis refused to dissipate or allow me to loosen my grip on the scriptures. Each time I tried to unclench my fingers the pain instantly escalated from stinging to burning. The scratches erupted with a shearing sting each time I tried to unclench my fingers. Rashad reached into his shirt pocket and took out a pouch of something that looked like snuff. He took a pinch of the powder and rubbed it into the back of my hand, immediately the pain and numbness disappeared.

"Give it three minutes, and it won't hurt no more." He looked at my hand, turned it over to examine the callous behind my thumb knuckle. "What's this from?" he said. "You got some weird habit?"

"It's from the thumb rest on a tenor saxophone." I said, as I jerked my hand back and tried, again, to open my fist.

"I play conga drums," he said. "Rhythm is my thing. All you pretty boys ain't nothin' without the rhythm."

"What was on that chicken foot? Snake venom? Essence of black widow poison? I like to know my dealers." I flexed my fingers, my fist loosened up, Rashad arched his eyebrows.

"W'make you t'ink hit a potion? Might be she summon de de'bil on you." He chuckled.

"Oh, the Devil huh? Yeah, makes perfect sense."

"You feelin' better now? Gettin' your head right? She put a Hag on you' honkey ass all right," he was pleased with himself all of a sudden.

"Oh, I got the Hag alright, but not on my honkey ass, it's sitting beside me."

Rashad took a joint out of his coat pocket, lit it, holding the smoke deep in his lungs then tried to talk while holding his breath.

"I take it, you don't b'leve in de' forces o' darkness, dat it?"

"Man, I grew up on Johns Island. I know there's plenty more shit flying 'round here than most people understand, but that doesn't make it magic."

He handed me the joint, his hallucinated costume now replaced by his street clothes, still his complexion, eyes and hair retained the vibrant ebony features of African warrior. I took a drag, careful to position the end between my thumb and forefinger so I could take a hit without letting my lips touch the joint.

"What's the matter, you think my spit is poison?"

"Right now I don't know what I think. I know I'm tripping on something, some kind of drug. One I'm unfamiliar with. Maybe I'm trying to keep you from catching something from me. Ever think of that? Besides, that voodoo crap only works on people who believe in it."

"Hoodoo."

"Voodoo? Hoodoo? You do!" I started laughing. "It's all in your fucking mind, man, don't you understand, just like church, religion, even the shed blood of Christ or the mantras of Buddha. None of it works unless you believe it."

"You right. The truth is whatever you believe it is."

My headache had subsided as well as my fuzzy thinking. The tracers were gone but the acid luminosity of my Technicolor vision, the surreal surroundings only intensified. Glowing inside like a fighter plane cockpit, the Thunderbird hummed over the pavement. Air whooshing past the partially lowered window expanded the flying sensation. Whatever Rashad had rubbed into the scratches had my whole body feeling warm and relaxed. Either that or I was peaking.

"And since I don't believe in it," I continued, "there had to be some kind of snake oil or yak dung on that chicken foot to make my hand freeze up. Your mama know about boiling Heavenly Blue Morning Glory seeds?"

"So, you admit you don't believe, but you know from experience de' claw foot worked." He was staring into the darkness as he took another hit off the joint. "An' what ezactly, mus' you see in order to convince you, my man?"

"Forget it," I said. "I've got no interest in seeing anything but this bag delivered and my poor ass back home in my bed." A neck muscle jerked, I rolled my head from shoulder to shoulder, on top of the visuals I was getting quite stoned. "And I sure as hell don't need anybody else's beliefs crammed down my throat or scratched into the back of my hand."

"Dat include de' Scrong Man?"

I was surprised he brought up the subject so close on the heels of Montague's warning.

"Yeah, him too, more or less."

"Don't know why you feel that way. I happen to know he's got divine plans jus' for you."

The juju bullshit was wearing thin and starting to really piss me off.

"Divine plan or not, I've got a job, a band and my own plans for the future. I won't be making middle of the night numbers drops while worrying about the devil or any of his cohorts chasing me through sleazy dumps or being concerned whether or not the Lord is watching over me while I drive like a maniac out in the country with the dope smoking, gun toting, son of crazy voodoo woman riding in my car questioning me about my belief system. Can you understand that?" At the end of my rant I realized I'd been yelling. Rashad put his hand on my arm.

"Easy brother, easy, you still feelin' invincible? Bullet-proof? Thas' good, thas' good, ain't 'fraid of no damn t'ing, are you? I see you, too, you know? Same as you see me. You got preachers and warriors in your soul blood, too. It's your own innocence savin' you from gettin' in way over your head. Python can hear ebery wo'd you sayin'.'"

"Who exactly are we going to meet? Is it Python, as in snake, or a Strong Man like a circus act, or some black con artist named Boots?" I snapped at him. "I'm getting my demonology all confused here, Rashad. Am I dealing with one demon with two names or two separate demons? Which is it, man? I'd really like to know, just in case the car starts levitating, can you dig it? I'd like to know who the Hell, from which Hell, it is I'm dealing with."

Rashad finished the joint and threw the roach out the window without answering. So, as is usually the case with arrogant, self-serving half-drunk assholes jacked to Jesus on drugs, I unleashed another volley.

"I don't like being lied to or played or taken advantage of, can you dig that? Brother? Brother Man? Brother Man in the Promised Land, Mr. Soul on Ice?" Rashad drummed the top of the console with his fingertips, his eyes focused on a point somewhere in his mind. "You think I don't know shit about being black, don't you? Well, you're half right. I wasn't born black, but I was raised by a black woman, and I have a blood brother who is black. You see this?" I was able to loosen my thumb enough to show him a pink scar dissecting my thumb print. "You see that? It's a knife cut I made, and Jackson Waldo Woods, a black man, just as black as you, has one just like it. We cut our thumbs and mingled our blood. He's my blood brother. Do you understand? Do you?"

"Watch out for Freddie," he said. "Word is he ain't happy with you."

"But people like you and Erlene and Reed are my real friends, right?"

"Don't be so cold, man. You walkin' a line thin as dem white lips o' yours, an' de brotha's are watchin', whether you know it, or not. You can think you got your act together, much as you want. Steady gig at yo' all-white club, servant nigga's dressed up like penguins, waitin' hand and foot on rich white folks. An' you, you gotch yo' R&B, a little money in the bank, a dip o' wicket every now and then.

But neither you nor any o' dem people got a clue who really be in charge. If you did, it'd turn yo' worl' upside down."

When he said that a light bulb went off in my head. Roy had said something similar when I asked him who held the lease on the building.

"Dem white folks will turn on you, if de' get half a chance, you need somethin' scronger dan peoples to fall back on, to lean on fo guidance when de goin' get scrange, like it's gonna get tonight."

"Out of curiosity, why do you and your mother go back forth between Geechee, Gullah and plain English?" I waited ten seconds then realized I'd taken my eyes off the road. A deer glowing caramel laced in bright white suddenly flashed into the path of the car. There was no time to hit the brakes. We drove right through it. No impact, no wreck, nothing. I looked at Rashad. Once again in warrior gear, this time with war paint decoration on his face.

"You saw the deer?" I said.

"Of course."

"It wasn't real."

"It was more real than you know."

"See, there you go, speaking plain English again."

"Man-to-man is one language, soul-to-soul is another."

"That makes no sense."

"Right now, you're like a child in kindergarten being forced into high school. There's so much you don't know. Which is why I'm pissed at Mama for pushing you off your true path and right into the river."

"I've got my own situation under control, Rashad. Now tell me, who really is in charge of this whole operation? Just level with me. And don't give me a bunch of hocus-pocus bullshit, man, I'm tired of that. Just the straight-up skinny, so I'll know who I'm dealing with."

"Is dat a fack?" He nodded in spurious admiration. "Let me tell you a somethin' 'bout bullshit, Josie, my man. Dis's a Gullah story I learnt a long time ago from a gran'father, who had it pass from his great gran'father, who was a slave on Rice

Hope Plantation." The deeper into the explanation Rashad went the thicker his Gullah accent became.

"Once 'pon a time, dere was dis freak storm down south, and a hummin'bird get e'sef caught up in it. He try to make it back to his nest, but 'e got too cole too fass. Fack is, 'e got so cole, he fell t'dah ground an' was mos' abut to freeze to death, when a big ol' bull come by and drop a load of bullshit right down on top of his poor, half froze ass. Well, de mess smell tur'ible but it wuz warm and it thaw out de poor bud wings and body. By 'n by he came to 'e sef and git'e circle-ation back and 'e start scrugglin' to free 'e sef from the mess' of bullshit e' in. Mind now, dis mess smell bad ain't no lie 'bout dat, an' de hummin' bud can't wait to get 'e sef free from um, but dis mess ain't near as bad as de one previous. In dat mess previous, he gwine freeze, you dig?"

"Dear God," I said, "Yes, I dig."

"So, dis hummin'bud scruggle an' scruggle 'til he most reach de top o' dis pile o' bullshit das been drop on he head and 'e manage to get 'is head out to whey 'e kin see de light-o-day and all the fight mos' gone out from um. And just when he can't scruggle no mo, de farmer's old tom cat come pa'ruse'n long in de pasture an' when he pass by 'e h'year de hummin'bud say, 'Please fo' free me from dis mess I's in, please fo' free me from dis mess I's in.' So, de ol' tom, he reach in wid he paw an' 'e snatch de hummin'bud out de cow pie and eat' em. You dig what I'm sayin' to you, man?"

"Not really," I said. "Sounds to me like the hummingbird had a real bad day."

"De moral o' dis story is jus' as true today as 'e was back den. De moral is dat er'rerybody know dat life is full of uncertainty an' er'reybody bound fo git dey fair share. Jus' remember dis, dough, de one who shit on you ain't always your enemy, and the one who snatches you out dat shit ain't always your friend."

"That's it?"

"Think about it."

"Thanks for sharing that piece of wisdom with me, Rashad. Especially in the original dialect. Personally though, I prefer to check the weather forecast before I venture out too far away from my nest."

"It's de freak storm, dat get you man. De unpridickable one. De one you can't see coming. Like de one you fell into tonight. It ain't never de one you plan fo. You go confusin' de two, you gone wind up gettin' eaten alive. You know de law o'de jungle, idn't?"

"Eat or be eaten," I said.

"Das right. So knowin' dat, wha's de question should be on anybody mind if dey fin' dey self in de jungle?"

"I don't know, why you don't tell me." I shook my head. "I mean why don't you tell me?"

He stared out the window. We were approaching the curve right before the dirt road leading back to the Davis Farm. Rashad was back in his un-hallucified street clothes. He reached in his belt and pulled out the .45.

With lethal precision he dropped the clip, checked it, and popped it back into the grip. I heard the clack-clack of the breech block going back across the barrel, cocking the hammer, picking up a bullet from the top of the clip and sliding it up the feed ramp into the chamber on the return trip. It was all so loud and clear, every nuance of the metallic racking echoed like I was in a steel drum with a microphone.

"Das de tree up on de leff han' side. Slow down, kill de lights."

I pulled off the road about thirty yards from where the oak limb bent down to the ground and turned off the engine. The clouds moved off uncovering a half-moon whose alien light played tricks with the shapes and shadows undulating beneath an oak shrouded landscape. Spanish moss hung silver in the woods on either side of the road. The brush between the trees rustled and snapped as the amplified nocturnal noises of opossums and raccoons went about their business in the dark. An owl hooted, another answered, then a third. In my mind's eye a gold strand of light triangulated their position.

"I don't see a car," I said.

"You won't either, 'less he wants you to see it." He leaned close to the windshield, studying the area in front of us. "Get out slow and tuck de bag up under your arm."

I did as instructed. My scratched fist had recovered and I'd regained control of my fingers. I opened the door, slipped out, easing my way toward the hood. Rashad moved up beside me and adjusted his overcoat.

"You ready?" he asked quietly.

"As ready as I'll ever be." I answered.

"You didn't answer my question 'bout the jungle."

"What question?" I said.

"The question that's on everybody's mind in the jungle."

"And you didn't answer me about the dialect bouncing back and forth."

"Gullah is code for closing ranks. It is the language of solidarity, it speaks soul-to-soul. Do you understand me? When a black speaks Gullah to a white, it's a show of respect for the life inside the listener. Gullah acknowledges a shared past, a history stretching back hundreds of years. Mama was right about one thing. You and others like you are soul bridges."

"That's some heavy shit man, made even heavier by this drug." I rubbed my eyes.

"You still feel invincible?"

"I'm not afraid, if that's what you mean. It's just a bag drop."

"There are some things you won't understand, can't understand, not for a while, not until you're fully crossed over. Some things only time can teach you. And that time starts with us surviving tonight. A bridge understands that before a group can be truly free, its members must close ranks."

"That's what we're doing here tonight? You and me? Closing ranks?"

Rashad looked me straight in the eye and whispered. "The question on every-body mind in the jungle is, 'can I eat that or will that eat me?'"

"Good question," I said.

"Dis old Tomcat will eat us both if we ain't careful."

"This gig isn't worth the money I'm being paid."

"It's too late to be worrin' 'bout dat now," he said. "Besides, think of de won-derful education you got tonight."

"Yeah," I said, "it's been a real sociology field trip. You ready?"

"OK," he said. "Let's do this."

We followed the contour of the dark ditch bank as closely as possible without sliding in until we came to the bent oak limb. Turning down the dirt road beside the tree was easy enough, but it was so dark in the shadows we couldn't see much more than five feet in front of us.

Bootsy Williams was waiting for us in an open spot around a curve in the dirt road about twenty yards back from the highway. He was leaning back on the trunk of his Buick Electra 225 smoking a cigarette with one heel propped on the bumper. The car was parked in the moonlight out from under the shadows of the ancient oak trees. If he had anyone with him, they were out of sight. He was so black I couldn't make out any facial features beyond a silhouette that showed he was wearing a hat cocked strategically to one side. I could also tell he was wearing a white shirt and tie, and a dark suit. Judging from the amount of shirt showing I assumed he was wearing a vest. Rashad was so close behind and to my left, I felt his pistol handle against my elbow.

"Remember," he whispered. Mama said. 'No gold tooth, duck and run.'"

When Rashad reminded me of his mother's words, it dawned on me: If this guy wasn't Bootsy, Rashad was prepared to kill him. When I got within five yards of the dark figure, he cleared his throat.

"That's close enough," purred a low, smooth as silk, Lou Rawls voice. "I trust you gentlemen have a message from the good Lord, for a poor sinner like me."

"Are you Bootsy?" I asked. My voice was calm though my mouth was dry as a cracker..

"Are you looking for someone named Bootsy?"

"Not really looking, I just have something that belongs to him and a mutual friend asked me to make sure I put it into his hands personally." I was glad it was so dark. I was trembling like a wet dog on a cold day, but my voice sounded firm, steady.

"Let's see the package," he said.

"Let's see some proof that you're Bootsy."

"What kind of proof you wanna see?"

"I was told you would know without my having to ask."

Rashad pulled up tight against me. I felt his coat rustle, sensed his fingers grasping the pistol and I looked down to see which way to duck. Bootsy shifted his weight, reached into his pants pocket and pulled out a matchbook.

"I'm going to light another cigarette," Williams said. "Tell your brother not to get excited."

I watched him slowly extract a cigarette from a pack and put it up to his lips. He struck a match, cupped his hands while letting the flame light up his face. He smiled and I saw the gold tooth on the left incisor.

"See what you needed to see?" he asked with a half joking voice.

"All I was told to look for," I said.

"Now, it's my turn to inspect the merchandise." He held out his hand.

I reached for the bag but he stopped me with his palm like a traffic cop; my left side involuntarily froze in place, wedging the zippered pouch tight against my armpit. "Not that, not yet. I wanna see your hand."

I looked around at Rashad. He nodded toward my right hand, still death grip clutching the folded scrap of paper. I held it out and Bootsy struck another match over the scratches. He grunted, turned my fist over and snapped his fingers. My fist flew open, my hand went numb, frozen in place, and he removed the folded Star of David, then snapped his fingers again. The muscles in my hand relaxed, the feeling returned, and my fingers starting tingling like they'd been asleep. He inspected the writing.

"Now, the bag," he said.

I handed the money bag over to him and watched him weigh the two strapped stacks, one in each hand. "Are we done here?" I said.

"There's a little package I need to send back to Charleston."

"What kind of package?" Rashad said.

"No kind of a package unless you plan to carry it on foot," I said.

"I've got a car," Bootsy said, talking right past me like I wasn't there.

"Well, I'm leaving." I started walking back the way we came.

"Wait a minute," Rashad said. He looked back at Bootsy. "How much?"

"Five," said Bootsy.

"Ten singles, up front, and we'll take it." Rashad said.

What the hell do you mean, 'we'll take it?'" I snapped.

Bootsy reached in the bag and slipped five hundred dollars from each of the two straps, folded the bills and handed them to Rashad. He opened the trunk of the Buick revealing a cardboard box with holes punched in the top. When Rashad picked it up and started back toward the main road, something inside started scrabbling around and I recognized the sound of chickens. Rashad picked up the box and started toward the car.

"Wait a minute?" I said. "You're paying us a thousand dollars to take a box of chickens back to Charleston?"

"Shut up and go to the car, man," Rashad ordered.

I shook my head and took a few steps back in the direction we'd come, then I turned around to face the man with the gold tooth.

"What if my hand wasn't scratched?" I said.

Bootsy laughed and made his hand into the shape of a pistol and pretended to shoot me.

I got behind the wheel while Rashad put the chickens in the trunk. I was searching the glove box when he tried to get in.

"What you huntin'?"

"My little black book."

"Why you need that?"

"I wanna find a phone number, if that's alright?"

Under my insurance papers I found my address book. Opening it up to the "I's" traced the entries down to the Internal Revenue Service. Then, I flipped over to the C's and located Janet Collin's address and phone number. I didn't know if either of the numbers were still current, but I was going to find out.

Backtracking the same path we had taken from Charleston, the road was empty except for one car, which passed us coming from the opposite direction. Ordinarily I wouldn't have paid any attention. I couldn't tell from the headlights coming at me what kind of car it was, but when it passed us I looked in the rear view mirror and recognized a cinnamon colored '66 Riviera with a black vinyl top. The same kind of car Bill Reed drove. I couldn't see the driver, but I could tell by its speed Bill was probably driving. That pissed me off, because he could've made the drop himself without involving me.

Rashad noticed the car too, turning all the way around to watch the taillights until they disappeared. We hadn't spoken since we got back in the car. When we crossed back over the Intracoastal Waterway, I decided to ask the obvious question.

"What's the deal with the chickens?"

"Dey fo' Mama," he said.

"Did you or didn't you, know about the chickens before we drove out here?"

"Don't matter either way," he said. "Dey wif us now."

"Just curious," I said. "But while we're on the subject, what kind of chickens could be worth five hundred dollars just to deliver them."

He started laughing, pulled out another joint, lit it and said, "Pretty special fuckin' chickens, don't you think?"

The insanity of the moment finally got the best of me, and I started laughing along with him. He handed me the joint, and I took a careful drag.

Still laughing, I said, "Those're Voodoo chickens, aren't they? Matadors?"

"You catch on quick," he said.

"So, what do you guys do with them?"

"This guy," he pointed to himself, "don't do nothin' with them, that's all Mama's stuff." I sensed he wanted to say something else so I waited. "Besides, it ain't the chickens, it's what's in the chickens," he said.

"You mean the blood?" I said.

"I didn't say dat, you just assume' dat." He hit the joint and offered it, but I waved him off.

The sky was glowing across the horizon's edge. Out by the ocean; it would soon be daylight. I wanted to be in my bed when the sun came up.

I dropped Rashad off at the St. James. Before he got out of the car, he opened a tin about the size of a can of shoe polish, dipped his thumb in and rubbed a salve into the scratches. A red flannel, drawstring pouch seemed to appear out of nowhere. With his thumb and fingers he sprinkled a reddish powder, which looked and smelled like ground cloves, onto the ointment, then rubbed it into the back of my hand. The scratches were still raw so the powder went straight into my bloodstream. My whole body went calm.

"What is that stuff?"

"High John the Conker Root," he said, "But you don't believe in 'bullshit' remember?"

"I said I don't believe in all that Voodoo religious bullshit."

"What 'chu think dis is?" He held up the pouch containing the powder, dangled it upside down, and then shook it. The dust swirling out of the bag transformed into ten hundred dollar bills which gently floated into his open palm.

"Here's seven hundred," he said as he laid the bills on the dash. "Five for your half and two for the car. You need to get the window fixed."

I didn't refuse the money. I didn't say anything one way or the other, I just nodded and he shut the door and removed the chicken box from the trunk. Rashad walked around to the driver's side window and bent down to speak to me before I drove off.

With a big grin on his face and chuckle in his voice, he said, "I was surprised when you didn't say anything back there, when he called me 'yo' brotha.'"

"You didn't say anything, either. What did surprise me, though, was how quickly you took him up on his offer to bring that box back to town without even asking me," I said.

"Like I said. You'd be surprised what you can get out of a chicken."

"Yeah, but just saying the words don't make them true."

He nodded. "Especially, usin' recipes written by Scrong Man."

"Yeah, I'm sure I'd love Chicken Cordon Bleu a la Voodoo."

He slapped the driver's door with his free hand and shot me a peace sign.

"It's Hoodoo," he said.

"Hoodoo?"

"You do."

I shook my head and drove off, watching him cross the street in the rearview mirror. Then I caught my own attention, saw my own eyes in the mirror like I was another person looking at my own self through a different pair of eyes. I was grinning from ear to ear. Rashad stood in the doorway, watching me pull onto Lockwood Boulevard. He was back in full warrior gear with a game rooster under each arm.

When he disappeared, it dawned on me, in spite of all the dark intrigue, the acid or whatever it was, the drop hadn't gone all that bad. After all nobody got shot. But the biggest surprise of the night came when I realized I really didn't dislike the guy.

In fact, he reminded me a little of Jackson; except for the on again, off again, Gullah dialect. What did bother me was seeing Reed's car come flying down Maybank Highway right after we'd left. That bothered the hell out of me. But after counting out seventeen hundred dollars for three hours work, I got over it, for a while.

CHAPTER TWELVE

Dawn was breaking at six-thirty Saturday morning. The streetlight in front of 3 Savage had either burnt out or been shot out by a BB gun. Not wanting to disturb J. Reynolds Rigney, III, and seeing no other cars parked nearby, I turned the engine off about twenty feet back from the driveway and tried to coast to a stop in front of my apartment. This was a stupid idea since turning off the engine meant killing the power steering which led to wresting the steering wheel like one might wrangle a calf at a rodeo.

Like so many times in the past, once again I was coming down alone. I tiptoed up the back stairs, careful not to let the steps creak. Taking my shoes off at the top of the back porch, I slipped inside the apartment without letting the door squeak and managed to get to my bedroom without bumping into anything.

A shower would've helped me sleep better, but the running water would surely have an irate Rigney banging on the ceiling within ten minutes. Instead I lay down on the bed without taking my clothes off or pulling back the covers. The events of the previous day circled my subconscious like images painted on the blades of a slow spinning ceiling fan. From the rain to Freddie, to Bobbie and her band, to Bill and the money, my band, Roy, Erlene Brown, Rashad, Williams and the chickens and back again. The dream kept me tossing and turning until almost 10 o'clock before I finally heard Vivaldi's "Four Seasons" softly playing downstairs. I got up to take a bath.

I used to stare into my own eyes in the medicine cabinet mirror. Letting the drug play my peripheral vision, filling my face with all kinds of monsters. Admittedly, I freaked a little the first time the Werewolf showed up. The alien wasn't nearly as scary as the wrinkled-up troll, or the hollow-eyed zombie, even the mummy paid a visit. After all the witches, warlocks, gargoyles and hobgoblins came and went, there was a parade of hybrid animals. A rabbit with ram horns, a pig, a couple dogs, a tiger, elephant, all of them with my eyes. All them staring at me, as if I were understanding something, like they were part of me, parts of my soul; someone other than the man in the mirror. But, because I never forgot I was on a drug, I busted them. After the third time, I started taking notes. I wrote down a description of each monster. And over time I proved, beyond all doubt, there hadn't been one single monster in my mirror that I hadn't seen in a movie. Finally, I started calling them out as soon they showed up. I'd name the movie, and they disappeared. I got so good at pulling up monsters out of my own imagination; I started doing it for entertainment. Laughing, joking, making fun, having a running commentary with my inner demons became one of my favorite games. So, I knew a little something about dropping acid.

And the drug Erlene Brown clawed into my hand, the shit still working in my head, eyes, and mouth, wasn't LSD.

When the water got hot, the mirror fogged up. I'd decided to play with whatever was in my system; give it a chance to reveal its true nature. A wash cloth was draped over the edge of the sink so I wiped the moisture off the mirror. There was nobody there but me. I tried the peripheral vision trick. Nothing. The water was still running so rather than piss off JR, I turned it off.

Stepping into the bath my feet went into the water with the sound exaggerated. More like the Paradise food truck that had splashed me earlier, than a foot in a tub. I slipped under the water until it covered my shoulders, head, and my face. The water felt thick, like the oil in a lava lamp, the bar of soap felt so slick I dropped it half a dozen times before I caught it with both hands. When I sat up to lather, blood rushed to my head, stirring up whatever residual potion still circulated through my system. I soaped and rinsed and soaked until my fingertips started to wrinkle, then stood up. The moisture beaded off my body like rain of a freshly waxed car. I stepped out of the tub feeling cleaner than I'd ever felt after an acid trip. Nobody I knew ever talked about how clean you feel at the end of an acid trip. I noticed it because it was the first hard evidence during this whole experience that Erlene had used some sort of lysergic acid diethylamide derivative when she cooked up her claw-foot juice. The clock on the dresser read 10:30 when I finally gave up the ghost and got to sleep.

The automatic timer on the stereo was set for 2:00. I was supposed to call Roy at 2:30 Saturday afternoon, so I set the stereo to come on playing "Spanish Key" off the *Bitch's Brew* album by Miles Davis. That was my favorite way to wake up. The automatic timer failed, of course, and it was already 3:00 by the time I woke up. The night before seemed like such a bizarre nightmare, I had difficulty believing it actually happened. I was thankful it was over. But I was late calling Roy, which presented a new set of problems.

I threw on a shirt, jeans and sneakers and ran down to the corner drug store to use the pay phone. Luckily Roy was still at The Merch. He answered the phone in his usual way.

"Vincent here," he said.

"Roy, it's Josie, sorry I'm late, long night."

"No problem," he said. "My guy couldn't make it anyway, so we set it up for later. He's going to call me with the time."

"So, am I going to get to meet this mystery man?" I said.

"He's got no problem with that."

"Good, so you think I still have a chance to pull this off?"

"I guess there's always a chance, we'll just have to see what happens." Roy sounded vague, which was understandable given his circumstances, but I got the impression that maybe somebody was in the room with him, listening to the conversation.

"Look, I've got to come down there anyway to get my flute. Are you going to be there a little while?" I said.

"No, I've got to go, but I'll be back later tonight. We can talk then," he said and hung up. Roy's phone manners were weird. He never said "hello" or "good-bye." When he had said all he wanted to say, he hung up.

The sun was bright and the humidity in the air had me sweating as I walked back down Savage Street. Rigney was futzing in his kitchen when I walked back into the yard. We gave each other a good-natured wave.

I brushed my teeth and combed my hair then hustled down to The Merch on the outside chance Roy might still be there. I really wanted to talk to him face to face, and I was starting to feel like he was avoiding me. His car was gone by the time I pulled into my spot.

As I walked in through the porthole door, a particularly jubilant Montague greeted me.

"What'z de word?" he said.

"Thunderbird," I answered.

"What'z de price?"

"Thirty twice."

"What'z de reason?"

"Grapes in season."

Thunderbird Wine was the cheapest wine you could buy, 60¢ a fifth.

"Cap'n boss man, why you lookin' so haggard and down en de mout'? If you still ain't found no sweet thang to come home to, maybe today is yo' lucky day 'cause old Montague can hep you out?"

Montague Bonneau was an easy man to love. Talking to this chief cook and bottle washer at The Merchant Seaman's Club was like talking to Uncle Remus. He was behind the bar garnishing two huge ham, cheese, bacon, and turkey club sandwiches with pickles and olives. They were so big I could only eat half of one. A blue dot flash bulb went off in my mind. Half of a sandwich, exactly like the ones he was making, was in the bag Rashad had pulled out of the Thunderbird's console. Staring over the wire-rimmed lenses of his bifocals, he gestured for me to sit down. He pushed a plate to the edge of the bar, along with a glass of beer.

Grey-haired, pushing sixty, with flared nostrils, high angular cheeks, he was blessed with the lean, faultfinding mouth of a mother who governs her children with omnipotent sarcasm. He enjoyed teasing me about not having a steady girlfriend.

Cooking wild game was his specialty, but women were his real first love. The women loved him, too. He was full of free relationship advice, constantly trying to set me up with girls who came into the club. His manner was so comfortable he was the only Negro in The Merch allowed to initiate a conversation with a white woman, no matter who she was with.

Montague's reputation as an expert with wild game had spread quickly after he prepared quail stuffed with breaded oysters for a group of downtown businessmen. They all belonged to a hunt club out on James Island. The hunters' wives hired him to cater a luncheon for a charity function at the Children's Hospital. The big hit of that event, a fried shrimp stuffed with crabmeat, wrapped in bacon, had the whole town talking. Roy Vincent hired him immediately and put him in charge of the kitchen at The Merch. Every steak, lobster, shrimp, chicken and pork chop had to meet his standards or it never got served. Because of Montague's skill in the kitchen, The Merch took in almost as much money from food as it did from set-ups at the bar.

"I hate'ta be de one to bring home de sad truf, I sho' hope you ain't mad wid me."

"You feed me and give me beer, why should I be mad?"

"You got a w'isitor back de in you dressin' room. She's a girl. She said she was a friend of yours and dat you was exspecking her."

"Really?" I said between bites. "How long has she been waiting?"

"Bout an hour or so. Why you ain told me you had a girlfriend...?"

I started to pick up the second sandwich when he slapped my hand. "You worse dan a no-mannahs nigga, boy. Dat uddah one fo' yo' lady friend. Woman gots to eat, too, you know."

The swiftness of his pop on the back of my hand startled me so that I almost choked. That's when I noticed the scratches from the night before had totally healed leaving only three pink lines. I jerked my hand back and tried to act like I hadn't noticed, but I was too late. He grabbed my hand and turned it over. Trying to talk with my mouth full, I said "Well damn, Montague, I don't even know who's back there."

"Don't talk wid yo' mout' full. De girls don't like crumbs in dey face," he said, as he paused staring intently down at the sandwich with a solemn look on his face. His whole demeanor had changed.

"What girl? I don't see a girl," I said.

Montague took a bar towel and dabbed my mouth and chin. He poured another glass of beer and set a bag of potato chips on the bar. I knew he'd seen the scratches and I knew he knew I knew, but neither one of us said anything.

"Hush up now and try to ack respeckable. Take dis san'wich and dis glass of b'er an' a bag a chips back to her an' ack like you got some breedin'. She's a pretty girl an' Gawd don't axe me why, I think she likes yo' ungrateful, little thin-lipped white boy ass."

"I don't even know who she is and already you've got me feeding her lunch."

I picked up the plate and crossed the room toward the stage, closely watched by Montague from behind the bar. He'd worked the kitchen for the last five years and seen thousands of people come and go through the doors of the club. I couldn't figure out why he'd taken such a liking to me, unless it was the family thing because Montague and Roy were very close. The thought crossed my mind like a comet. Roy must've told him my deadline for buying the club had been moved up. I stopped outside the dressing room door and listened, but I couldn't hear anything. I didn't have a girlfriend, and I couldn't think of anyone who would have the nerve to pretend she knew me or that I was expecting her. I pushed the door open with my foot.

Bobbie Storm was leaning forward in a chair with her feet apart, elbows on her knees, with my flute held up to her lips. She peeked up at me, gave me a warm inspection, dropped her eyes and pretended to execute a run, and then set the flute down on top of its case. She did it with that nonchalant air of familiarity that exists between people who've known each other for years. I was surprised that she knew the correct hand position for holding a flute. I didn't walk all the way into the dressing room. I just stood in the doorway, staring at her, with the sandwich plate in one hand and the beer in the other.

"What brings you here?" I said.

"I was bored, nothing else to do. Are you surprised to see me?"

"More like curious."

On the one hand I was extremely glad to see her, but I was ticked off because she'd taken my flute out and put it together without asking me. The dressing room was the one place where the band could keep private property private. She'd overstepped the boundary. By making herself at home in my private space, with my flute, it was as if the onstage me and the offstage suddenly met each other in front of a stranger. She'd accidentally touched a nerve I didn't know I had.

"What can I do for you?" I said.

She took the food out of my hands and set it on the dressing table, cast her eyes around the room, taking in the tuxedo jackets hanging in the closet, the James Brown and Ray Charles posters on the walls, the stacks of sheet music piled on an old Silvertone amplifier. She was acting a little too curious for her own good, as if boredom wasn't her only reason for being there. I immediately felt stupid for leaving my flute in the dressing room. At the same time I felt relieved I'd had the good sense to put my horn in the trunk.

"I would've thought you guys had a place with soft chairs, thick carpets, private bar, mirrors ringed in lights — you know, rock star furniture."

"This is where we get dressed. The public doesn't come back here uninvited." I walked into the room, picked my flute up, inspected it, then took it apart and put it back in the case.

"Aren't you going to practice or something?" she said.

"What does it look like?"

"You upset about something?"

"Maybe."

"Is it because of me?"

"Why would I be upset with you?" I widened my eyes in an unreserved gaze. "Why, I even brought you lunch, compliments of the chef."

"How nice, Montague and I had a nice chat. We discovered we have a mutual friend in Alabama." She breathed in, blew it out, looked down at the floor. "My husband's still in England. I don't have any friends here."

"Your husband is your husband no matter where he is."

"I can't argue with you there." She tried to catch my eyes, but I avoided her, letting the remark hang in the air. Her voice tightened. "The other day you said that improvisation was like mental telepathy. I came by to find out for myself if that's really true."

"It's not something I can conjure up at will. It doesn't happen like that for me," I said. "Others can, players like Sonny Rollins, but I need at least one other person to play off of. I can't turn it on and off like a light switch."

"Why not?"

"It's not something I can force. The truth is I don't know the language of jazz or improv. I don't speak the lingo. I hear music, I blow in the mouthpiece, my fingers work the keys." My mind tried to shut up, but my mouth kept talking. "I know enough about playing the saxophone to fool people into thinking I know how to play a saxophone." The truth spilled out of me like vomit. I'd never admitted this to myself, much less someone I barely knew. She picked up the sandwich, took a small bite, chewing it slowly to keep up her naïve front.

"Why are you doing this to me?"

I looked at her. She was still chewing. My hand went to my temple. Did she ask me the question or had I imagined it?

"Doing what?" I answered coldly.

Either she didn't hear me or she was ignoring me. "Pushing me away." This time I was watching her. Her mouth had not moved. Yet I could've sworn she was talking to me. Now I let my eyes meet hers, she was about to tear up, her face was flushed, she swallowed.

"I had a very long night. Way too much to drink," I said.

"What has the world done to you?" She ran her finger over the mic James Brown was cradling in the poster. "I've never had to track a man down and beg him to pay attention to me. Yesterday you told me you couldn't read music; that you'd taught yourself to play by ear. When you spoke, it sounded like you were talking about a woman you were in love with. I was touched. I came here. I found you. I want to know what it's like." She bit her lip and got the next words out with difficulty. "I want you to teach me how to love it like that. I have money. I am as talented as your other musician friends, and I think…" She stopped talking, dropped her head, and started to tremble, then to cry.

I had an English teacher who was a big fan of the Canadian humorist, Thomas Chandler Halliburton. The teacher liked to quote Halliburton every chance he got and one of those quotes stuck with me: "Every woman is wrong until she cries, and then she is right, instantly."

CHAPTER THIRTEEN

Impulsive decisions have cost me dearly. My mind wasn't right, and I knew it. I understood immediately how difficult it had been for her to fight down her vulnerability. She was engaged in a tremendous battle of wills, a war with herself. Trying to summon the courage to go after something she wanted this much was a reckless cry for help. She hadn't fooled Montague by trying to pass herself off as an old friend of mine. Just to get into my dressing room was totally out of character. I sensed in her a desperation so deep it was like discovering a new emotion. It gave me a chill. Suddenly, in a moment like I'd had with Rashad, I saw a little girl crying beside a grave. I gasped as an overwhelming wave of grief flowed through my body, and I knew in that instant, I'd recognized the pain she was feeling. My head cleared, the image faded like the monsters in the mirror, and she was back sitting on the chair, fully composed.

"Where'd you learn to play a flute?" I nodded toward the flute case sitting on the dresser next to her. "You were holding it correctly is why I ask."

"I played in high school." She paused then continued. "You must like that flute. You've cleaned between all the keys and pads, it's spotless."

"Yes, it was a gift from a very special friend."

"Tell me," she smiled, "when did you know you wanted to be a musician?"

"When I was in the fourth grade, I played "On Top of Old Smokey" on a little plastic recorder for the whole class. I played it without the music, and the whole class cheered, except for Julia White. She just sat and stared at me with a dreamy smile on her face. She knew I liked her, but she'd ignored me until that day. We were sweethearts after that. Her smile changed my life. She had a birthday party and asked me to play the recorder. My first private party, and I started ad-libbing all the songs in the little book. Her parents clapped louder than any of the kids. They kept making these funny hand signals. I found out later, both her parents were deaf."

I looked down into her eyes. She was hanging on every word. I suddenly felt foolish and embarrassed. "I'm sorry. I didn't mean to get mushy on you."

"Oh, I wouldn't call it mushy. I'd call it sweet." She smiled. I heard her voice in my head. Not my ears, not in the outside room, not with sound vibration, more like a thought. "Only a true artist would be strong enough to open up to a total stranger and reveal something so personal."

I reached down and took her hand and motioned for her to stand up. I opened the flute case and assembled the instrument slowly, one piece at a time, carefully aligning the foot and the head with the barrel. Then I walked her out to the B3 and had her sit down on the bench. I adjusted the stage lights so that we were in a blue semi-dark haze.

"Ever played a Hammond?"

"I've seen them, watched others play them, I like Jimmy Smith."

"Turning one on is a ritual for a true Hammond player. Lot of people do it incorrectly, especially hard rock and roll keyboard players, who use them as gimmicks. To them, a B3 is no more than a one elephant ride at a gypsy circus. They couldn't care less about the soul of the instrument so they don't give it adequate respect."

"In other words, they miss the whole point of having one."

"Exactly. This instrument has electric motors, gears, oil, and has to be cared for like an antique car. The heat generated by the tubes, the room, all contribute to the viscosity of the oil. Dust can build up inside the cabinet. It's not just an organ, it's a system, and because this system speaks directly to the human heart, people respond to the sound on a subconscious level."

"I feel like I'm in church."

"I wouldn't go that far, but I did find this one in a church."

"What kind of church?"

"AME. Why?'

"An all-black church."

"I suppose so, most AME churches are black."

"Abraham went to an AME church."

"Who's Abraham?"

"The blues singer, from Hamilton, my home town, I told you about him last night."

"Is he the one Montague knows?"

"Yes. They're related. Not sure if it's by blood or marriage, but they know each other."

"Well, it's a small world," I said.

"I didn't mean to get off the subject. Where were we?"

"These two switches, marked START and RUN," I put her hand on the switches located in the upper right corner of the cabinet, above the top row of keys, "are used in sequence. Push the start button up with your thumb and hold it for five seconds."

The electric motors started spinning, gaining speed until a steady wind-up whirring coursed inside the cabinet. "Now you know the motors have come up to speed, keep your thumb on the start switch and use your index and middle fingers to push up on the run switch." I coaxed the two fingers into position. "Now hold down one of the keys until the sound comes up."

"It's like waking up a pet bear."

"Why do you think we call it the Beast?"

Sitting on the bench beside her, my leg was pressed against hers I felt heat, physical heat. I blew air into the flute to warm up the cool metal. Her hands trembled in her lap, and I put my own right hand on the top of her thigh and gave her a friendly pat. She put her fingers on the keyboard and whispered in a faint voice, "Oh God, I don't know the first thing about playing this thing, what do you want me to do?"

"Hold D minor7, four counts; E minor7 flat5; A7, back to D minor 7."

"Summertime?"

"No, not quite, I'll play the melody, you follow me."

"Like this?" She formed the second inversion of the chord.

"Keep the root in the bass with your left hand. Like this... "

I held the flute with my left hand and softly put my right hand down across hers until I had her fingers forming the tonic chord in four slow beats.

"Play the '1,' then go to the 'V7 suspended' and repeat it," I said softly.

"How do you form the suspended chord?"

"Play a Bb major triad with a C in the bass. Go through that change twice, then play the III chord, with the A in the bass." I showed her where to put her fingers.

"You mean, put the C in the bass under the Bb Chord, then back to the I, then to the III?"

"Exactly." I was surprised she didn't notice the three pink scars.

Her left hand instinctively followed the bass line, and I put both hands back on the flute, allowing the melody to flow through me, through her, into the Hammond to her and back again. Her hands began to float the way I'd seen them in the Swamp Fox Room only this time her eyes were closed. I heard the chord structure shift slightly as she moved from one change to the next and back.

"Now, from the III, go to VI, then IV for two beats, then move the Bb up a half step to B to form the diminished, two beats and raise the A flat to A, keeping all the other notes, while dropping the bass back to F or the 1." I walked her through the changes carefully and lifted the melody up to the next octave, so the flute hovered above the Hammond like a spirit.

"What is this, it sounds familiar but I've never played anything like this. It almost sounds like orthodox church music."

I took a breath. "It's called improvisation," I said. "We're making it up as we go along." She was so mesmerized she hadn't realized we slipped out of a straight F major blues into an atonal modal structure.

We reached out to each other mentally and carefully placed the notes beside and on top of each other weaving a fine lace pattern with no recognizable melody. Just notes floating over chords; a flute over an organ. After what seemed like only a few minutes, I let the melody die off in a breathy low C holding the note until the 'sustain' ran out on the organ. Thirty minutes had passed in what seemed like five.

Silence engulfed us when the melody ended. We sat motionless, listening as the beautiful music we had created drifted into the void. I put my arm around her shoulder. "Welcome home, soldier," I said.

"It was so pretty, so beautiful, so bittersweet, I wanted to hold onto it a little longer."

"To quote Eric Dolphy, 'When you hear music, after it's over, it's gone, in the air. You can never capture it again.'"

"In the air and gone."

"Pretty much."

In the dim atmosphere of softened stage lights, sitting next to her there at the organ, I wondered why I'd let myself get so close to her, why I'd let her get so close to me. I felt like I'd confessed a secret to someone I didn't even know. Then, wondering if it was possible that the stranger could be feeling the same? My eyes were still burning, the drug hadn't completely worn off and it was a battle trying to determine fact from fantasy. It had been a long time since I'd visited the vault in my heart where I stored the real experiences which dictated my life course. I wasn't even sure I wanted to understand it. Introspection was not a natural talent for me. Besides, according to Freddie May, I was the father confessor type, "Chicks love that fag charm of yours," he'd said.

I'd been disillusioned with the world for so long, nothing got through that didn't fuel my cynicism. Now, viewing it from a heart touched by hope, I felt like a soldier who has completed a long tour of duty. I longed to fly home, but I couldn't shake the fear of the plane blowing up before it got off the runway.

Bobbie was still sitting with her eyes closed when the door behind the stage opened and someone came in behind us. Jack had come in early. He walked to the stage, looked at us, nodded and walked over to his amp.

"Making sure everything's ready for another Saturday night in paradise," he said.

Suddenly, without even thinking I was Josie Chapman again, all business, everything that just happened forgotten.

"Jack's into arranging," I said, "he likes to keep people guessing."

"Hello," Bobbie said. Jack nodded.

"Last week, it was the theme from the movie 'Exodus,' the week before that we worked up the 'James Bond' theme," I said.

"People dance to those songs?" she said.

"We play them during the third after everybody's drunk. They get a kick out of it."

"You're getting stuck in a rut with these movie themes." I laughed.

"Let's work up something in 5/4, 'Mission Impossible' or 'Take Five?'"

Bobbie shifted her weight next to me. Her eyes were open, but she was still staring at the floor. I was sure she was only half listening.

"'Mission Impossible' sounds good to me," he said. "I already know the chords and Wayne can pick up the bass line. Monk will dig it to death."

I glanced over at Bobbie. She was watching Jack, hardly breathing.

"Come over here a minute, will you, Jack? There's someone I want you to meet." I put my arm around her neck and pulled our heads together. "He doesn't bite." I gave her a little kiss on the forehead and asked her what she'd like for dinner.

"Just you," she said.

"Rib eye, baked potato, green peas, salad, Bordeaux?"

"That'll work." She took a tissue out of her pocket and wiped her eyes.

I turned back to Jack. "I'm sorry, man, this is really embarrassing. This is the piano player from the Swamp Fox. She, that is we, were just giving each other a music lesson. Bobbie, meet Jack Howerson. Jack; Bobbie Storm."

Jack, forever the consummate gentleman, shook hands with her. I swiveled around the edge of the organ bench, swinging my legs out from under the keyboard, and engaged in a face rubbing, stretching yawn. I scratched my head and ran my fingers over what seemed like a day's worth of stubble on my chin. My skin itched. I scratched my head, rubbing my hands over what felt like a day's worth of beard stubble. After a moment, I looked at her.

"Well?" I said. "What do you think?"

"About what?" she said.

"Was coming here this afternoon the right thing to do?"

"I'm sure it was," she said.

"Everything you expected?" I stood up and stretched again.

"No, it was more like making love than I thought it would be."

"I wasn't expecting that." Jack said, then started unpacking his guitar.

I didn't really wanna know what she was expecting, or what she wasn't expecting, for that matter. I knew that once we started getting into what was going on in her mind, besides the music, I'd be saddled with all kinds of responsibilities. About that time Monk, Gary and Wayne walked in. Jack and I worked with them on the "Mission Impossible" theme until we had a tight arrangement. When the other horn players arrived, Jack showed them their parts.

I'd only eaten half the sandwich Montague made, and Bobbie had hardly touched hers. I knew she must be getting hungry. She'd hung around the club all afternoon. She walked through the kitchen, the restrooms, generally casing the whole club. When the band put the finishing touches on the "Mission Impossible" theme, Bobbie and I sat in a back corner booth like a couple of regular sweethearts.

Montague brought us each a steak, with salad and baked potato. Over dinner, she was quiet, even restrained. She was dressed for her gig at the Swamp Fox.

"You know I can't stay, I have a gig," she said.

"I love it when girls say 'gig,'" I said.

A sharp pain hit my left temple. I clenched my teeth.

"What's wrong?"

"Oh, nothing. A bit of a headache, couple aspirin, couple drinks, I'll be fine."

"Are you sure it's just a headache?"

"Like I said, long night, too little sleep, nothing I haven't been through before. I'm fine."

I kept waiting for her to suggest we get together again. I was relieved when she didn't. I was already in over my head, and crashing on Erlene's "Love Potion No. 9" wasn't helping."

"It's quarter to four, you know. Don't you start at four?"

"Five on Saturdays."

"Well then, you've got plenty of time." I figured about two minutes before I'd have to hit the restroom.

She obviously had something else on her mind, but I didn't know how much longer I could keep from throwing up. She couldn't finish her dinner, which was understandable. The steak Montague fixed her was big enough for two people. I couldn't finish what was on my plate and I'd been hungry.

When the rest of the band was on stage ready for a sound check, I placed my napkin on the table and smiled at her. "I have to go," I said. Drops of sweat formed on my top lip. She finished her coffee and began the self-conscious fidgeting of a person who didn't want to go, but felt out of place in the present circumstances. As I started to get up, she looked across the table as if she was going to say one thing but decided on something else.

"How long do you have to play tonight?"

"We go from nine to one, if the crowd is thin."

"Then what? I mean, are you going out for breakfast before you go home?"

"Maybe. It depends."

"On what?"

"On whether I'm hungry for breakfast or happy just to raid the kitchen."

I could see where this little conversation was heading. I remember thinking that this is the problem with relationships: having to explain yourself. That's why I lived alone. Other than tip-toeing around Rigney, I didn't have to explain my actions, or the decisions leading to them, to anyone. She looked at me like she'd seen a ghost.

My mind started racing. An entire monologue ran through my head. "That's what separates being friends with a woman from being involved with one. One minute, I'm minding my own business, going on with my life. The next minute I'm explaining where I'm going and what I'm going to do and when and why I'm doing it that way instead of some other way. Worst of all, if I didn't do what I said I would, she'd be asking why I changed my mind."

Women treat you like you teach them to treat you. Bobbie asked what I was doing later to keep track of me. If I let her, I'd have to be careful she didn't start thinking I'd rather be alone than with her. Next I'd be worrying about whether or not I'd hurt her feelings. If I hurt her feelings she might cry and if she cried Halliburton's Rule would kick in and I'd be sunk."

"So you ... uh ... don't have anything definite lined up?"

"Nothing definite." I said. "When I'm not working, I improvise."

She slid out of the booth. "I want to thank you." She smiled.

"For what?"

"For the music, the dinner, the attention, you know," she nodded at the red glass bar candle flickering on the table and said, "the candle light." We both snickered. "I was wrong to invade your privacy. You've been very sweet. I enjoyed our time together."

"Me, too."

"So, I guess it kind of ends with the first lesson, huh?" She bit her lip.

I could tell she was getting in over her head. She knew how I felt about her being married, but that didn't keep her from trying a different approach. The old "no-strings-attached, no-harm-intended, undemanding, I'll be around if you wanna see me" routine. It was a modern variation on the damsel in distress theme, with a twist. The twist is the quiet, diminutive, polite way she was screaming for help.

"I enjoyed it ... I really did. We'll have to do it again, sometime," I said.

"Do you remember how it felt, right at the end?" She said. "Does it feel like that every time?"

"It does until you get comfortable with it. Like everything else." That stung her. I knew she'd wanted it to be unique.

"But it was a little different, wasn't it?"

"Different in what way?"

"You said you couldn't turn it on and off like a light switch. That you have to click with the other person."

"That's true, to a certain extent. But you have to be familiar with the language of music, too … and you definitely are."

"You mean because I read?"

"No, because you've got soul." I walked her to the door trying not to throw up or piss my pants. "You have a natural sense of self-expression, very pretty, like your face." I paused, bit my lip, tilted my head, and stared.…

"But?"

"But, we're not always sweet in real life. Sometimes we feel like kicking ass, raising hell, and making noise. You know, rock and roll." I laughed.

She slipped on her jacket, smiling to herself, absorbed in some consideration of what I'd said. At the door, she stood on her tiptoes and kissed me lightly on the cheek, keeping her eyes riveted to mine.

At the last moment, I almost suggested we meet for breakfast, but then I remembered again that she was married and, goddamn it, I just could not let myself get involved with a married woman, even if her husband was on the other side of the fucking ocean.

"Thanks again," she said, and walked out the door.

She couldn't have been easier to like or more enjoyable to be with. All I could figure was her husband was either the world's biggest jerk or too stupid to realize what he had.

I watched her car pull out of the parking lot; then literally, ran to men's room where I hung my head over the toilet and puked until my nose started bleeding. My skin was crawling, my muscles were screaming, I even felt my jaw trying to lock up. I washed my face, gargled some water, and remembered I still had two Darvon in my pocket.

I went to the bar, grabbed a highball glass and poured it full of Wild Turkey, popped the pills, chased them with half the whiskey and looked in the mirror behind the bar. I saw my reflection, but I didn't recognize myself, I looked like an old man, in the face I mean. I had my own body, my own hair, but my face looked like pictures I'd seen of my great-grandfather from his days after the Civil

War. I started to get scared, but remembered my first rule of drug survival: never forget you're on a drug. Nothing you see is real. I drank the last of the whiskey in the glass while staring at the image in the mirror. "Back off, motherfucker," I hissed, and like a dog skulking off with its tail between its legs, the image faded and I was back.

The guys were warmed up and jamming on a standard 12-bar blues in E-flat. I'd been practicing a Coltrane run for weeks, one of those screaming note clusters the uninitiated call noise. I kept a practice horn in a stand at the back of the stage so I wouldn't have to bring the Mark VI down to the club to practice. I grabbed the horn and began to play. I'd transposed the riff from Coltrane's version of "My Favorite Things," an exquisitely complex piece of music that ordinarily cleared my mind, but I didn't feel like tearing the roof off of anything. Instead, I blew a laid-back blues riff I'd ripped from an old Stan Getz album and found myself drifting in and out of the melody to "I Concentrate On You."

When we finished, Jack counted off the five beats signaling the beginning to "Mission Impossible" and I picked up the flute and fell right in with the melody line. I couldn't really think about what I was doing, but I'd done it so many times, I didn't really have to think.

Letting Bobbie go was the smart thing to do. Putting some distance between us was the only safe course I could take. Had she been divorced, I could see pursuing it, if for no other reason than to let the emotions run their course. A married woman never needs the disastrous, predestined ordeal of having an affair with a professional musician. And the musician doesn't need the jealous husband blasting into his crib and blowing his brains out. Nothing ends a musician's career faster than his lover's husband putting a few bullet holes in him. Ask Sam Cooke.

Still, I couldn't shake the feeling I was making a mistake. Somewhere in the back of my mind something was trying to warn me again. It irritated me to even consider another man's wife as my girlfriend because he would always have a legal claim and I'd always be the bad guy. That thought really pissed me off at myself because I was doing the same thing to her in my mind that I'd just wanted her to stop doing to me. I felt a hand on my shoulder.

"You feeling all right?" Jack said.

"Huh?"

"The rest of us were wondering how long you were going to stand there staring into space. You stopped playing halfway through the tune. We were curious as to how long you were going to stand there doing nothing?"

I looked around at the other guys. They were about to bust a gut trying to keep from laughing at me. The Darvon-whiskey cocktail had stopped the spasms; it was a high I was used to. Nobody's face was moving, no trippy lights, no muscle cramps, no sweat dripping, no undulating floors or walls, just a stomach ache from heaving and a good solid chemical/alcohol stone. I kept thinking, "you've got this, you've got this, motherfucker, you have got this."

"I think the boy's in lo-o-o-o-v-e." Gary, the drummer made a kissing sound with his lips on the back of his hand.

"She's married," I said.

"Uh, Oh," the band whistled in unison.

"Now, now boys, don't go teasing the sax player," Jack told them. "Y'all know how sensitive they can be."

"OK, show's over," I said. "Let's get back to work."

We ran through the tune until it was tight and then a couple more times for good measure. When I walked off the stage toward the bar, I saw Montague sitting on the counter with his feet propped up on a beer keg. He had his arms crossed and a big grin on his face that broke into laugh when he saw me stop and look at him.

"What the hell are you laughing at?" I said.

"Oh…nothin'…be'sept you." He slapped his knee.

"What'd I do that was so funny?"

"Ain't what you did. It's what got done to you."

"You mean that girl?"

"Uh, huh."

"That's ridiculous, besides she's married," I said.

"Married or not she likes you, brother." Gary yelled from behind his drums.

"Oh, yes indeedy, I sho' do think you right about that, yes sir, you most definitely right on that ba'ticular account." Montague was almost singing as he burst into a wave of side splitting laughter that had him crying while he was falling all over the counter. "Yes sir, you sho' is right 'bout dat gal wanted to learn to play. And yo' drummer's right 'bout that other thing too," he said looking down his nose.

"What other thing?" I stood there with my hands on my hips, watching him dry his tears on a bar towel.

"'Bout her wantin' to play without music. Dat's a mos' definite, fo' sure." He started laughing again.

I was about to get pissed but decided to roll with it instead. Best defense, etc., and all that bullshit.

"Hey, maybe you're right," I said "Maybe we'll fall in love; she'll leave her husband, or he'll leave her, and we'll get married and live happily, ever after."

"Dat may berry well be, but you got a lotta stuff to go through before it ever gets to dat point. And the fun's just beginning."

"Montague, you're crazy if you think I'm getting mixed up with her."

"And you is crazy if you thinks you ain't already mixed up wit her. I knows what I'm talking about. I seen 'em too many time."

I shook my head, "You're wrong." I told him. But way down deep, where nobody goes but me, I knew he wasn't.

CHAPTER FOURTEEN

My Saturday night pre-performance ritual included reciting a prison poem before I went on stage. It was more like a chant I whispered under my breath in the dressing room.

"Deep down in the jungle where the ground grows rich,
There's a pool-shootin' monkey that's a son-of-a-bitch.
The baboon gang was goin' tight
So they hung around the pool hall, day and night.

Along about ten, the shark walked in,
You could tell he was a shark by the way he wore his clothes.

Spade black slippers and dark blue slacks,
A Chesterfield coat with a slit down the back.
Monkey said, "I don't know the bastard's name,
But I'm going to shoot him just one damn game."

They put up ten for the stake,
And flipped a coin for the break.

Monkey won the break for the one, two, three, four, five, six, seven;
Which left a combination on the eight, nine, ten, eleven.
With the twelve on the rail and the cue on the spot,
The monkey ran the table in five damn shots.

Baboon said, "You might win rotation, still don't mean you win.
Before you leave here, you'll gimme back my ten."

Monkey swung around with a hard right straight,
And flew out the door like a B-38.

One of his friends, sittin' on a stool,
Said, "That's a yellow motherfucker, but he can sure shoot pool."

I timed it so the poem ended precisely as I stepped onto the stage. The poem held a special meaning for two reasons. I learned it from the prisoner who wrote it. And second, because it was always 'along about ten when the sharks walked in.' This particular Saturday night was full of sharks.

From the floor, they always appeared evenly dispersed throughout the room. Viewed from the extra six inches or so the height of the stage added, I could watch the people gravitating toward each other like fish in a pond. They formed miniature versions of the same social structures that existed throughout the city. A gray-blue haze of cigarette smoke enveloped them in a humming, clinking fog, that took on a life of its own; becoming more animated with each passing hour.

By midnight, The Merch was its own universe. A coterie of stars from each local group circulated through a gossamer cross-section of the community. Near the back, a big man with pink skin, freckles and thinning red hair, negotiated his way through the undulating swell of humanity. Strawberry Barrineau made eye contact with me from twenty feet out. Smiling brightly, he moved from one group to another on his way toward the stage.

Jack turned to Gary and said, "Strawberry's on his way up."

Behind me, I heard a collective sigh rise up from the drummer and the bass player. Strawberry wanted to sing his favorite song, "Sweet Potato Pie." Strawberry was the hoodlum de jour in Charleston. A notorious heroin dealer, he appeared to exist above the law. Every band in town had "Sweet Potato Pie" on the song list just in case Strawberry took a notion to sing.

As a kid, Strawberry Barrineau made a name for himself as a softball player. Picture in the papers, regional championships, a fierce competitor who toured with several teams playing in some kind of softball league circuit. Word on the street was they even got paid to play. Which translated meant the side bet money depended on who threw the game.

When Strawberry decided to sit in with the band, he stalked the stage like a carnivore. The red hair fit his head like a mop. The dopey blue eyes slit above a big nose and grin. Drifting toward me from out of the blurry-eyed audience, with a cigarette hanging out one side of his mouth and a toothpick hanging out the other, he looked like an albino gorilla imitation of Ronald McDonald. The stale cigarette smoke cloud hanging over the stage, not usually a problem, irritated my eyes. A sweet smell wafted up from Strawberry as he climbed on the stage. Spearmint gum mingled with the scent of menthol Kools. The musky odor of sweat combined with the strong perfume of Canoe cologne. Filling the space next to me, he grabbed my microphone with his left hand while transferring the cigarette between the first two fingers of his right, which also held a glass of beer. This was exactly the same way the girls of The Merch held their beer and cigarette in one hand when they shagged. I'd never noticed a man doing it before.

I took my sax out of its stand on the edge of the stage, hooked the neck strap into the ring on the back, and then wrapped my arms around the bell.

Strawberry had been known to wobble.

Obviously enjoying the attention, he talked slowly. The crowded dance floor was as raucous as a fraternity party. Only the waiters, the bartenders, and Freddie May standing by the kitchen door signaled to the band that the help was less than impressed.

Strawberry was leaning on the mike stand when I counted off the slow blues beat of the song. He closed his eyes and motioned me over to the mic, angling it toward the bell of my horn. He looked into the audience and called over a girl with her blouse unbuttoned past her bra.

"Hummm, 'ear ba'bee, Daddy Sugah gonna sang you all's a purdy song."

A lanky, hopelessly drunk, overblown woman with an absurdly rounded figure and a plain freckled face leered back at him. She had shallow, vicious green eyes, a lean straight mouth, and masses of frizzy blonde hair. The man she was with looked like he was just along for the ride. After we played the first few bars without him singing, I asked, "Something wrong?"

"Fine-en nah groove," he slurred. "Hep me… hep me-e-e," belch, fart, throat clear, gag, cough and spit, "fin' nah groove." Then he drank half the beer in one gulp, wiped his mouth with his hairy red arm opening up a three inch scratch with the toothpick that he didn't even notice he was chewing.

Finding the groove in "Sweet Potato Pie" is easier than finding your face in a mirror. But Strawberry was so wasted; I doubted he could find the holes in his nose with his finger. After a few more bars, I whispered the words in his ear, the song itself usually lasted a little more than three minutes. Unless he got stuck in "nah groove." He really liked going through the lyrics with a woman staring up at him from the dance floor. Once he got started on the "Gimme, Gimme sum-mah-um Sweet, Sweet Potato Pie, Oooh so good," part, he was hard to stop.

Following the verse, Strawberry Barrineau suddenly felt compelled to demonstrate his prowess in the area of dance. With both microphone and beer glass raised high, he initiated a gyroscopic sequence of moves referred to, by the local shaggers, as the "Dirty Hunch." He gyrated down the handrail with the all precision of an unbalanced washing machine busting its bolts.

Two minutes into the Strawberry wallow, Freddie drew his index finger slowly across his throat. We went through the coda twice and on the third pass started bringing the song to a close. Strawberry, of course, was totally lost in his own reverie. Jack shook his head and looked at me.

"Take it out," I said. And the band ended the song.

Strawberry bent over the rail and kept right on singing. His girlfriend was slobbering right in the mike with him. They were growling the "Gimme, gimme some" part when Strawberry began to wobble and the beer started sloshing in his glass.

It was all over but the crying, as his final dirty hunch rotation sent him somersaulting over the edge of the stage railing onto the parquet tile of the dance floor. He took the woman and her date down with him as he sprawled out flat on his back and passed out cold.

The woman, with her dress now hiked up around her waist, had lost one shoe. The shoe, sandwiched between Strawberry's body and the floor, was barely visible. When she tried to pull the shoe out from under him, she popped the last button on her blouse. This, in turn, released one boob, which bounced around like one of those toy eyeballs on a spring.

A howl went up from the rest of the onlookers that emptied the gambling tables as well as the bar. While the dork she'd been dancing with was trying to pull her dress down, he slipped in the spilled beer and, accidentally, goosed her with the toe of his own shoe. This, in turn, prompted the goosee to return fire by wheeling around with the recently recovered shoe, clipping the gooser right in the nose causing blood to splash all over the dance floor. By the time Freddie May, Sinclair, Nukes and Beep got to them, the woman and the dork were in a bloody, beer-soaked, drunken free for all tripping over the sprawled, incoherent Strawberry Barrineau who lay belching and farting in a puddle of his own puke. That was damn sure something you don't see every night.

I told Jack that we needed to take a break until somebody could clean up the mess. Wayne, the bass player, threw the switch to the jukebox while Nukes and Beeps carried Strawberry into the men's room. Sinclair and Freddie had the woman and the man divided into separate piles. I cradled the mic in its stand and tried to straighten up the wires on the stage. I'd just put my horn back on its stand when I heard a voice behind me say "That was some show." Turning around, I looked straight into the shimmering gold flecks of Bobbie Storm's hazel eyes.

"We pride ourselves on audience contact," I said.

"At least you don't have baboons like that trying to marry you every night."

"Hey, don't kid yourself, I've had my share."

Bobbie laughed and stuffed her hands down into the pockets of her jeans. She was, obviously, waiting for me to finish with the wires. I knew why she'd come by. She wanted to sit in with The Magnificent Seven.

With my back turned, I indulged myself in a private victory smirk. There is no greater thrill in music than knowing you're going to blow an audience away. Being the only person in the room who fully understood the potent combination of talent about to take place, I decided against having a drink before we went back to play. My head had cleared, and I wanted to be as straight as I could be. I didn't want to miss a single note.

Bobbie was an engine; a high performance, super-stock, power plant waiting only for the right vehicle. The Magnificent Seven was that vehicle. I stepped off the stage, she took my arm like a girl walking home from school with her boyfriend. Montague was staring at us, his hand on his chin.

"Was it as good for you this afternoon, as it was for me?" she said.

The obvious double meaning meant she now trusted me enough to flirt. Translation: She thought we could be friends on a professional level.

"I thought we sounded good together. I think my band will impress you."

"If they're all as good as you, it'll be like dying and going to heaven."

She stepped on the foot rail, slipped onto a barstool and I took the one next to her. I wasn't surprised that when our elbows touched, she didn't pull back. Montague's harrumphed; his eyes rolled to heaven.

"What would you like to drink?" I asked her.

"I'll have whatever you're having."

When she swiveled the stool, letting both her knees trace the side of my leg, Montague bit his bar towel to keep from laughing. After regaining his composure, he casually placed a coaster in front of each of us.

"Montague, I'd like to introduce you to a fellow musician. This is Bobbie Storm, she sings with the band over at The Apartment Club."

"We met earlier," Bobbie said. "Hello again, Montague."

"When did you two meet? Earlier I mean?" I said.

"This afternoon, remember? I told you, Montague and my friend, Abraham, knew each other."

I was drawing a blank. There was a hole in my memory, but I couldn't worry about it. It would sort itself out.

"How do, Missy," Montague said, graciously tipping his head forward.

"Two black coffees, Montague." I shot him the order and a smirk/glint that was telepathy for: "Don't start any of your girlfriend-boyfriend shit."

"I need cream and sugar," she said smiling at Montague.

He winked at her and pulled two cups from under the bar. I was watching her watch the room in the mirror behind the bar. She'd never played a club like The Merch. She was trying to get a feel for it, trying to sense the fabric of the atmosphere, the tension. When Montague poured the coffee, she didn't even notice. I had to tap her knee to get her attention. She still had her knees pressed hard against my leg.

"You don't have to be afraid. You'll do just fine," I said.

"You really think the band will like me?" she said.

"I'd never get my hopes up high enough to contemplate heaven," I said, "but my guess is you'll at least feel like you've been in church."

"Like this afternoon?"

I just looked at her without blinking and grinned. She turned to face me and let her eyes track my face from my eyes to my mouth and back again. It would have been easy to kiss her right then. I thought about it and decided not to confuse the issue.

In the bar band business, it pays to be careful who you flirt with. The girl in the audience, that guy on the stage, that man at the bar, you never know what they're thinking. You never know how they're taking that look on your face or what they think you meant by what you sang or played. When it's late their emotions are running neck and neck with their blood-alcohol levels.

"I had a guy come up to me tonight and ask me to marry him," she pulled the statement out of thin air.

"Are you going to do it?" I quipped.

"Hell, n-o-o!" She playfully hit me on the arm. "He was so drunk he could hardly stand up. I get so sick of that."

"It goes with the territory," I said. "It could be worse."

"How?"

"You could get drunk enough to accept." She hit me again.

"You better stop picking on me. I'm trying to be good," she said.

"You're very good. And the crowd is going to love you. So stop worrying and drink your coffee, I wanna go over a couple of tunes with you before we go back to the stage."

Bobbie and I finished our coffees, and I walked her back to the dressing room. Everybody in the band, except Jack, was out in the club so the three of us had the room all to ourselves. We went over the basic arrangements for, "Sheer Curiosity," "You're Killin' Me," "Love Light," "I Don't Want To Cry," "Heat Wave," "Summertime" and "Georgia On My Mind." Bobbie didn't have any trouble with the key signatures and hardly looked at any of the chord charts. Her attention centered on the melody line moving through the chord changes, on the lookout for holes she could fill with her voice. She'd introduce each phrase after Jack's cue, then he could move it around anywhere without losing her. Bobbie followed him instinctively. I suspected she secretly liked following a good leader, someone who could guide her in and out of the changes, while still allowing her to explore the area between.

I was hoping she wouldn't get lost and freeze up when we got back on stage. Her other band had relied on her to guide them. Her guitar player was pretty good at what he did. He just couldn't do anything else. Jack, on the other hand, had been playing and arranging professionally since he was fourteen years old. I'd been following his lead for months. It would be interesting to see how far outside the musical structure he'd be willing to go with her. Even more interesting would be to see if he'd set it up so she'd have to get back by herself.

After the fiasco with Strawberry, the crowd was wide-awake and wired for some hard driving soul music. The vibe in the room was perfect for blowing the doors off the room. Bobbie walked on stage and looked down at the red carpet and whispered. "I've got butterflies in my stomach."

"Stop worrying, butterflies are good. Worry when you stop having them."

The crowd noise didn't bother her. She'd heard it all before at Reed's place. What got her rubbing her arms were three horns and a B3. She was about to channel the spirit of music in a way she'd never done before. We'd slipped her on stage without anyone noticing, so she had her head down, whispering with her eyes closed. I counted off "Sheer Curiosity," Jack laid down the opening riff, which caused her to jolt upright. She wrapped her fingers around the mike, with it still on the stand and started rocking slowly on the balls of her feet. Still whispering, she lifted her head, stared out over the crowd and focused on a picture of something far away. She sniffled, coughed once, then looked me straight in the eye as she snapped the mic out of its cradle and started from way down low and issued a slow stream of four-bar phrases, just vocal sounds with no words, floating on top of the chords. There was nothing recognizable as the beginning of the road house blues classic.

Gary kicked his bass drum, alternating with a left hand rim shot on the snare, Monk was all over it, "Hell, yeah!!" he yelled from the Hammond console. He started bouncing his palms across the keys. Wayne alternated his fingers between the top two strings of the bass adding a low rolling drone under Gary's ride cymbal and floor tom. The rhythmic combination of sounds kept building under her vocals to the breaking point; still she continued to hold back. She repeated broken passages of the lyric, faster and faster, but then stopped short of pushing the tune into full swing. Jack and the band rode the riff until she started on a different set of arpeggios. It didn't matter to us how long the beginning took; we were all into whatever she wanted to do. She was waiting for some kind of kinetic window to open in the wall of rhythm and sound pulsating at the edge of the stage. Her voice refused to relinquish control of the music. She slowly started to dictate and manage every detail of the sound coming from the rhythm section.

Something much heavier than the sum of the parts was about to rip through The Merchant Seaman's Club and change forever the way music was played in Charleston. Bobbie's deep, throaty gravel voice rose up from her soul, her eyes closed down to slits, Gary and Wayne thump, thump, thump, thumped the count off under the guitar. And Bobbie Storm throttled up The Magnificent Seven like a 747 rolling down a runway. When she released the melody, every chin in the room was on the floor. Bobbie: *"Whoo-oo! / They cut my power / and the phone is dead. /"* She growled. *"Got a drop cord from the neighbors / run to the lamp beside 'a my bed . /"* "Ho-ly-fuck," Jack mouthed. *"Sink's full of dishes / I got clothes all over the floor. / My truck won't start / my dog won't bark / and a lawyer's at my door. / Tell 'em I'm runnin' on sheer curiosity. /"* Horns: Punch!-Punch!-Punch *"Don't know what's next / but I damn sure wanta see. /"* Bobbie lifted off: *"Runnin' on sheer curiosity /*

ever since that boy / got the best of me. / Woooowhooo! / He got the best of me! /" Bobbie cut her eyes at me and grinned. *"That lawyer told me / 'he don't want a thing. / Keep the house, keep the car, keep the furniture / and keep your diamond ring!' / Oh-ohhh, I said Hey lawyer / does'at mean he ain't coming back? / Lawyer said, 'he's just thankful for the clothes that're on his back! /'"*

A chorus of *"Runnin' on sheer curiosity / wooo-hoooo,"* rose from a bevy of Jesus testifying finger wagging Doo-wop bitches, rushing the stage. *"Don't know what's next / but I damn sure wanta see! /"* Bobbie held the mic over their heads, *"Runnin' on sheer curiosity / ever since that boy got the best of me!"* We took it to the bridge. Bobbie: *"I know I shoulda known better / than to think that he could change. / Livin' down in the Lowcountry / can get a little scrange. / We got people down here use hoodoo / black cat bone and monkey paw. / Ain't too many boys / from New York City / gonna cut it on Wadmalaw. / Wooooohoooo-oooooooooo-whoooooo!"*

Cadillac horns pierced the air, Bobbie over the top: *"Runnin' on sheer curiosity / ever since that boy got the best of me!"* Stinging harmony brass punctuating chorus lines drove the men wild. Bobbie swung around, jacked her thumb in the air indicating a modulation, "Take it up, 'You're Killin' Me,' on three!" She mouthed "one – two – three!" The Mag Seven pivoted on an eighth note, modulated a full step, Bobbie swung back with the new verse of the different song in a different key, *"It's in all you don't say / somehow she's taken you away / Wooo-oooo woooo, baby! / She's killing me! /"* Bobbie snarled: *"I can no longer deny / I'm slowly dying inside / oooh, oohh ohhh, baby, baby, you're killing me. / Yes, you're killing me! /"* Gary's eyes closed, Wayne worked the groove with his head down. *"I'm tryin' to tell you what baby / baby / baby / you're killing me! /"* Jack ripped into a wailing guitar solo, the horn section kicked like three semis in a road race, Bobbie looked back at me and grinned.

The bridge leveled out, Bobbie glided into the next line. Her palm covered her heart. *"Listen! / I know by your scent / when you leave her she's spent / ohhhh baby / you're killin' me. /"* She aimed her finger like a rifle at the audience, *"It's not all in my head / when you lay in our bed / oh-ohh-baby, you're killin' me?"*

A guy lunged toward the stage tripping over tables, chairs, trying to get to the band. *"Why's it so hard to decide / which of us you wanta be beside? /"* Bobbie stared directly into my soul, *"Wooowhoo, baby / you're killing me? /"* She winked at me, *"I look into my own eyes / wonder what I might do / oh, I wonder, if I'm capable of killing you? /"* She pointed her mike at the doo-wop bitches, the whole band stopped.

They all sang, *"Yes, You're killllling meeee!"* Bobbie pointed straight up, let go primal animal howl, Gary took an insane two measure drum fill solo, pounded out the count, Jack's eyes closed, he throttled his wa-wa petal, sweat drenched his face and shirt, and we took off right back into "Sheer Curiosity."

"The raccoons by the trash can / they got mad today / wooo-wooo-wooo / since I quit eatin' pizza / well, so did they. / The cooters and the snakes / they all worried 'bout me too. / They all scratchin' round the screen door / wonderin' 'What's she gonna do . . .? / I told 'em we're runnin' on sheer curiosity / ever since that boy got the best of me / runnin' on sheer curiosity / don't know what's next / but I'm damn sure gonna see! /" The brass heralded the bridge coming around again, Bobbie slung her head back, reached out and clenched her fist like she'd grabbed the mane of a wild stallion, then hit a high falsetto hallelujah wail. She rode it, tried to choke it and sustained it over the entire chorus before she tagged the end with a perfect vibrato and immediately switched back to "Killing Me." Bobbie: *"I don't wanta have to kill you baby, baby, baby!"* Gary's synchronized his double back-beat kicking bass drum with his floor tom-tom mimicking a locomotive in a thunderstorm. Bobbie to the girls up front: *"I've done all that I can / to stand by my man! /"* Monk's head rolling like a white Stevie Wonder; Bobbie: *"But something keeps getting' in the way. /"* Horn players rocking up and down. Bobbie: *"Baby, baby, baby, baby, baby, / I don't wanta kill you darlin'."* Two rim shots, Bap-Bap, Bobbie: *"I got the feelin' y'all! /"* Drums: Bap-Bap, *"Hey!!"* Horns: Punch!-Punch! *"I got the feelin' now!"* Punch-Punch. *"Do you feel it?"* Gary slashed the cymbals. Monk wrung out the high end B3 solo with his right hand, his left popped rhythm, he pulled out all the stops and toggled the Leslie on and off, feet dancing on the foot pedals. A big guy with a voice like a submarine dive horn yelled, "Blow man, blow!" The

room was jamming. Nukes and Beep in tuxedo shirts danced in the back of the room. Montague and Sinclair, arm over arm longnecks in hand, were jukin' and jivin'. Barry shutdown the blackjack table. Bobbie: *"I'm tryin' to tell you what's happenin' baby, baby, baby!"*

The Magnificent Seven, now fully transformed by the magical chemistry every musician lives for; mystically levitated into the synergistic utopian cloud where every note is perfect, where you can do no wrong. I stepped down from the row of horns, making my way to the backup mic. A shiver went up my back when my sax cut through the PA system. When my lip touched the reed my sax came alive in my hands. I growled some old school Memphis funk. People were chanting "Go! Go! Go!" I screamed into the mouthpiece, the most complicated Coltrane combination I knew leaped from the bell of my horn. I stopped thinking, my fingers picked the notes, spirit hands revealed patterns I could've never dreamed. It was amazing. Harmonics that had eluded me for years leaped from the Mark VI. I didn't even have to try, the horn was playing itself. There were no wrong notes, every phrase embellished the one before it. The melody line came back around and Bobbie apparently decided to blow the doors off the place. She stepped up beside me for a call and response with the audience.

Bobbie: *"Let me hear you say / Oh, Hell Yeah!"* Audience: *"Oh Hell Yeah!"* Bap-Bap. I thought I was dreaming. Bobbie: *"Let me hear you say / Oh Hell Yeah!"* Audience: *"Oh Hell Yeah!"* Bap-Bap. Bobbie: *"I can't stand it!"* Bap-Bap. *"I can't stand it!"* I was in a trance, an out of body experience. I dropped the bell of the horn, grabbed a lung full of air and started a 12 bar chromatic walk up, one pattern after another flew out of the sax with each key change, the Mag Seven fell in behind me, from the bottom to the top each passage building on the one before it. When we hit the 12th bar, I bit into the reed nailing a three octave D above high C and laid into it while the chords changed color under the note. Trumpet and trombone automatically kicked in with the rest of the band on the "Bop! Bop! Bop!" lick signaling the return to the lead line. Bobbie: *"I'm goin' to find a way out / I got to find a way out' /"* She vamped with the band for another thirty seconds, then tightened up the ending before taking it home. Jack signaled the cut off. I went back to the horn section, relishing a screaming applause, and Bobbie's grin.

I don't think she was ready for the response she got, but I understood exactly. Music had transformed me on many similar nights out on the road, but nothing like this had ever happened to me. Bobbie had innocently shown me how to let go of fear, putting me into a mental state that yielded completely to the music. It was irrational. For years, I'd longed for my musical soul to yield, to give in totally to the impulsive, instinctive extinguishing of the will.

People yearn for that kind of release, but their minds won't let them have it because they won't allow themselves to become vulnerable long enough. It's just too dangerous for most people. But, I didn't say any of that to Bobbie Storm. She was so high on an adrenaline rush, nothing I could say would make it any better. She was happy, her confidence in her ability had taken a giant leap forward and I'd had a hand in the process.

At the edge of the stage, she held my hand, her eyes shining, "I thought for a moment, I'd died and gone to heaven."

"That's what it's all about," I said. "You've got the juice."

She believed me. Walking back to my spot in the horn section, I glanced across the room to where Freddie was standing with his arms crossed watching. I thought to myself how wrong he was about the music business in general, and musicians in particular. There was a real bond, a brotherhood he would never understand, between these musicians and me. He believed getting paid well for performing canceled out any need for real emotion. He's going to learn, I told myself, musicians aren't that simple.

The feeling artists have toward each other doesn't follow that eat or be eaten law of the jungle, unless the artist has a major character flaw, uncontrollable drug habit or a serious ego problem. If they do, then the god of enough rope brings the musical cosmos back into balance.

The Magnificent Seven, with Bobbie Storm at the helm, kicked serious ass until four in the morning. We gave it everything we had to give spiritually, emotionally, and physically. It meant more to me that Bobbie had at last learned what it meant to fly, than the money I'd earned or the peacock pride I took in the evening's success.

"Just like church," she said as I walked her to her car.

"Yeah, I'm feeling a little born again this fine Sunday morning."

Watching her drive away, I indulged in a little free-form philosophical musing toward my view of my work. Bobbie saw the real me no one else had ever seen. Becoming her pure self, who I knew she was, who Montague had told me she was, and the take-no-prisoners, white girl, soul singer everyone in The Merch now knew she was, that's what pushed me now, drove me. Acceptance was all I'd ever wanted from the world of music, on my terms, not somebody else's and she gave it to me, in spite of the risks involved. I was star-struck.

A cool night offshore breeze carrying the tangy salt air scent of the harbor drifted across the parking lot. Hands in pockets, I turned back toward my parking spot, thinking I'd better pack up. I looked down at the asphalt, still smiling when twenty feet from my car I froze. Bootsy Williams, legs crossed, hat strategically tilted to one side, was leaning, against the door of my car.

"I have nothing to say to you, step away from my car."

"Josie, Josie, Josie, my dear boy, I don't expect you to say anything. I expect you to listen." An icy chill shivered through me.

He walked toward me, to within five feet of me. His skin was a dark eggplant purple; his teeth were perfect gleaming white except for the gold incisor. "Ease up, there's nothing here to harm you, quite the contrary; I have a message for you."

I started to speak, but he snapped his fingers and I froze solid, unable to move a muscle. I was getting claustrophobic in my own body. My adrenaline level was so high I thought I'd explode. He snapped his fingers again, and I collapsed on the pavement. Then I felt my arms go up, someone was picking me up, but there was no one near me other than Williams.

"Forgive me," he said, "I have a limited amount of time, and can't afford further interruptions. The thing is, Josie, you've found favor with, how should I say this…" he paused, "the powers that be. Or rather, the power that is. Do you understand what I'm saying to you?"

I tried to speak, but couldn't unlock my jaw, my teeth were still clenched.

"Sorry, I'm being rude." He waved his hand. All the muscles in my face relaxed. "Well?"

"You're a hallucination." I said, "A figment of my imagination, I'm still on a drug."

"Perhaps this will convince you." He pointed toward the street light, turning it on and off with a snap of his fingers. Then he pointed at my car, it started, the lights came on, the windshield wipers went back and forth, the sequential turn signals blinked. The broken window rolled up and down. I was so terrified, I thought menthol was coursing through my veins. In an instant, he closed to within two feet of my face. I looked at his suit. It was made from reptile skin.

He closed in to within a foot, the clothing rippled as if it were alive. I could feel his cold breath on my cheek. My eyes locked on to his, for a few seconds I knew his eyes were my eyes, like the monster faces I'd seen in my bathroom mirror when I was tripping. My body went limp, I was on the verge of fainting, his voice deepened, echoing in my ears, "This is the message I have for you, Joseph Chapman: 'The fear of Strong Man, is the beginning of wisdom. Arise, accept your calling. You are but one Bridge. Many others will follow. You must prepare yourself to embrace your destiny.'"

CHAPTER FIFTEEN

I woke up alone in a cold sweat behind the wheel of my car. The dashboard clock read four-thirty. Exhausted, hung over, and shaking like a leaf, I fumbled for my keys, stabbed at the ignition switch, almost breaking the key off trying to start the car, and realized I was parked by the curb in front of 3 Savage Street. Blacking out while driving was not in my survival skill set, but I'd heard about others who had done it without having a wreck. What got my attention was how I'd managed to parallel park. I had no idea when I left The Merch, how I got home, or if I even drove the car. What I did remember was my second face-to-face confrontation with Bootsy Williams.

The shaking was coming in contractions when I managed to get out. My horn was in the back seat. I didn't remember putting it there. In fact, I never put it there – it always went in the trunk. Someone walking down the sidewalk suddenly vanished. Voices floated over my head; someone whispered my name. I knew for certain, I was finally losing my mind. A dog barked, a black cat darted into the street, hissed at me and disappeared. All I could think about was getting inside and getting into bed.

Because I couldn't trust the stereo to wake me up anymore, I set my old alarm clock to what I thought was three o'clock in the afternoon. Then I pulled out my old Zenith AM/FM radio. Made in 1950, it was a birthday present from my grandmother the year I turned fifteen. The dial used to glow green in the dark, but over the years the radium paint had faded so much the numbers were barely visible. A gold plastic crest, fashioned in the shape of a shield topped by three crown spikes, representing The Royalty of Radio, was stuck on in the center of the speaker grill. I used to lie in bed staring into those glowing numbers, listening to WTMA while my parents argued, counting the minutes until I could get out on my own.

"The Mighty TMA," with 5,000 watts of power, insured Doug Ramsey played all the hits perched in a Plexiglas booth built atop of the Patio Drive-In. He played requests and made dedications from as far away as Moncks Corner. I'd stay awake until all hours listening to the Four Tops, The Temptations, The Beatles, The Rolling Stones, Eddie Floyd, Sam & Dave, and James Brown.

The clock radio's volume and tuning knobs got messed up during a fight I'd had with my old man. The click, which usually preceded the on/off of the volume knob, no longer clicked. Even though the radio came on exactly the same way it had for twenty years, there was no way to tell if it was completely off or turned down as low as it would go. Something inside was broken.

Every Sunday morning, I listened to Brother Green's broadcast from the Tabernacle of the Divine Redeemer. On Sunday mornings, I'd become conscious a few seconds before the broadcast, then turn it way down to keep from waking up the rest of the family. I'd turn the radio down low, often putting it under the covers with me. That's where I learned the basics of black gospel music. Brother Green's preaching and singing rivaled Reverend James Cleveland while The Sisters of the Silver Moon Choir kicked in behind him with hand clapping, "Amen", "Hallelujah" and "Praise Jesus." Right about the time Brother Green started praying for "all de los' sheeps and de brothers down on de prisoner farm," like clockwork the signal would fade in and out like somebody in the control room was playing with the volume output control. I'd put a pillow over the speaker until it quit.

A few times I smacked the sides, or turned it on and off two or three times, thinking a tube was loose, Nothing seemed to work, which I always thought was odd, since it only happened when Brother Green started quoting scripture. So, I got to hear the music, but never heard the entire sermon.

You see, there was no way to keep the volume from fluctuating after my old man broke it. He was blind drunk the last time he knocked my radio off the bedside table. Usually, when he and my mother were arguing about how much money they owed her parents, I'd turn the volume up so I wouldn't have to listen to them scream, or hit each other. The last time I did that he came in and slapped the radio so hard he knocked it off the table. Then he slapped me for being a wise ass. He'd hit me more times than I could count, ever since I was old enough to walk, but until that night he'd never hurt the radio. I picked it up, put it under the covers with me, turned it back on and turned the volume almost off. Then, I amplified the music in my mind.

By the time I was fifteen, that radio was pretty scratched, chipped and cracked from all the times it hit the floor, but it still worked. Late on that last night, it was raining really hard when he came home soaking wet, drunker than usual, but just as broke as always. He'd already back-handed my mother and left her sobbing on the sofa when he heard my radio playing and decided to take out his self-hate first on it and then on me.

Screaming profanity and lumbering like a wounded half-drowned Cyclops, he stormed into my room and knocked the radio across the bed to the floor. Then he turned on me. Only that night, I wasn't a little kid anymore. When he came at me, he slipped on the wet floor, tripped over a lamp cord and fell flat on his back. I went at him like a buzz saw. Fists, feet, teeth and going for my baseball bat when my mother pulled me off him. There's no doubt I'd be writing this from prison, if she hadn't stopped me when she did. So, it's not like I don't know what it's like to want to kill somebody, or how far I'd have to be pushed, before I'd actually do it.

When he got up, he stumbled out of the house cursing my mother and me. I picked up that old Zenith and plugged it in. It looked OK and the music coming through the speaker sounded fine, but there was a rattle inside. Something internal was broken. It never worked the same again.

My old man didn't come home the next night or the next. The third night he came in packed his stuff and left without saying a word. I didn't see him again until his funeral three years later. He'd made the mistake of going over the counter after a bartender who wouldn't sell him another drink for his girlfriend. One shot to the heart took him down for good. Court called it self-defense. I never shed a tear.

When I think back on that time, I realize how damn grateful I am to that bartender. Nothing works like a gun for getting the job of killing done. Proper tool for the proper job was what Old Man Davis used to say. That's why I didn't carry a gun. If it's not worth killing over, it's not worth fighting over, and my old man was the only person I'd ever wanted to kill. I could've gotten a new radio I guess, but I kept the Zenith because, sometimes, late at night when I was alone and it was quiet, especially when it was raining, I could listen to the gospel station, look at the green phosphorous dial and know I'd never have to hear my parents fighting over money or anything else again; never have to hear the sound of a woman being slapped, cursed and not be able to do anything about it. That's when I felt the safest: alone, at night, in my own bed, with rain hitting the roof, and plenty of money in the bank. Can't forget that little ingredient. Knowing I didn't owe anybody money or allegiance meant I didn't owe anybody any explanations. I liked it that way. Still do.

I would've never said anything about my past if I didn't think it was important. But with things shaping up the way they are, I need all the help I can get. I want it understood that I'm not, by nature, a violent man. And it's not because I don't know how to be violent; it's because I choose not to be violent. Most of the time. Of course, there are some things worth killing over. For me those things are also worth dying for. I feel like I need to make that clear before I go on with this story.

Lying in bed that particular Sunday morning I was drifting in and out of two different dreams. Listening to an AM jazz station out of Savannah playing "Sketches of Spain" by Miles Davis while overlaying the previous night when Bobbie Storm and the Magnificent Seven leveled The Merchant Seamen's Club, the cosmic nightmare in the parking lot, trying to figure out how I got home, all while watching a green eyed tornado swirling off the coast.

I knew the alarm was about to kick in, because I heard the click. Even though there was no click, hadn't been an on/off click since the radio got broken. But I heard a click. Even if I've only had an hour's sleep, I still hear the click. Even after eight years. You know, anything to keep from waking up my old man. Even with him dead. That shit from childhood sticks with you. I'm telling you, that shit does not go away.

So, in order to do the least amount of damage to the tune, I thumbed the on/off button real fast three or four times to make sure the volume didn't fade in and out. There was no need; the volume didn't change. Rather, at that exact moment I touched the knob, the DJ cut in with a news flash. A local farmer from Wadmalaw Island was missing; apparently a victim of foul play.

I thought I was dreaming the whole thing; thought it was more residual payback from Friday night. In that hazy twilight between half awake and sound asleep; the words were soaking into my consciousness like rain on fresh-plowed earth. At first, I was too numb from lack of sleep to understand exactly what the DJ was saying. My mind was searching for meaning like a stranded sailor searching for a beacon on the horizon. The broadcast started to vacillate unintelligibly, then the frequency locked in and the message suddenly leaped from the speaker. The damn alarm clock went off, and I didn't hear the farmer's name. I switched channels for about five minutes, then I heard it and my heart stopped.

"Mr. Alfonso Krytorious 'Bootsy' Williams, aged fifty-three, owner of Fiddler's Creek Farms on Wadmalaw Island, was reported missing this morning. William's car and several articles of clothing were found on a deserted dirt wagon path between Highway 17 South and Bee's Ferry Road early this morning. Williams' coat, pants and shirt were in a trash heap, a few yards from the car. The jacket and shirt had three bullet holes and heavy blood stains. The car also had blood stains on the front seat. But there is no sign of a struggle and no body has been found. No explanation has yet been given, and the Charleston County Police are continuing their investigation, saying they would be questioning several people in connection with the incident."

I sat straight up in the bed; a shot of adrenaline rushed into my blood stream, and I almost went into a panic. I could see Bootsy in my mind's eye: the cocked hat, sneering eyes, the dark snake skin suit, patent leather snake skin slippers and his foot propped on the back of his Buick. And Rashad close behind me with his hand on the pistol, the s-s-scratch of the match as Williams lit up his face to show me the gold tooth. I'd been with that same man just a few nights before;

trying to deliver a bag full of money as a favor to Bill Reed. Then I remembered seeing Reed's car flying down Maybank Highway in the direction of the bag drop. I automatically thought the worst. Bill Reed killed Williams, took the money and buried the body only God knows where. Then, earlier this morning, his back resting against the driver's side of the Thunderbird, me paralyzed, unable to speak, and the unearthly voice telling me, "This is the message I have for you, Joseph Chapman: 'The fear of Strong Man, is the beginning of wisdom. Arise, accept your calling, you are but one Bridge. Many others will follow. Prepare. Embrace your destiny.'"

I don't know how long I sat there, my back and face cold and sweaty, and my eyes burning. Five minutes felt like an hour. I heard someone coming up the stairs. When they reached the door of my apartment, they stopped.

I could see the outline of someone trying to look through the window into the kitchen. I got up and opened the door and looked into the sunglasses of Bobbie Storm, absolutely the last person on the planet I needed to see. She wasn't dressed like she was going to the beach. She was wearing dark slacks with a pale blue cotton blouse tucked in neatly. A pale peach scarf was wrapped around her head and tied under her chin and a floppy straw hat big enough to double as an umbrella came down almost to her shoulders. Huge, black sunglasses covered all of her eyebrows, most of her cheeks and forehead. She reminded me of Jacqueline Kennedy disguised for a shopping spree, wholesome and sweet, with a gentle uniqueness and slightly flirtatious air about her. And something else, the giggling, girlish look of her lips and the way she cocked her head to one side when she smiled up at me suggested that she wasn't just dropping by to discuss music theory. I was glad to see her and scared of her at the same time. She knew how I felt about seeing a married woman. I opened the door, but didn't invite her in. She was not making it any easier for either of us.

"So, when does your husband get back from England?" I said.

"He flew in late yesterday."

She walked past me into the kitchen toward the coffee pot like she did it every morning and stood on her tiptoes. Stretching up to reach the cabinet caused the fabric of her slacks to tighten against her seat exposing a thin panty line.

"I can't get last night out of my mind," she said.

"Try practicing the piano with your eyes closed."

"I don't want to practice," she whispered, "I want a cup of coffee."

"Please. I can't get involved with you, not now," I said. "I don't have the answers you need."

"I'll pay you." She dug into the front pocket of her slacks and pulled out a roll of bills.

"I don't need your money."

"It's two hundred dollars." She thrust the bills toward me.

"That's enough, really you're being rude."

"I can't help it," she said. "I want to learn from you; I'll do anything to be near you."

"When the student is ready, the teacher arrives, huh? You really expect me to believe that's all this is about?"

"I have nowhere else to go."

"We play a few tunes together, and now you're ready to start a whole new life." I really didn't need this shit, but she wouldn't budge. "Listen, you don't want to get mixed up with me. Especially not right now. I have enough problems of my own. I don't need you or your military husband, complicating my life any more than it already is."

My head felt like it was in a vice, the pressure behind my eyes, my jaw muscles tensed up. She sat on the sofa with hands between her knees, staring at her feet.

"Who the hell do you think you are?" I said, "Get a life, for God's sake. If you wanna have an affair, find somebody who's in a position to have one. Or better yet, if you don't want a real relationship, ditch your husband and go on the road. Do whatever you want. Just leave me out of it. My plate is full. I can't handle another crisis right now."

The coffee pot whistled, she got up fixed two cups, handed me one and sat back down.

"Bobbie, I'm just a sax player. That's all I am. I work all night getting paid to blow on a piece of brass plumbing. I come home, sleep most of the day, get up and do it again. There's no room in my life right now for a normal daytime relationship with you or any other woman, married or otherwise. How can I put this so you'll understand? How's this? Not only do I not *need* it, I don't *want* it. At least not right now. Not at this pivotal moment in my life."

"I don't believe you," she said stubbornly. "You will never convince me that you don't need anybody else. That's just another song you've been singing to yourself, all your life."

"What do you know about my life?"

"I can see right through you, Josie," she said. "The problem here is you can't see through me. I'm not who you think I am." She had a sting in her voice I'd not heard before.

I snapped, I suppose, because I knew instinctively something heavy was brewing behind Bootsy Williams' death. If Bill Reed was involved in it, almost certainly by extension, so was I. I suddenly grabbed Bobbie's hand and pulled her toward the bedroom.

"Let's go," I said.

"What?"

"I don't want your money. Let's just go straight to bed and get it over with. That's what you're really here for, isn't it? Why waste time talking, come on in here and show me what you've got!"

I was a stranger. I didn't recognize myself. My eyes were burning from the salt of a heavy sweat. My shirt stuck to my wet skin, and I could feel her glaring at me from behind the glasses. It made me even stranger. I was electric with sexual tension. My body started shaking; it reminded me of how I used to feel when I got high right before walking out on stage for a big concert. I couldn't even focus on her face. My chest felt tight. I wondered is this how a man feels before he rapes a woman? She stood rigid as a statue, then lifted her hand up, cautiously, and softly touched my cheek.

"You wanna see what I've got?" she asked, her voice emotionless as she slowly removed her glasses, letting me see her face. Both of her eyes were black and blue, almost swollen shut.

Then she took off the hat and scarf revealing patches on her scalp where her hair had been pulled out by the roots. As she slowly unbuttoned her blouse, the bruises on her breasts came into view. Around her rib cage, the bruises were the color of eggplant. One mark on her shoulder had the unmistakable signature of teeth marks. She started to weep slowly as she unzipped her slacks, pushed them down to the floor and stepped out of them. Her legs were covered with red welts. When she slipped out of her panties and turned around, I could see the perfect imprint of a belt buckle on her buttocks.

I lost the strength in my legs, and dropped to my knees in front of her and pulled her body close to me. I put my cheek on her stomach, an overwhelming sense of helplessness swelled in my throat. I stayed like that for a long time, with her stroking my hair, her own sweet tears trickling down on the back of my neck, my hot face pressed into the even hotter skin of her stomach. I was hollow, empty, hungry, hurting, and sick. Sicker than any drug crash, sicker than I'd ever been in my life. When I finally broke, I cried until I was limp as a rag.

Somewhere during this gut-wrenching ordeal, I felt her hands reaching for my arms, gently working me back up to my feet, pulling and letting go like a delicate tug on some inner rope. It was as if she were pulling me up from inside myself, from an inaccessible void deeper than words can go, from a location that had nothing to do with who we were as people. The gentle tugging motion drew me closer, and I gave in to the wretched bizarreness of it. It had an identity of its own; we were two spirits caught in the same limbo, looking for a way to make it back to the real world. I'd never experienced a wave of emotion like that before. Not on acid, not on hash or mescaline or any other drug. She understood, even though I didn't, what she was trying to share with me. Looking back I realize this moment represented my first true spiritual connection with another human being. Our wounds recognized each other. On the outside I was putty, on the inside I was terrified. A weaker man would have contemplated suicide.

Before she got dressed, I rubbed Vaseline on the bruises. After helping her get dressed, I began putting together a picnic basket using a five-gallon bucket. I grabbed some cheese and bread and crackers. A jar of pickles was way back in the fridge, beside a bottle of Black Cat chardonnay. There was a package of frozen chicken in the freezer; I grabbed it, a bag of French bread and another loaf of stale bread. I'd decided to take her out to the Davis Farm, sit on the floating dock, in the sunshine, do a little crabbing, feed the turtles, watch the boats and see if I could regain my sanity. I felt my cheeks starting to get hot and, by the time she gathered up her bags, I felt the all too familiar knots burning in my chest. I started getting a headache, and my eyes were getting red. By the time we walked out the door into the bright sunlight, I felt like a spring that's been wound too tight. A cold constricting lump tightened in the pit of my stomach. That's when I knew I wanted to kill her husband.

"Something has to give or I'm going to crash and burn." I told her. I could handle Bobbie having a crush on me. What I couldn't handle were the cuts, welts, bruises and the goddamn teeth marks. The rage surging through me reminded me of when I'd grabbed the baseball bat the last night I saw my father alive. That was the rage rising up in me again and I was fighting it back.

"Me, too."

"But, don't you see? Your problem is not my problem. I can't help you."

"I'm not asking you to do anything. All I want right now is a friend I can trust."

OK," I said, "on one condition, and I am serious as a heart attack about this." I figured she was going to use me for something, or try to, but what the hell, so was everybody else. "You leave me out of your personal life. Whatever's going on between you and your husband, especially this thing he's done to you …," She was staring down again, "… you're going to have to handle it yourself." I waited. Nothing. "Report him to his commanding officer, call your congressman, or leave him and go back to your parents. Just don't even think of asking me to get in the middle of your personal life." She patted my leg. "I'll be your friend, I'll listen to you, we can jam together in public, but that's it. Agreed?"

"Agreed." She smiled.

"No more coming over here alone. That's how guys like me get shot."

"I understand," she nodded, "or should I say 'I dig'?"

"This is not a joke."

"I'm sorry. I'm not thinking straight, at the moment."

"You're right, you aren't and I don't care how you say it, as long as you understand, I'm not going down with a bullet in my head because I got caught screwing another man's wife." I got no response. "You have no idea how seeing you like this fucks with my head, even though you're the one who took the hits. If it was up to me, I'd talk to a couple of the guys down at the club, and sub out a major ass-whipping on your old man. Probably would bring more heat than either of us would want, but it's always an option."

"I wouldn't want that. Beating him up would only make matters worse for everyone, especially me. I'll figure out something. All I want is someone to talk too, and I feel like I can talk to you."

There's a kind of bonding trick some women use when they start playing a guy. I'd been suckered into the needy female trap a time or two, or three, but never with such obvious collateral damage. A pool hustler friend, Eldridge Tucker, (author of Tucker's Rules, I mentioned earlier) used a con he called "laying out the lemon", and this situation reminded me of it.

Basically, you pretend to be vulnerable, the damsel in distress gimmick, to convince the mark you're a soft touch, easy to manipulate. Only Tucker did it with wannabe pool sharks. But it'll work on any sucker, if they aren't aware of the con. What happens is this; after you "lay out the lemon" which means making yourself look weak, you wait. When put-up-or-shut-up time comes, the mark thinks you're the real sucker, not him. You appear easy to manipulate, he challenges you to go double or nothing, you take him up on his idea, then you cut off his nuts. Take him, for all he's worth.

So all this time I was thinking, if Bobbie thought I had a streak of helpless victim in me, too, she might try to convert me to her way of thinking, even going so far as allowing me to think it was all my idea. Then she could step in, save me from my life of solitude and, in the process, use me to save herself. I would've been a damn fool not to consider it a possibility.

If that was what she was thinking, then she was the best I'd ever seen at hiding it. I had no intention of having sex with her. If she was bluffing I needed to call her on it, get her to leave me alone, so I could concentrate on the situation with Bill Reed and Bootsy Williams. That's what I'd been thinking. Until I saw how badly her husband had beat her up. So it startled me, when I realized, that during these awkward moments, we'd possibly isolated the lowest common denominator we shared; our scars recognized each other.

Maybe I shouldn't have been surprised. Impulsive decisions based on too little information had screwed up my life for years. You'd think a man would learn from his mistakes. Being with Bobbie hadn't changed the sick angst I felt over Bill Reed, or the foregone conclusion I might somehow be implicated in Williams' death, if he was in fact dead, which I figured he was. That is, if his Saturday night appearance was nothing more than a drug induced hallucination. Call it what you will, but I felt like the whole world was starting to close in on me. It was the worst, most helpless feeling I'd had since I'd gotten back to Charleston. Seeing the tornado coming right at me, powerless to stop it or get out of the way, just like my dream. Bobbie knew I was dealing with a problem much bigger than my relationship with her. She picked up the bucket and tried to take my hand. When I pulled back, she nodded.

"Friends," I said.

"I wanna see the farm," she said.

We walked down to my car without touching each other and drove to Wadmalaw Island. Once the blanket was spread out on the dock, I opened the wine and poured two plastic cups. The sun was bright, the air still and cool. First one, then a dozen turtles had spotted the stale bread floating on the water. They were already paddling in our direction, trying to beat the minnows to the feast.

"When we were kids, we'd spend a couple Saturdays a month out here. We'd hunt deer, turkey, even snakes," I said. "This section of the farm used to be part of a working plantation."

"Why snakes?"

"Only water moccasins and the occasional rattlesnake were legitimate targets. They'll kill a dog if it gets too close. You ever see a dog bitten by a snake?"

"No."

"Trust me; you don't want to either," I said. "Besides, it's just the country version of crowd control. There will always be plenty of snakes in the lowcountry."

"Apparently."

I pointed out an open spot between a stand of giant Live Oaks. "Right over there, they had a pig pen and behind it were three of the biggest chicken coops you can imagine. They were built with big wagon wheels, and screen wire bottoms so they could be moved. That way, when old man Davis wanted to fertilize a section of ground, he'd just roll the coop wagons over it."

"That's ingenious," Bobbie said.

"The horse stalls, corral for the cattle, and a tanning shed were over beside the pig pens, kept all the bad smells in one place; which could be good or bad depending on which way the breeze was blowing. We have mostly off shore breezes here, so the smells blew away from the main house."

"Tell me what's really going on here." She brushed her hair back away from her ear. She didn't get right in front of me; rather, she kept her face turned a little to one side.

"Why? Why do you want to know?" I asked quietly.

"Because I think we're a lot alike. That's why."

"I was about to force myself on you or have you forgotten?"

"Maybe, maybe not. The important thing is you couldn't."

"Then you know that about me," I said.

"That you're incapable of taking a woman by force?" She asked politely.

"Yes."

"I knew you weren't like that the moment I met you. That's not a secret; girls like me know instantly. What I want to know is what's going on inside you that nobody knows but you."

"I'm not that deep. I'm just an average guy with no big secrets. You can learn everything worth knowing about me, listening to me play."

"Please stop trying to put me off. It doesn't matter to me if you're not a deep thinker, although I don't believe that for one second. What matters is feeling you can't express your deepest emotions. Not to me or anyone else."

"I hardly know you. We met, what … two days ago?"

She didn't even acknowledge what I said.

"Why do you feel music is the only way you can vent your frustrations? You've got so much more to give. It's all those other facets of your soul that make me want to be with you. I think you actually use music to keep your distance from the rest of the world. You use that horn to get next to people without actually having to be near them. You feel safest hiding in plain sight behind the invisible wall between you and your audience. Actors call it the fourth wall. That's you're real home. Isn't it?"

Bingo, she nailed me. No outsider had ever gotten that close, that fast. A real player, woman or man, wouldn't dare to say a thing like that because it's understood. I've heard actors call it the curse. It's like being a pool hustler; or a jazz musician, you either have it or you don't; you either get it or you don't. You just don't go there; it's like sacred ground, and you have to be invited. Very few women can handle a relationship with an artist who's married first and foremost to his work. When an artist is married to, or rather addicted to, his work. He's more than a little bent. There's not a whole hell of lot left over to share with so-called normal people

It's a sad fact, but it's still a fact. Same holds true for female artists married to straight men. That's another one you can take to the bank. I bit my lip and threw some stale bread to the turtles. Then the seagulls got in on the deal by diving down and robbing them.

"Damn sky rats," I said.

"Sky rats?" She sounded puzzled.

"The seagulls," I said, pointing to the birds. "They're like rats, only they fly."
She shook her head like she didn't understand.

"How do rats make a living?" She shrugged her shoulders. "By eating the garbage we humans throw away. Same with those seagulls, they'd rather hang around here and eat stale bread than go make a real living catching fish. Sky rats. They remind me of people like Tommy Bennett."

"Why do you close your eyes when you play a blues solo?" she said.

"I close my eyes when I play any solo."

"Not like you do playing blues."

"It's an effect – it's entertainment. The audience loves thinking I'm giving them this fabulous insight into my soul or the cosmos. Or channeling some magic message from the Blues Gods." I was being so sarcastic, hoping she'd back off.

"I don't believe it's an effect," she said, "and neither does the audience. What do you see when you're soloing on blues changes that you don't see the other times?"

"I see a father mourning the death of his son."

"And?"

"I see a young man mourning the death of his father. I see men in prison, men being whipped, women in tears, and poor people in hopeless situations doing the best they can to survive."

"Why do you picture those particular images?"

"Because that's what the damn blues is all about; the bittersweet irony of holding onto hope in a hopeless situation."

"Give me an example."

"OK. Take the song 'Danny Boy,' for instance. It's not a traditional blues song but it will work as an illustration. Look at the song from a father's point of view. In that song, his boy is going off to war. If the war doesn't kill him, then there's the chance the old man will die before the kid gets back home. Either way, there's a good chance they'll never see each other again. Their shared history is encapsulated in the chord progression, melody line and lyrics of the song. Those three elements, chords, melody and lyrics, when combined, expresses the love they feel for each other at the moment of departure, what's so complicated about that? A lot of love went into the tune. I try to express that love by adding my own sense of what it might feel like to think I'll never see a loved one again. I use a tenor saxophone as the instrument because the range of a tenor sax is the closer to range of the human voice than any other instrument except a cello. Both these instruments by pass the intellect and speak directly to the human heart. Other than these technicalitiess, 'Danny Boy' is another sad song. Everything is right there in the chords and the changes; the song means nothing to me. I've never had a son to love or a father for that matter. The only meaning the song has is the meaning people give it. It's just a sound I'm manipulating."

Bobbie looked up at the sun through her dark glasses. I could see the edge of the bruise around her cheek and felt bad about the way I was talking to her, but, damn it, she was the one pushing the thing. I tried a different track.

"The other night," I said. "I met a woman who uses voodoo or black magic or some kind of witchy shit to control her own son. Or so he says. I don't believe it, but that's neither here nor there. He believes it so it works for him. My point is she didn't give a damn about how he felt about anything. When she's around, he's as cold-blooded as a lizard. When she is not around, he's like a cross between a child, a warrior and a zombie. Parents have no idea how hard they can be on their kids, even the grown ones. My childhood wasn't all that great; in fact, when my old man died, I was relieved. I wish I could've had a relationship with my father, like the one in 'Danny Boy,' but I didn't. So I close my eyes and imagine it and it makes me feel sad for the loss. This manufactured emotion translates to a bend in a note here, a sustain there, and I go with the flow. Does that make sense?"

"It makes perfect sense."

"I think about how cruel and manipulating the world can be, like the voodoo woman was to her son, and the war was to the father and son in 'Danny Boy.'

Like my father was to my mother and to me. Like your husband has been to you. And, you know what? It makes me very sad, hurt and angry, all at the same time. You still with me?"

"I'm listening." She tore off a piece of bread and tossed it toward the turtles. A seagull snatched it before it hit the water.

"I try to translate all that pain from my head to my lungs, mouth and fingers, then play my horn. That emotion gets translated into a series of notes and easily recognizable, tonal embellishments which exit as a sound from the bell of the horn. There's a definite amount of time that passes until the song is over. Then I open my eyes, say 'screw all that pain and suffering,' change gears, change mindsets, count off 'Midnight Hour,' and we rock and roll. Got that?"

"Got it."

"Three seconds into the next tune and old 'Danny Boy,' his father, my childhood, my old man, my mother, the old woman, her son, the war, all the damn wars and everything else associated with the blues is in the air and gone. You understand? It's in the air and gone, just like everything I've said during the last five minutes. It means nothing. It's only a song, a sound, a vibration on an ear drum. Some people even think it's noise. The only meaning it has is the meaning you or anyone else gives it."

"You make it sound so mechanical."

"It is mechanical. I just happen to be a pretty damn good mechanic."

"You don't think the audience knows when you're faking it?"

"The audience doesn't care if I'm a mechanic or not. They're there to be entertained. So when the song is over, and I see some drunk crying in his beer, I feel I've either provided him a release, or given him permission to grieve or just make a damn fool of himself. Doesn't matter to me how he uses what I give him; I've done something special for him. Something only I could've done. In that moment. Do you get that? Do you understand what I'm trying to tell you? Who else, in the club, could've pulled those emotions out of the guy with that kind of precision, or cared enough to do it right? In that moment. I can't do that to them while looking them straight in the eyes, so I close mine. Knowing what I know about how music works. It would be dishonest, manipulative."

"Or, maybe, too honest?"

"I've been playing since I was a kid, Bobbie. I know all the tricks. These people try to thank me, tell me how I made them feel. They might as well be telling Noah about the flood."

"What do you mean?" She was pressing me now.

"Noah was in the Ark with the windows closed, like you up on the stage. Noah had to remember what happened a long time after the people it happened to were gone. I just remember what happened and use my horn to tell the story instead of words," I said. "I don't know what the song means to them personally. I just play it, the best I can, deliver this rather vague tonal message and let them come to their own conclusions."

"You'll never convince me you don't feel at least some of the emotions coming out of your horn."

"I feel it. I do. I feel it until it becomes as predictable as a habit. You think Sinatra doesn't know exactly how to push the audience's buttons," I said. "You're just jealous because you think you can't do it without having to feel it, which is stupid because, sometimes, you have to manufacture the emotion simply because it's your job to walk on that stage convince the audience you know what you're doing, even when you feel like shit. Why? Because making people feel something they want to feel, but can't manufacture for themselves, is your fucking job. It's called show business because your job is to show people something, that'll make them feel something, they wouldn't feel if you hadn't shown it to them. Convincing the audience makes the money flow; that's the business part of show business. It's what I'm being paid to do. As a performer, you can't cry every day over the same sorrow. If you did, you'd come off like an amateur or a lunatic. You have to learn how to rise to every occasion, in every circumstance, and fortunately or unfortunately, for me anyway, sometimes I have to resort to gimmicks in order to trick myself into believing each time is the first time."

"I think you're the one who's afraid of sounding like an amateur," she countered.

"This conversation isn't going anywhere. We aren't here to talk about my feelings, or lack thereof. You want to know how this game is played. All I can tell you is how I play it. I wasn't blessed with the creative genius of a Duane Allman or Janis Joplin. Once you've worked side by side with a true genius you learn real fast exactly what they have that you don't and never will. The best you can hope for is the audience gets what you're trying to do, in the moment, because the moment is all you've got. If they get it, then you've done your job. You've put on a show, and you get paid." Of course, I was hedging; I knew damn well what she was driving at.

"I bet there isn't a single person, in the world, you trust or tell the truth to," she said. "So, how can you call yourself honest?"

"What's this honesty bullshit? I'm being as honest with you as I can be. I'm not complaining about my life. I made my bed, I sleep in it. And I'm sorry if explaining how proven, musical techniques are used to deliver a certain kind of song, so it elicits the proper response for the audience strikes you as dishonest. After all, it's only music, not the Cross of Christ or the cure for cancer. It's only music, not life and death."

"I see. So with you, it's all about the gimmicks. I get it, I do." With that, she got up and brushed herself off.

"My job is to make people feel. I offer them an oasis of fun or a moment of freedom from their humdrum lives. I play in a band; that's what musicians do. We entertain people by providing them with a safe means of escape. Like I said, it's only music doing what music does."

"But, to you, it's just a job? You don't get anything out of it, but money?"

"I enjoy my job. It's a fun job. Learning a new song or a new lick beats the fuck out of painting houses or bussing tables. I enjoy watching people have fun. When it stops being fun, I'll quit. I can't do for people what my music does for them. Trust me, I don't plan on doing this the rest of my life."

And I bit my tongue the moment the words left my lips. It was the same fucking mistake I'd made when I was talking to Freddie. Goddamit! I thought. Two times in two days I'd gotten emotional and unraveled my mouth and let another person I hardly knew learn something about me that was none of their fucking business. I was losing my grip, I'm telling you. I wanted to own The Merch so bad. I wanted out from under all this heavy drama shit so bad, and I was losing my fucking grip. The harder I tried to hang on the harder it got to hang on. Why couldn't she just leave me alone and let me play my horn and do my job and buy my club, and get back on top of my life the way I used to be? I didn't think I was asking for too much. I had to get a grip. I just had to.

I folded the blanket. We walked back to the car and drove home in silence. When we got back to my apartment, she followed me upstairs, went into my bedroom and looked at the pile of books lying on the floor. She picked up my copy of Manchild in the Promised Land.

"I wouldn't say you were exactly rejoicing in the life you live. Would you?" She said softly, as she took my hands in hers. "Look at how you live. Look at this apartment, this room. You've got enough books on every subject from physics to history to implement the Dewey Decimal System. So, don't try to sell me the 'I'm just a mechanic line.' You're searching for something. You're looking for the key to unlock whatever is trapped inside of you. The only thing that really interests you is finding out who you really are. Or at least, who you think you're supposed to be."

"You're my shrink now?" I asked, grinning as only a true cynic can grin.

"No, your horn is your shrink," she said softly. "That's what keeps you focused. But, you also have an intellect, insight, and the ability that go way beyond playing in a rock and roll band. But you conceal them all beneath this accommodating performance. What did you mean when you said you didn't plan to be a musician for the rest of your life?"

"Do you know how fast people get used up in this business, how fast they forfeit their youth, and before they realize it, they're playing 'Sunshine of Your Love' at the Ramada Inn for forty bucks a night?"

"Then, why waste your life on people who don't give a damn about you or your dreams? What are you accomplishing by making every night a Saturday night party?"

"All this coming from a woman who, just forty-eight hours ago, said she'd wanted to play full-time for as long as she could remember. I don't get it, Bobbie, who are you trying to convince? Me? Or yourself?" I let that sink in for a moment. "I watched my old man beat my mother from the time I was a baby. We never had any fun, no birthdays, no Christmas, nothing. He started on me when I was about three and didn't stop until he left. My only escape from that world was the music on the radio. For years my only regret was not killing him myself. A clinical psychologist friend, who used to come hear me play, said playing in a band was my way of making up for all the parties I never had as a kid. How fucked up does that sound?"

"I'm not convinced, but for the sake of argument, let's assume it's true."

"You lost me. Are we talking about the same thing?"

"What would stop you from taking some of the energy the shrink said you were channeling into music, and channel it into something more productive?"

"Why do people like you insert themselves into my life for no apparent reason other than to analyze my feelings? You posed the question on the dock, in so many words. What's really going on here? Why don't you tell me, since you're the one who seems to know all the answers?"

"You could run your own business."

Funny how you, of all people, should broach this subject."

"What's so funny about it?"

"Not funny ha-ha. Strange, weird and little coincidental, funny," I said.

"Josie, listen to me for a minute. I may not've been where you've been, or seen what you've seen, but I haven't exactly been living under a rock, either. Now, you've seen the big time, you've already played with the genius stars."

"Yeah, but ..."

"And figured out you aren't star material."

I threw up my hands.

"Let me finish. Hear me out and I won't mention it again. OK?"

"Do I have a choice?"

"Now you're accepted playing this 'joint,' your words not mine, which is no comparison to the life you're used to, and yet even in this you insist on running the band, controlling every aspect of it, while apparently trying to convince me or yourself, I'm not sure which, that because you're no longer a rock star, you don't really care anymore? That it's all gimmicks? That simply because you've realized you're never going to be a star, that you don't have any ambition?"

So there we were, at last, down to the heart of the matter.

"Let me get this straight. You're accusing me of faking lack of ambition?" I burst out laughing. "Even as a kid, the ultimate question, always lurking, ready to pounce, has been: 'When are you getting a REAL job?'" I couldn't stop laughing. "I've got a job! I go to work! I pay taxes! I've even worked my way up to manager for God's sake! What The Fuck's Wrong With That!?"

As I said earlier, back then nobody in the "real world" considered being a full-time musician a "real job." The public always saw me as some aberration. Doing something where I used my talents to entertain instead of building a "real" business. Like the stars I'd backed weren't legitimate businesses with taxes, expenses, employees, drivers, roadies, all who provide jobs for real people who use the money to feed real families?

"Do you think The Allman Brothers aren't a real business? Or The Rolling Stones? Or any of those groups who played Woodstock?"

"I never said they weren't."

"I've considered starting up my own booking agency, becoming a promoter, a professional road manager; I even considered starting a rock and roll music school. I've also considered becoming a stockbroker, a history teacher. I even considered becoming a writer." I told her everything but the truth.

"I can see you as a teacher or a writer, even a promoter."

"But not a musician?"

"Not at forty or fifty years old, not a full-time sax player in a nightclub, or some other 'joint.' No, I can't see you wasting your talent using 'gimmicks' to make drunks feel better about themselves for a couple hours on the weekend."

"Why are we having this conversation?" I said.

"Because you agreed to be my friend and friends talk about things."

"I honestly can't see any difference between any of the fields I mentioned and what I am doing right now. It's all rock and roll to me."

"But I'm right, give me that."

"Right about what?"

"You really don't want to do this for the rest of your life, do you?"

"I'll give you this. I do know I'm never going to be a rock and roll star."

Bobbie had been right about one aspect of my life. I'd been searching for something. I didn't want to commit to the constricted requirements of a real job. I wanted to call my own shots. The idea of answering to a boss or a supervisor or some other authority figure didn't match up with my game plan. Which is exactly why I'd wanted to buy The Merch, which until the previous Friday, I'd thought was the answer. What a joke. Needless to say, I didn't share these thoughts with Bobbie Storm. It was pretty clear she was an exceptional woman. Conceivably, she was also a bit of a threat. Threatening to me, at least. It struck me as odd how this girl showed up in my life with questions so similar to the ones Freddie had hit me with, especially since it was his idea for me to contact her. The whole thing started sounding a little too much like The Twilight Zone for me.

The discussion ended then because someone else was knocking at my door. Montague called me out on the porch with some urgent news and told me to shut the door behind me.

"De's a po'leece detec'ive down to de' Merchant axing Mr. Roy all kind'na question 'bout 'chu."

"What kind of questions, Montague?" As I said earlier, it'd crossed my mind that I might, somehow, get tangled up in the particulars surrounding Bootsy Williams' disappearance. "'e axing 'bout yo' comin' an' goin' an' wha' peeples yo' runnin' 'round wit."

"Did you hear anything Roy said?"

"Mr. Roy ain't crack 'e teeph. But de po'leece 'e unravel he mout' evebry chance he git. Said 'e knows you."

I should've been coming up with a plan for dealing with the cops. I should've been doing anything other than trying to work out the blues licks of life with Bobbie Storm. Scared to death is what I should've been, but I wasn't. Nobody could pin anything on me. I hadn't done anything but drive. I had my story straight. A friend asked me for a favor. What are friends for? If not to drive out to Wadmalaw Island, at four o'clock in the morning to pick up a box with two chickens in it. My ass was covered.

In fact, when Montague said the cops wanted to talk to me, I actually felt a sense of relief. It was going to be a hassle, I knew that, but only because they'd try to turn it into one. No one person could prove I was anywhere, at any time, with any-particular-body, unless they talked to Rashad and Erlene Brown. Neither of those characters was going to talk, but the situation might give me a little leverage with Bill Reed. Montague was watching me think this through. He bit his lip looked around the yard, obviously he had more to say.

"You kin laff if yo' wants t'. But I tink yo' is fixin' t' fin' yo'sef in a worl' o' shit." Then he reached forward, took my right hand, turning it over slowly as he lifted it to reveal the pink lines across the back. I looked at him, waiting for the inevitable. "Wha' witch done dis?" he asked softly, "an' don' lie t' me, boy."

I wanted to tell him the truth; do the right thing and own my part in what had happened. Instead, I remembered how running my mouth had worked out earlier and said nothing.

"Josie, yo' bes' be list'n t' me now, son. Yo' gwine be in a world o' hurt, sho' nuff, yo' keep fuggin' 'roun', not listenin' t' me. Scrong Man got 'e mark on yo', boy. Yo' bes' be b'leivin' what I tell yo'. Whey's dat cross I gib yo' d'other evenin'?"

"It's still in my horn case," I said.

"Dam' sho' betta git it an' wear it roun' yo' neck, 'cause yo' gone need all de' hep yo' kin git, yo' dam' sho' is." In his eyes I was a condemned man. "Why yo' ain't come to me when dis shit happen?"

"To be honest, Montague, I'd rather not discuss it, right now," I said.

"Aw right." He said crossing his arms. "If'n das de way yo' want 'em, das de way e'll be. But hark'en at me, boy, I's may seem foolish, but Gawd use' de' foolish t' bring de wise t' shame. Das' in de Book, firs' Corinthian one, tweny-six an' seben. When Scrong Man come fo' yo', yo' gon' need me an' I don' wan' yo' t' be 'fraid to ax fo' hep, idn't it?"

"If I need help, Montague, you'll be the first person I'll call," I said.

Montague let go of my hand with a little shake, like we had sealed some kind of deal.

"Aw' right, den," he said. "Das mo' like it."

He turned and walked back down the steps. At the bottom, he turned and looked back up at me.

"I'll get it, and I'll wear it, I promise," I said.

"Was that Montague?" Bobbie asked, as I came in from the porch.

"Yeah, some VA rep is giving him a hard time because a real Merchant Seaman wasn't allowed into the club last night. I've got to go down there to explain that we're a private club before the Feds start trying to make trouble for us." The lie was as spontaneous as a blues riff. It came out of thin air, without a moment's hesitation.

Tucker once told me, "You can shear a sheep a thousand times, but if you skin that sucker, he's dead." He was right. I just didn't know how right.

CHAPTER SIXTEEN

Detective Charlie Thigpen was in the parking lot waiting in his car. He was the county cop asking all the questions. Running into old enemies is not unusual in a town the size of Charleston. Neither was the idea of former hoodlums showing up on the police force hiding behind a badge. I stuck my head through the cruiser's open passenger side window. On the door of the glove compartment was a bumper sticker that read: "I don't give a damn how you did it up North."

"You looking for me?" I said.

"Josie Chapman." He smiled as I got into the car beside him, a kitchen match hanging out the corner of his mouth. "Well, well, well, if you ain't a sight for sore eyes." His eyes scoured me. I was wearing a black t-shirt under an olive drab button up, faded jeans, and leather biker's boots with a brass ring strapped on them. Hardly the Charleston bubba he was expecting. Freddie May was pretending not to watch us from the entry foyer.

Too dumpy for one of the Lowcountry's finest, Charlie looked more like left over parts from God's own junkyard. Hands better adapted to removing tight lug nuts from the lock rims of eighteen-wheelers, than taking notes were attached to short, freckled arms that didn't quite match in length. One eye drooped, and both eyebrows were bigger and fuller than most mustaches. His fat-laden cheeks, black eyes set close together, formed a swollen facial symmetry dominated by a hulk forehead set over a bulbous, clown nose. He reminded me of the poorly drawn caricature of W.C. Fields where each tooth had its own brown frame from years of chewing Red Man. His gut hung over his belt, the buckle, and most of the belt itself, encased in a dark blue, polyester fat bag shirt. A mustard stain dotted his acetone clip-on tie which he'd attached to his shirt by a promotional Smith & Wesson tie bar he'd probably picked up at some gun show. He thought he knew everything.

What Detective Charlie Thigpen didn't think I knew was this – he was the dirtiest cop in Charleston County. During the time I spent at The Apartment Club, I'd watched Bill Reed pay him off like clockwork every week.

He took up as much room as he possibly could, sprawling his boorish presence and pig demeanor over most of the car's front seat. His hair needed washing. His nose hairs needed trimming. He needed to shave, brush his teeth, and his high-pitched nasal rasp of a voice could peel paint. "I was just about to ride down to the Battery, take a walk," he said quickly. "We can talk down there."

When he shifted positions behind the wheel, he sounded like a schooner popping its sails while sloshing in heavy seas. He spit his cud of Red Man out the window and started the car.

We drove slowly down East Bay Street to South Battery, then parked in the shade by the Civil War cannon on the corner. Thigpen turned off the ignition. "We'll talk right here, in front of God and everybody."

"This spot doesn't have much of a view," I said.

"I happen to like this view. Nothin' to distract from the conversation." He was such a jerk.

His eyes turned to slits as he rubbed his chin while making the match swap sides without using his hands. Under the shade of the oak trees, he added more intrigue to the situation by opening a black leather-bound book entitled South Carolina Law Enforcement Regulations Guide. Thigpen slowly thumbed through the book, pausing every few pages to scrutinize me.

"So, where were you Friday night?" he said.

"What, no foreplay?" I said.

"Oh, I'm sorry, let me try a softer approach. Where the fuck were you Friday night, dipshit? That better?"

"Friday night, I went from my apartment to the Swamp Fox, then to The Apartment Club, then to The Merch."

His eyes reminded me of a gorilla's eyes. I knew he wasn't stupid, but I also knew he didn't relate to most humans one on one. I mean, when I look into the face of a gorilla, or just look at a photograph of one, it almost looks human, like it can think. A gorilla looks pretty smart for an animal.

"Anyone see you?"

"Oh, I don't know, if you add them all up, probably somewhere between one and two hundred people."

You look into the eyes of the beast. Subconsciously, you assign them your ideas of the human qualities you think go with those eyes. The furrowed brow, the bashful, bamboo eating, grape peeling, furry-human looking creature reminds you of a human. You're drawn to it. You want to relate to it somehow, to talk to it, to touch it, to communicate with it.

"You go anywhere else?"

"You mean Friday night; did I go anywhere else on Friday night?"

"Don't be a wise ass, Chapman. You don't wear it too good."

Then, in a flash, the beast turns on you. Roaring, rushing, beating fists on its chest, bearing down on you with a mouth full of big white teeth and you remember seeing one of these creatures on Wild Kingdom. I loved that show.

"No, Officer. I was in The Merchant Seaman's Club all Friday night." Which, technically ended at midnight.

"How late did you play?"

"Friday night?"

"Yeah, asshole, Friday night."

"Until midnight."

"Now that's a goddamn lie right there! I rode by the place at two-thirty and it was still going strong, I could hear the band from the parking lot."

"Yeah, but that wasn't Friday night. You asked me about Friday night."

The gorilla I saw on Wild Kingdom could stretch a steel belted radial like a rubber band. And suddenly, as if it was a new thought, I remembered why they call gorillas animals. I was thinking about this while Thigpen fumbled with his notebook. He took in a deep breath, and then breathed it out slowly, like venting air brakes on a Greyhound.

"OK, that's the way you wanna play it, that's the way we'll play it. After you arrived at The Merchant Seaman's Club on Friday night, September 11, 1970, what time did you leave?"

It struck me that the gorillas on Wild Kingdom looked much more intelligent than Thigpen. Gorillas, after all, don't go looking for trouble. They don't enjoy being mean. They don't sit around plotting bodily harm. It struck me as ironic that I'd have felt safer with a wild gorilla than with this knuckle-dragging throwback to the dawn of civilization.

"There's something you need to know about me," he said. "I play by the rules with people who play by the rules. You start making up your own rules, I'll start making up my own rules."

"That's cool."

A horse drawn carriage, with two tourists, pulled up alongside of us. This was before the diapers, and the horse dumped a load right when the tour guide started pointing out the historic aspects of each of the houses across the street. Thigpen ignored the poop but listened to the spiel with strained enthusiasm.

"That kid knows his stuff," he said. "I'm all about history, especially recent history." He paused to make sure I was paying attention. "You know, anything from this morning clear back to my childhood just fascinates me. I remember all of it. How about you, Chapman, you like recent history?"

Here it comes, I thought, and there's nothing I could do to stop it. So I took a defensive position, took a mental step back and made sure Charlie didn't sucker me into throwing the first punch.

"Listen, Thigpen ... "

"It's Officer Thigpen to you."

"Officer Thigpen, I don't know what you want from me. Whatever it is, though, just get it out. If you're going to arrest me, arrest me. I'm not good at games. I've got two ways of doing business, too. I can be professional or personal."

"Real road warrior, huh? You learn to be a tough guy out on the road?"

"Just the opposite. I'm into peace, love, light shows, Hare Krishna, shit like that."

"So, what brought you back here?"

"Ah, some foreplay at last. I was beginning to think you didn't care."

"Don't fuck with me, Chapman. I ain't in the mood."

"You're wearing the Man's badge, driving the Man's car, carrying the Man's gun, on the Man's clock, and licking your fingers, thumbing through the Man's rulebook. So, I'm assuming you want to do this professionally. So, interrogate me or arrest me or take me back to The Merch, because I'm not going to hand you my chain and say, 'Here, Officer, please jerk this for me.'"

A bead of sweat broke out on his upper lip, he gritted his teeth. "Gee, Chapman, if I didn't know better, I'd think you have no respect for the law."

"The way I show respect for the law is my business and falls under the Constitutional right of freedom of speech, which, I might add, it's your solemn duty to protect." I faked respect when I said this.

"I hate the Union." He said, as he stared at the cannon on the corner.

"The war's been over for more than a hundred years. Let it go," I said.

"I hate the word 'Union,' Jerk-Off." His face turned red.

"But I didn't invent the Union I simply joined because that's what I had to do in order to work. And while we're at it, why's it a problem? I thought you Democrats supported unions."

"I mean 'Union' as in the War of Northern Aggression sense of the word." I knew he said it to piss me off. "Yeah, I guess you're right. We should just play by the rules and put the past behind us, the distant past with its wars and unions. The more recent past is more difficult to push aside."

"What, exactly, are we talking about?" I said.

"How's it going in the music business these days?"

"Are we on the record or off?"

"On the record."

"For the record then. I'm a musician and a band manager. I work six nights a week at The Merchant Seamen's Club as Director of Entertainment."

He had his official blue police pencil out now, making official notes in his official fucking notebook. There was #1 with a circle around it followed by a period and a colon. Next to the colon were the words "plays in a band."

"Exactly what kind of entertainment do you direct?" He built the #2.

"I manage the band business, stage, and payroll and make sure everybody shows up on time."

"Does your job description cover managing the gambling and whores?"

"Let me think for a second." I cupped my chin with my hand. "Nope. Well, I say no. But. If you consider being a musician a gamble and drinks and tips are considered part of your paycheck, then you could say the band whores itself out nightly. Oh, and somebody is always trying to fuck us or fuck with us, so if you count that, then yes, gambling and whores are part of my job. Just like they're part of yours."

"What's that supposed to mean?"

"It means, if not for the musicians, gamblers and whores, you'd be out of a job."

"You're cute, real cute," he said, scratching his head with the pencil point before writing "manager" by the #2. Then he lit a cigarette and offered me one.

"I don't smoke."

"You don't smoke cigarettes, but you smoke pot, don't you?"

"You mean marijuana? That's against the law."

"And you say you're a member of the local musicians 'union? Do you have a membership card?"

I leaned up on one cheek, took out my wallet and showed him my card.

"I hate unions," he snarled.

"I thought we just plowed this field," I said.

"They're ruining the free enterprise system; stifling entrepreneurs, the little guys can't ever get ahead, know what I mean? Unions breed all sorts of corruption, dope, whores, gamblin'. Especially gamblin'. Hell, inside that, you got your craps, your ball games, your poker and blackjack."

"I wouldn't know," I lied.

"And of course, last but certainly not least, your numbers." He said that last word fully stretched over to my side of the car and he dragged the word out "nuuumm-berrrzzz." Then he leaned back, with his arms folded across his chest, and stared at me. "It ain't right. All that money flowin' and guys like us have to make ends meet on next to nothing." He was baiting me.

"You're breaking my heart, Detective. Can we get on with it?"

"Yes we can, Union man. Where were you between 3 and 5, Saturday morning?"

"I was at home, in my bed, asleep."

"Alone?"

"Yes, alone."

"There was no one else with you, no one who could confirm your story?"

"Well, let's see." I cupped my chin again. "No, last time I checked my two room flat I didn't see anything indicating I had a roommate, so I'm pretty sure I live alone."

"I'm talkin' about whores, asshole. You didn't haul a whore back to your place after work?"

"Why do I need someone to confirm my story? It's not a 'story,' I was home between 3 and 5."

He finished his cigarette, flipped the butt into the street. The son-of-a-bitch.

"Littering is against the law," I said. He ignored me.

"Let's just say without anyone to verify your story, all you've got is your story."

I felt the hair on the back of my neck send a signal to the pit of my stomach. "I get the feeling I'm more than merely the current object of your affections," I said.

"Nice sense of humor and intuition you got there, straight out of the Laugh-In show. Now, tell me about your dealings with Mr. Bill Reed and Mr. Alfonso Krytorious 'Bootsy' Williams?"

"Reed and I were business associates at one time. I helped him out by playing in the house band at his nightclub in West Ashley."

"The Apartment Club?"

"Yes, The Apartment Club is the only club he owns. I'm absolutely sure you're familiar with where it is, what goes on there." I let that one hang in the air a few seconds. "As for Mr. Williams, I don't know the man."

Thigpen's body odor overpowered the car. I needed to get some fresh air or gag. "Give it up, Chapman!" he barked suddenly. "You held a bag for Reed. Hell, you dropped the bag for Reed. You dropped a bag for him Friday night, then, you did old Bootsy in and took all the money. Admit it."

"I have no idea what you're talking about. I told you, I was home alone Saturday morning."

"I'm talking about Friday night."

"I thought you asked me about Saturday morning."

"You know, I could always take you down to the jail and charge you with it and the word will be all over the city. It'd work wonders for your resume. You'll be lucky to land a job playing 'See You in September' at the Carousel Lounge in Sumter. That what you got planned for the rest of your musical career?"

"Not exactly. Then things are never what they appear around here. You, of all people, should know that," I said.

"Well, then, if the way things appear ain't exactly the way they are, just tell me the truth about the last little bag drop you made for Reed, Josie. Man to man, off the record. Maybe I can help you."

I kept my lies as close to the truth as I could. Trying not to get lost, I improvised on the basics of Friday night at The Merch. Of course, I left out everything that happened between three and five of the Saturday morning in question by simply replacing the events with the words, "I was alone, in my apartment, asleep in my bed."

"And you expect me to believe that?" He said.

"I just play the songs, man. I don't write the music."

"How much was in the bag Reed gave you?"

"I don't know what you're talking about."

"What do you know? Or Better yet, have you ever heard of somebody called The Strong Man? Or The Python?" His question startled me.

"Yes, as a matter of fact, I have heard both terms used as recently as forty-eight hours ago," I watched his eyebrows arch. This would be fun, I thought. "One of the waiters at the club has been telling me all sorts of things about Strong Man."

"Who's the waiter?" he asked, pencil poised.

"His name is Montague; he's in charge of the kitchen."

"Did he tell you who this Strong Man is?"

"Yes. Indeed, he did." Dead silence.

Thigpen's belly was about to pop the buttons off his shirt as he opened up his hands like he was setting a bird free and said, "WEEELLLLLLLLLL?"

"You wouldn't believe me, if I told you," I said.

"Try me," he said.

"Strong Man is a demon. Well, not a demon in the classical sense; fallen angel is more accurate." I watched him scribble the word then draw what looked like a winged hieroglyphic. "In fact, he is the ruling spirit of divination over Charleston. He lives out in the harbor, only comes on shore when a major division is getting set up." I stopped to get his initial reaction.

"A demon, huh? You mean, like a ghost?" He shook his head like he had water in his ear. "You telling me this Strong Man is some kinda evil spirit?"

"Yes," I continued. "And no. He's a spirit, and depending on who you talk to he's evil, but sometimes, if he likes you, he's your best friend. Oh, and he also wears a snake skin suit."

"Are you on drugs? Right now?"

"Strong Man's sole purpose is to control an elite group of four spirits, called spooks, whose job is to divide the city's leaders into four small groups and play them against each other."

"Like a gang?"

"Kind of, but an invisible gang."

"How do they do it?"

"You sure you wanna hear this? I don't wanna insult your intelligence."

"Then you don't believe in the shed blood of Christ, Chapman. But that's not important. What is important is that we find this black guy, Williams' body and the money bag you gave him. Whether you killed him or not, I don't care, but I do think you know where the body and the money are?"

"Do you still wanna know how they do it?" I said.

"Sure, I'm dying to find out. Can't you tell?"

"There may be more truth to that statement than even you realize, but as you said, that's not relevant to the moment. What is relevant is the method Strong Man uses. He uses people who think they're powerful, who think they're smart, especially those who nurture their pet prejudices. Take you, for instance, and your love of all things Confederate." His eyes went to slits. I decided to hammer him. "Anytime the subject of race, religion, crime, vice, civic and political corruption, anything which creates groups with attitudes which morph into layers of Charleston society, Strong Man's demon hordes are in on it. But that's not the best part."

"Are you sure you aren't on drugs? Right now, I mean? Are you high on something? You been smokin' sash?"

"Are we on or off the record?" I said.

"Off the record."

"No. But if I was smoking something it wouldn't be part of a window or a piece of drapery fabric."

"What're you talking about?"

"Never mind."

"Go on, what's the best part about this snake suit character."

"Well, what really pisses Strong Man off is people moving into his territory; people who disrespect the natural order of Charleston society. He really doesn't like assholes who blow into town stay a couple years, buy a house, and then start acting like they own the whole city. Take Freddie May, Bill Reed and you, for instance."

"Me?"

"Yes. You weren't born in Charleston were you, Detective?" His eyes narrowed. "And yet you run around town showing your ass acting like you own the place."

I braced myself in case he decided to throw a punch. "Strong Man uses race as a gateway into the other three segments of society: Politics, Money, and Prostitution. He then drives them to war with each other. Blacks kill blacks, whites kill whites, blacks and whites kill each other, primarily, for three main reasons: Power, Money, and Whores." Thigpen's eyes were slits. "Once he's eliminated the usurpers, he re-populates Charleston with leaders who show proper respect for the entire population. This restores balance; preventing the city from being overrun by transplanted assholes who blow into town thinking their money gives them carte blanche to act like they own the place." I wish I'd had a camera.

"It's the Yankees, ain't it?" His mouth was hanging so wide open the toothpick was standing straight up, stuck to his lip.

"Not just the Yankees. He controls them all, Thigpen. Strong Man is working each and every one of the major groups."

"You kidding? Man, if you're fuckin' kidding me, if this is your idea of a fuckin' joke, then you're definitely on my serious shit list." If he'd been a blood hound, he would've slobbered.

"You asked me what I knew. Here's the truth about Charleston, Charlie: If it wasn't for old Strong Man keeping things in order, why between the Yankees, niggers, hippies and queers, southern whites wouldn't stand a chance."

"You think this shit's funny, don't you? You think I'm a dumbass. I got news for you Chapman. I know you had something to do with this, and I'm going to prove it. We'll see who gets the last laugh."

It was all I could do to keep a straight face.

"What I know is what I overheard down to the night club." I'd instinctively covered the back of my right hand with the palm of my left.

"For the last time, where is the money and the spade's body?"

"I told you. I don't know anything about Williams' body or any money."

"You know more than you're telling me. And this bullshit about a demon better square with that cook, because when I do find out you're lying, your life will be a livin' hell."

"You be careful Charlie. You have no idea what you're dealing with."

He started the car and pulled away from the curb.

"I take it we're finished here?" I said.

"Yeah, we're finished," he said, "for the time being."

We drove back to The Merch in silence. I got out, shut the door, then I couldn't help myself. I walked around to his window and said, "Niggers and Hippies and Queers. Got a nice ring to it don't you think? Sounds like 'Lions and Tigers and Bears.'" Then I leaned in closer to his window, smiled and said, "BOO!" I thought for sure he'd shit himself.

"Fuck You!" He yelled.

I watched him wheel out of the parking lot then stop down the street. I got in my car and pulled away. In the rearview mirror, I watched him watch me pull out. I figured he was waiting for me to leave. I circled the block in time to see him get out of his cruiser and walk toward the front door of The Merch. The truth hit me like a freight train. He was in with Freddie and in with Reed, he was taking payoffs from both of them. I knew it; I could feel it.

When I got back to the apartment, Bobbie was gone. If it hadn't been for the blinds being up and sunlight in the room, I would've never known she'd been there. The light showed up the dust that had accumulated over the past months. I started to clean up a little, but after washing a few dishes and making the bed, I decided to drop the blinds and get back to the business of worrying about the mess I was in. While I could lie as well as anybody, I didn't think Thigpen bought the story I'd tried to sell him. Lying to the cops, even a crook like Charlie Thigpen, might have crossed the line. So, on the one hand, I was kind of glad Bobbie was gone. But then, on the other hand, I realized how alone I was; not having someone to share this problem with sucked.

I mean, it was like the melody line on top of the chord, one supports the other, the sum is greater than the parts, sort of thing. You've got to be one hell of a player to carry the song all by yourself, with no backup. Being a horn player, I knew that better than anybody. It wasn't so much about missing Bobbie; as feeling totally alone. She was the only person I'd met in years I felt I could be honest with, but only a few days into the relationship, I'm already lying to her. I mean, how fucked up is that?

I started daydreaming about her, remembering how she wanted to be with me, little looks she gave me. And now that she was gone, I don't know, it scared me a little. There was no reason for me to have to get in touch with her. She was married to another man. There might even be a kid somewhere. Her old man might be looking for her with a gun or some such craziness.

He'd already beat her up. I couldn't call her if I wanted to, I didn't know her number. Still, it bothered me that she left without leaving a note or anything; really bothered me. She'd been overly persistent trying to get close to me. Then I realized that until this thing with her husband knocking her around came up, all I'd known about her was that she was a mild-mannered piano player at the Swamp Fox Room by day and a kick-ass rock and roller at The Apartment Club by night. There were too many coincidences. Freddie wanting me to check out Bobbie, who worked for Reed. Then Reed coming by The Merch with the bag, the Freddie May-Bill Reed connection, now Thigpen showing up right after Bobbie came to see me. Something wasn't adding up, I thought, or maybe it was and I hadn't figured it out the math yet. The truth is I didn't know what to believe.

The only good thing I was reasonably sure of was the drug Erlene had scratched into my hand was out of my system. I took out my flute and ran a few scales; they flew through my fingers like butter. I didn't even have to think. I tried a few Pharaoh Sanders licks, same thing, picture the run, and blow into the lip plate, the notes leaped from the instrument so fast, crisp and clean, it scared me. I flipped through the latest issue of Downbeat. Someone had transcribed a Yusef Latiff solo. I looked at it and understood every note. Suddenly, I could read music.

None of this made any sense. Something in the potion Erlene used on me had unblocked part of my mind. I looked around my apartment. I hadn't touched my Civil War books in months. When I picked up The Battle of Gettysburg, it was light as a feather, the pages turned when I touched them. The sun dragged across the afternoon like it was pulling an anchor. About four o'clock, I finally dozed off on the couch, but I should've stayed awake. All I dreamed about was Bill Reed laughing, Bill Reed cursing, Bootsy Williams with his gold tooth, down at the Battery with Charlie, Freddie May threatening, Bobbie Storm all beat up, Bill Reed's gold chain and diamond stick-pin, Fort Sumter in the distance, dice cuff links, then Williams dead. I'm backed up against the guard rail on the Battery with my back to the harbor and everybody looking at me. When I turned around, all of a sudden, the first dream ended. I was staring out at Charleston Harbor, watching a massive blue-gray waterspout form against a clear blue sky and start heading toward the city. It looked more like a cylinder than the tapered cone of a tornado. And there was this other minor detail: the waterspout had green iridescent eyes. I woke up in a cold sweat.

If the book on Gettysburg hadn't been lying on the floor beside me, I would've written it all off to a nightmare in the middle of the afternoon. I sat up, wide awake, but trembling. Rigney had Vivaldi's "Four Seasons" on his stereo. Instead of sleeping on the couch, I should've been doing whatever it took to cover my ass. I should've called Roy, let him know what was happening, maybe called Goldman, his lawyer, for advice. There were options; I had time, but I was sleeping on the couch, in a kind of stupor. There's no simple explanation for my inaction except that, like a terrified cat treed by a pack of dogs, there was nothing left to do but fall.

I even started thinking I'd brought it all on myself, thinking I'd created the situation. After all, it did fit in with everything else. Think about it: A supposedly bad man, a man who supposedly hurts and kills people finally, supposedly gets what's coming to him. Somebody, supposedly, had to take the fall, why not me?

Charleston grows a weird variety of criminal. In half the murders some idiot, other than the murderer, gets looked at. Every wannabe-connected-street-urchin acts like he knows who did it and why, but he "ain't sayin'," because, one: he doesn't know shit, and two: he's afraid of getting hit himself. As if. Maybe I had some of that novelty hound in my own blood, some overt ego deep inside, exacerbated by the drug, that wanted to be identified with his death. And maybe it's not as weird as some people think.

For this reason: if these "associates:" of the deceased and his friends are believed to be "connected" then, to quote Shakespeare, "they give to the airy nothing, substance and a name." The "airy nothing" being themselves, and, since by a sort of bizarre social osmosis, they get to share in the "substance," i.e. the notoriety of the crime, without actually having to risk any personal involvement, they suddenly appear to know something everybody else is wondering about. When the truth is they don't know jack. Well, if ever there was an airy nothing in Charleston, it was my clueless ass lying on my couch that Saturday afternoon, gathering more substance and name by the minute.

It also, wasn't like I had no experience with death. I'd seen guys OD. I've watched shoot outs where somebody got killed. I watched my father's funeral, watched my mother die. I'd hunted and killed animals. I'd lost friends in Vietnam. Friends I went to high school with had died in car crashes. It wasn't the death part that bothered me. It's no secret that I knew people, who knew people who could get things taken care of, but I'd never pulled the lever on anyone personally, because I always saw death from behind the fourth wall. It was something that happened to other people, I merely happened to be in the neighborhood. But Thigpen was talking real murder and using my name in the same breath. This was my first up-close brush with death as a crime. A crime which had my name associated with it. I'm not saying I couldn't do it if I had too. I'm saying that in this particular moment I was operating way beyond my depth of hands on experience and the dreams weren't helping any.

So, when Gary Edwards, my drummer from The Merch, stopped by and asked if I could sit in on baritone sax with The Charleston Swing Band that evening, I went to the closet, grabbed my bari and was out the door and gone in ten minutes.

CHAPTER SEVENTEEN

The regular baritone sax player couldn't make the swing band gig. The parts required minimal reading skills, running eighth notes in two-bar clusters, a twelve-bar solo here and there, nothing I couldn't handle. Soft, mellow and undemanding, it was exactly what I needed to test my newly acquired reading skills. This particular night, the gig was at The Officers Club on the Naval Base.

Gary Edwards was the lightest skinned black guy I ever met. So light in fact, most people, including those who frequented The Merch, didn't know he was black. His father, Reverend Gary W. Edwards, came from a long list of black preachers. The family lived in a predominately white section of downtown Charleston.

Gary knew his father had business interests outside the church, but he never discussed it. At one time or another, the money from every major betting pool in the city passed through the Reverend's hands. Cold hard cash from simple point spreads on anything from the local high-school ball games to high stakes pool tournaments up at Tuckers found a way of circulating through Reverend Edward's net of connections. He wanted a better life for his son so he sent him to Berklee College of Music in Boston, where he earned a degree in percussion.

Gary Jr. had no use for the road. Jazz was his thing, and while he was not opposed to playing soul, R&B or even Rock & Roll, it was the big band sound he liked best. He was twenty-five, short, wore prescription sunglasses 24/7, and liked to drape his coat over his shoulders like a cape, a gimmick he stole from Buddy Rich.

His light bronze complexion complimented his straight black hair, and he carried a pair of drumsticks everywhere he went. He never touched alcohol or tobacco, but he drank Coca-Cola constantly. Gary Edwards fancied himself the ultimate local, on call, cool, jazz musician. When the Ice Capades were in Columbia, they called Gary. If Aretha Franklin was playing the Myrtle Beach

Pavilion she called Gary. If the Ringling Brothers Circus was touring the southeast, the bandleader always tried to get Gary. He had offers for big money from all over the country, and he turned them all down. His practice schedule intimidated the hell out of most area musicians. He took a practice pad with him everywhere he went.

I'd always admired him for sticking close to home. He said it would kill his mother, if he left town. She used to tell him that he was her "eyes."

After I took over the gig at The Merch, Gary and I'd had a long talk. Our goals were the same. We wanted to make our living as working musicians. The only difference being he didn't know I was planning to buy the club. He just wanted a regular gig, paying enough for him to live at home without working a day job. Over the course of the previous months, we had become closer, but we still didn't hang out like Jack and I did. So, when he picked me up, I was surprised to find him in an unusually talkative mood.

"Mama says I'm her eyes, you know?" He told me. "I'm all she's got that isn't connected to the business. She says I'm her eyes because I'm the only one she can see escaping from the night train."

At the time I didn't know what he meant by the term "night train," but as conversation progressed I came to realize that the "night train" was Charleston's underground economy.

Gary's father was "The Preacher." There was also "The Night Mayor" and "The Landlord." These men were all legitimate black businessmen by day, and leaders of a sophisticated crime syndicate by night. A lucrative enterprise, with roots tracing all the way back to the Underground Railroad of the Civil War.

"I don't mind staying here with mama," Gary continued. "At least I don't have to go looking for work like most other cats. Daddy's doing what he was born into; it's the only thing he knows how to do, so I can't blame him. Besides, I get to blow with some bitchin' players from time to time."

"What exactly does your father do, other than preach? Or is he not really an ordained minister?" I said.

"My old man is a tough son of a bitch," Gary said. "He comes from a family of preachers with roots stretching all the way back to slavery. Daddy is just carrying on the tradition he was born into. God only knows how much money he has spread all over. Never held a day job his whole life, but the people love him; he has plenty of honor out in the street. But lately, since 'The Farmer' disappeared, things are different."

I couldn't believe what I was hearing, but I didn't say anything. I wanted to wait to see what else Gary volunteered before I started asking questions of my own.

"I was lucky enough to have a mother who wanted something better for her son," Gary said. "She says that knowing I can play better than anybody else makes her proud. She told me that when she sees me play, she can see a future that's bright and honest. I'll stay here as long as she needs me. If it weren't for her, I'd probably be holding a Bible instead of these sticks."

Gary was as down to earth a guy as I'd ever known. He was the leading drummer in the Lowcountry, not simply because he could out play every other drummer east of the Mississippi, but because he took time with his family. He took care of his mother. He was the only truly great musician I knew whose personal life hadn't suffered because of his art; or whose head wasn't as big as a balloon. I respected him as much as any man I knew, but I needed to find out who these other people were, even if it meant deceiving Gary.

We'd never been very close off stage. He always kept his private life private. When he started to let me in on what was really happening with his family, it was about as close as we ever got. Now, for some reason, Gary wanted to talk to me. He stopped the car, abruptly grabbed my arm, and turned me around the way a parent would a child. It startled me for a second.

"Listen," he said. "Something's been on my mind for a while and I don't know how to bring it up, except to come right out and say it. You're in a world of shit, man." His eyes darted back and forth from one of my eyes to the other. "I know you've got this gift, man, the thing that can't be taught. You've sown your wild oats, you've seen the mountaintop and it looks like you might even be ready to settle down in one spot for a while. Am I right?" he looked me in the eyes while still holding onto my arm.

I shrugged and said, "I'm not sure what I want right now."

"Well, I know what you don't want," he said. "You don't wanna get caught on the Night Train with no way to get off, and that's where you're headed."

What he said was totally out of character for him. I understood where he was coming from. He'd never suggested he knew anything about my dealings with Reed or anyone else. I don't think he ever suggested he even might know who The Night Mayor, The Landlord and The Farmer were. His advantage was knowing he didn't need to know. He was protected by his bloodline. He didn't have to work full-time with anybody; in fact, he could work or not work as he chose, totally free from the local music scene or nightclub politics. But for whatever reason, that night in the car, heading to the Naval Base, he'd decided I needed a Come-To-Jesus reality check.

"You're thinking too deep, Josie," he said. "Your eyes, man, and your mind. You're a long way from here. You must have something heavy on your mind."

"I don't talk much lately." I said, wondering how much he knew about the Williams incident.

"It must be hard on you, everywhere you go, people looking at you, knowing how high up the ladder you got. Wondering if you can still cut it." While he was still talking, he put the car in gear and pulled back into the traffic. "I was born into a family that prided itself on maintaining the lowest of low profiles. I never had a problem with fame. Nobody really knows who I am. I used to envy guys like you when I was younger, but I don't anymore."

"I never envied guys like me either," I said.

"You know what I mean," he continued. "That's why I've waited until now to have this little chat. I had to wait until you figured out what fame can do to a guy like you, make you a prisoner, make you a junkie for approval, or worse, make you a target."

"Is there something specific you're trying to tell me, man? Because, if there's a message here, I'm not getting it." This time I was searching his eyes. "I mean, don't get me wrong, I know we have a lot in common, but I'm getting the distinct impression this conversation is not about the music business."

"Josie, a talented person like you has to be exceptionally careful who you let into your inner circle. Because the influence you exert on those very same people will come back to haunt you. Are you listening to me?"

"Yes, I'm listening."

"Once you know the truth, the real hard down truth, you influence the way they think and vice versa. They take their cues, good and bad, from you. And the next thing you know these same people, who praised this wonderful talent of yours, until they got you rolling, try to jump on your back for the free ride and before you know it, you start running out of steam because of carrying all these people on your back. Too many talented people forget that talent is a gift. You dig? A gift is not something you squander on ungrateful parasites."

"How long have you been planning this speech?" I said.

"Long enough," he went on. "I just wanted to wait until you realized that the world sets up guys like you, just so you can get your chops busted. You hear about it all the time. They come and they go, but why do they go?"

"I don't know, Gary, why do they go?"

"Because they took their gift for granted. Like you did."

"Where do you get off judging me, man? I never took anything for granted. I worked my ass off to learn how to play that horn."

"Listen, Josie, I like you, man, but I think sometimes you take this music thing too seriously. It's just sounds, you know. It's not a living, breathing entity like a family. Nobody cares about 99.9% of all the great players that have come and gone. That's not true with a real family. Family is where the truth is, family is what makes music possible. Family and friends, man, that's where it's at."

"Gary, have you ever played in front of 20,000 people and when you finished have them jump to their feet as one, man, screaming for more?" I said.

"No," he answered.

"Have you ever made $2,500 a night thirty nights in a row?"

"No."

"Have you ever had people stand in line to get your autograph, night after night? Or have them recognize you somewhere and point you out to their friends? Or been on stage looking down at them when something your band plays causes them to start climbing on top of each other to get closer to you. To just touch you?"

"No. Nope, and no, again." Gary said. "Now, let me ask you something."

"Shoot."

"Have you ever seen them do that for anybody but a handful of institutional rock legends, like the Stones, McCartney, Clapton or Elvis? Or the latest group currently on the hit parade? Have you ever seen them do that for a nightclub house band? Night after night?"

I didn't say anything.

"Have you ever seen guys, with a hundred times more talent than the best superstars you know, never even get noticed? Have you ever heard the old saying that for every star, there are a thousand just as good or better who will never make it? How many marriages stay together because the husband or the wife is the target of all that attention?"

Gary was starting to get on my nerves.

"What I'm trying to tell you, man, as gently as I can, is simply this. You've had your shot, and you didn't make it. If you had made it, you wouldn't be here with me going to gigs like this at the Naval Base, which is exactly where you were five years ago. The wild ride is over, man, face it and quit trying to fight it. You're almost twenty-five years old. Everybody famous that you worked with is either dead or a has-been. It's over, man, and if I didn't respect you for what you've accomplished, I wouldn't be telling you this. If you were meant to be a star, you would be one by now, with all the money and the house and the women, the whole bit. But it ain't happ'nin', Josie. You gotta move on to Plan B.

"I don't have a Plan B. This is all I know."

"Which brings me to my last and final point, brother man. The young man's game is over, Josie. Even as we speak, your Plan B is being formulated. If you don't start paying attention to what's going on behind your back, you're going to get your head handed to you, if you'll pardon the expression, on a silver platter. Before you know it, you'll be two things: old and bitter. That's if your luck holds out."

"And if it doesn't?"

"You'll be dead before you're thirty."

With that, we pulled up to the Base gate. I still hadn't looked at him during this last burst of character analysis.

"Tell me something," I said finally looking at him.

"What?"

"If your father is The Preacher, who are The Farmer, The Landlord and The Night Mayor?" I watched his face for the reaction.

"I can't tell you that," he said.

"Why?"

"Because if they find out you know, they will assume I told you and that will put my family in jeopardy." He pulled into a parking spot across from the back door to the Officers Club.

"So you know about the situation I'm in?" I said.

"Why do you think I said everything I said to you tonight?" he asked.

"I was trying to figure that out, myself," I said.

"I would say, just guessing, that you've figured it out. But, in case you haven't let me say this and this will be the end of it, for the time being at least. Take your worst fears about your present situation and make your plans accordingly, that is, if you plan to stay in Charleston. If you're planning to leave, I'd do it soon. But regardless of what you do, check your ego at the door, 'Pride goeth before a fall,' according to the Good Book."

"Just tell me this. Is Bootsy Williams The Farmer?"

"Matthew 11:15, look it up."

By the time, I got out of the car, I'd copped an attitude toward Gary because he wouldn't level with me. If he'd been anybody else I would've told him to shove it. Why was I, all of a sudden, fair game in a big potshot contest? Nobody, to my knowledge, knew the real reason I came off the road. And of course, because of his father, he'd figured out what was really going on, so he knew exactly how to wrap the bitter pill in sugar, and slip it to me while still retaining his plausible deniability.

I shouldn't have gotten so bent out of shape. Gary was a good guy, and he said what he thought. But the needle was too close to the nerve and the medicine stung; besides I didn't need somebody hitting me that close to home and my tolerance level for other people inserting themselves into my life was getting pretty low. Especially, if Gary knew something about the trouble I was in and wouldn't tell me.

I had all the implications of my conversation with Gary running through my head when I walked in the back door to the kitchen of the Officer's Club. Waiters were scurrying everywhere with trays, while several waitresses refilled champagne flutes and wine glasses. There was a bartender free pouring mixed drinks at a station next to the kitchen door. I figured the South Carolina liquor laws didn't apply to the Naval Base. Either that or the Officers' Club manager knew somebody.

The crowd at the "O" Club was wrapped a little tight, but the food was good. There were big carts of sliced ham, rounds of roast beef, salads and fresh vegetables. I remember a big silver bowl full of boiled shrimp surrounded by potato salad. The guest list included about a hundred officers having drinks and chatting. No civilians were dressed up, which was unusual since every other time I'd played there was a formal event. These were not the hip people, the local social elite, but, rather, represented a significantly more liquid financial base in the city.

An Admiral, a Commander, and two Captains huddled up with local suppliers to the base. I spotted businessmen I'd seen in The Merch. There were a couple of car dealership owners, a chemical company president, harbor pilots, several food service executives and a half dozen government subcontractors.

All these people were tapped into the river of federal money flowing from the Charleston Naval Base. The base was the fountain head from whence all blessings flowed into the Holy City. If you won a lucrative government contract like paving a runway or supplying parts to a fleet of trucks, it was like busting Vegas. And if you did good work and you covered yourself after the contract had been let and took care of your benefactor, then your name stayed at the top of the list. The next time a project came up the guy at the top of the list and the two guys in slots two and three got together and decided which one of them would get the job, and they rigged their bids accordingly. That's the way it'd just been explained to me. Oh, so little did I know.

The big hand-painted sign above the stage with red, white and blue ribbons and balloons all over it said: Charleston Salutes Captain Mark Ward, Officer of the Year. I didn't recognize the name at first. Then I saw the newspaper article tacked to the bulletin board and remembered seeing his picture in the paper. Ward was one of the new Navy's elite submarine commanders. He looked like he'd posed for a "The Few, The Proud" Marine billboard. Chiseled features and solid as you would expect – after all, he controlled a billion-dollar boat with two hundred men on it that could blow up the world. When I looked at him close though, I got a chill. Something in my head reverberated, my ears started to ring and I knew instantly his spit-shine image was more attributable to his uniform and the trappings of office than anything that showed up in his eyes.

He looked to be thirty-five or so, bronzed with black hair that had the perfect look of a regular beauty parlor cut. His big, square chin with straight, white teeth you could see from across the room, every time he talked. When he wasn't talking he was smiling.

"Do you know anything about government contracts?" Gary elbowed me out of the stare I had going at Ward.

"A little, why?"

"You need to know more. This is where the real money is."

I thought I knew more than most about Charleston's money flow, but I was coming to understand that the real insider was Gary's father. How else would he know?

"Look at that guy," I said. "What kind of ego does it take to handle a ship that could start World War Three, at the touch of a button, and still suck up to these business people? He's all teeth and handshakes with every one of them. There's a kind of professionalism in it that reminds me of show business."

"You're very observant and not too far from the truth on that, Josie."

"No, I just know a player, when I see one. This guy is a hustler, and he knows it. How many other men, officers or otherwise, would give their pensions to be in his shoes?"

Gary shrugged. "He's just a guy who spends ninety days, at a clip, underwater."

"Yeah, but he's also the trigger man on sixteen missiles, any one of which is bigger than WWII."

Before the first set, an officer in dress whites with a chest full of metals, walked to the podium, tapping the side of his glass with a spoon.

"Ladies and gentlemen before we launch into the evening's festivities, I would ask you to join me in welcoming our newest Port Operations Officer, Captain Mark Ward."

Captain Ward took the podium for what I figured, having played this gig before, would be a few moments of self-aggrandizement.

"Good evening, everyone. It's customary to address a gathering of Steel Boat jockeys by acknowledging the motto of each unit represented. But since we have such a mixed lot of distinguished guests from 'outside the fence' tonight, I think we can forego some of the military rhetoric. So, on behalf of the United States Navy, I'll just say welcome one and all like a normal human being." A polite round of applause followed. "I would like to thank my base commander and all the Bubbleheads working the Atlantic Fleet Polaris Weapons System as well as the crews of the tenders, support staff, and certainly the City of Charleston and area businesses for their ongoing, generous support of the most important Naval Base in America."

Gary leaned over his kit and whispered, "That means he's got the money and you don't; and that's how it's going to stay."

CHAPTER EIGHTEEN

"I'm proud to be stationed in Charleston," Captain Ward said, "and I want to assure each of you that, while there will be a few minor adjustments in the way the Navy transacts business with civilian contractors, these modifications will only serve to improve the Navy's commitment to increasing our presence in Charleston and the surrounding area. Without going into too much detail, I will share this one item I'm sure will be of interest to you all. As many of you know, the Naval Tactical Data System, or NTDS refers to a computerized information processing system developed by the United States Navy in the 1950's and was first deployed in the early 1960s for use in combat ships."

Glasses stopped tinkling, whispers ceased immediately, every eye in the room was fixed on the speaker. "Now that this technology has been implemented into every aspect of command and control, the United States Navy has been transitioning to a centralized accounting system. Moving forward, these changes have already resulted in speeding up the wheels of commerce and facilitating a much smoother flow of goods and services between the base and private sector. The abbreviated version is outside vendors will no longer have to wait six months to get paid. In most cases, the turnaround time has been reduced to ninety days." Applause erupted in the room, followed by raised glasses, and more than a few hoots and hollers.

"Charleston," he continued, "has been a major force for good in our great country for over 300 years and I'll stake my command's reputation on the successful continuation of fair and equitable relations between the U.S. Navy and our host city. Here's to the best kept secret in the United States, Charleston, South Carolina."

Ward lifted, then sipped his champagne, turned from the podium, and the master of ceremonies simply said, "Have fun."

Sizing up an audience isn't rocket science. Like ducks, fish and wildebeest the collective conscience of a pack of humans, joined in a common cause, is pretty easy to read. Individual animals are basically the same. For the most part every monkey acts like the other monkeys. You can't take the true measure of a human being until they're cut from the herd. The crew of hot-shot wannabes in the room was there for one reason: To insure their spot in the pecking order. I scanned the room of smiling faces; saw a few people I knew. Most of those people never frequented The Merch. They swam in different social streams during the day, but everyone in the room that night participated in the food chain. Naval Base Command decisions would affect them one way or another. They all seemed very pleased with themselves.

Those who recognized me kept their distance. I never quite understood how some men justified being all buddy-buddy with me when they're high, drunk or both, hanging out in the club gawking over the girls; then, when they're socializing with their peer group, pretended they didn't know me. Probably why I preferred street people over the Nouveau Riche. I know, I know, better Nuevo than not rich at all, but give me a break; money can't buy class. It was nice for a change, just being one of the guys in the band because I didn't have to contend with the slobbering bullshit of assholes who, because they suddenly had money, thought they were better than the rest of us. Bill Reed was a perfect example of this stinkin' thinkin'.

I don't want to come off sounding hypocritical here. What I mean is, not putting them down, you understand, because Charleston society, like all societies, needed a certain amount of civic corruption. A decent level of vice, endorsed by a handful of corrupt leaders, in order to justify the legal system, was good for business. For me to say otherwise would be the pot calling the kettle black. Without a cadre of respectable, duly elected, self-appointed crooks versed in systematic manipulation of the city's resources for personal gain, the holier than thou do-gooders would be starved for mortification. They'd've been bored stiff, with nothing to bitch or gossip about and nobody to preach into hell. But these people, at this particular gathering, even dressed up as they were, lacked the sophistication bred into old money corruption. By that I mean family fortunes passed down from generation to generation.

By the time 1970 rolled around, each successive trust fund supported generation was becoming more and more pressed to actually do something worthwhile for a living. Old money knew instinctively how to bridle their greed, knew how to camouflage their wealth. The same way their ancestors bridled the slaves who generated it. But the level of greed in the room, on this particular night, was stupid-obvious. Everybody was all about getting more than their fair share of the Navy money, which was taxpayer money, mine included, that flowed through the system.

According to J. Reynolds, my all knowing landlord, more than a few Charlestonians adhered to a brand of sociopathic thinking similar to European monarchs of the 17th Century. They sincerely believed their station in life required the masses to not only recognize their superior standing in society, but also compensate them for merely existing. These third and fourth generation elitists felt entitled to the highest standard of Lowcountry living, for no other reason than this: Their parents, grandparents and great grandparents spawned them.

Their chief aim in life was continuing to perpetuate the Plantation Mentality by exploiting the labor of Charleston's black citizens, without the bothersome and time consuming task of actually owning them. As a consequence of this stroke of genius they could "be a rich somebody" without having to do a damn thing other than show up, get drunk and fog a mirror.

In the absence of slaves to mistreat, and with the state government, their family fortunes and their gene pools pretty well tapped out, they decided their self indulgent lifestyle could best be supported by swindling the Government. And what better way to achieve this end, than by defrauding the United States Navy?

Ward's announcement, of the introduction of a computerized accounting system, required an adjustment in the level of sophistication employed by these upright citizens in how they would go about defrauding the United States Navy in the future, hence this particular guest list. Of course I didn't know any of this at the time. But I was about to learn.

I looked up at the red, white and blue balloons. *One nation under God, with liberty and justice for all.* The American Dream. What a joke! Try to sell that shit to the people living right downtown on fucking America Street.

Charleston History was full of exploits of these frozen chosen who single-handedly manipulated the system to their advantage. I had to hand it to them. They knew how to get the money, and in good old America, land of the free and home of the brave, money does have a way of talking and bullshit definitely walks. I guess they thought I should've felt privileged to be allowed to serve in my humble capacity that evening, to breathe the rarefied air of the social elite and share the same space with this august body. But with things going the way they were for me, at the moment, I knew these same people, or some exactly like them, would drop the trap door from under my feet at any given moment; leaving me hanging by precisely the amount of rope needed to do the job.

When Ward finished his little speech, we kicked off with Glenn Miller's "In the Mood." The dance floor filled quickly with properly dressed officers, high dollar civilians, swinging and swaying to the music. Tinted spotlights trained on a spinning glitter ball cast an array of tiny multicolored light dots racing all over the ceiling and walls. The place reminded me of the "I Want to be Loved by You" scene from Some Like It Hot.

I didn't look up from the stand very often. My sudden ability to read like a trained musician still fascinated me. Nothing else had changed beyond what I'd already accepted as a newly discovered heightened sense of awareness. No physical side effects, no sweats, no cramps, none of the nausea from the last forty-eight hours. I'd begun to think maybe the drug Erlene used wasn't so bad after all. I knew from experience how LSD had changed my perspective on life. Why not accept this hoodoo by-product as a good thing? The running eighth notes were no problem. I looked at the sheet music, knew instantly what the notes were, key signature, timing, the whole thing. Honestly, it felt great to see all those dots make sense for once. Ordinarily, when it came time to play, I would've followed along enough to know when it's my turn.

"In The Mood" has dueling solos in the middle where the two tenor saxes trade licks, back and forth, before the trumpet comes in with a bluesy chorus of his own. Some bands use two tenors and some use an alto and a tenor. I have had both sides of the duet memorized since I was twelve so when Gary told me to take the lead on the bari and bounce it off the tenor player I nodded. What happened next blew my mind.

The tenor player took the call side of the solo and I took the respond side. Last time I did this, we both stayed seated, but for some reason, the tenor man decided to stand up. I was going to stay in my seat, but when my time to solo came, my body jolted up of its own free will, and I ripped the solo to shreds. I mean I burned that mother down. It sounded so good I even looked around to make sure it was me playing. All I had to do was think about the basic notes in the solo, put my hands on the keys and blow into the mouthpiece. The horn felt like it was alive in my hands. The trumpet player ripped his solo as well, and when I looked at Gary, his eyes were wide as saucers. When the tune was over, Gary had the three of us take a bow and everybody clapped like they'd seen Glenn Miller rise from the dead. I felt like I'd just gotten out of a time machine.

We did a set of Glenn Miller, Dorsey and a couple by Harry James, then took a break.

"Where did that come from?" Gary asked, as he took me back to the kitchen to meet the cooks and raid the food racks.

"Practice, I guess. . . I don't really know. Sometimes, I get lucky just showing up," I said.

One of the perks allowed the hired help was checking out the industrial refrigerators; which looked more like meat lockers. With the door open and my head and one arm stuck inside, I was checking out stainless steel bowls full of various dishes set aside to refill the hors d'oeuvre trays. People complained about government waste, but the Navy had the best cooks in Charleston, and the best of the best worked in the Officer's Club.

I settled on the shrimp and potato salad. Gary found some plates and silverware. We were standing off to the left of the big Vulcan ovens, leaning on the stainless steel counter tops. I'd just put a fork full of potato salad in my mouth when the swinging doors leading to the ballroom opened slowly and a woman wearing dark glasses, a black silk pantsuit and scarf peeked through the crack, apparently looking for something, or someone. My jaw stopped in mid-chew revealing a mouth full of half-chewed potato salad. I was speechless because, earlier that afternoon, I'd rubbed Vaseline onto the bruises that were now hidden by that pantsuit.

Gary spoke first. "Could I help you find something?"

Bobbie Storm eased into the room, holding her arms and rubbing them like she was cold and shy all at the same time. She looked past Gary and smiled discreetly at me while mechanically running her hands up and down the arms of her jacket. She was obviously nervous, and she kept looking back over her shoulder, at the doors behind her. She was fumbling for something to say.

"Hi. Uh, I'm Kela Ward, Captain Ward is my husband. I'd like to request a song, if it's not too much trouble."

Something rose up in my blood stream. Not adrenaline, not anger, not fear, but reptilian cold, as in ice water flowing through my veins.

"No trouble at all, if we know it," Gary said politely.

He noticed immediately that while she was talking to him, she was looking at me. Then his automatic manners jumped to the forefront of his brain.

"My name is Gary and this is Josie Chapman; he's sitting in with us tonight. What would you like to hear?"

"Well, I, that is, my husband and I really enjoyed the solo Mr. Chapman played earlier, and we were wondering if you could play a song that featured him, you know, playing without reading the music, oh what do you call that…?"

"Improvising," I said, looking straight at her.

Her dark hair was pulled straight back and done in a simple French Twist similar to the way she looked the first time I saw her in the Swamp Fox Room.

A graduated string of pearls accented her white silk blouse. Except for the tiny bruise on the back of her hand, everything about her was perfect. I had to hand it to Ward. He was a methodical son-of-a-bitch. No one would suspect that under her clothes, she looked like a punching bag.

"Yes, improvising, isn't that where you kind of make it up as you go along?" She was doing a fairly good job of faking ignorance. Gary still hadn't recognized her, but he was getting suspicious.

"Yes," he said cautiously, trying his best to figure out what was going on. "But you have to have some sense of where you're going. I don't know if we have any-thing on our list that lends itself to that sort of thing."

The wait staff were still working out of the kitchen. I was trying to maintain my composure, too, but I felt like my eyes were bugging out of my head. Gary turned toward me, Bobbie, I mean Kela, or whoever the fuck she was, put her finger to her lips and shook her head.

When Gary turned around, he caught the tail end of the headshake and knew some nonverbal communication had transpired behind his back. Kela lightly touched his arm.

"Well, Captain Ward and I would appreciate anything you can do." She smiled, shook Gary's hand and had reached past him to shake mine, when the doors opened behind her. The alleged "Man of the Hour" rolled up like he was on wheels.

Teeth aglow, he called his wife back to the party with a bark. "Kela, we have guests, I need you out here with me, not hanging out in the kitchen with the band." He shot Gary a toothy grin and added, "She loves music. You should hear her play the piano." His smile disappeared as she walked past him, through the doors. Then he locked his eyes on mine just long enough to let me know I was different from Gary and let the smile reappear until all the teeth were showing. When Kela got behind her husband's back, she turned giving me a look both apologetic and frightened.

Ward was still staring at me when he said, "Gentlemen, I think it's time to get back to work, don't you?"

"We've got five minutes left on our break. Then, we'll start," Gary said.

Obviously unaccustomed to back talk, Ward whirled out the door like a man possessed. Through the glass, I saw him blow past his wife, grab her arm above the elbow and maneuver her into the crowd.

"What the hell was that all about?" Gary snapped.

It had happened so fast I didn't have time to react. By the time I realized who Bobbie or Kela was married to, the potato salad was rolling over in my stomach.

"I don't know what you're talking about," I said.

"The hell you don't," Gary hissed. "That's the same girl who sat in with us the other night. You had lunch with her, and she looked at you like you were her long lost lover; her husband looked at you like he'd kill the both of you, if he ever caught you breathing the same air. Now, what the fuck is going on?"

"I've got to go to the john," I said and left the kitchen for the restroom.

Hanging my head over the sink, I splashed water on my face. My eyes were burning and my stomach hurt. Adrenaline, the real thing this time, was running through my chest, and my hands were shaking. Tears of rage were welling up in my eyes as I fought hard to get control of myself. The whole incident, seeing her scared like that, seeing the monster parading around like a white knight, had me feeling totally helpless. I broke down and started to cry out of sheer frustration. In the mirror, I saw Montague's face, I heard his voice, clear as a bell in my mind, "Here's a little piece of advice you can take to the bank," the voice said, "never push a man who is so angry he starts to cry. A man who starts crying in anger, he is as dangerous as a man can get. You are the man. Get control of yourself before you go suicidal and do something stupid."

I looked at my face in the mirror and tried to focus on the facts. If Kela's following me into the kitchen was a cry for help, then why did she leave my apartment so abruptly this afternoon, without so much as a note? She should've told me who her husband was in the first place. Why hadn't she told me her real name? She did tell me her husband was in the Navy. She didn't tell me he owned it. How could she expect to be with someone like me when she was locked into a marriage with someone like Captain Mark-fucking-Ward? She was the wife of one of the most powerful men on the Naval Base, for God's sake. And she was in a city where that shit carried some weight.

I understood why she'd want to leave her husband. Nothing is worth staying with somebody who beats you, but that was her problem. I didn't get her into that mess and I, sure as hell, couldn't get her out of it. I understood why she wanted a life outside her husband's shadow. But knowing what little I did about basic human nature, I was convinced that this wife would never be allowed to play piano in a downtown lounge and have the blessing of the fleet. That spread was too wide for the system to accept. I could only imagine the reaction she'd get, if the powers that be knew she was singing in a rock band at The Apartment Club while hanging with a musician in his apartment.

The more I thought about it, the more convinced I became that I could only make her situation worse. Seeing her with her husband confirmed the cold truth. She had some big decisions to make on her own, and I was not the person to help her make them.

The band had already gone back up on stage, and I was still a nervous wreck. Just being in the same room with the guy, who had beaten her, stirred me with the same rage and fear I'd felt when my father beat my mother. That's when I realized I was still capable of picking up a baseball bat and doing it again. That thought finally sobered me up enough to go back to the bandstand.

By the time I picked up the bari and sat down, the band was already into the first number. They were playing "Mood Indigo." I knew Gary picked it so I wouldn't be missed. When I turned the sheet music to the song, there was a pack of Alka-Seltzer sitting on the page. I looked back at Gary, he motioned for me to look on the floor under my chair. He had set a glass of water there. I looked back at him and he said, "Drink that and stay away from the potato salad." Then he grinned and went back to paying attention to the song.

When the song was over, Gary looked over at me again.

"That Alka-Seltzer help any?"

"Yeah, it helped, but my stomach isn't right," I said.

"After this set, go to the john and stick a finger down your throat. You'll feel better after you throw up." Gary chuckled.

"I'll just ride it out, if it's all the same to you."

"Suit yourself," he said. "My mom used to make me do it every time something I ate made me sick. It's gross, but it works. I'm telling you, you will feel much better."

I muddled through the rest of that set without taking any solos. Every time one of the arrangements called for a baritone sax solo, I passed it off to the alto player or one of the trumpet players. When we finally took our second break, Gary came off the drums and put his arm over my shoulder.

"Hey man, I'm sorry I got on your case back there," he said, motioning over his shoulder toward the kitchen.

"Don't worry about it," I said.

"Well, we must not've made too bad an impression on the guy." Gary was smiling at me.

"Oh yeah, why's that?"

"Because Captain Ward invited the rhythm section, and you, over to his place after the gig. He wants us to play some background music while he entertains a few close friends. He specifically asked for you to be included in the group. He's paying us $200 bucks each, for two hours work."

I just looked at Gary for a second while I thought about what he had just said. Then it hit me. Ward wanted to get me close to his wife to watch how we interacted with each other. This guy was some piece of work.

I told Gary that, even though I could use the extra money, I felt too bad to stay out until four o'clock in the morning playing in somebody's living room or, worse yet, out on his patio. I told him I needed to get some rest or it would screw up my gig at The Merch tomorrow night. He didn't like it but said he understood and would get the alto player to take my place.

As soon as the last note of the last song was over, I grabbed the bari from its stand and was out of my chair packing up. I happened to glance up at one of the mirrors hanging on the wall and caught a glimpse of Mark Ward talking to some young blond guy with glasses while he watched me out of the corner of his eye. He knew. And he knew I knew he knew. I got the horn in its case and was heading for the back door when Gary caught me by the arm.

"Hey man," Gary said. "Don't you wanna get paid?"

"Bring it to the club or mail me a check," I said and turned for the door. I knew I sounded rude so I stopped and looked back at him.

"I really am sick, man. I need to get in bed and stay there for a while."

"That's cool. You go get some rest. I'll catch up with you tomorrow."

When Gary turned to walk away, I looked over his shoulder. I could see Kela sitting at a table with another officer while her husband floated from one group to another. She was holding a full drink glass in her hands the way you hold a cocoa mug on a cold day. She stole a quick glance at me, then turned back to her guest. The guy she was with was obviously drunk and completely full of himself. He took a drag off his cigarette and blew the smoke up in the air, then laughed and coughed and patted Kela on the knee. Then he swallowed what was left of his drink and traded Kela his empty glass for her full one. I watched Mark Ward watching his wife like he had her on an invisible leash. The chill from the open door got my attention, and I turned toward the back door and the parking lot.

So this was the damsel in distress I was supposed to rescue. The same one who, just a few hours ago, I'd concluded was able to take care of herself. The Joan of Arc who was going to save me from myself and right all the wrongs in my life. I realized, at that moment, that of all the idiots I'd ever known or heard of, I was chief among them.

The anger I felt at everyone, from myself to the drunk with his hand on Kela's knee, made me seriously contemplate taking Gary's advice about sticking my finger down my throat so I could go ahead, throw up and get it over with.

As I made my way toward Gary's car, I heard the back door to the kitchen close again and saw the blond-haired guy with glasses Ward had been talking to come out of the building and walk swiftly to one of the staff cars sitting in the parking lot. He watched me walk to the cabstand, open the back door of a parked taxi and put my horn inside. Then, when I got into the cab, the blond guy got into his car. I told the driver my address, and we pulled into the street with the staff car following the cab all the way out to the base gate.

The cabbie showed the MP at the gate his pass, then the guard waved the blonde guy through with a smile. I figured he would just make sure I left the base, but I was wrong. He followed me to the Texaco and piddled around under the hood of his car while I got a bottle of aspirin. Then he followed me all the way to Savage Street, where he parked under a street light half a block away.

If he was a cop, why was he in a Navy staff car? If he wasn't a cop, then why was he following me? Why would Mark Ward put a tail on me simply because he knew I'd met his wife? If he was that possessive, why let her play out at all? I wasn't going to get involved with Bobbie or Kela or Mrs. Ward or whoever she was. He could have me followed from now until he pushed his doomsday buttons, I didn't care. My only problem was trying to decide how I was going to get flush on the Bootsy Williams mess.

I sat the bari case on the steps and went around the corner through the neighbor's backyard, so I could come up on his blind side from the opposite direction. The guy was slumped down in the seat smoking a cigarette with his left elbow propped up in the driver's side window. He was watching my house in his rear-view mirror so he didn't see me cross the street. When I was within five feet of his arm I duck walked the length of the car. He busted both knees on the bottom of the steering wheel when I suddenly popped up beside his head at open window. "Why are you following me?" I said.

He bolted upright so fast he hit his head on the roof of the car and bumped his knees under the steering wheel. He looked at me like a startled burglar trying to come up with a satisfactory explanation as to why he is in your house while you're not supposed to be home.

"I'm not following anybody. I don't know what you're talking about. Now get away from me before I call the police." He reached for the keys in the ignition, started the car and dropped it down into drive. For a split second, I thought I was going to hit him. I even thought about going in through the car window and grabbing his keys while pinning his neck against the headrest with my elbow. Instead I did something that even surprised me.

"Hey, don't rush off," I said. "I've got a message for your boss."

He stopped the car and looked back at me with a smirk on his face. "Oh yeah, what's that?"

I walked to the window, leaned in just a little and said, "Tell him I'm sick about all the misunderstandings." Then I jammed my finger down my throat and puked all over him. Gary was right. Throwing up did make me feel better.

CHAPTER NINETEEN

I spent most of the next day staring out the window, watching for cars. The blond guy never came back. Nobody except the neighbors had parked anywhere on the street. Maybe one of them had taken up the job of watching me. Since I'd never knowingly been followed before, I didn't know how these things worked, but through my new eyes I learned quickly how to spot strangers.

By six o'clock, my mind was ready to go to work, but it was too early. The tenor case didn't feel heavy at all. In fact, the case felt so light I looked inside to make sure the horn was there. A walk would kill some time, Ashley Avenue to the Battery was only a couple blocks, then a right down toward the Coast Guard Station would be good exercise. The joggers and tourists had all gone in. The only other visible humans were two lovebirds making out in a red Chevy Nova. The sun was going down, the salt air smelled fresh and strong.

With only myself to worry about, being alone felt good, safe. A warm, salty offshore breeze had just brushed my cheek when I suddenly knew someone was watching me. I say I knew because the menthol adrenaline chill reminded me of saying goodbye to Bobbie, who I now realized was Kela, in the parking lot of The Merch. How everything had seemed fine until I suddenly saw Bootsy Williams leaning against my car. This feeling felt like that.

Picking up my pace, the horn weighed less than a briefcase. There's a break in the sidewalk where a ninety degree curve is perpendicular to the paved entry into the Station. Street signs mark the end of Murray Boulevard and the beginning of Tradd Street. Joggers often turned around there so they could continue to run by the water. Fifty feet beyond the Coast Guard Station gate, I'd be completely out of sight to anyone following me. It was a good place to turn around without drawing attention, I could cross the street, double back and meet anyone behind head on. When I hit my mental mark, I wasn't even winded.

Headed back up Murray Boulevard toward East Bay, now on the opposite side of the street, I passed Ashley Avenue. After another half block, I saw a car suddenly break, then the turn signal started blinking. Like a stray dog loose in the street, the car darted right onto Rutledge the moment the driver realized I'd reversed course. I don't know how I knew; it didn't matter, but I was certain I was being followed. I kept walking toward the Ft. Sumter Hotel. I looked for other cars, people, any unusual activity, and didn't see any.

Inside the hotel lobby, I pretended to use the pay phone. A few minutes passed, plenty of time for the driver to cut the block. Another five minutes passed and the car still hadn't come back. The receiver was resting on my shoulder with the recording telling me to please hang up. The doorman stepped over and politely informed me the lobby phone was for residents and their guests only. I put the receiver in the cradle and walked across the street to White Point Gardens.

When it comes to keeping your story straight, frame of reference is paramount. The more concrete facts you nail down, the better off you'll be. There's a trick to that, and if you don't know this one, you should. This has nothing to do with anything, but covering your ass. Believe it or not I learned it from an English Professor. So, if you're willing to bear with me for a second, I'll give you a mental gift between friends. Because if you ever find yourself in the middle of a fucked up mess like the one I was in, you'll be glad this little chop is in your gig bag.

There's a bench on the East Battery side of the park. When I was younger I'd sit there to read. Fort Sumter is not visible if you're sitting on it, because the high wall of the Battery is in the way. To see the fort, you have to stand up beside the cannon. It's the 3.5 mile expanse of water between the cannon and the fort that, according to Montague, Strong Man calls home.

Dr. Nan Morrison, one of the English professors at the College of Charleston, walked by one day while my head was buried in Go Tell It on the Mountain. She sat down and handed me a book called The Book of Five Rings, written by a samurai named Miyamoto Mushashi. I'd never heard of him. She said if I liked Baldwin I'd like Mushashi. She said the two books shared themes for people trying to figure out their place in the grand scheme of things. I thought it was pretty cool that a professor would give a kid a book like that, not even knowing my name. I found out who she was by hanging around the college until I saw her again. When I asked one of the students about her, the guy acted like he'd seen a ghost.

"That's Dr. Morrison, the hardest teacher in the English department," the kid said. She didn't look so tough. In fact, I thought she was cute. She reminded me of a sexy librarian. I still have the copy she gave me, still read it. The Book of Five Rings is in my head; especially Mushashi's explanation of mental strategy, "if you can make your opponent flinch, you have already won." I recognized that one, because that's exactly what a pool hustler does to a player; only it's called making the other guy choke. I'll get sidetracked if I try to go into detail here, but trust me, when it comes to covering your ass, understanding the mind of Mushashi will help you, as Sinclair says, to "Stand your shit straight up."

The bench by the cannon was also my favorite place to contemplate the meaning of life in general, and mine in particular. Chilly on a warm evening, self-confident and worried about being followed, confused while clear-headed, I was a mass of contradictions. I closed my eyes, distant thunder rumbled, as visions of the raging battle swirled through my imagination. How many people died because of this cannon, I wondered. With all the cannons in the world, I wondered how anybody could be afraid of an English teacher.

My gig at The Merch didn't start for another three hours, so I had some time to kill. Dwelling on how many people had died in the different wars was one way to keep my mind off subjects like Bill Reed and Kela Ward. The moon was coming up, and the sky was a deep sapphire blue. Somebody sat on the bench beside me.

"Fancy meeting you here." Kela was sitting beside me, her eyes staring straight ahead. It was now obvious she'd been following me on foot. "Nice night for a walk," she continued. "Do you come here often?"

"Often enough, Mrs. Ward," I said.

"Did you recover from the party Sunday night?"

"I need to get going."

"Is your stomach still upset?" She ignored my last sentence. "Gary said you didn't feel well."

"Something I disagreed with tried to eat me." I shrugged. "Getting sick is one of my gimmicks. I use it to get out of close calls. Not too many people I know can puke on demand. Really, I need to get to work. Maybe I'll catch you later at the Swamp Fox." I got up to leave.

"That's it?" She said. "I track you down hoping for a chance just to talk to you and you blow me off?"

"Me? Blow you off? Mrs. Ward? Or is it Bobbie Storm? I'm confused."

"My first name is Kela. Bobbie Storm is my stage name."

"But Captain Mark Ward is still your husband. Right? Because, all you told me was, that your husband was in the Navy,"

"You're not being fair," she said, "I didn't lie; I told you my husband was in the Navy. I just didn't give you his job description, that's all."

"There's a big difference between being in the Navy and running the Charleston Naval Shipyard." Any way you wanna cut it, she'd misled me. To my way of thinking, if a person you trust withholds vital information you could use to make an important personal decision, they might as well lie. The outcome is the same "OK, let's get all our cards out in the open so I can figure out how much time I have left on the planet."

We walked up the Battery past Elliot Street to Exchange Street and went into Perdita's. The only four-star restaurant in Charleston, Perdita's was dark with lots of old paintings and an air of hospitality unmatched in the city. Since it was still early on a Monday night, the only people in the restaurant were the waiters and an older couple talking at the bar.

At the waiter's suggestion, we took a table for two by a window on the harbor side of the building and ordered two coffees. The waiter lit a candle in the center of the table, and Kela slipped out of her jacket, allowing it to drop over the back of her chair. The harbor wasn't visible from that window, but the window allowed some of the sharper sounds from the waterfront to drift in. I heard a tugboat horn off in the distance and thought about how nice it would be to simply sail away from all my troubles. A few moments later, a steam whistle pierced the distance, bringing my mind back to the table.

Sitting with Kela in a public place like Perdita's was scary enough; the thought of sending her back to Mark Ward was even scarier. When she touched my hand, I saw the little bruise on the back of her hand had started to turn yellow. I rolled up the sleeve of her blouse and looked at the bruises on her arm.

"Looks like the Vaseline helped," I said, even though several of the bruises were still dark purple. "I need this like I needed a hole in the head," I thought. And one was probably going to lead to the other.

"I've been following you since you left your apartment," she told me. "I was afraid to come up the stairs. Afraid you might tell me to go to hell."

"You could've told me your husband was an important officer. You could've told me your real name. You knew I'd find out sooner or later." I took a sip of my coffee and stared out the window.

"I'm sorry I was such a coward." She took my free hand in hers. "When you walked out on that bandstand, I became physically ill. In the kitchen I was trying to tell you, but Gary was there, and then Mark followed me. Then when you left without saying anything, I almost cried. I hated for you to have to find out like that."

"I've been lied to before," I said. "It's no big deal. I'm used to double standards. Fact is I'm getting right fond of the service entrances of life."

She was starting to sniffle. "I have to be so careful," she said, "I'm sorry I didn't level with you from the start. I needed to know I could trust you."

"Your husband is a very powerful man. He knows all the right people. Using your maiden name would get you into a lot more trouble with him than using your real name would with me." She didn't say anything. There wasn't much she could say, since it was true.

"He knows some of the right people, but he's not really connected with any one particular group in Charleston. All his connections are out of town and a few of those people know people here. He's trying to bridge the gap."

"Sounds like an ambitious guy," I said.

"He has a one word vocabulary: More."

She finally sipped her coffee, for the first time. We sat there quietly contemplating the moment. The breeze off the harbor had picked up, rustling the oleanders outside the window. The ringing of a buoy bell floated in from somewhere out in the harbor. The distant ringing reminded me of an antique clock chime.

"Mark's a Neanderthal." Kela shifted her weight in her chair.

"Yeah, so I gathered," I said.

"Anything standing between him and what he wants gets slashed and burned, including our relationship."

I looked out over the empty room and thought about the ramifications of a personality like Mark Ward having his finger on the trigger of one of mankind's ultimate sunset cannons. I'd already made up my mind that I was seriously out-gunned. The words of Sun Su came to mind: "The most foolish mistake a single soldier can make is to attack a fortified city." There was no way a relationship with Kela could work without somebody getting hurt.

For most of the conversation, I hadn't let the discussion go much beyond small talk. Kela had touched me deeply, there was no place I'd rather be than with her, but she was a prisoner in a fortified city. No matter how I juggled the pieces, there was no way to turn this puzzle into a picture. So, I didn't hammer her anymore.

Every relationship gets tested on a regular basis. Music is like that too, so are the musicians who play the music. That's one reason music is so powerful. The music creates a spiritual relationship with the listener, just like a person. Some relationships pass the test while others fail. My relationship with Kela exploded early enough to keep the collateral damage down to a minimum. I'd let her see I wouldn't be taken for granted or manipulated. I would survive; because I always survive. Kela's fate was out of my hands. Depending on how she handled her submerging relationship with her nuclear husband, it could go either way. God might've been in His heaven, but the world still needed work and I wasn't about to fire her sunset cannon.

Make no bones about it, I was concerned about what this woman's husband would do to her, if he suspected she was having an affair. And, honestly, I was afraid of what he might do to me, if I actually slept with her. Assuming, of course, that she'd even want that. There would be no defense, no excuse, no reasonable explanation, because I would've crossed, not just a line, but also my own damned line.

If, on the other hand, she was just using me as an escape route out of a bad marriage, then my decision was still right. How I felt about her at the present couldn't be considered a viable part of the equation. It had to end. There was no other way.

I turned and looked into eyes welling up with tears.

"Listen Kela," I said softly. "I know exactly how trapped you feel. I was trapped once, too, a few years back, by my own father. It was horrible, but I rode out the storm, making sure I never got caught in another one. But I can't help you with this. I'm way out of my league."

The tears broke and ran down her cheeks as she braced herself for the next velvet-covered cannon ball. Trying to be compassionate while cutting her off made me sick. But it had to be done.

"You've got to stop pursuing me or you'll get us both killed," I said.

"Does that mean you won't teach me?" Her voice started to crack.

"Teach you what, Kela? You already know how to play, you've got the education, you're working, you've got two paying gigs and everybody thinks you're great. So you've got a marriage that needs some work...OK, a lot of work, but there's nothing here you can't handle."

"Stop it!" She grabbed both my hands in both of hers like someone begging for their life. "I need you to teach me how to survive!! For God's sake! Can't you understand that?" She started sobbing. "I am lost. I'm just stumbling around. My life is making me up as it goes along. If I'm going to live through this, I've got to learn how to improvise, and I don't mean on the piano, but in every aspect of my life. Like you have."

She stopped long enough to look out the window and gather her thoughts. When she turned her face back toward me she pulled a Kleenex out of her coat pocket and blew her nose.

"All I ask is that you teach me, Josie. Will you just give me a few basic lessons? Will you just teach me the basics of how to fight back? Tell me where to start, that's all I ask."

Well, there it was, the truth, at last. I looked at her long and hard, waiting for the right words.

A dozen clichés from past leaders I'd read came to mind. All of them trite and worn compared to what she needed. I started to say several things like "you have to be strong;" "you have to be convinced you are right;" "you have to have confidence, self-esteem, and a sense of who you are and your purpose in life." The more I thought about it, the more stupid I felt. How could I tell her what to do when I didn't do any of that stuff myself?

For some reason, the big Civil War cannon I sat beside earlier came to mind. My mind's eye arced over the trajectory the cannon balls would have flown on the way to Ft. Sumter. I thought about the battle that started the Civil War, and war in general. I felt like I was behind enemy lines.

Thinking about all the spilled blood and lives wasted in the name of all the great causes, the bottom line came to me softly on the whispering breeze blowing in from the harbor seasoned by the distant dinging of the buoy bell. A voice in my thoughts I was starting to recognize as a voice separate from my thinking voice said. "Perception is strong and sight weak. In strategy it is important to see distant things as if they were close and to take a distanced view of close things." I knew instantly it was a passage from The Book of Five Rings. My head shook, then my body, like a wet dog shaking off water.

"What's wrong?" She said.

"All this damp weather. Maybe I'm coming down with a cold," I said.

She reached over putting her hand on my forehead. "Are you high on something, or coming down off some drug?"

"No." I said, then drank a full glass of water. "OK. Let's do this."

She stared at the table with both hands cradling her face.

"When was the last time he hit you?" I said. "Before this latest incident?"

"In Norfolk, a little over a year ago. But it was only open-handed slaps."

"He used his fists this time and a belt, and he bit you. Right?"

"And he pulled my hair when he dragged me down to the floor."

"Did he try to rape you?"

"No."

"He ever give you a reason?"

"A reason?"

"When he slapped you in Norfolk, how'd he justify it?"

"He blamed me for not getting promoted."

I didn't say anything, only looked at her.

"He said his superiors didn't think it was appropriate for his wife to be..."

Her lip started quivering. "He was a logistics specialist on The Queenfish. An attack submarine, I think, mapping the ocean floor under the arctic ice cap. The tour lasted almost ten months."

"How long had you been married? Before he went to sea?"

"A month." She took a sip of water. "We'd dated in Alabama. High school cheerleader falls for college football star, you know the drill." She gazed out the window. "He'd made Lt. JG by the time he was twenty-three. My parents knew his parents, he was home on leave, we met, we dated, and the rest is history." Her mouth started to quiver again.

"No need to relive the whole story," I was struggling for something to say, " I shouldn't..."

"I'm glad you asked. I need to tell my side. Hear myself say the words."

"OK. Say it. Say the words."

"I dropped out of Julliard to follow him to Pearl Harbor, the Queenfish's home port. While he was at sea I took classes on the base. I wanted friends, I wanted to meet people. There was a piano at the NCO Club, they'd let me practice. Which led to playing in the lounge of The Officers Club. One of the officers taught a class in forensic ballistics, said I could take his class, so I signed up. Fast forward four weeks, we were at the shooting range and he tried to kiss me. I slapped him, he got pissed, called me a prick tease. After Mark's tour, he was transferred to Norfolk, assigned to The Sturgeon."

"Another submarine?"

Kela nodded. I put my hand on hers.

"Yes, you can do this, just say what he said."

"He said, his superiors told him it was inappropriate for his wife to be, in his words, a bar-hopping gutter slut." She collapsed in waves of sobbing tears.

"What about this last time?" I said. "He got his promotion, how'd he justify this last round?" She froze up. "I can't help you if you don't tell me what's changed since Norfolk."

"If he finds out I told anybody, he'll kill me."

"What's changed between the slaps in Norfolk and this …this …?"

"Assault?" She said.

"I was thinking attempted murder, but assault works."

"If he'd wanted to kill me, I'd be dead."

I didn't know what to do, what to say, what to think. The beating was bad enough, but the humiliation he'd heaped on her…was…the words escaped me. Then in a moment of clarity, an epiphany arrived unlike any I'd ever experienced. My new inner voice said, "Reed."

"What is it?" Kela said.

"How'd you get the gig at The Apartment Club?"

"Bill Reed came into the Swamp Fox, like you did."

"How'd he figure out you could front a band?"

"He didn't. That came later."

"Later, after what?" I said.

"After I sat in with his house band during a rehearsal."

"You ever front a band in Norfolk?"

"What are you getting at?"

"Nothing. You wanted my help, I'm trying to help."

Something didn't add up. I pulled the trick where the next person to speak loses. Seconds turned into three minutes.

"I did front a band in Norfolk," Kela said.

"And your husband didn't have a problem with that?"

"He was a bubble head, on a ten month tour."

"So he didn't know."

"Not until after he got back. By then I was the perfect Navy wife. Until we went out one night and I was recognized by a fan."

"I gather this bit of adulation from a fan set off the Norfolk slap fest?"

Kela nodded. This settled one part of the mystery. Still missing was the reasoning behind this latest escalation in Mark's physical violence toward his wife.

"You can't fear pain." I heard myself say.

"That's it?" She blew her nose, sniffling. "I can't be afraid of pain? What's that supposed to mean? You saw me naked, remember? You put Vaseline on my cuts and bruises. Now your best advice is I'm not supposed to fear its happening again?"

"Tell me the difference between Norfolk and Charleston. Aside from the promotion?"

"He'll know if I'm lying. If I tell him I haven't told anyone, when I have, he'll know."

"And?"

"He'll kill me. He'll make it look like an accident on a trip; he's good at that sort of thing."

"The fear of pain is the major motivator in the world. Everybody wants something; everybody is afraid of something. Everything people are afraid of inflicts some kind of pain. It doesn't always involve a beating. People fear any threat standing between them and what they want. Your husband beat you because he wants to control you. He wants to control you because something about you threatens him."

"Look at me. Mark's a foot taller and a hundred pounds heavier."

"I understand. I really do. But if he's not afraid of the physical pain you could inflict on him, then he must be afraid of something you know. Some knowledge you have. There has to be something. And if you know what it is, then you're at a definite advantage."

"I'm not following you," she said.

"You can respect the pain, or the prospect of pain, resulting from his hitting you. I'd even say you should be prepared for it, because, sure as the sun rises, it is the only thing he can hold over you. But you don't have to live in fear of pain."

"That doesn't make sense."

"You remember hearing about the gang wars during the thirties?"

"What's that got to do with this?"

"When the Italian mob and the Irish mob were in competition with each other in Chicago, word got out the Italians were planning to hit the Irish bosses. So the Irish loaded up several cars full of guys with Tommy Guns, and proceeded to shred the Italians' homes with bullets."

"So?"

"Back then nobody was afraid to die. The possibility of getting killed didn't scare them. What terrified those guys was getting caught and tortured. In other words, what came right before death, which was pain," I said.

"Go on," she said.

"When asked why they gunned down the Italians without provocation, the Irish said they'd engaged in an act of 'Preemptive Self Defense by Proxy.'"

"What exactly are you suggesting?" she said.

"You need some sort of preemptive self-defense plan in case he comes at you again."

"A way to protect myself?"

"Even if there's a risk you could get hurt or killed," I said. "But without knowing what's changed since you left Norfolk, there's nothing more I can tell you. Because I don't know the risks, I can't put myself in your shoes."

"I understand," Kela said.

"If it were easy, anybody could do it, and the world would be one big Disneyland. Life, as we know it, has a lot of pain. If one of your major motivating factors with regards to your husband is the avoidance of the physical pain he can inflict on you, then you'll live in fear of him for the rest of your life. Everything you do, every decision you make, every thought going through your head, will be designed to avoid getting hit." I let that sink in. "On the other hand if he feels threatened by you, then you need to know exactly why and figure out how to use that to your advantage."

"You just described my marriage."

"I can't help you there. I can tell you one of the reasons Freddie May hates my guts is he knows I'm not afraid of him because he can't hurt me without hurting himself."

"I've seen him. He looks like he could get dangerous if you crossed him."

"Kela, look at me," I said. "A fucking baboon can get dangerous if you cross it. The ability to kick ass doesn't make a baboon human any more than it makes a human being smart. Violence is the last resort of the weak."

"I never thought of it like that?"

"You can only fight the way you practice." The words blurted out of my mouth like someone else had spoken.

"What?"

"It's a quote. From a book I used to study."

"Why did you say it?"

"I didn't mean to, the words slipped out. The point is, the more you fear pain, the more power the fear of pain has over you. When you no longer fear pain, you no longer fear. Period. Then you can fight. Because, the bottom line is: Pain, in all its forms, is the only thing weak people fear. Which is why violence is the last resort of the weak. Even Mark is afraid of something. Probably not death, and probably not physical pain, but that motherfucker is afraid of something."

"My guess is public humiliation or embarrassment before he gets what he wants." Kela stared out the window. Her tears were gone.

"What does he want?'

"Money, for one thing. Lots of money. A lot more than he'll ever make in the Navy."

"Survival step number one: Discover what your adversary fears, and let him see that it doesn't scare you." I folded my arms, thinking I was thoroughly convinced of my own ludicrous absurdity.

"This is the most morbid view of life I've ever heard," she said, folding her own arms across her chest. "I can't believe you said that."

"Yeah, well, the truth is whatever you believe it is, but here's a fact; nobody's beaten the shit out of me. Not lately. And you know why? Because I'm not afraid of pain. And if a motherfucker does decide to kick my ass for no reason, he better kill me. Because he will die, one way or another."

And, for the first time in my life, I believed it. Her tears stopped, some of the tension eased up. She seemed to relax a little.

"It's not easy." I felt like I was on a roll. "In fact, it's very difficult. Standing up to fear means going against a fundamental survival instinct. And this is only one of the basics, and it's not an original idea. Didn't Roosevelt say, 'The only thing we have to fear is fear itself?' You think he made that up? Here's the 1645 samurai version of the same concept: 'Under the sword lifted high, there is hell making you tremble. But go ahead, and you have the land of bliss.'"

She was looking at me like I was trying to explain a math problem. In retrospect, I think how stupid my words would've sounded to anybody who'd never been beaten or abused. There's no way to explain the low-grade depression a battered person learns to accept as normal. I knew the words sounded shallow, even as I was saying them, but they were the best I could come up with at the moment. They'd only make sense to a person who understood the elongated, exaggerated pain of systematic humiliation. Could I have said it differently? Sure. Was there a better, clearer way to explain how I learned to survive in, and make sense of, this fucked up world? Maybe. Did she consciously understand what I was talking about? Probably not, at least I didn't think so. Not consciously. Subconsciously? Abso-fucking-lutely. Like I said when I first saw her bruises, scars recognize each other, even if the wounded people don't.

"There's an old saying, 'you can't scare a man who's not afraid to die.' But it's misleading. A lot of people say they aren't afraid to die, or at least they think they're not. And that's because they've never done it before, so they have no reference point. These same people, though, are definitely afraid of what comes right before death."

"So," she breathed and sat up straight. "If we're not afraid of pain and not afraid to live and not afraid to die, then what are we afraid of?"

It was a good question, one that deserved an honest answer.

"We, that is, you and I, are afraid that your husband will either try to have us killed, or try to kill us himself, before we have a chance to have any say-so in the matter."

We laughed. The tension was finally gone and we were left with deciding what to do next.

"So basically, we're afraid of getting caught," she said. "If we do this," she moved her finger back and forth between us, "thing."

"Exactly. Death before embarrassment, remember."

"So, what are we going to do about it?"

"Well, I don't know about you, but I'm going to The Merch, eat a club sandwich, drink a shot of whiskey, chased by a beer, try to play some music, and not get sloppy."

"And...?" she leaned forward again, wrapping my hands in hers.

"And... And start preparing my mind and body to accept the pain which will inevitably accompany the consequences of my actions." I smiled and drained my coffee cup.

"Would you like to join me?" I flirted. "I'm famished."

"I can't," she said. "I'm expected for dinner at the OC, then the Swamp Fox by ten."

"It's Monday night, call in sick, tell them you can't make it," I said.

"It's the Fleet Commander and his wife. Mark can't show up alone." She shrugged her shoulders and pressed my hands. "It wouldn't look good, and Mark would know I wasn't sick. Besides, I need to work up to this. I've been afraid all my married life and old habits die hard."

"That's cool." I shrugged too. "God forbid, things shouldn't look good for Mark." I decided to put a cap on our conversation. "After the Officer's Club thing, I was so upset with you I swore I'd never see you again," I said.

"I know," she whispered.

"Then I felt so sorry for you I wanted to grab you and take you away from it all."

"I know that, too," she said.

"The trick is to not drive yourself insane as you march to the beat of your own drum; knowing full well, nobody hears it but you. "

"I don't worry about going insane. I pretty much live in my own mind."

"I hate to break it to you, but when you live in your own mind; you're living behind enemy lines."

CHAPTER TWENTY

From our table by the window I could see part of Prioleau Street. I didn't say anything to Kela when a blue-gray sedan, like the one that had followed me from the Officer's Club, pulled over to the curb two blocks from the Harbor House Restaurant. The headlights went out, and I watched for someone to get out. Instead the driver rolled down his window and lit a cigarette, cupping his hands around the match so I got a quick glimpse of his features. He was white with blonde hair. He looked like the guy I puked on, who'd followed me from the club, but I wasn't sure. Then the headlights of a car moving toward him shined right in his face, and I recognized Charlie Thigpen, the cop who had questioned me about my dealings with Bill Reed.

It did upset me a little, since I figured that, thanks to Thigpen, most of the Charleston County Police Department probably believed I killed Bootsy Williams. I was getting more than a little paranoid thinking everywhere I went I was either being followed by the cops or one of Mark Ward's windup toys. Then I remembered my brand of paranoia was more like a heightened sense of awareness.

"I gotta go," I said, quickly, trying not to sound alarmed.

Kela looked a little startled when I abruptly stood up and grabbed my horn case. I patted her on the back like an old friend, reached for my wallet and threw five dollars on the table.

"Hang in there," I said, and started walking out of Perdita's toward the door that opens onto Exchange Street.

"Thank you," she said. "I'll call you tomorrow." She blew me a kiss, and I waved back. From that point on, my mind was on the driver in the car.

I turned left onto Prioleau and walked straight toward Thigpen. The car started up. He was waiting for me to pass him so it wouldn't look obvious. When I crossed the street, he made a slow U-turn and came up behind me. Intersecting

East Bay, I went left and walked the distance to Longitude Lane, an alley that's more like a driveway than a street. There are three concrete posts dissecting the middle that split the lane into halves. It is impossible to drive a car from one end to the other so I sprinted down toward Church Street and doubled back to Tradd. After walking against the one-way traffic on Tradd Street to Ashley Avenue, I caught the bus to Charlotte Street, where I cut across the parking lot and came up to the back door of The Merch. I thought I was home free.

As cool and full of intrigue as the whole chase scene appeared to me, none of my back alley ducking and dodging made a difference. When I came in through the kitchen door, Montague nodded toward the front door.

"Sinclair's looking for you," he said.

When I got up front to Sinclair's stand, I looked out the front door and saw Thigpen's empty cruiser parked under the street light in the back corner of the parking lot.

"He done bun gone from dey 'bout half-a-our," Sinclair said without looking back at me. "Drivin' unmarked dis time. He gotch'u numba all right, dat' for damn sho'."

I grabbed the key for the band room from under the counter and smiled sarcastically, as I went back through the porthole door and headed into the dressing room. I opened the door and picked up the towel I use to dry my horn from under the bench at the end of the room. I looked up slightly and saw two dirty, highly scuffed, black wingtips, topped by the soiled cuffs of two navy blue trouser legs, then the mustard and ketchup stains on the shirt.

Thigpen banged into the room, eyes blazing, and slammed the door behind him. When he did, the lid on my horn case fell down with a soft thunk. I lifted the lid and retrieved my sax, like nothing out of the ordinary was going on.

His next move surprised me even more. He opened his jacket took out his gun, took off his badge holder and laid both of them on the chair seat. Then he locked the dressing room door.

Rules and regulations, the Bill of Rights, basic freedoms and most other constitutional rights were not regular fixtures in Thigpen's intellectual tool kit.

I backed up against the cabinet so I'd have some room to kick and checked the umbrella stand for the sawed-off baseball bat we kept there for emergencies. If he was thinking he was going to whip my ass off the record, then by God, he was going to know that he tangled with somebody who could give as good as he got.

Thigpen started wringing his hands, pacing, shifting his weight, hands on hips, hands through his hair, hands on his face and chin, thinking.

I kept waiting for him to throw the first punch. Outside the door, I heard the jukebox start up with "Hold On, I'm Coming." I knew Sinclair was right outside the door listening. A key slid into the lock, and I saw the bolt turn until the door was unlocked. Thigpen, of course, was too preoccupied with his little tantrum to notice. He was buzzing and puffing and foaming at the mouth, turning beet red as he rolled up his shirtsleeves.

"Something bothering you?" I said.

"Yeah, you might say that." He hissed and pointed his finger at my nose, about an inch from my face. His fat legs were just far enough apart to give me a clear shot at his groin.

"Your story don't check out! Erlene Brown said she heard from her night clerk that you came by the St. James and picked up a package that'd been left at the front desk. She said she heard you delivered that package to Bootsy Williams on Wadmalaw Island at exactly four a.m. Saturday morning."

"Did this Erlene Brown say where she heard all this?" I said.

"Let me finish," he barked. "William's was last seen at midnight when he left his house. His bloody clothes and car were found at six a.m. by a couple of deer hunters." He stuck two fingers up in front of my face, "That's two, count 'em, TWO hours, Chapman. You can drive from Wadmalaw to Columbia in two hours. You had plenty of time to do the job. You're going to jail."

"OK! OK," I said "Since you brought up Erlene Brown, I'm going to level with you. OK? Will that be all right? If I just go ahead and level with you?"

"I'm listening," he said.

I told him about Bill Reed dropping the bank bag off in the very room in which he was standing. I told him about going to the St. James, Erlene and the chicken foot. I deliberately left Rashad's name out of my story to see if Thigpen knew about him.

"I didn't even leave the St. James until 3:30." I shifted all my weight to my left foot. "The route I took to Wadmalaw was straight down Maybank. I'll put you in the car and retrace the whole trip."

"You're a liar, Chapman. You lied to me when I asked you the first time. How do I know you're not lying to me now?"

"I didn't have to tell you this," I said. "You don't have the first witness, much less a body. I didn't kill the guy. Simple as that. I gave him a bag full of money and a piece of paper with scriptures from the Bible on it. He was wearing an alligator or snake skin suit, and he put a box full of chickens in the trunk of my car and I drove back to the St. James. I passed Bill Reed's car going in the opposite direction about 4:15. I dropped the chickens at the St. James and came home. Smuggling chickens is all I will admit to, but Williams was alive and smiling the last time I saw him, which was around four a.m. on Saturday morning right out there in the parking lot, snake suit and all. If anybody killed Bootsy Williams between 3 and 6 it was Reed, not me, and he rose from the grave the next night."

"You're a lying' son-of-a-bitch!" he howled.

He thought he had sprung his trap again. If I kicked his fat ass, or if I didn't, he was still the one in control and hell-bent on seeing me behind the grillwork.

In an instant, another spark of total clarity flared up. Something inside of me summed up the buffoon as a fat, sloppy, pig idiot and decided I'd had enough of his swill. Suddenly, he stopped pacing, took a deep breath and sat on the chair by the door. He forgot to turn the badge over so he jumped up when the sharp pin stuck him in the ass. The jukebox stopped playing.

There wasn't a sound from the other side of the door. I relaxed my stance a bit and stared into his eyes.

Without raising my voice, I asked. "Was there a point you were trying to make when you took off the gun and badge and rolled up your sleeves?"

"Yeah, there was. I was going to quit the force just long enough to beat the ever-loving' shit out of you," he grinned.

"I see," I calmly pointed toward the door. He still hadn't realized it was unlocked. "And that bit about locking the door; that was so I couldn't get away? Right?"

"You're catchin' on quick Chapman."

"So, while you were beating the, how was that? 'Ever-loving' shit' out of me, the fact that you had your badge off and your gun lying on the chair, that'd make you a private citizen. And as such you couldn't be charged with police brutality, acting outside the line of duty or any of the bullshit in your little regulation book. Stuff that would make you guilty of a crime if you were wearing your badge and gun, right?"

"Right," he snickered.

"Would that mean, then, that I'd have the right to defend myself without having to worry about getting arrested?"

"You would be welcome to use any means at your disposal, for all the good it would do you," said the smug bastard, who was just about to get the surprise of his life.

"Thanks. I just wanted to verify that, you know, before I made a big mistake and got myself into even more trouble with the authorities. You understand, don't you Mr. Charles? Or is it Detective Thigpen?" He hated to be called Charles. He hated me, but not quite as much as I hated him. "If you decide to do that again, Charles, could I suggest you go ahead and kill me."

"You're crazy, Chapman, I wasn't going to kill you. Just rough you up for lyin', that's all."

"The lie you accuse me of is a police matter. This taking off the badge and gun…that's personal. You see my problem here, Charles?" I leaned toward him.

"Just forget it, Chapman."

"I never forget anything, Thigpen, especially a low-rent threat from a double-crossing motherfucker like you."

"Is that a fact?" He stood up and puffed out his chest.

"That is a fact. So next time, either plan to kill me or put the thought out of your head before you drop the gun and badge, because if you let me survive, even a slight roughing up," I pushed right up into his face, "I will take a 30-06 and, sometime, a long way down the road, when you least expect it, I'll blow your fucking head off from 300 yards out and nobody, especially you, will ever know it was me."

"You're nuts, man, I'm going to nail you for this murder."

"What murder? There's no body! How can you have a murder without a body? If I'd killed the guy I'd've taken the money and been long gone."

"You were the only person Reed would trust with a five-figure drop."

"Bullshit. It's a setup! We're talking about an illegal gambling operator who's been running small town numbers rackets between Georgetown and Myrtle Beach for the last three years. Now he's trying to set up here." I let that sink in. "You think the powers that be don't know who he is? I was nothing to Reed but convenient. He's used lots of people for his drops. He used me for this one because he needed a scapegoat. Reed's who you want. Not me."

"Bill Reed is not a murder suspect. He has four witnesses for where he was at four a.m."

"He's a professional criminal, Thigpen!" I yelled. "That guy has more notches on his gun than you've got dents in your car, he's dropped people in Atlanta, L.A., and New Orleans. He's had more people killed than you've arrested. Either that or he's just another lying piece of shit trying to make a name for himself. Either way, he's in Charleston now, doing what he does best. What's with you? Anybody could've done this, why've you got a hard-on for me?"

"Because, I can't charge Reed with anything that'll hold up in court."

"But me, you can charge?"

"He's clean on this one, his girlfriend, Janet, says he was with her all night. You're the only other person with motive and opportunity. Also, this particular incident happened here in my county. Besides, nothing Reed did in the past is an excuse for your actions here and now."

"I'm telling you, he's gotten away with murder before and he's getting away with it now."

Thigpen shifted his weight so he was staring at the wall across the room. He was talking to me, but not looking at me. During that brief interlude, his voice softened, and he laughed.

"Scared the crap out of you, didn't I?"

"You don't frighten me. I've had my ass kicked by guys who'd eat you for lunch."

He started chuckling, then laughing out loud. "You sure looked scared with your back up against the wall. Thought you were gonna piss your pants. You really play with Janis Joplin?"

"Yep."

"And the Allman Brothers?"

I nodded.

"Chicago, the Temptations, Jerry Lee Lewis and all those people?" he continued.

"Sure did."

"So, how'd you get in with that circle?"

"I was good at my job. Word got around."

"That a fact?"

"And I always stayed friends with the right people."

"What'd you do, launder their money? Get 'em drugs? You ain't that good a player. What else'd you have to do?" He tried to sucker me back into a non-threatening conversation.

"I took jobs nobody else wanted. Management, tax records, banking, basic business stuff, but if you guys don't back off, I'm going to be looking for another line of work."

"Hey, I'd play some of those gigs you've played. I'd play right here in The Merch if I could get girls to follow me around like a little puppy, like that little piano player from the Swamp Fox Room." He was back on the interrogation path.

"She's got nothing to do with this."

"Ouch, stepped on a toe, did I?" he smirked. "Mr. Brick Wall got a few loose mortar joints. Maybe there's more to this thing than just the money angle."

"She plays music, just like I do. That's why they call us musicians. It's a real world, taxable income-paying job. I get a W-2, same as you. It's work. That's all, I'm not obsessed with the job or the money or the women or any of the other more obvious aspects you so amply pointed out. The girl on piano at the Swamp Fox is another musician and a married one, at that."

He flipped open a pocket notebook and took a pen out of his shirt pocket. The pen bounced on the top lip as his eyes went to the ceiling and then back to his notes. One by one, he checked items on the list, adding up the facts. I could hear the waiters and busboys coming in, the back door opening and closing. It was getting close to 7:30. In another hour, the first real customers would be coming in to start partying with drinks and an early dinner.

"Out of curiosity, what does a gig like this pay?" Thigpen stretched.

"Nothing compared to what I made on the road. I get a double cut, because I take care of all the books, equipment, taxes; stuff I've always done."

"All those groupies and women that follow bands around, none of them ever got their hooks in you long enough to make you wanna settle down and get married?" The idiot had gone from a potential fistfight to discussing career moves, to marriage and children.

"Unless I was really a star, working only when I wanted to, I wouldn't saddle a woman with the burden of being married to somebody in this business. It has a way of destroying relationships. I've seen it happen too many times."

"You know, Chapman, I started at the bottom, reading meters and worked my way up. I did it being a good cop. You had it all, the attention, the money, fame and the girls. What doesn't make any sense to me is why you'd want to dump it all to come back here."

"I told you, I got tired of the road. I wanted to come home for a while."

"You sure you didn't get into some kind of trouble?" He was fishing.

"If you have a weakness, the road will find it," I said.

"Reed got something on you? Something to convince you to make the drop?'

"Yeah, he did. It's called money. He paid me a thousand dollars to drive out to Wadmalaw and buy some chickens."

"Twenty-thousand dollars for two chickens?"

Confirmation. Ice water in my veins again. He went from 'five-figures' to 'twenty-thousand dollars, and he knew how many matadors had been in the box. Did he know about Rashad? I hate to categorize people because as soon as I do, somebody proves me wrong. But I swear, the Thigpens of the world are all alike. It must be the mindset. We studied mindsets in Political Science. Miss Liddy said, "You don't see fighter pilots on submarines, do you? You don't see submariners in fighter planes, do you? You don't see welfare workers in the IRS and you won't see preachers in Charleston County police cars." Miss Liddy was way ahead of her time when it came to teaching high school. "It's all in the mindset."

Here's one for free, you can take this to the bank. When a cop questions you, they're free to lie about whatever they want, present fake evidence, anything if it will get you to talk. By pretending they care, all the Thigpens in the world, disguised as cops, think they can fool you into making some kind of Freudian slip. Trust me, they don't give a rat's ass about you. Thigpen was bullshitting while I was stumbling along, trying to figure out exactly what he knew. Familiarity breeds contempt.

"Well, I know you weren't dying to play six nights a week on East Bay Street," he said.

"Anything else you wanna know?"

"Yeah. When can you come down to the station and spend a few hours on the record."

"Any time."

"OK, I'll call you."

"No problem."

"Don't you miss the road, though?" He clipped his pen back onto the notepad and slipped it back into his shirt pocket? "I still don't understand why you would give it all up to play in a joint like this, unless there was more money or more women or more something… anything. You got to help me understand this."

"It's not all it's cracked up to be, Thigpen. It is a lot of really hard work. It takes a lot of energy and self-sacrifice. You have to stay at it night and day. Just look at how many people who were famous when we were kids, or even last year, that are gone. Show business eats people alive and only the strongest of the strong survive. You're either on your way to the top or on your way to the bottom, very little in between, except white lines and Holiday Inns. Sometimes, in order to survive, you have to do things you aren't proud of."

"Like what?"

"You're a cop – you should be able to put it together. I got tired. I'm not the first and I won't be the last." I was praying for the conversation to end.

"One more thing, why didn't you tell me you and Reed had a big blow up, the night of the murder, about you leaving The Apartment Club gig?"

He slipped the "motive" question in under the conversation like the fifth card in a blackjack game. You either win or you're busted.

"You didn't ask," I said.

"Of course, you're not guilty, so you won't say anything to make it sound like you are." He was studying me again. "The clothing showed signs of a struggle along with the evidence of the gunshots. There was blood on the ground around the car and on the front seats, which were ripped by the way, like somebody or something had clawed the upholstery." I consciously covered the back of my own right hand with my left to hide the scratches. "No use trying to cover it up, Chapman. I've already seen the scratches on the back of your hand. You wouldn't happen to know why they appear to be spaced about the same distance apart as the ones on Williams' car seats, would you?" he was closing in again.

"I told you. I don't even know how to fight. Besides, you don't see any other marks on me, do you? You don't think somebody like Bootsy Williams could engineer his own disappearance and make it look like murder? If Bill Reed didn't kill him, then maybe he got drunk and fell in some bushes. Maybe his wife caught him fooling around with his girlfriend. How should I know? I personally don't believe the guy is dead. I told you, I saw him here after the gig, early Sunday morning."

"Dressed like an alligator?"

"See, there you go, asshole, putting words in my mouth."

It was a smart aleck answer, and I shouldn't have said it like I did. But Thigpen was trying to trick me into confessing to a murder I didn't commit. He would set me up with one line of questions, then slip these unrelated questions in when he thought my guard was down. He was trying to make everything I said sound like a lie.

He reached in his coat pocket and pulled out some pictures, then shuffled through them one by one. He offered the stack to me like he was passing some envelope full of payoff money. All the time, watching how I'd react.

The first picture showed Williams' shirt covered with blood from the waist up. The next shot was from farther back, showing the whole front seat of the Buick, rips and all. Blood was everywhere and the back seat held the suit coat with three holes in it.

"Williams' jacket got scratches and rips in it, huh?' I said.

"No," Thigpen said quietly. "We think that was more an act of vandalism that happened after Williams was shot. There were no bullet holes in the seat either, so apparently he took a couple of slugs in the chest area, here... and here...." He used his pen to point to the tiny dots on the coat in the photograph. He was watching me react to the pictures. "Then, whoever shredded the jacket and shirt, took them off the body before they shredded the car seat."

It was stupid. I got up and handed the pictures back. The room was hot and muggy, and I needed some air-conditioning and something to drink. My mouth was dry, and Thigpen smelled like sweat and Old Spice. Claustrophobia was setting in on me. I put my hands on top of my horn case and looked down at the gold tenor sax lying on the soft wine velvet. That was the first time my horn and case reminded me of someone lying in a casket. Next to it, in the accessory compartment, was the little wooden cross Montague had given me. Under the cross were the folded invoices. I ran my hand over the horn and then over the velvet lining to the leather exterior of the case. Then I picked up the cross and put it in the compartment where I kept the saxophone's neckpiece. For a moment, it was like I'd never seen the cross before, like it was a mysterious object which somehow ended up in my horn case.

"And you think I did this? You really think I killed this guy?" I asked quietly.

"Stranger things have happened," Thigpen said.

"That was no blowup," I said. "That thing between Reed and me wasn't any kind of blow up. He just threw the thing about leaving The Apartment Club up in my face to get a reaction out of me, so I'd drop the bag for him." I watched the words register. "I did it for the money. Off the record, of course."

I picked up Detective Charlie Thigpen's badge and gun and started to hand them back to him. Then I hesitated and put my hand on the doorknob to the dressing room.

"By the way," I said, turning the knob, "the next time you lock a door to keep me from getting away, remember you won't be able to get away either."

"You tryin' scare me? You couldn't fight your way out of a soup bowl."

"You're right, I don't know how to fist fight. Never took the time to learn. Learned how to shoot instead, less damage to my chops. Important detail to a sax player. But you knew that. So, you think you can come waltzing into my life now and intimidate me because you think I'm a wimp, don't you? You believe that and, at the same time, you also believe I'm capable of murdering a man in cold blood, stealing thousands of dollars, shredding his clothes and his car, and dumping his body, then going on with my life, as if it was a walk on the beach. It doesn't make sense, unless…" I stopped and looked at him without finishing the sentence.

"Unless what?" He asked bluntly.

"Unless…" I decided not to say I suspected he was in on the frame.

"Unless what, Chapman," he insisted.

"Let's just say that when we were kids, I told you I don't fight. I knew then, like I know now, that fighting would injure my hands and my mouth, but Charles, son…" (Redneck idiots hate it when people younger than themselves call them 'son'), "don't think for one minute I can't take care of myself." I paused long enough to let the words sink in. "You'll notice the door you locked has been unlocked from the outside."

Thigpen looked at the latch, then back at me. I opened the door and there was Sinclair, Montague, Conroy, Dexter, Beep, Nukes, Tyrone, Maurice and Marion, each one holding a chrome microphone stand. Thigpen grabbed his jacket off the back of the chair.

"Y'all think this shit's funny, don't you? Y'all think you got one over on me, don't you? Well, I'll tell you something Mr. Smart-ass – I'm an officer of the law and…" I held up my finger and wiggled it back and forth like a schoolteacher "no, no, no no-o-o," I said. "Not when you take this off." I held up his badge, "and tell me you're off the clock. When you take this off, motherfucker, you're just another fat, mean, bully picking on us little kids."

He grabbed his gun, snatched the badge, then muscled through the seven black faces, toward the porthole door. About half way across the room, he stopped and yelled, "And you niggers ain't seen the last of me, either." When he tried to open the door it was locked.

Sinclair sat his microphone stand down and walked alone over to the door where he took out his key and started to unlock the door. Just before he turned the key, he looked at Thigpen.

"'Scuse me boss, lemme git dat doe' fo' ya'. We knows how you feels 'bout folk getting' 'en de way wheen ya'll is een de process ob beatin' de… what was it fellas?" From the back of the club all the guys yelled as one man "the ever-lovin' shit!"

"Yeah boss, dat's it, beatin' th' ever-lovin'-shit, outa folks." Sinclair smiled. The place burst into laughter.

Looking at the pictures of the crime scene took me back in time to the early days of my career. Jerry Lee Lewis played a week long gig at the Folly Beach Ocean Plaza Pier in 1964. He stayed at the Charleston Inn, on Lockwood Drive. Each night I'd sit on the steps of the Pier waiting for him to arrive in a big black

Cadillac. The Vistas opened for him and our horn section sat in with his rhythm section. Morris Tyrant, Jerry Lee's drummer, had a shoebox full of pot mailed to the post office at Folly Beach. That was my first drug experience, the day my life took an irrevocable turn. I didn't even drink when I was seventeen. I'd never heard of weed before the Summer of '64, the summer I got high.

Rockin' Jerry Lee didn't get up until noon. He'd start drinking J&B Scotch almost immediately. There were two fifths in his dressing room. He'd go through both in one night. All that business about throwing chairs, standing on the piano, playing with his feet; is all true. He did it every night not five feet from me. I didn't know where he came from, but I knew I wanted to go there. After the gig he'd get in his Cadillac, I'd get in my Mustang, he'd go his way, I'd go mine, but both cars drove down Folly Beach Road, which consisted of a two lane strip of asphalt flanked on either side by intermittent tidal creeks, junk yards and boiled peanut stands, scrawled across the belly of James Island. But the majority of the main road, especially the side roads, were as desolate as the backdrop in the crime scene pictures. No way could the kid I was back then have predicted the mess I was in. I walked to Thigpen's car to return his pictures.

"Don't forget these," I said.

"Thought you'd like to keep them as a souvenir," he said.

"A souvenir of what?"

He backed out of the parking lot and pulled out onto East Bay Street without saying anything. I walked to the edge of the street and flagged him down. He stopped and rolled his window down.

"One more thing, just out of curiosity, since we're being all up front and shit, how did you know there was twenty-thousand in the bag, and two chickens in my trunk?"

He grinned the same, stupid grin that shows up on the face of every bully asshole who realizes maybe, just maybe, this time he'd let his alligator mouth overload his hummingbird ass.

CHAPTER TWENTY-ONE

He ain't the only one," Sinclair said. "I bet one's going through yo' house while that one kept you busy."

"Going through my house? Who's going through my house?" I said.

"Th' man. Or somebody like 'em," Montague said. "Tha's how dey do, when dey's afta sum'body. And dey's afta you, boy."

I called Reynolds. He told me a plain-clothes cop, with a search warrant, showed up about an hour earlier. Which was odd given County officers never served a warrant (search or arrest) inside the city limits without a City escort. It wasn't required by law, but was considered 'etiquette/good departmental relations.' The County was free to come and go as they pleased, which only aided and abetted the level of corruption, kickbacks, payoffs, you name it. But for something like this, even a cop as crooked as Thigpen treaded lightly.

"He was here alone until a few minutes ago when the ugliest white man I've ever seen suddenly appeared, flashing his badge," Reynolds said.

"Did either of them say what they're looking for?" I could hear his shallow breathing.

"No, they are walking past my front door right now. The ugly one has a notebook, he's jotting down the things the other cop is saying."

"They're trying to bust me for something I didn't do, Reynolds! But it's going to blow up in their faces."

"Well, it certainly looks bad for the neighborhood." Reynolds hung up.

I turned to Sinclair, who had overheard the conversation.

"They won't get away with this. You wait and see."

"Ain't for me to wait an' see," he said. Then he clicked his teeth and sighed as if he had caught a kid stealing cookies. "Mr. Roy'll be the one waitin' to see. He's who yo' answer to."

Sinclair would pass judgment on me for the slightest indiscretion, taking the tone of a condescending baby-sitter with his righteous indignation. His pompous gaze reminded me of the "just you wait 'till your father gets home" look. He had to know this was about my being involved with Bootsy Williams' disappearance.

"Some other boy was pokin' his nose 'round here 'bout noontime," he sighed.

"And?"

"I don't know who he is. Freddie and him was yackety yackin' 'bout some shit while he was lookin' around yo' e-quip-mint en snoopin' 'round the back of your dressin' room. I told 'em wasn't nuttin' back dey belong to him."

"What did he look like?" I said.

"Like all o' ya'll," he tisked, "too white and ghostly looking, black hair, needin' a bath. He ain't said nothing about who he was. But he's been in here before."

"God Almighty Sinclair, was it the same guy who was here last Friday, when I came in to talk to Freddie?"

"I think so, look like him anyway, had his hair different, and not so junk-a-fied."

I was pissed at Sinclair for taking so long to tell me this. I bolted out the door and caught a cab to my apartment. About five minutes later, the cab dropped me off, but Thigpen and the other cop were already gone. That was all I needed, the cops snooping around in front of the neighbors' watchful eyes. God, the neighbors this and the neighbors that. They all thought I was a drug dealer anyway, so this would definitely confirm it for them.

The apartment had been carefully searched rather than ransacked. Nothing was torn up or scattered all over the rooms, but I could tell they left nothing to chance. Each of my record albums had been opened. I was afraid they'd scratched the vinyl, but it appeared that they just left their fingerprints on the edge of each record. They were checking the inside covers. My kitchen sink, cabinets, closet, everything had been searched and the only mess they left was in the bathroom. After going through the medicine cabinet, none of that stuff was put back.

A couple things did bother me, though. One was the shoeprints on my bed. I couldn't imagine why, until I looked up at the ceiling. The cops had checked inside the light.

The other thing I saw really made me sick. One of them had taken my soprano sax, put the mouthpiece on it upside down and tried to play it. I could tell because the reed was still wet with the guy's spit. It grossed me out to think of Thigpen playing around with my horn. Then I remembered Reynolds said he never went upstairs. I immediately wondered what he was doing during the time he got there and the time he walked past the front door. The searcher had also gone into the back of my old Zenith. This impersonal assault on my belongings made me more vindictive than ever. But for the time being I'd settle for finding out who was putting on the frame.

While checking my belongings, I started wondering exactly how many people were involved in this nightmare. I decided to start an investigation of my own. The St. James' phone number was disconnected, and Erlene Brown's phone number was unlisted. So, I decided to go see her in person.

On the way across town I noticed a dirty, white, Chevy van following me. The shadow shit was getting old. My best option was to stay out in the open, in broad daylight, where everybody could see me.

A dark cloud of people, mostly women and children, of various ages, fifteen to twenty deep, was hanging around the front of the St. James Hotel, swatting flies and fanning themselves with various parlor fans when I pulled up in the T-Bird. They were listening to an AM radio station blaring gospel music from inside the lobby. All eyes were on me when I stepped out onto the sidewalk.

The van I'd been watching in the rear view mirror pulled over to the curb about half a block away. I had to walk through the group milling about in the street. They were listening to the same gospel program on various transistor portables.

The tiny foyer of the St. James was even dingier in the daylight. Erlene Brown was lounging in the split-pea green, cracked, peeling Naugahyde Lazy Boy recliner, previously occupied by the fish man. She pulled a nylon stocking over her head and wore the same dirty, flower print dress she'd had on the last time I saw her. With its broken leg lift, busted recliner handle and torn upholstery, the chair looked like a great candidate for the dump. Erlene was glued to her own portable radio listening intently to the gospel program, constantly adjusting the volume so the people outside could hear. Like the fish man's Magnavox, the radio had its own set of foil flags set at full sail. Erlene had a Bible in her lap with a small note pad and pencil. With one hand she stuffed popcorn in her mouth; with the other she wielded a green fly flap.

Something resembling petrified food taken from the bowl found in King Tut's tomb was heaped in an aluminum pie pan sitting on top of the TV. Two at a time, the flies fell when the green swatter lashed out. The pie pan was obviously a trap, and the flies, of course, were idiots.

The song on the radio was a straight gospel jam with everybody who could yell praising Jesus, shouting "Amen!" and "Hallelujah!" I stepped up to the counter under the watchful gaze of everybody standing in the doorway.

"Well, well, if it ain't Snow White's little brother, Lily." Erlene didn't look up except to smack a single fly checking out a grease streak on the blank TV screen, its crushed body quickly joining the carnage of its brothers on the floor.

"Well, if it ain't Pat Boone's big sister, Ba," I returned.

Trying to appear angry, I leaned forward on the counter, looking down on her, with my white-knuckled fists on the counter top. Dumb move. A fly landed on my knuckle and, faster than a snake strike, she nailed it with the outside tip of the flap. It stung like the pop of a wet, rolled-up dishtowel. Startled by the sudden flash of green plastic and the sting, I jumped backwards, right hand grabbing left, my palm smeared with fly parts and fly blood, stumbled over the coffee table and fell flat on my butt, in front of the entire entourage. A wave of snickering floated through the crowd by the door as Erlene leaned over the counter, supporting herself on her knuckles and stared at me like a crazy woman looking into her first camera lens.

The whites of her eyes were jaundiced and blood shot. Her lip curled and bunched up under her nose. For a split second, I imagined her fly swatter as a spear. All she needed was a bone in her nose, a couple of disks in her lips, a shrunken-head necklace and she could've passed for a clap-bill Ubangi. I picked myself up right about the time the preacher on the gospel station said that Rev. Gary W. Edwards would now lead us in today's consideration of God's Word. With this announcement, all talking and snickering ceased immediately. The only sound in the room besides the radio was the passing traffic.

I guess it was just a coincidence that Sly and the Family Stone's "Dance to the Music" was playing on somebody's transistor down the street. But as soon as the "boom-jacka-lacka-lacka" part came up, the radio suddenly went silent.

"Where is Rashad?" I asked as I got up off the floor.

"Shush, Bowyee," she said, taking up her note pad and pencil. "Brother Edward gonna give today's text." A second later Gary's father, came on the radio.

"Brothers and sisters," he said, a great dignity rising in his voice, "Today's message is taken from the 23rd Psalm verses 6 & 7, where it says, speaking of the humble man, 'Only goodness and mercy shall follow me all the days of my life.'"

With those words, everybody listening to the radio, pulled out scratch paper and jotted down the verse. Except Erlene, who simply wrote the number 7 in her notebook.

"And in the face of such admonition, we all must ask, 'Why Do The Heathen Rage?' For this reason," Rev. Edwards continued. "As it says in the book of Ecclesiastes, Chapter 8, verses 17 and 18, 'though a wise man thinks and yes, even claims to know, yet he will not be able to find out.'" Again Erlene only wrote down the number 18. "And why? Why, brothers and sisters? Why do the heathen rage? It is because, as James points out in Chapter 1 of the book bearing his name, the man wise in his own eyes cannot see that he is unclean and defiled in the eyes of The Lord. We must take care of widows and orphans and remain unblemished as verses 26-28 makes clear. The raging heathen know not the Lord, but their lust and iniquity, Amen?"

As soon as Erlene, along with everyone else within earshot of the radio, wrote down the number 28, a shriek went up from some woman outside the door and sigh from everyone else. Almost immediately after the last scripture was quoted the crowd around the door disbanded, leaving me alone with Erlene and her fly swatter. She turned off the radio and turned on the TV.

"What was that all about?" I said.

"What da hell's it to ya?" she snapped, working her lips over the question like a fresh bamboo shoot.

She reached under the counter and pulled out a label-less soup can, spit snuff juice in it, then pulled back from the counter and sat back down in the Lazy-Boy. In the light of day, Erlene Brown was just another crook working some scam in the dark side of Charleston's underground economy. The voodoo act was a front, the old Mojo Woman routine was getting old.

"I need some answers, Erlene," I said.

"Das Miss Brown to yo, bwoyee, you mus' be fool idn't it? Comin' in yeah ackin' like you one ah we people. Who you t'ink you is, enyway?"

"I'm the guy somebody is trying to frame," I said.

"Now, who'd go to all dat trouble? When yo' be so easy to kill outright."

I took a napkin out of my pocket and wiped off my hands then laid the napkin on the counter. Through the front door I could see a cop questioning people down the street.

"Either somebody took Bootsy out, or somebody is trying to make it look that way," I said. "Either way, the arrows are pointing to me. So, could we drop the Geechee bullshit and have a serious conversation, I'm in trouble here. I need to find Rashad. He's the only person who knows where I was when Williams supposedly disappeared. Which he didn't, by the way, because I saw him the next night."

She ignored the last part. "Could'ah bun you, could'ah bun him, could'ah bun enybody." Two more flies got flattened, one on top of the TV set, then another on the useless telephone.

"I dropped that bag as a favor to Bill Reed," I said. "Rashad was with me the whole time. Now the cops think I killed Bootsy Williams, dumped the body and took the money. They're just waiting for enough evidence to arrest me."

"You ain't too cool, is you, bwoyee?" She said this in almost a whisper because she was stalking a fly that had wandered out onto the foil flag antenna of the TV. The flick was light and lethal, and the TV flag never fluttered.

"Listen lady," I leaned forward again, "somebody, somebody you know, is trying to make me look like a murderer. I dropped one bag to the guy, and your son was with me."

"So, why you here talking to me, 'stead o' yo' jive ass honky frien' Reed? He de one got yo' into dis'. He de one should be gittin' yo' out." She refused to let go of the accent.

"Just tell me where I can find Rashad. He and I were together, he knows I didn't do it."

She started fussing and cussing and shuffling around behind the counter. First, she put one hand on one hip, then the other on the other hip. Then she started the talking in tongues bullshit, slapping the fly flap on the counter even where no flies landed.

"You white boys all bun de same. Mens like Reed bun cheatin' me and mine fo' two hundred years and when de haag get on yo', yo' come a crawlin' back to da' mama fo' ta heal ya'. Each and ebery damn one."

"Miss Brown, please, you know Rashad was with me the night Bootsy Williams disappeared. I need to find him so he can tell that to the police."

"Rashad? He ain't talkin' to da po'leece, boy?" Both hands were on her hips now and her eyes gone to heaven. "Bwoyee, now I know yo' head bun feek-ee." There was a Geechee word I'd never heard. "Wha' make yo t'ink the po'leece gone believe anythin' that Rasta boy gone say? He ain't sayin' not nothin' to no po'leece."

"So, you would rather see me go to jail for murder than help me?"

Erlene reached up under the counter and pulled out a little leather pouch pulled together with a drawstring. She opened the pouch, pinched off a piece of something and stuck it in her cheek. "Ain't nothin' for free. You gotta scratch my back, if'n you wan' me to scratch yo own."

"What do you mean?" I said.

"I need a little heppin' hand in yo' honky, white man world. You'll do me a favor or two. Can yo' git behind dat?" She worked her finger back over her gums.

"The numbers gig doesn't have anything to do with this, does it?" I said.

"Like hell it don't! I' yo think I'm gon' hep yo' out de kindness o' my black heart, yo' crazier than a flea climin' up a elephant's ass wid rape on he min'. Wid out me yo' jus' another white jive-ass honky caught in yo' own white net o' lies. Wid me an' my peoples heppin' yo' an' yo' heppin' us, we can all make de money an' life'll be sweet as cane sugah. But y'all ain't getting' nuttin' fa' nuttin'. Now y'all got to decide which Massa yo' gone serve. Can't serve two, cause one gone stan and one gon' fall an' you gon' fall wid 'em or stan' wid 'em. Y'all got to learn from the dirt dauber an' de honey bee. Either yo' got hive full of honey or y'all got nothin' but mud hut full o' dead spider. You mess wid de wrong ting and boy, Scrong Man will be eatin' you alive."

"You don't scare me," I said. "I grew up on Johns Island with people like you. One of my best friends was raised by a woman who was a real root doctor. I'm not afraid of that Hoodoo bullshit. You'll have to find a bigger fool than me to buy into that line of crap."

"You keep on, tryin' to do it yo' way," she continued sarcastically. "You'll be beggin' me fo' intercessory prayer on yo' behalf fo' you done goin' through dis fire. You'll be creepin' and crawlin' jest to get my back door, pleadin' fer me to stan in de gap fo' ya."

She swatted another fly on top of the TV, reached for the snuff can and took another pinch out of the bag. "You do dis one las drop now an' I'll git y'all out dis trouble. 'Sides, it'll hep make up fo' dis one you messed up."

"Who messed up? I wasn't the one packing a gun on the drop; that's your boy. Rashad was carrying all the heat."

"Rashad ain't shot nobody, you de one needin' his hep, heah, not de udda way 'roun'."

"Last time I did anyone a favor, I got into the trouble I'm in right now. I've had nothing but trouble from you since the day I met you."

"Still, you the one they want, not me," she said.

She spit into the soup can and wiped her mouth, then in perfect accent-free English said, "I'll speak to Rashad when I see him. I don't know whether one of you killed Bootsy or not. Fact is I'm tired of Bill Reed's mouth. He asked me to help him with this one last drop. Then he was supposed to keep his nose out of my business." She spit and swatted another fly.

"You're crazy, aren't you?" I turned from the counter and started for the door. When I reached the stoop and was about to go out, she shook her head and glared at me with the same crazy look she had the night of Bootsy's murder.

"You honkys're all alike," she said.

"What?"

"White jive-asses, y'all all alike."

I shook my head. "You don't know me from Adam. You, of all people, passing judgment on me because of the color of my skin." She shot me the bird with no more thought than she'd give swatting a fly.

"I'm not like Bill Reed," I said.

"Mo' so den not. Ain't nothin' fo' yo' boys to shoot a nigga that' getting' too big fo' 'is britches. Been goin' on fo' t'ree hunnah year 'o mo'. No needin' stoppin' it now."

"I didn't kill Bootsy Williams."

"Humph," She grunted and shrugged her skin and bone shoulders. She was looking at me straight on, while tracking a fly by the edge of the pie pan. "If y'all say so." Then smacked the fly without taking her eyes off mine.

Believing dumb things has always come naturally to me. But without a doubt, the dumbest thing I ever believed was being a musician would, in some way, make me immune to the uglier, seedier side of life. Somewhere along the line

I got the insane idea, that if I became an artist I'd somehow rise above it all. Truth is, there's a seedy side to every business, and the Bootsys, Erlenes and Bill Reeds were everywhere, alligators waiting below the smooth surface of every pond, for idiots like me to wander too close to the edge.

Talking to Erlene Brown forced me back to confronting the ugly truth I'd ignored. She'd treated me as if I was as two-faced as any racist Klansman. Whether I was guilty or not didn't make any more difference to her than the flies she popped. I was seeing Charleston through a completely new set of eyes. Whatever myth I'd fooled myself into believing, that I was somehow above these people or the music business simply because I considered myself a working artist, was just that: A Myth.

For the first time I saw the truth clearly. I was no different from the people I'd been dealing with. For me to come to that realization was one thing. But going beyond it, knowing everyone else knew I was just another has-been version of himself, who hadn't figured it out yet, was an eye opener. Since I couldn't beat Erlene, I decided to join her.

"OK," I said. "You have a deal; I'll help you, if you'll help me. Just tell me what you want me to do and I'll do it. If…"

"If, what?" she said, suddenly swiveling in the chair, glaring at me with a wicked grin on her face.

"I want to know what's going on and who's behind it?"

"Das my precious little thin-lip white bowyee," she said, rubbing her hands together. "Now we gittin' somewhere. Sit yo' skinny white ass down ri'chia', son." She pulled out a folding chair and patted the seat, "Yes'sa, I do b'lieve chile, dat you got some edju-cation coming." Then she picked up her Bible and handed it to me. "Look up the 23rd Psalm," she said. "Read verses 6 and 7."

I hadn't opened a Bible since I was in Sunday School at the Ashley River Baptist Church, in what seemed like a hundred years ago. The book of Psalms was in the old testament next to Proverbs, I remembered that much. When I found the scripture, I read it to myself and thought I'd missed something.

I read it again. There was no 7th verse.

"There's no 7th verse in the 23rd Psalm," I said.

"Exactly," she said, as she smiled and spit in her snuff can. "Now go on back to ol' Montague and tell him where you been and what you learned and who you learned it from.

CHAPTER TWENTY-TWO

Montague was stacking highball glasses on a shelf. Whatever I was doing wasn't working. The net was tightening, the frame was squaring up. Too much had changed, since I'd left Charleston for the road, and nothing I'd learned either touring or since I got back prepared me for a life sequestered in the midnight port city fishbowl. He didn't look up when I walked to the bar.

"You got a minute, I need your advice," I said.

"Been tryin' to give you ad'wice for some time now." He was still refusing to look at me.

"You know what's going on, don't you?"

"Ain't much I don't know, been tryin' to tell you but yo' head is hard."

"I'm sorry."

"Been tryin' to tell you Scrong Man is watchin' you, but you jes' keeps on ackin' fool."

"You're right, you're absolutely right. I'm apologizing now. I'm ready to listen."

"Fust, you tell me how you got them scratches on your hand."

"I thought you knew everything."

"See, dere you go again, bein' a smart ass."

"I just figured you knew the whole story."

"Ain't heard it from yo' side."

I laid the whole story out in as much detail as I could. Everything from Freddie telling me to "check out the girl at The Apartment Club," the St. James, Erlene, Rashad, Bootsy, all the way back to when he showed up at my apartment to tell me Thigpen was looking for me.

"I left the St. James about ten minutes ago because she sent me back to you. What's a Bridge?" I said, "That night Erlene kept calling me a Bridge."

"We'll get to dat in a minute. Tell me what'cha said to the law?"

"Everything I knew, even about Williams showing up after the gig Saturday night."

Montague spun around. "You didn't tell me nothin' about Boots bein' here, on my property."

"Your property?" I said.

"I works here. This's my job site. I gots dominion ov'r this space. Dey all know dat. He got no bidness bein' here." Montague took a few moments to absorb this piece of news. "Dis change eberyt'ing, and not fo' de good."

"There were moments," I said, "during all these conversations, when they didn't speak with a Gullah accent. Did I imagine that?"

He stared directly into my eyes until the tension reached the level of two people about to argue. The experience was so strange. He appeared to grow larger, not expand like a balloon blowing up. Rather, he seemed to become a larger version of himself. I blinked, shook my head and when I looked back at him, he was back to normal. "I tell you, Montague, whatever drug Erlene clawed into my skin has messed me up. I'm seeing things, hearing things. Sometimes I feel great, then I feel sick, my imagination is running wild, Montague, and I can't control it."

"You wearin' the cross I gave yo'?"

"It's in my horn case."

"I tol' you it would protek you but yo head too hard to listen to old Montague. What make you think I got anything ta 'say can hep you?"

"Erlene sent me back to you. I'm not asking you to do anything. I'm asking you to help me understand what's going on. How did I get caught in the middle? Knowledge is power, right?"

"Knowin' how a thing is different from its appearance, yeah, thas one thing and a good one to know. But knowin' what it's gonna do next, and bein' right, thas somethin' else entirely."

"What's that supposed to mean?"

"Don' mean nothin' except whatever meanin' you give it. But if you know what a thing is fo' true, you can predict what he's gonna do."

"I think I'm losing my mind. I think Erlene poisoned me."

"She ain't poisoned you, boy, she jus' opened you up too early."

"Explain that." I crossed my arms.

"Two rivers flow 'round Babylon," he said. "The Tigris an' de Euphrates. An' two rivers flow 'round Charleston, the Ashley and the Cooper."

"OK."

"Now these rivers symbolize the trickling flow of wealth to the parched and dry regions, which is us, black folks and poor white trash like you." I didn't flinch. "You had dat one comin', you know dat." He winked at me. "Now one river is white and one river is black, but both flow through the heart of Charleston at night." He leaned in over the bar, "You followin' me, boy?"

"Yes," I said. "There's a black river and a white river flowing through the city at night. The rivers symbolize money. The black and white are the people involved in the money flow."

"Ezackly," he said. "You remember the scriptures you took to the bosom of Abraham?"

"You mean that Star of David paper she put in my hand before she clawed the shit out me with that chicken foot?"

"She had to seal you boy, Scrong Man always seal His servant, even if the servant is unwillin'." He watched my reaction, then continued. "The s'triptures you carried to the Farmer are the same one's Rev. Edward quoted today on his Gospel hour. Here, look 'em up." He pulled a King James Bible from under the bar.

I grabbed the Bible and looked up Ecclesiastes 8:17-18. There was no verse 18. In the book of James 1:26-28 there was no 27 or 28. I looked up from the Bible into a notebook Montague was holding in front of my face. There were the numbers 7, 18, 27, 28.

"Yes, I know about the numbers. Erlene showed me."

"You remember that gal you heard hollerin' down the street when everybody else was sighing?" I nodded. Montague pointed the notebook like a wand. "Well, these here numbers are the ones she picked last week, so tonight she's going to receive one thousand dollars in cash."

"They're running an illegal lottery," I said. "Not only illegal, but rigged."

"Ezackly."

According to Montague, the blacks in Charleston have always had a method for dealing with the tyranny of white oppression. From the time the first slaves were brought up from Barbados, a code of honor based on silence has been passed down from generation to generation, in the black families of the Lowcountry. From the time of the Underground Railroad until the present day, there have been two economies, two sets of books, two sets of values and a fully-functioning double standard in place to maintain the status quo. As times and people changed, so did the nature of business after dark. This wasn't all news to me. I knew people gambled, I knew some of the prostitutes, the joke which passed for liquor laws. Since I'd gone on the road, I'd never been involved in any of this stuff.

"But where does the money come from?" I said. "How do these people afford to bet on the numbers when they're so poor?"

"They got jobs," he said. "Look right over there to the Medical University Hospital. How many black folks you think work in that one place or Roper Hospital next door or the St. Francis or The VA or the Navy Hospital or Baker? Thousands, son. There's tens of thousands of black people workin' every day in this city that'll gladly put up a dollar a week to buy a little hope. You saw what happened last summer? When they went on strike? A lot of people nobody knows about, died behind that strike."

I didn't say anything about the two dead soldiers found in the gas station restroom.

"You know exactly what I'm talkin' 'bout. Don't you, boy?"

"No, I don't."

"You axed me how you got caught up in this mess. I'm tellin' you now."

"I'm not following you."

"Oh, you's followin' me just fine. Don't try pretendin' you ain't. You can't fool me, boy. Ol' Montague knows most everything. 'Bout most everybody. I know you hep'ed catch them men what killed our solider boys."

"Who else knows?"

"Nobody, less you tell 'em."

"How did you find out?"

"You didn't get kicked outa yo' band for no reason."

"Oh, I know how that came about."

"You didn't lose yo' job, son. You got called home."

"Yeah, right." There was no way Montague could've known what went down in Columbia unless he'd been involved in it somehow. The only link I could fathom was the connection between the two dead soldiers with family involved in the hospital strike. I'd suspected for years that money was running up and down the road between Charleston and Columbia, but I thought it was all liquor and gambling protection payoffs. This was the first clue I'd run across indicating and confirming the whole state was in on the con.

"How much money are we talking about here?" I said.

"I can't tell you, but I'll tell you this," he said, "it's nothin' compared to the white river."

"What about the white river?" I said.

"Ah yes, the white river." He got up and walked to the empty front door of The Merch.

"Look up the Ashley to the harbor," he pointed toward the city marina. "Then go around the Battery up the Cooper River to Bushy Park."

"That's where the Navy Base and the Weapons Station are located," I said.

"Ezackly."

"You mean the white river flows from the Navy Base?" I said.

Montague nodded and walked back inside. "Those big ships and sub'arines and bull'din's and houses constantly need fixin' and the parts to fix 'em got to come from somewhere." He reached behind the counter and took out a regular

Phillips head screwdriver and a sheet metal screw, laying them side-by-side. "How much yo' think deas're worth?"

"I don't know," I said, picking up the screwdriver, "probably a dollar or so."

"How about this?" He held the sheet metal screw like a diamond.

"A penny?" I shrugged.

"Try $90 for the strew'drivah and $10 for the strew."

"But that's insane, I'd never pay that much," I said.

"Of course you wouldn't," Montague explained, his English improving with every sentence, "not shopping in a hardware store, and certainly not to hang a picture in your livin' room. But have you ever heard of a 'CHIT'?"

"No."

"A CHIT is an old sailing term for something like a Navy purchase order. Say you're a by-the-hour civil service employee working 9 to 5 in the supply depot and the chief supply officer shoots a requisition CHIT across your desk for a piece o' equip 'mint or a part. The order has a part number, so you don't know if it's a hun'red boxes of screws for a galley counter top or a seal for the re'actor on a nu'clear sub'arine. All you see is the requisition order number, the part number, and number of units. If de CHIT is stamped URGENT, NATIONAL SECURITY, then you don't question anything about the order, you jus' handle the paperwork. You understand?"

"What if it's not marked 'National Security'?" I said.

"Then, they have to take bids."

"And if it is?"

"The supply clerk can send it to anyone on the list, and the Navy pays whatever comes back on the invoice. No questions. It's all done by a computer. Even if you could buy the same box of screws down at the local hardware store for $1, the Navy's price is $1000."

"You're telling me somebody could put in an order for a thousand dollar box of screws that would only cost one dollar in the store and nobody would question it?"

"Hundred dollar hammers get ordered all the time," he said.

"And the Navy just cuts a check? How does this help the person with the National Security stamp?" I said.

"The order goes to a vendor 'outside the fence,' like a phony construction company, owned by a friend of his. The company normally has two sets of books. When the invoices go to the Navy, the onlyist thing the clerk sees is a CHIT number and an amount. He ain't allowed to question the order because it's stamped National Security. If de CHIT number and de invoice number match, the computer spits out the check. You with me?" I nodded. "Check goes in the bank under a separate account number, company owner waits ninety days, writes hisself a check from the account, cashes it and meets up with the commander or his representative at a public place where cash can change hands without anyone noticing. Am I making myself clear?"

"You mean, like a nightclub with an illegal gambling game already set up?"

"Ezackly."

"Wouldn't the person running the game have to be in on it?"

"No, sir, especially not the operator, or the owner, why risk adding more cuts to the pie?"

I sat back in astonished disbelief, a million images running through my mind. I saw Mark Ward at the Officer's Club, all teeth and smiling at me like a wolf. I saw Bill Reed, at The Apartment Club, transferring numbers from invoices like the ones I picked up by the dumpster and Freddie May, at The Merchant Seaman's Club, copying numbers off a sheet of notebook paper exactly like the one Reed used. Bootsy Williams' gold tooth glowing in the match light as I handed him a satchel filled with new bank wrapped hundred dollar bills. Thigpen cross-examining me in his squad car, all the time knowing how much money was in the bank bag. I saw Montague handing me the little wooden cross. There was Kela's face, all black and blue, and Roy Vincent sitting behind his desk coughing after downing a shot of Scotch.

Then suddenly, off in the distance of my mind's eye, I saw a dark gray funnel cloud with huge eyes watching me off Battery Point, swirling, churning, and moving on shore. All these images were somehow related, I knew, but I couldn't figure out how I figured in.

"You have a vision?" Montague said.

"What?"

"You look lost in thought," he said. "You had to 'spect somethin' like this was going on."

"Who all is involved?"

"Boy, your ignorance is amazing. I haven't told you anything half the people in this city don't know. This is a generational thing that's been going on since the first slaves brought Python up from Barbados. Strong Man has controlled this city since Charleston first had permanent residents. Only the players' names change. What you don't know is, the players are handpicked."

"Wait, wait, wait, who is this Python and who is Strong Man?"

Montague slid the Bible back and opened it to the tenth chapter of Daniel.

"Read the thirteenth verse," he said.

"But the prince of the kingdom of Persia withstood me one and twenty days: but, lo, Michael, one of the chief princes, came to help me; and I remained there with the kings of Persia."

"Stop right there." Montague said. "Who's this prince of Persia, who withstood him twenty-one days?"

"I have no idea," I said.

"The prince of Persia is a fallen angel. Persia is his geographical domain. Keep reading."

I didn't read the passages aloud, but struggled through the Shakespearean thee's, thou's, thine, thy and knowest from whence's silently. After I read verse twenty, "Then said he, Knowest thou wherefore I come unto thee? And now will I return to fight with the prince of Persia: and when I am gone forth, lo, the prince of Grecia shall come." Montague stopped me.

"Right there," he said, "who came to fight dat prince o' Persia? Huh . . . huh? An' who's the prince o' Greece?"

"Montague' I love you brother," I said. "But I still don't see what this has to do with finding out who is trying to frame me? And why?"

Montague grabbed me by both shoulders, put his face within inches of mine, his eyes piercing my own. I heard his voice in my mind, but without the Gullah accent. "Python was the name of the African god the slaves brought with them to Barbados. Over the centuries the name changed along with the location of the slaves. Strong Man is the name their descendants call him now. Charleston is his dominion. Strong Man is a fallen angel who watches over the city."

I thought right back at him. "This is the same story you told me when I started working here years ago, before I ever went on the road. I thought it was an old folk legend. I even told Thigpen something similar, because I thought it would be fun to see his reaction."

"You were a mere boy then," said Montague telepathically. "You're still too young, but now you've been pushed into the truth. There is a vile cancer in Charleston. Strong Man needs you, so He called you in from the road, that we might rid ourselves of it."

"God almighty, man, how did I get myself into this shit?" I put my head in my hands, running my palms over my face. "And I'm supposed to suddenly believe all this is real, that there's a demon ruling all the crooks in Charleston? And he's somehow singled me out to be the fall guy for one of his cohorts who got whacked for getting greedy?"

"One man's demon is another man's God."

"How do you know which is which?"

"Strong Man is neither god nor demon. He is truly a fallen angel."

I shook my head, forced my mouth open, and dragged my fingers down my face. "What's the difference?"

"Demons only desire is getting what they want. They're the spiritual equivalent of what humans know as psychopaths. A fallen angel honors his commitments."

I started laughing. "None of this makes any difference to me. I'm just the poor fool who stumbled into this Hoodoo drama. Gods, and Angels, and

Demons, oh, my! I'm losing my fucking mind and it's hilarious. Where does it all go from here? What is my next stop, Montague? Oh, I know … Hell! My next stop is Hell!!"

Montague didn't bat an eye, he simply watched and waited for me to crash. Then he poured a whiskey on the rocks. "You done?"

"Yeah, I'm done." I threw back the glass. "Who's trying to frame me, Montague?"

"You can't guess? After what I just told you?"

"Bill Reed?" I said, and he smiled.

"But why me?"

"Why not you? Somebody has to take the fall for what he's done."

"Who else's in on it? I wanna know who's out to get me. Reed ain't doin' it by himself." I felt like I was so close, yet so far away from what I needed to know.

"You right 'bout that. He can't do it by hisself and he ain't. But's ain't my place to say who all the players are. For 'dat yo' needs to see th' Landlord."

"So we're back to Gullah now?"

"Because we back here on the ground, back to our human selves. Talk to the Landlord."

There it was again, that title, The Landlord. I knew The Preacher was Gary's father. The Farmer was Bootsy Williams. But who was The Landlord, and who was The Night Mayor?

"This is more confusing than tripping on Erlene's bad acid," I said.

"And rightly so," he said. "The Devil be's the author of confusion, stands reasonable, if you gets in bed with the devil, you bound to be confuse'."

"But Strong Man isn't the Devil. Right?"

"Right. But the Devil's got his people workin' in the City. Tryin' to take over, so's a real demon can move in and take over Charleston."

"So, why do you speak with a Gullah accent most of the time, then switch to perfect English, for no apparent reason?"

"Because first of all, I'm a Bridge, like you. Second, I'm black. Third, I'm smart, but most of all, I'm a Seventh Son Charlestonian. Seven generations of seventh sons born to seventh sons, which means I'll talk any damn way I feel like talking. Seriez-vous plutôt je parle français?"

"Why do I understand what you said? I don't speak French."

"Bridges connect. The Cooper River Bridge connects downtown Charleston to Mt. Pleasant. They're suspended over obstructions like rivers, and railroads, and valleys. They're shortcuts to the truth, they rise above the natural. You are a Bridge. You have the ability to connect with any living creature, man or beast, plant or animal, at its highest level of communication."

"Does that include a demon?" I said.

"I don't know, but it definitely includes a fallen angel."

"And this all happened because Erlene scratched some magic potion into my hand, with a fucking chicken foot?" I said.

"No, she was wrong to do that, she pushed ahead. She opened your mind too early, like picking fruit before it is ripe, then waiting for it to ripen on its own. Sometimes fruit picked too early goes bad. Same with a Bridge."

"You know, I find this almost impossible to believe."

"You ever heard the old saying, 'Just cause you believe it don't make it so?'"

"Yeah."

"The reverse is also true. Not believing don't make it not so."

"What now?"

"You need to go back to the St. James. Clear the air between you and Sister Erlene. She's waiting for you."

"How do you know?"

"She said so."

"When?"

"Just now."

"Come on boy," I heard Erlene Brown's voice in my mind. "Come on back to Sister E, and let's get you straightened up, so you can fly right."

Montague nodded toward the door. "You got some edgy-cation coming."

Erlene greeted me like a sister would a brother or a mother would a son.

"You feelin' better now, after talking with old Montague?"

"Not really. To be honest, right now I'm running on shear curiosity."

"Sounds like a song title."

"It is, I wrote it, I'll sing it to you someday."

"Before we go into the real deal about your current situation, I need you to make one more drop. It's simple, in fact, maybe too simple. But it will be a good test to see if you're on the right path," she said. "All you have to do is deliver the two matador game roosters to Rashad at Mosquito Beach. In return, Sista E'll show you all true things, including the people framing you."

I took the squawking box outside and put it in the trunk. I remember thinking 'you guys need to settle down' and the noise from the box suddenly stopped. From where I was standing, I could see the smokestack of a tug boat coming toward the bridge so I waited just long enough to make it across before the gate went down. On the other side, I looped through the parking lot of the round Holiday Inn, so I could double back, then get back on Savannah Highway, before cutting across to Folly Road. The white van following me got caught by the drawbridge before it could cross the Ashley River Bridge. By the time the tugboats and barges had passed the bridge, I was over the Wappoo Cut, heading for Mosquito Beach.

A black '68 Electra 225 was parked next to Rashad's Coupe De Ville. Since this was a Monday, I figured the fish shack would be empty, but I decided to go on in, anyway. I knocked on the door and looked around at the litter of beer cans and wine bottles floating in the marsh grass. I couldn't believe I had to do this. A slim black man, who needed only a loincloth and a spear to fit right onto the cover of National Geographic, cracked the door and looked at me with his yellow and brown eyes. I'd always been comfortable with the black musicians and the guys who worked around the clubs, but like a dog sensing fear, I understood immediately this guy did not like my white skin.

"Wha' chu won't?" He squinted at me.

"Whose car is this?" I said. His head lifted up so he could look over the top of mine as he looked out the door. In the background, I heard WPAL then the crack of pool balls. Rashad was singing along with the radio. The gospel hour was winding up again and the hallelujahs were coming in fast and furious.

"Who at de doe, Tyrone?" Rashad's boots clicked against the hard wood planks as he walked toward the door. Tyrone pulled back and was instantly replaced by the Rasta man. In the daylight, his face was pockmarked, his hair natty, with stains on his shirt and pants. His black sunglasses reflecting the bridge and marsh grass made him look more like a machine than a man.

"What's the word, hummin'bird?" he said. "I hear you're lookin' for me."

"You've got to help me, Rashad."

"I don't have to do nothin', but die."

"You're my only chance…" I put my hand on the door, but he didn't back up or offer to let me in. "The cops already been here. Nice surprise seein' 'em here, droppin' yo' name. The boys here don't cotton to the pig stickin' his nose in our bidness, 'specially don't like it when a white boy put 'em on us."

"That's ridiculous," I said.

"Hey, the man said you told him I was wit' you. Now, why you wanna say a thing like that?"

"You were with me. You were with me until five in the morning. You, me and a trunk full of chickens. Which I am supposed to deliver to you here, I might add. But I never said anything about you to the cops."

"You can't prove I was with you, my man, besides I don't need no cops snoopin' in my bidness. None 'o us need dat right now. Right fellas?" They all nodded, growl grumbling like junk yard dogs before they attack.

When Rashad finally opened the door, I saw four other black men, all African looking, standing around with pool cues in their hands, looking at me like I was crazy. They were all taller than Rashad with various trinkets hanging around their necks and beads in their hair. The body language was obvious: "Get lost whitey, while you still can."

"What's he doin' here?" The tallest one said.

He took a drag off his cigarette, blew smoke out of his mouth and sucked it up his nose.

"Fellas, this here is Josie Chapman, the cracker boy who told the cops I was with him the night Bootsy disappeared." They laid their pool cues on the table and started walking toward me.

"That the honky with the horn? Hey, ain't he one blows in that all-white club where the only niggahs they let in are the table bussin' Toms to bus the tables them white folks eats at? Get him a rag, Rashad; let's see him wipe down the tables here in the Snake Pit. We'll show him how we niggah's like to have our tables cleaned."

"Now Lenny, he didn't come here to start trouble," Rashad said.

"Move over Rashad." Lenny grabbed a bar towel and a beer bottle and started walking toward me. "I was with Rashad that night," he said.

"And I'm a midget jet pilot," I answered.

"What? You don't believe me, boy?" Lenny's nostrils flared when he stopped right behind Rashad. "Because, if you was with Rashad, then how come he was here with us that night?" Lenny's face was as badly pocked as Rashad's; he had a scar running from his ear to the corner of his mouth. For some reason, possibly my natural instinct for suicidal tendency, I was no longer afraid of them. In fact, Lenny was the one getting nervous. I suspected these guys were the mules involved in the number's operation that had been milking the black community. If word got around they'd killed one of their own, the whole scam would go down in flames and take them with it.

"You definitely fixin' to get hurt, boy" Lenny warned as Rashad looked over my head.

"Right, I got the picture," I said as I turned to leave. Erlene controlled all these guys. If they screwed up, she'd get them in ways even I didn't understand.

As I walked down the steps, Lenny stepped out on the porch and yelled, "betta git yo' boney ass ouch'eah, fo' I buss a knot upside yo' haid. Fuck wid me boy an' they ain't but s'hree ways I'm gonna cut you: long, deep and fre-quent-ly."

The rest of them howled with laughter while banging the butt end of their cue sticks on the floor. I shook my head, looked at him, and thought of the hypocrisy they perpetrated on their own people and how they were ready to pin it all on me because I was white. I opened the trunk and removed the portable chicken motel.

"You son-of-a-bitch," I said. "You're a disgrace to your own people." As I started walking back toward the porch I heard the door slam shut, followed by the click-snap-lock of the slide sending a bullet into the chamber of an automatic. I could hear them howling with laughter on the inside. I set the box on the steps, then looked into Rashad's eyes and a thought took over my mind, "Tell him to back off before the whip comes down on him and his friends."

Rashad took off his glasses, his eyes widened. He touched Lenny's arm and nodded toward something behind me. Lenny's entire demeanor changed, he dropped the clip from the gun, racked the bullet out of the chamber, then dropped the pistol on the ground. I was by myself and there were five of them counting the three inside. But these two weren't looking at me, they were looking at something behind me. When I turned around my car was gone. It had been right behind me. I didn't see anything. I stepped off to one side, and half my car re-appeared. Something invisible was between my car and me. If I hadn't remembered I was on a learning curve, I would've panicked. I stepped back and the Thunderbird looked like it was behind a wall. Everything else was visible, the marsh grass, the water, but my car was hidden. I took a few more steps to my right until the length of the car came into view. Along with the car I saw a broken pier, an oyster boat, and a dock with a faded life ring hanging from a nail.

I looked at Rashad, "*What's going on?*" I thought to him. Lenny looked at me, then at Rashad, then turned and broke for the fish shack like he'd seen a ghost. Rashad picked up the pistol, clip and bullet, stuffing them into his pocket.

"Strong Man is standing in the gap right now. He needs you to do that."

"You know I'm new at this, what's it been less than four days?"

"Montague talked to you, right?"

"He explained a little, I have to go back to the St. James for another lesson."

"I don't know who you are, boy, or what your family line is, but you're more than a Bridge."

I didn't show my hand, didn't let him see me sweat. "Well, we all have our little gifts, don't we? Now, are you going to help me, or not?"

CHAPTER TWENTY-THREE

J. Reynolds Rigney, as usual, was sweeping the sidewalk in front of the house when I got home. He was from an old Williamsburg County family that had made their money in tobacco farming and fertilizer. Complete with the genteel manners and a bow tie, J. Reynolds plied his trade as a landlord with British wit and milky white skin, green eyes and a furrowed, old money brow. Completely at home with either a broom, garden rake or apron, Mr. Rigney ran his real estate holdings like a stern schoolmaster: Quick to praise the praiseworthy and equally quick to chastise the late-paying sinner. Not at all like the hardcore property owners who were native Charlestonians, J. Reynolds would never break into a renter's apartment and set their belongings out on the sidewalk because they came up a few days short on the rent. He was cool and deliberate in his sweeping and in total control of every inch of sidewalk fronting his property.

Renters paid exactly on the first of the month. Mr. Rigney had taught business accounting at the Palmer College for most of his life and was still in demand as an accountant. He had visions of one day finding the right student to open a small firm handling only old Charleston money. Often, he would check my records for the band's revenues and taxes. It was J. Reynolds who showed me how to set up the books, post receipts, file 1099's and W-2's.

"Why Joseph, you're all out of breath." He started sweeping right in front of the gate so I couldn't get past him. "I was just thinking the other day, how proud I am of the way you've handled your little band business. Things are still going well, I hope."

"Yes, sir, thank you."

"This dreadful incident with the police department has some of the neighbors upset, I mean search warrants and all such nonsense! Mrs. Peterson was in a shambles."

Mrs. Peterson came in every other day to help J. Reynolds keep the property tidy. She had keys to every locked door.

"They're tactless," I said with disdain. "They don't care who they hurt or embarrass, especially the innocent taxpayer."

"Innocent, yes…well, I certainly…" His green eyes fastened on mine, "why, of course, you're innocent. And I don't even know the charge…uh, I mean circumstances, but I am a good judge of character. That's why I rented to you in the first place, because I knew there would be no problems. I consider you a professional and a gentleman." He paused then passed the broom over the sidewalk a couple more strokes. "I mean really. Joseph, we just can't have any more of these un-pleasantries. It's bad for the neighborhood. Don't you agree?"

"Yes sir, I agree. These bureaucratic imbeciles cause much more trouble than they prevent. I'll go down tomorrow and lodge a formal complaint on behalf of the entire neighborhood…"

"No, no, no," Reynolds said as if he were reprimanding a child for an incorrect response on a math paper. "We don't wanna stir up a WASP nest."

"I get it. I mean it. I'll have the officer in charge come by and explain the misunderstanding in person." I offered.

"That's not necessary either, Joseph. I would just as soon the neighbors not have to look out their windows at yet another of those vile patrol cars."

I felt silly doing that little dance with Mr. Rigney. He was no dummy. It was just his way of saying, "I don't know what kind of crap you've got yourself into, but don't let it follow you back to a piece of my real estate again." And he knew I knew exactly what he meant. I walked through the gate as Mrs. Peterson ducked back behind the curtains of the downstairs window. She scurried out, fussing with a porch plant, as I walked by. She looked from side to side in the empty yard, as if she wasn't sure we were alone.

"Some policemen went through your apartment," she whispered.

"Thank you, I know."

"They had a search warrant, said they were going to search the whole place for evidence. I told them not to break the door down; that I would give them a key. I hope you don't mind."

"Of course not, there was nothing else for you to do," I said.

"They let me stay up there while they searched. I made sure they didn't steal anything.

"Thank you, Mrs. Peterson," I said. "Did you get a good look at my place? Please don't tell the neighbors what a bad housekeeper I am."

"There's a girl up there now," she said. "Mr. Rigney doesn't know. She came right while Reynolds was at Burbage's buying disinfectant, after those rude policemen left. They didn't look or act like our City police officers."

I looked at her in shocked silence, then bounded up the steps. When I opened the door, Kela Ward stood up. She'd been straightening out the bottom bookshelves. She walked over, brushed my hair back lightly and kissed me on the cheek.

"You're in some kind of serious trouble," she said. "What can I do to help?"

"For one thing, you shouldn't be here," I said.

I walked past her to the refrigerator to get a beer. "You need to put as much distance between you and me as you can."

"I can't do that," she said as she put her hand on my arm. "I'm not going back to him. I want to stay with you. If you're in trouble, I can help you."

"You don't even know what kind of trouble I'm in."

"I've seen all kinds of trouble. I've lived all over the world – Lebanon, Germany, The Philippines…" She tried to put her arms around my waist. "I've seen people die from hunger, get blown up by bombs, and gunned down in the street. I've seen people in trouble."

"So the mouse finally roars; seen it all, done it all, nothing new here and yesterday you were asking me for survival tips."

"I thought a lot about what you said. I know how to be supportive. Being a witness to trouble doesn't make you a combat veteran. It's time for me to start fighting back."

"I know you've traveled with the Navy," I said. "You've seen civil unrest, which is nothing like what's going on here. I'm no political rebel; I'm not even part of some grand scheme of things. I'm a nightclub musician who is in over his head, in a criminal mess with no connection to any honorable cause."

"So what if you are? You'll get through this and then, you could be a lot more. Much more."

"You mean, you see me as something other than a musician?" I said.

"Music isn't the be all and end all of life, is it?"

"To me, it is. This is all I know." I lowered her hands from my waist.. "I'm a respected member of the music community and I enjoy what I do." I guided her to sit with me on the sofa. "I can play as much or as little or for as long as I want. Nobody else is going to pay my bills or buy my food or put a shirt on my back. What's that old saying? I made my bed and now I have to eat cake?"

"Stop it, Josie, don't make fun of me. Your bed is not finished, and you're still young enough to do whatever you want. You could get your masters. I could work…" She stopped short of finishing the sentence.

"You could what?" I said. "What did you just say?"

She looked down at the floor and mumbled the words again. "I could work while you finished school."

She stood in front of me, the bruises on her arms were yellowing. I was so determined to justify my life as a musician, I hadn't been paying attention to what was happening between us. She slowly lifted my chin with her fingertips and searched my eyes.

"Are you suggesting, what I think you're suggesting?" I said.

Her hazel eyes darted back and forth from one of my eyes to the other.

"I'm not suggesting anything, I'm ready to move past suggesting," she said, as she leaned over and kissed me.

Kela had put herself in a terrible situation to be with me. Her marriage to an idiot faded into the background and a scarier thought surfaced. What if they managed to nail me for murder? What would she do then?

"You don't know what you're asking," I said. "The cops think I killed a man named Bootsy Williams. I'd been with him the night he disappeared."

"I read about it in the papers. He owned an old farm on Wadmalaw Island?" she said.

"That's the guy. I did a favor for your boss, Bill Reed, which involved meeting Williams. The next day some hunters found his car, his bloody clothes full of bullet holes. The police think I shot him and hid the body."

"The paper said the car was found on Saturday morning. That Friday night you played until 3 am and went to breakfast," she said.

"No, Friday was the day I met you at the Swamp Fox, then sat in with you at The Apartment Club. I know where I was Friday night."

"They can't prove it, if they've got no witnesses and no body."

"In the nightclub business, nobody's word is worth much, Kela, the people who did this knew exactly what they were doing. Somebody went to a lot of trouble to set me up. They're watching me, tailing me, they even know you've been coming here."

"I don't give a damn what they know." She collapsed on the sofa. "I didn't come this far to give up now."

Well, that was it for me. The wall came a tumbling down, brick by brick. I sat beside her and nestled my chin in the warm right angle of her neck and shoulder. She was wearing a white cotton peasant blouse pulled down around her shoulders. A ribbon tied in a bow at the top was all that held it together. I wanted to untie that string and take her to bed, to feel her breasts against my chest, to feel her breath on my skin. Her eyelashes blinked as they moved lightly over the wrinkled cloth of my shirt. As much as I wanted to be with her, wanted to protect her, wanted her to protect me, a sudden rush of fear, almost panic, welled up in my chest. She sensed it and tightened her grip on me. Slowly, the fear melted into the warmest glow I'd ever experienced. I didn't know much about metaphysics, but after what I'd learned from Erlene and Montague, I'd stopped doubting the unseen forces surrounding us. I was a long way from nirvana, but I'd never experienced a connection, or peace and oneness with another human being, as I did with Kela at that moment.

I was so entranced I think I drifted into the dream state between sleep and waking up just before consciousness when I rubbed my hands down her shoulder the elastic in the peasant blouse moved down showing the top of her breast.

"I'm sorry," I said. "I'm not trying to undress you."

"I know Josie, but I wouldn't mind if you did."

I didn't say anything.

"I could sit here like this all day," she said.

Thirty minutes passed with us sitting in my living room holding each other. During that time, my feelings for her ran the gamut from loving her like a lover, a sister, a mother, to loving her as a friend and wanting to take her to bed. With each wave of emotion, she would hold me tight until the wave subsided. We started to breathe in sync, but each time the emotions completed a cycle, I was back in the real world holding another man's wife.

"This is crazy," I whispered.

"I just want you to hold me a little longer."

She nuzzled my neck and I pulled her back so I could look in her eyes.

"Kela, we can't do this. Your husband's insane. He'll hunt you down, possibly kill you."

"I don't love him. I don't want to be with him. I'm not going back to him even if I have to stay in a motel. I want to be with you. I love to be with you, watching you work, helping you become the man I know you are. You're so much more than a bar musician."

She placed her ear next to my heart and sighed.

"I'm a business man who makes his living playing music. What's wrong with that? Tens of thousands of people do it every day," I said.

"But how many old people do you see doing it? How many men and women in their fifties and sixties do you see playing clubs? What kind of family life do they have?"

If I hadn't known better I would've sworn she'd been talking to Gary. I couldn't believe I was getting this from her after hearing it from him.

"What makes you think I want the responsibility of a family?" I asked.

"That's something I know I want. You want it, too. You don't realize it yet, but a sense of family is what's missing from your life. You use music to push it aside because you don't consider it a viable possibility."

I dropped my arms and put a couple of inches between us.

"An artist should be able to discern an honest emotion when it hits him over the head, don't you think?" she said suddenly. "You've been running from yourself, just like I have. My parents sent me away to school when I was twelve; my husband used me to get himself in with the right people. Everything I've done has been in an attempt to get close to the kind of love I never had but always wanted and knew existed. You're just like me, only afraid to admit it."

"I don't need anybody, I really don't," I said.

"You say that. And I believe you think you mean it, but there's no real conviction in your voice. I'll never believe you want to spend the rest of your life alone."

"I am the product of my decisions; I am my choices," I said.

She stood up and opened the blinds. The light cascaded onto the floor.

"You know," she said. "For the last fifteen years, I've done precisely what you're doing. I've lived my life trying to make other people happy. My parents, my teachers, my friends, even my husband, in spite of how he treats me. I can't once remember anyone asking me how I felt about anything. Last Friday, when we played together, the first thing you asked me when it was over was how I felt about it. I knew then there was no turning back. Ever since then, I've become less and less afraid of my husband. He hit me because I stood up to him. When I wouldn't back down, he kept hitting me. When it was over, I knew that once I left, I'd never go back to him. Well, I've left. I'd rather die than go back."

"This is more than I can handle," I said. "With everything else falling down around my ears…" I paused and looked at her again, "The man really is sick, you know."

"Well, I can't help him, and I can't go back," she sighed. "I'll never go back to living in fear of him either. But I know he'll come looking for me."

"Maybe, but he won't find you. Not where I'll take you."

I knew immediately I'd crossed the line; there was no way I could leave her to fend for herself against a lunatic barbarian. Everything in my life had taught me to protect myself, at all cost, to make sure my back was covered. I'd tried to protect my mother and failed. Now, suddenly, all those old feelings flowed into my soul. The feelings of rage and territorial imperative welled up and a new feeling flowed into my soul. Kela felt like family.

We sat on the floor and talked all afternoon. She told me about growing up in Alabama, the daughter of a military father stationed at Redstone Arsenal, then living in Germany after marrying a man much like her father except she'd never seen her father hit her mother. We cuddled, we cooked a meal together—looked through my record collection. I showed her my scrap book and how I kept up with the careers of the sidemen I'd worked with over the years, which ones were now working with big stars, which were studio musicians on which records.

By 7:30, I'd dressed and was ready to go play. She had the night off from the Swamp Fox Room. "You wanna come with me?" I said.

"I'd rather stay here where it's safe, if that's OK with you."

"Fine with me. Don't know how it will square with JR downstairs, but it will be nice to have someone to come home to."

"I'll have your breakfast ready when you get back."

She kissed me again, this time on the cheek. It was an innocent gesture and it made me feel like I was part of something nice. I turned the doorknob to leave and then she said for me to wait a minute. She ran back to the kitchen and returned with a brown paper bag.

"I've always wanted to fix a man his lunch and put it in a brown paper bag to send with him off to work. It's a sandwich to eat during your break." I took the bag out to the T-Bird.

I sent a question to my subconscious: "When was the last time a woman made you lunch, put it in a bag and sent you off to work with a kiss?" The answer came back quickly: "Never." I felt very good for the first time in a very long time.

The feeling lasted exactly the fifteen minutes it took me to get to the parking lot of The Merch. Then the monster popped up full-blown, right in front of me as Thigpen stepped out into the street light halo. He propped one foot on the bumper of his car and lit a cigarette, looking at his watch like I was late for an appointment. He had another guy with him, a short, stocky Italian-looking dude in an overcoat who ignored me as I approached the club.

I walked right past both of them without speaking and went inside looking into Sinclair's mind through his eyes. He cut a look toward the back of the club. The clock behind the bar read 7:46.

Another blonde haired man, different from Ward's twink I'd puked on, was sitting in a corner with his back to the wall, going over some notes on a yellow legal pad. With his light olive suit, burgundy club tie, powder blue oxford cloth shirt and tortoise shell glasses; he looked more like a clean-cut all-American accountant with an attitude than a cop or one of Mark Ward's pets.

The legal pad could've been a prop, but as I walked past there appeared to be some kind of schedule with times listed in order. He was checking one set of numbers against another and checking his watch against the clock on the wall behind the bar. When I got to the stage, he glanced up at me, but went right back to whatever it was he was working on. I knew he was there to see me, but for the moment I didn't seem very important. All I could think of was how the cops were in the parking lot watching me. They were at my house. Now they were even inside the club. I figured next they'd be under my bed. I laughed to myself when I remembered my mattress sat on the floor. This new guy didn't fit the stereotype.

I went into the dressing room and joked with Jack and Gary. "Why is the Man all over the place? We havin' a barbecue or something?" I said.

They both shrugged their shoulders, trying to act like nothing was wrong, but the vibe was in the air, I could feel it in my skin. Jack and Gary knew something was up. I sat my horn on the shelf and went into the restroom. The blonde guy followed me and when he pulled up beside me in one of the stalls, I looked right at him, down at his dick, then right back into his eyes.

Thigpen's man came in next. He went into a stall with a door on it. Mr. GQ acted like he didn't know the other guy, which I thought was strange, since I just assumed they were both cops. When I went to the lavatory to wash my hands, he zipped up and came over to wash his. I turned to walk out, and he pretended to straighten his tie in the mirror and walked out right behind me. It was getting painfully obvious that both sides were starting to put the pressure on me. If they got any closer, we'd be wearing the same pants. I went over to the bar and poured myself a beer from the tap, all the time watching pretty boy in the mirror behind the bar. When he saw me watching, he worked on his papers. I'd catch his eye, he'd quickly look away.

I took my beer and sat next to him at his table.

CHAPTER TWENTY-FOUR

"Hi, my name is Josie." I extended my hand. "I get the distinct impression you're here to keep an eye on me. Can I buy you a beer?"

He leaned back, flashing his beautiful smile, and tapped his chin with his pencil. "Excuse me," he said politely, "but I'm afraid you have me confused with someone else."

I slid my chair around so that I was sitting beside him. "Don't worry, no one can hear us. Besides, I saw the way you were watching me in the men's room."

"I don't think, I ..." he started to slide his chair away, "You definitely have me confused with somebody else ... I'm not into ..."

"Hey, hey, hey," I slid my chair back to the other side of the table. "Don't suck your shorts up your crack, it's part of my job to keep up with the new customers. Most people who come in here are regulars, and I always enjoy meeting new people, especially when they watch every move I make and follow me into the toilet. Like I said, my name is Josie, I'm open-minded, I'm the sax player for Christ sake, can't go blowing on something long, round and hard every night and not be open minded, right? I manage the band. I'm nosey by nature. Besides you might be with the IRS or the South Carolina Tax Commission, you look so, how should I put this? Severe, that's it, severe. You know, with the paper and pencil and watching me use the urinal, I figure you gotta be a tax man."

I was grinning my redneck grin, the one with the crazy twinkle in the eyes the redneck gives a guy who's about to get sucker punched.

"Look, buddy," he said. "I'm not with the tax commission and I don't give a damn how you look in the restroom. Now, get away from me or you'll regret..."

"Get away from you?" I looked him straight in the eye and continued to grin. He locked his fingers together on top of his legal pad. The French cuffs, the alligator watch band, the perfectly manicured fingernails, extended from the suit coat fucking perfectly. Teeth clinched, he grabbed my shirt, I was still smiling.

"I wouldn't do that, if I were you," I said softly and showed him my other hand in my coat pocket. "Now, unless I'm mistaken and I might be, about all the things you're not, I'll just bet 'ready-to-die' is not real high on the list. So, if you aren't a cop or the tax man, then tell me why you're in my night club, taking notes on me? When we're not yet open for business?"

He stowed his legal pad and pencil neatly in his brief case. What I was doing was crazy, but I was going crazy anyway, so it made sense, at the time. Even though he was smaller than I was, he was in much better shape. I knew I wouldn't stand much of a chance if he decided to have a go of it. I figured Thigpen's buddy would step in if things got out of hand. I pointed the pocket of my jacket toward his stomach.

"Who are you working for?"

"I don't know anything about anything." He snapped his briefcase shut and acted like he was going to walk away from me toward the door.

"You know, I've got nothing to lose by blowing a hole through you, right here and now." I said quietly. I learned the tactic from the *Book of Five Rings*. When the castle is surrounded, open the gates of the city and leave one lone sweeper in the courtyard. The enemy, suspects an ambush and retreats. It was suicidal, but sometimes it worked.

"The police will be all over you," he said.

"That man scrolling through the jukebox is with the County Police Department, he works for the Neanderthal detective holding court in the parking lot. The detective's name is Thigpen, he follows me everywhere I go because he thinks I killed a man. Why don't you call him over?" I paused and watched him. "Here, I'll call him for you."

"No, wait!" He was half way out of the seat glancing nervously back at the cop.

"How about you calm the fuck down." I drummed my fingers on his briefcase. "Show me some ID."

"Excuse me, but that should be 'what else I've gotten myself into?' Now, tell me who you are or I swear you will not walk away from this without a trip to the County Emergency Room." I put my hand on his arm and squeezed it. "If you know anything about the rumors circling around me, then you know I will shoot you, sooner or later. They all think I'm a murderer, anyway. Why not prove them right and get it over with?"

The briefcase was one of those $400 rosewood and alligator jobs. I flipped the latches, opened the lid and rifled through the contents. His business card wallet along with his government ID and several file folders were tucked into a pleated accordion fold out.

"Curtis Mitchell, U.S. Navy, born September 19, 1947, you're dressed kind of snazzy for a sailor. Have you won any medals dressing like a male model?"

"You're in way over your head, Chapman," he said coolly.

"So, you do know who I am," I said.

"You told me your name."

"I told you my first name. Oh, look you have a nice pistol, too. Now, we really do have something in common. What were you going to do with that, Curt? You going to shoot me? I didn't know sailors who dressed like male models and acted like tax collectors who didn't want to call the police, even when a crazy hippie had the drop on them in a night club, carried pistols. That's a new one on me. Why don't you tell me who you really are; maybe you'll get out of here in one piece."

"I'm sure you can figure it out," he said.

"Captain Ward? You work for him?" I said.

"Obviously." He straightened his tie knot.

"Why is somebody working for Ward in my club, taking notes on me?"

"You're so smart, it should be obvious. I'm doing my job." He snapped his briefcase shut, took out a handkerchief, wiped his lips, brow and then snapped his shirt cuffs.

"The Navy thinks I'm a threat to national security? I'm flattered."

"My commanding officer thinks you're a threat to his security."

"Interesting." I closed his briefcase, clicking the latches shut. "So, he sent you here to talk to me?"

"He sent me here to warn you," he said.

"That's why you're following me, Curt?"

"Not really. It's because you've been seeing the Captain's wife. I suspected she'd be here tonight. Since she didn't show, I decided to take a few notes on you while I was here. Nothing personal, you understand?" Curt leaned back in the chair with his arms folded across his chest.

"Oh, I think I understand." I began closing in on his eyes. "Your boss beats his wife black and blue from head to toe, and then he sends you to make sure nothing happens to her while she's with me. Is that it?" I was right in his face.

"I'm not aware of any beating," he said.

"Then you aren't paying attention, Curtis. You don't mind if I call you Curtis, do you? Because, if you had been paying attention at the Officer's Club, you would have seen the bruises on her hands and face." He was stonewalling me. "But that's probably somebody else's job. Just like it'll be somebody else's job to pull you out of Hell Hole Swamp if you, or Ward, or any of you motherfuckers, do anything to hurt her. You remember that Curtis, the next time the Captain gives you an assignment like this one here tonight." I stood up from the chair.

"You're a real tough guy, aren't you, Chapman?" he laughed. "You remind me of those clowns in the Three Stooges' movies. I do what I'm told, or rather ordered to do."

"Tracking an officer's wife is not part of the Navy," I said.

"Captain Ward is part of the Navy, I work for him. That's my first responsibility, the Navy comes second." Curtis wasn't backing off the 'just following orders' bullshit.

"God, I love this country," I said. "Do me a favor, will you, Curt? Tell Popeye if he wants to take notes on me, I'll be happy to oblige him."

"I'll relay the message, sir." He had a smug stupid grin on his face. "By the way, you don't have to resort to pulling a gun on me to get my attention. He buttoned his jacket and composed himself. "Besides, you don't have a snowball's chance of hiding anything. Captain Ward knows all about it. He has all along."

"All about what?"

"You and his wife."

"Man, you're some piece of work, Curt, you know that?"

"And you, sir, are a fool," he said crisply. "This is my last stop on this tour, not my first. I was finishing my report, not starting it. We know everything about you, your associates and, last but not least, your present situation." He set his briefcase down, unsnapped it and pulled out the legal pad again. "Would you like a litany of your activities over the last two weeks?"

"Well, clue me in, will you? What do you know about me the night I supposedly murdered Bootsy Williams?" I figured I might as well go for it.

"The Navy, that is Captain Ward, believes you're involved in a plan to embarrass the Charleston Command. I think it's called blackmail."

"WHAT?" I yelled it so loud Thigpen's monkey jumped.

It dawned on me what a tar baby this thing was turning into. I was being framed for murder, accused of robbery and now blackmail. Mark Ward was using my friendship with his wife as an excuse for the U.S. Navy to follow me as insurance, in case I tried to blackmail him.

"I guess I should seriously consider going out back and shooting myself, get it over with. I mean, I'm the only person in this high drama who hasn't really done anything, except deliver a money bag and a couple chickens, and all the heat was on me."

"I'm afraid I don't have the slightest idea what you're talking about," he said.

"Then what 'present situation' of mine are you referring to?

"Let me make it perfectly clear, then, Mr. Chapman." Curt pulled out a handkerchief, moistened his glasses with his breath and proceeded to talk while cleaning his glasses. "As I'm sure you know, my commanding officer and his wife are going through a difficult phase in their personal relationship. My commanding officer…"

"Why don't you just call the wife-beating son-of-a-bitch by his name?"

"Would you like to hear what I have to say, or not?" He was all business.

"Sorry," I said. "I just remembered how your commanding officer's wife's body looked the last time I saw her naked." Curtis placed his hands palm down on the table, stretched his fingers, huffed a deep breath, then puffed.

"As I was saying, my commanding officer is concerned for the security of the Naval Base because of Mrs. Ward's knowledge of some rather delicate information." He was trying hard to read my reaction. He must've known I didn't have a clue what he was talking about.

"You guys think Kela has told me some big Navy secret, like how deep a submarine can go, or some other spy bullshit?" I said.

"Not exactly," he said. "Captain Ward isn't concerned about his wife divulging her knowledge of national security issues. He's worried by her poor choice of confidants, you in particular. His personal life is just that: personal. Put yourself in his shoes."

"You're one pompous piece of crap, you know that, right?" My head was buzzing, my shoulders were aching, and my ears started ringing. Then I started laughing like a crazy man. "You mean to tell me, that Ward, who less than forty-eight hours ago, beat his wife within inches of hospitalization, is worried about being embarrassed because she might 'confide' in a nightclub musician?" I was dumbfounded. "Curt, she had teeth marks on her for God's sake! He beat her with the buckle end of a leather belt! She was covered with welts and some of her hair was pulled out. Does that mean nothing to you, man? I mean, what the fuck was I supposed to do, Curtis? She came to me rather than the police or the hospital. Your fucking C.O. should thank his lucky stars I was there for her."

He rubbed his chin. While he was thinking, so was I. This couldn't be simply about Mark Ward beating his wife. There had to be more to it. Why would Ward go to all this trouble to hassle me? Then it hit me. Something Erlene Brown had said about how money was funneled out of the Naval Supply Depot using national security as an excuse to rush the paperwork through, was starting to make perfect sense. Mark Ward was defrauding the Navy, and he was afraid I knew. I was sure of it.

"You're a slime ball, Curt, a government flunky, slime ball for hire," I said.

"I've been called worse, but I think it was in the third grade. "Besides, he's onto you, and it's only a matter of time before you get enough rope to hang yourself. One doesn't reach Captain Ward's position by being stupid." Curtis collected his briefcase and proceeded to glide toward the door.

A still small voice spoke a thought to me. "*Ask him about Douglas.*"

"Hey, Curtis, wait a second." I caught up with him at the porthole door in time to put my hand on it. "How's Douglas?"

He blinked three times as the color drained out of his face. *He and Douglas are lovers and Douglas is married.*

"Does Douglas' wife know how close you two are, or I should say, can get?"

"I have no idea what you're talking about?"

A picture of a martini with an olive, a pearl onion, and a twist of lemon appeared right in front of me, then a New Year's Eve noisemaker fell in it and I saw Curtis and another man making out in a bathroom stall with red wallpaper. The words "Sick Twist" formed above the scene. I put my palms together and rubbed them like a man with cold hands, then did a pointy finger wag and grinned.

"Do the words "Sick Twist" ring your chimes there, Curtis, old buddy, old pal, old chum...bucket? That's a play on words; chum bucket is a pail full of fish guts."

"I know what a chum bucket is."

"You and Douglas have a favorite drink don't you? That silly martini with the olive, onion, and lemon twist. That's a sick twist, isn't it? A few of those and you two start giggling, head to the men's room? You know the one you went into on New Year's Eve with the red wallpaper, where the two of you were making out, calling your little love affair a sick twist?"

Curtis stumbled back into the wall. I was sure he was about to faint. "Hey, hey, there now, little buddy! Don't go getting all rubber-legged on me."

"How did you find out? You, of all people? What are you, a Russian spy or something?" He was sweating like a whore in church. "You have no proof, none! This...is a baseless...false accusation...I could bring you up on charges."

"Wrong, asshole. Nobody, but you and me knows what I said to you."

"How did you find out?"

"You really want to know? I mean, do you really, really want to know, because I'll tell you, if you really wanna know."

"How did you know?"

"You have to say it like I said it."

"I really want to know."

"You need another 'really'".

"I really, really want to know."

"I made a deal with The Devil. He tells me things about people like you."

"That's absurd."

"Why, Curtis, son, why do you find this so hard to believe? You've done the same thing yourself. Your Captain is Lucifer incarnate, can't you see that? Now, you run along to your boss, like a good little fairy, and you tell him if he tries to hurt his soon-to-be ex-wife, that Strong Man will cut his balls off and shove them down his throat."

"You're insane, you're certifiably insane."

"Why, thank you," I said. "That's the sickest twist I've heard today."

That last little remark really got me hot. It was one thing to get blamed for something you didn't do, like kill somebody. It was one thing to be blamed for screwing another man's wife when all you did was give her a place to stay so he wouldn't beat her to death, a place where she could be safe. But to be threatened because you might blow the whistle on a corrupt public servant, who parades around like the people's prince, was something altogether different. Mark Ward didn't give a damn about Kela. He was protecting his own personal river of money.

"You tell your boss that I'll be in Hampton Park, by the gates of the Citadel, at noon tomorrow. If he wants a piece of me, that's where I'll be."

"I'll tell him." Curt struggled with the door.

"Here, let me get that for you, there's a trick to it." When I reached past him to trip the security lock, I kissed him on the cheek. "Tell Dougie, Josie says 'hey.'"

"Someone is going to kill you, I can promise you," he snarled.

"You wanna know who is going to kill you Curtis, because I can tell you. The Devil will show me, and I'll tell you right here, right now. You wanna know? Do you? Do you, huh?" I felt invincible. In a split second, I saw Curtis, naked, hanging from a shower head with a bathrobe belt around his neck. He watched the vision register in my eyes, watched the smirk form across my face. He knew that I knew.

"And Curt, remind Captain Ward I live by an old African Proverb."

"And…wha…what might that be?" he stuttered.

"Call me a thief and I go to steal."

From behind the porthole mirror, I watched Curtis make his way past Thigpen. He almost tripped and fell getting into his car, put it in reverse, then park, then drive, lurched forward, slammed on brakes, back in reverse. He arched backwards into the traffic, horns blowing, people cursing. Thigpen, along with his companion, gawked at each other, then back at the front door.

I turned around and walked toward the bar. Thigpen's flunky was still flipping through the Rockola's Hit Tracker. The rest of the band were milling around. I looked at the clock, 7:46.

"Your clock stopped."

Montague placed a Wild Turkey Manhattan on a napkin. "Ain't nothin' wrong with the clock. It'll catch up to itself."

"What did you think of my conversation with Ward's puppet?"

Monk walked up and ordered vodka with a splash of cranberry juice.

"Why didn't you guys warn me about that guy?

"What guy?" Monk stirred his drink with his finger.

"The guy in the suit, he was just here, I've been talking to him the last five minutes."

"Was it outside?" Monk said. "We weren't outside. We didn't see a guy in a suit."

Sinclair saddled up beside me, then Montague and they exchanged a look. I looked at both of them and started to press the issue with Monk when Sinclair nudged my elbow. Montague made one slight head shake. I let it drop.

"There're two plainclothes cops in the parking lot – the goon who's been asking questions and some other mafia-looking dude," I said.

"I don't know what you're talking about. They weren't there when I got here. County or City?"

"Probably County waitin' on a piece 'a trim." Monk sipped his drink.

"Probably right. Never mind," I said. "Hey, turn off the organ before you leave tonight."

Monk walked back to the dressing room. The jukebox stooge looked at his watch. He shuffled back through the front door like he needed to check in.

"You two saw the guy I was talking to, right? You heard the conversation, too. Tell me I didn't imagine the whole thing. Because if I did, I'm checking myself into the psych ward."

Montague wiped the bar top while Sinclair lit a cigarette.

"Montague…?" I put my scratched hand on his towel hand. He stopped wiping and looked down at the scars. Sinclair looked at Montague. "Montague…? Am I losing my mind?"

"She opened you up too early, but that's sailed with the tide. To answer yo' question, no. You ain't crazy. Your eyes and ears have been opened. Scrong Man is building you into a Bridge. As the teacher say, 'Boy, you got some education comin'. We best be at bringing you…" he looked at Sinclair, "…how you young folks say it?"

"Up to speed," Sinclair took a drag off his cigarette.

"Yeah, up to speed," Montague chuckled.

Monk sat down behind the B3 and toggled the Start switch, the electric motor began to whir, gathering momentum until it reached a steady hum. Then he pushed the Run switch holding both until the sound rose up from the keys. Up to speed, I thought, everything needs to be up to speed. I looked at the clock, 8:27. I was back in real time.

CHAPTER TWENTY-FIVE

Hampton Park, at noon on a Monday, was almost deserted. Except for the ducks, squirrels, pigeons and seagulls, nothing moves but the breeze and a lonely human or two. The green grass, azaleas, camellias and ponds that make up the landscape are bright and beautiful as any park I've ever seen. July 4th brings in the brass bands, the Star-Spangled Banner and a John Phillips Sousa medley. Kids slurp snow cones, hold onto balloon strings and watch their parents try to hang on to the American Dream.

I sat on a park bench by one of the fountains near the bandstand. From that position I could watch three of the four corners of the park. Like a baseball field viewed from home plate, I had a catcher's view of the park. Only my back was exposed, but there was nothing behind me except a sandy parking lot.

Three men came into the park from each of the three corners, first one, then the other, then the last. Two moved into the sunlight, carrying newspapers, dressed in suits and wearing sunglasses. The guy covering the upper left corner crossed right on the diagonal like the Queen's Bishop moving to the center of a chess board. He threw some bread crumbs to the ducks near the fountain opposite the Gazebo. The other two stationed themselves at nine o'clock and three o'clock respectively, taking seats on the benches nearest them, while pretending to read their papers. They were too well-dressed to be with the police department, and the put-on casual body language made them look like they were trying too hard to go unnoticed. The way they ignored each other told me they weren't just out for a stroll in the sunshine to feed the ducks. For all I knew they could've been called in to dust me off. Wherever they were from, they didn't know how to dress to blend in with the people who frequented Hampton Park.

At exactly noon, a fourth man came on the scene. He stopped beside the guy feeding the ducks and nodded in my direction without looking at me. This one was more businesslike with a clean chiseled face, blonde hair and a briefcase. He looked straight at me while talking to the other man out of the corner of his mouth. After acknowledging the presence of the two men at the other end of the park, he walked straight over to me and sat on the bench beside me.

"Mr. Chapman?"

"That's me," I said.

"Are you carrying a weapon of any kind?"

I gave him my, "What kind of fool do you think I am?" look.

"Don't look surprised, Mr. Chapman. You threatened one of my men with a pistol, just yesterday."

"Oh, you mean this?" I said, as I pulled my hand out of my coat pocket and formed the image of a pistol with my thumb and index finger and pointed it at him. "Don't worry, it's not loaded."

"You're a real comedian, aren't you, Mr. Chapman? My source said you threatened to shoot him last night." The guy was as dry as the bread the other guy was feeding the ducks.

"Your friend needs to get a job selling clothes at Berlin's. He's a lot better dresser than he is a detective," I said.

"You seem to know a great deal about Charleston's little known peculiarities," he said.

"When I was a kid, I'd ride my bike over here," I said. "This park used to be a zoo."

I pointed out the open spots between the Azalea bushes and the giant Live Oaks. "Right over there, they had an elephant and behind it was a camel. The lion, two tigers, and a room full of snakes were over beside the monkeys. I remember this one monkey always jacked off in front of the preacher's wife. It was like the animal knew who she was. Everybody loved that monkey."

"Your point?" He said.

"No point; just a story about a caged monkey jacking off. Thought you might relate to it."

He sat with both hands on his briefcase and drummed his fingers on the alligator skin. It was an exact duplicate of the one last night's Mr. GQ was carrying.

"Let me guess," I said. "Your boss threw a Christmas party last year and gave each one of his flunkies one of these expensive briefcases, all at the taxpayers' expense. Right?" I couldn't help it; the whole scene was so B-movie.

Quickly, he unsnapped both locks at once. Inside was a kind of amp meter. When he flipped a switch, the needle sprang to life, then steadied itself in a green zone. I tried to read it over his shoulder.

"Does that mean I'm OK?"

"That means there are no heavy deposits of metal such as iron, steel, copper or lead within five feet of this device," he said. "You aren't carrying a tape recorder, by any chance?"

I smiled at the thought of having a tape recorder with me. "You guys are really into the Mission Impossible routine, aren't you? Should I get my tape recorder? Do you think I'm going to need one? Are you going to pull one of those deals where the tape self-destructs after we listen to it? I know where we can rent a mobile studio for about a five hundred an hour. What's going on here? Who do you guys think I am?"

"You're nobody, Chapman. But I thought you knew that already. My job's simply to make sure you stay a nobody." The guy was a real smart ass. I wanted to smack him. "You're alone, I presume. None of your jungle bunny friends roosting in the trees or hiding in the bushes?"

"Of course I am alone, except for you and your friends, and my guardian angels, of course. If I had anyone here with me, I'm sure you would know about it."

"My friends and I work as a team to protect the Captain. We all carry side arms and we will be watching every move you make." With that, he opened the briefcase again, lifting the amp meter up enough for me to see the .45 automatic under it. Then he unsnapped a folding section in the lid and pulled out a plastic bag full of breadcrumbs.

"Now, if you will excuse me, I think I'll go feed the ducks. Nice to have met you, Mr. Chapman. Please, try to remember what I said. We don't want to make a scene. One wrong move and we will shoot you. Just like that." He pointed his index finger pistol at me and wiggled his thumb.

As he went to feed the ducks, the other three men slipped back into the shade of the big oak trees. A blue-gray sedan, exactly like the one that had followed me, driven by the same guy I'd kissed on the cheek, pulled into the gravel parking lot behind the bandstand. I looked at my watch; it was exactly 12:10 P.M.

Mark Ward casually exited the backseat wearing a khaki windbreaker, jeans, T-shirt and sneakers. The sunglasses were the aviator type with dark, green lenses framed in brass. Just looking at him you'd never guess he controlled a fleet of ships, any one of which could start WWIII. He was chewing gum and looking from side to side as he made his way to where I was sitting. He looked bigger than I remembered, but twice as cocky, obviously nervous, and not used to doing business dressed like a Little League coach. He was trying too hard to be cool and the military body language wasn't working with the casual clothes.

When he made eye contact with me through the sunglasses, he carefully pulled a brown paper bag out of his jacket pocket, removed some peanuts from the bag, shaking them like a pair of dice before popping them in his mouth, Evidently, this was some kind of signal to the other four men because they abruptly disappeared from view, leaving the two of us alone in the sunlight. Out in the light his face showed much more strain than I'd noticed in the officer's club kitchen.

Actually, strained is not the best word to use. Tired is a better word. I could tell he was dying his hair to cover the gray streaks and his teeth were outlined in the brown stain of a chain smoker. I'd seen the look in the faces of musicians who had been on the road too long, in the faces of club owners who had spent too much time out of the sun and on the music company talent scouts who hadn't eaten a home cooked meal in years. These men all have one thing in common – they want it all and they want it now.

Seeing Mark Ward in the sunlight, wearing his softball outfit; realizing the power he had over so many people made me wonder why he'd stoop so low as to meet with me in a public place. He had to suspect I was on to his scam. Looking at his face, I'd have figured he would sooner have me knocked off by one of his government paid flunkies. An option which certainly wasn't out of his reach. He sat beside me and took a deep breath.

"So, Mr. Chapman, I heard you wanted to meet with me privately, so here I am. What can I do for you?" He shook more peanuts in his fist and popped them in his mouth.

"Do you always carry four bodyguards and a mini-mine detector with you to every private meeting you attend?" I said.

"My job is very unforgiving. One little mistake and 'POOF!'" he twirled his hand with the peanuts in the air to simulate a tornado.

"Must give you a tremendous sense of power to ride the world's oceans with your finger on the doomsday button?" I said.

"Actually, I feel much safer out there than I do here right now. Besides, you don't look like someone who would be all that interested in thermonuclear war. Probably never crossed your mind, has it?" He chuckled. "In fact," he continued, "I'd wager that your little mind doesn't move much farther out than the next groupie you're going to sleep with or copying down the lyrics of the latest Rolling Stones single and adding them to your list of words to live by."

There was a new theory going around. "It's all the rage," J. Reynolds Rigney had shared with me, "it's called the 'trickledown theory.' I thought it was a cute drug store psychology term until they ruined it by applying it to business. Now, it's the height of fashion amongst the name droppers."

Basically, it says the attitude of the employees in a business can be traced back to the attitude of management and, ultimately, back to the president of the company. I quickly deduced the attitude of Ward's men trickled down from their boss, who was the biggest idiot asshole I'd ever met in my life.

"Interesting that we've only met twice for less than three minutes and you think you've already got me figured out," I said.

"You're kind is easy to figure out, Chapman. You're simply a roach in need of a shoe, which will come to you in time. Right now, I'm here to set matters straight between us before you start getting any crazy ideas about being a hero." More dice-tossing peanuts, sun-checking, watch looking, staring in the direction of the bodyguards.

"Let me get this straight," I said. "You came all the way out here from your office, because I wanted to see you? You mean I've got that kind of pull; then you use the occasion to warn me, threaten me, and insult me? You've got four body-guards to protect you from me and you're all dressed up in a disguise, and I'm a roach that needs to be stepped on? Forgive me, Dr. Oppenheim, but I must say I am flattered. I simply told your boy Curt over there," I nodded toward his car, "I'd be here, if YOU wanted to see ME. You were the one having me followed; you were the one spending the taxpayer's money to follow a bug. How do you explain that, Captain? If I might be so brazen as to ask?"

"Listen, kiddo!" He'd watched too many Humphrey Bogart movies. Bogart liked the word "kiddo." Now I understood the rest of his body language. He was acting out; trying to imitate Rick in a scene from Casablanca. "I'm here to settle up with you and get on about my business. I know who you are, who you were and what you're trying to do. What do I have to do to get you out of my life?"

"What?! Me out of YOUR life? You inserted yourself into my life!" I said.

"I've had you followed because you're seeing my wife. I know every move you make. I can't stop my wife from hanging around goofy musicians, she's got this crazy idea of being a professional piano player, for God's sake, but I will not allow low-life barflies like you to use me to get you out of trouble with the police."

"That's about the most ridiculous thing I've ever heard a grown man say. Your wife, Kela, the one you beat the hell out of three nights ago, came to me to learn how to improvise on jazz chords. That's all, man. That was it. Then, all hell started breaking loose, and you had me followed everywhere. She shows up looking like a punching bag and is scared you're going to kill her. Then you come here and threaten to kill me. Excuse me, man, but you're looking more like the lowlife in this picture."

"Screw you, Chapman, I don't give a damn what you think. Last week, a man was killed and everybody thinks you did it. Next, you show up at my party at the base with a band you don't even play with. Then you hook up with my wife." He was really starting to breathe hard now. "I know you didn't kill the spook because I was having you followed. Trouble is, you can't prove you didn't do it without my help. You're so low on the ladder; you'll get stepped on by people reaching for the bottom rung. I'm here to get one message to you and that's all. Stay away from my wife or I'll let you hang out to dry on the murder rap. It's that simple."

I was spellbound by his intensity. A vessel in his neck popped out like a junkie's arm with a belt around it. "You think you can get away from me because you have the cops watching you everywhere you go." It was such a good idea I wondered why I hadn't thought of it myself. "You don't fool me for one minute. But I admit none of this came together until I figured out the guy that my wife was hanging out with and the murder suspect were both the same guy, you."

"Forgive me, I'm stupid. So, let me make sure of this again, so there's no misunderstanding," I said. "You had me followed the night Bootsy Williams was killed, because I spoke to your wife while she was working at the Swamp Fox, then you put all these pieces of the puzzle together, confront your wife with all this evidence and she doesn't see it the way you see it so you grab her by the hair and beat the hell out of her. She runs to my apartment because she's afraid you're going to kill her. Then you set your flunkies on my tail to gather evidence against me so you can blackmail me into staying away from your wife, by withholding the evidence I need to clear my name with the cops. And you're now saying that if I don't go along with you on this you'll make sure I get nailed for murder? Is that pretty close?" He'd backed up a little as I verbally closed in on him.

"I think you're beginning to see the picture," he said.

"God help us, if the rest of the submarine captains are as nuts as you."

That was, of course, the wrong thing to say. His face turned red as a sunburn and his eyes went wild with hate. If I hadn't been in my suicide mode, he would've scared me. But I had one advantage over him and he must have sensed it. I grew up with a man twice as crazy as Mark Ward, beating me. So when his anger peaked, I knew I'd faced worse enemies than him. Then he grabbed my arm like a vice grip.

"I ought to kill you right here," he hissed. "You think you can walk into my life and destroy everything I've worked for? You think I can't make your life a living hell from now on? I can take you anytime I want you, Chapman. Who do you think the cops will believe, a Naval Captain or a drugged out, burned-out hippie throwback who toots a horn for a living?"

"I may be wrong, but I get the distinct impression you're more worried than I am, about who they might believe. Especially, if I end up dead," I said.

"You didn't answer me. What'll it take to make you disappear on your own?" He growled.

"You mean like in how much money will it take? It bothers my conscience to waste the taxpayer's money. Or do you mean like your supplying the cops with my alibi? In other words, what price do I put on my friendship with Kela?" I tried to act puzzled.

"Either one or both and screw your conscience," he said.

"I don't want anything from you. Your wife wants to take music lessons from me. I was teaching her before the murder. Now she's come to me because she's afraid of you. I saw what you did to her, and I'm only here today to tell you face to face that, I've never slept with your wife; I've never even kissed her (it wasn't a lie, she kissed me), our friendship is centered on music. Or it was until you beat her. That said, if you ever hit her again, you'll live to regret it."

"Shut up and listen to me, hippie," he glared into my face, my arm still in his grip, "you're only alive right now because I can't afford to have somebody this close to my wife hit. She's my wife! You got that? You're a slug; you're lower than whale shit in the grand scheme of things. Unless you want your next gig to be playing a harp or a pitchfork, stay away from Kela Ward."

"You don't scare me. I've had my ass cut by men who'd chew you up and spit you out. Just remember what I said. You beat her again and not even your doomsday button will save you much less the four doo-wop bitches backing you up today. This is Charleston, South Carolina; even the mafia stays clear of this place. So, don't threaten me. I know too many people."

"You're even more of an idiot that I thought," he said. "I figured you'd at least have enough common sense to save yourself more trouble. I know everybody, who is anybody. I have more economic clout in this state than the governor; people who could buy you with the change off their nightstand. Am I making myself clear?" His chest was all puffed up like an ape.

"You'll get somebody to take me out of the picture, even if it means putting out a contract with a hired killer. Yeah, I'm clear on that," I smiled.

"I never said those words, exactly." He got up, tossed back a fist full of peanuts. "That'd be too obvious. I was thinking more along the lines of how hard it might be for you to play the saxophone with broken hands, no teeth and in a wheel chair." He stood up dusting the peanut husks off his shirt.

He grinned a crazy grin and walked back to his car. The other four guys followed him. When he opened the door, I realized my heart had been racing. I'd been determined to show no fear and not back down in the face of his threats. I'd pulled it off, too, but when it was over, I thought I was going to throw up. There was no doubt he could do whatever he wanted in order to take me out of the picture. So why hadn't he done it? He had the connections, the political clout, in the civilian, military and economic sectors. There was no telling what his little private hit squad could do under the guise of national security. He had the whole Navy at his disposal. I wasn't thinking clearly. I was going on the assumption that it was me who was going off the deep end. Something wasn't right. Yes, he had access to a wealth of tools by which he could dispatch me. He could hint to the Secret Service, tell a supplier to tell the mayor to tell the chief of police. But why hadn't he done that already? If he could do any or all of these things, why hadn't he done it? He knew I wasn't so close to his wife to get him looked at if something happened to me. It would be much less risky than meeting me in person because I spooked one of his flunky goof balls. I could only come up with one answer that made any sense. Mark Ward was more afraid of me than I was of him. But why?

As Curtis, the cute driver, started the car Ward rolled down the window and shot me the bird. I waved at him like I wanted to say something, and he leaned out the window.

"I was wondering something, Captain Ward," I said.

"I'm listening," he said coldly.

You should've seen his face when I asked, "Does the word "CHIT" mean anything to you?" He started to get back out of the car, but the driver said something. The car pulled out of the lot as he rolled up the window.

It was two-thirty in the morning before I started looking for Bill Reed. Knowing him, he'd leave Cricket holding down The Apartment Club, while he club-hopped all over town. Reed loved to run around checking out his competition and generally stirring up as much trouble as he could. I went to the A&N Club on Remount Road. Benny, the doorman told me Reed had already come and gone a couple hours earlier. He'd been in the Hoof & Horn on Dorchester Road right after he left the A&N. The AMVETS on Spruill Avenue hadn't seen him, neither had the guys at the Hayloft. Any other time, I'd be bumping into him everywhere I turned.

Charleston is small enough to hit all the major clubs in a few hours, even if you have to drive to North Charleston. If you wanted to be found, it was no big thing to just sit in one place and wait. Reed didn't like the idea of being found. He would rather do the finding. His numbers business would have him carrying a large amount of cash, which meant he would be traveling armed, and usually with a bodyguard. If I couldn't catch up with him, it would be because he didn't want me to catch up with him. Reed had a sixth sense when it came to knowing when to surface and when to stay low. When I finally got to The Joker, the word was on the street that I needed to talk to him. It would only be a matter of time before he found me.

The streets were deserted and all the old money was in bed. These hours belonged to people like me, the night runners. I pulled into Piggy Park, a drive-in barbecue joint on the north end of Rutledge Avenue, and pushed the intercom button under the plastic menu. Five minutes later a cute carhop in short-shorts roller skated up carrying a beer and a Big Joe Basket which came with the best fries, onion rings and hush puppies on the east coast. She didn't recognize me, or pretended not to. Either way she'd obviously decided to let me eat in peace, so, I gave her a twenty and told her to keep the change.

Slowing down long enough to enjoy one of my favorite meals helped clear my head, I considered my options and decided to start at The Brick, a club down near the end of the Peninsula, and work my way north.

Proper businessmen in seersucker suits and white bucks mingled with the blue blazers and tan pants of the legal community, the bankers and real estate moguls. But when the sun went down, the youthful faces of the college crowd and the local Bubbas, hoodlums, gamblers and drug dealers started making the rounds in the clubs. It was like living in two civilizations at once. The proper society folk in Charleston headed to bed by ten, except the ones who gambled at The Merch, which was about the time the rest of us were getting started. The funny thing to me was that the people who went to bed early were the same ones who had partied all night ten years earlier. Some tried to hang on by staying out until one or two, but the bottom line was that after two a.m., the streets of Charleston belonged to those who worked around the nightclub business.

You couldn't run the streets at night and work during the day, every day of the week, and live to tell about it. At some point, they'd all eventually end up in some bed, but for the time being there was only the night, the music and the perpetual party-hearty attitude of the street people. I ordered bourbon and water from "a member's bottle" at The Brick and had it put in a traveler. That's a cocktail in a plastic to go cup. There was one last place to look.

The Coconut Grove had nothing in common with a coconut or a grove. It was an old warehouse stuck back in the industrial park section on Pittsburgh Avenue off North Meeting Street. The club had been converted into a strip joint with topless go-go dancers and a lighted dance floor.

Within a hundred feet of the front door, eighteen-wheelers fueled up at Southern Truck Stop on the way from the docks to the rest of the world. A hundred feet in the opposite direction the ancient scrap metal crane at Friarson's salvage yard scraped, creaked and rumbled into the night, loading wrecked cars, worn out washing machines, refrigerators and any other metal scrap into freight cars heading for the refineries up north. Even at three in the morning, the music from inside the Coconut Grove was so loud it could be heard over the dirty din of the car crushers. I took another sip from my bourbon and water as I eased down Pittsburgh Avenue toward the back of the club.

The industrial side of Charleston was in full swing, even on a Monday night. The vibrations from the crane, the jolts from the big rigs rumbling out of the truck stop, syncopated with the beginning of Deep Purple's version of "Hush." Every kind of freak, queen and drug-head could be seen leaning on, out or into a car. Making-out, snorting up anything that would fit inside a straw or just puking against the building, the night crawlers of Charleston were doing their thing; not a cop in sight.

Reed's Riviera was around back parked next to a red XKE. The Jaguar was locked up tight, but Reed had left the keys in the ignition of the Buick. Anyone who didn't know Bill Reed would say this was a stupid thing to do. But Reed left his keys in his car on a regular basis just hoping somebody would be fool enough to steal the car. He enjoyed tempting fate; living on the edge made him feel indestructible.

If some fool did steal the car, a whole new game would be a foot. Reed then took matters into his own hands. Playing judge, jury and executioner, he would track the guilty party down and then, as he was so fond of saying, "Beat him 'til he can't walk, then beat him because he can't walk." Reed's favorite tactic was to find the fool in a club and pistol whip the hell out of him before he turned him over to the police. Anybody, who got in Reed's way, got the .45 upside the head. In Bill Reed's mind, the bad-ass game furthered his reputation. Word got out. It had been over two years since Reed had a car stolen. With his reputation firmly in place, leaving the keys in his car was as much a part of his power trip as the nickel-plated .45 in his belt.

Inside, the Coconut Grove sounded like a Hell's Halloween party. The band, The Magicians, was fronted by Mickey Driggers, alias Mandrake, who wore a black cape with red satin lining. The rest of the band members were in tux shirts, tux pants, red cummerbunds and red capes with black lining. They were a six-piece band with two horns, trumpet and sax, trying hard to cross Black Sabbath, Led Zeppelin, and Hendrix with James Brown.

Mandrake and the Magicians latest claim to fame was an original song called "Heads on Fire." Mickey bounded around the stage in something like a tie-died, floor length moo moo, jumping up and down, waving two giant bubble wands like he was trying to fly, wearing a flaming butane fueled helmet screaming "MY FUCKING HEAD'S ON FIRE!" One thing about this crew, you could tell they were all heavy into acid and proud of it.

Patrons of the Coconut Grove seldom drifted below the North Charleston city limit sign. Most were from all over the country, by way of the Naval Base, with a few locals wandering in and out, mainly waiting to see Mickey light up. A hand-scrawled sign on the door to the men's room read 'Times of dope will get you through times of no money better than times of money will get you through times of no dope.'

I weaved my way through the mob of sequins, patent leather and plastic miniskirts, crushed velvet bell-bottoms and freak hairdos to a corner by the end of the stage. Mickey winked at me from the stage. He was screaming the lead vocal to "Whole Lotta Love," doing all that moaning and breathing crap that goes in the middle, while the guitar player dragged a violin bow across his strings. When the drums kicked in, he looked down at me and yelled, "I'll never play country music again!" I laughed at him, remembering that six months ago, he was wearing a cowboy hat and boots, playing at the VFW up on Rivers Ave.

"What's happ'nin', Josie?" A shoulder rubbed up next to mine, and I looked over at Tommy Bennett. He was bouncing out of sync with the beat, his left hand cupped over a vein north of his right elbow joint in that loving way junkies do right after they shoot up. His clothes smelled like sweat, smoke and no bath for days, his shirt stuck to his chest.

When you gonna c-c-call me m-m-man?" He coughed, then spit, then shivered. "I just need a few more days to get my chops back up. Been practicin' ever-everyday. Every-fuckin'-d-day." His eyes darted around the room. A bead of sweat formed on his upper lip, his eyes a frosty glare. "Got them Wilson Pickett chops goin'. Got that first lick to 'Mr. Pitiful' down c-cold … you gotta hear me, man. I got it now." Head bobbin', mouth on the sleeve wipe, sleeve across the eye wipe. "Yeah, man, I g-got it n-now." He was fried.

"Why don't you blow with old Mandrake there, Tommy?" I nodded toward Mickey the caped mad man, formerly Copper Head and the Diamondbacks.

"Funny you shou' men-shunit," he slurred. "I'm blowin' with them on a number or two tonight. I just ain't into that psychedelic drag Queen, fuzzy hair, platform shoe scene, man, you dig? I'm into the damn blues, man, the low down and dirty damn mutha fugkin' blues, man. I ain't into no hot as hell capes and trippin' an' shit, you dig? Light shows, crash pads and Hare Krishna, fuck tha shhhhhit." Bobbing, weaving, sleeves, sweats. "I'm into soul music, man. Tyrone Davis, Darrell Banks, man, fuggin' "Open The Door To Your Heart," man, fuggin' Jackie Wilson, man, Chuck fuggin' Jackson, you dig?"The cough went deeper, to an almost TB deep kind of cough. "'Sides, these fuggin' people are all fuggin' crazy as fuggin' hell, man, I mean look at 'em, man." His eyes were tearing from all the coughing, he could barely speak, he took a bottle of Robitussin out of his pocket and took a big swig. "Always hated the damn Beatles. All that English crap."

I said nothing. Didn't look at him. Made no gesture of any kind, which was Charleston body language for "I hear you perfectly, but I really don't want to be seen with you." Still, Tommy might know where I could find Reed, which is the self-serving side of the same coin. "Gimme Motown and Stax any fuggin' day. Know what I mean?"

"Have you seen Bill tonight?" I had to yell to be heard over the racket.

"Reed?" Tommy coughed and inclined his face toward me. "Reed's in his mover and shaker mode flashing the .45. Somebody's going to get smacked 'fore the night's over. He's here somewhere but I ain't talked to him tonight."

"You sittin' in or not?" Mickey, the caped crusader, yelled from his position behind his Vox Continental organ, "We're doing the Arthur Brown thing again."

"I'm comin' man." Tommy opened his trumpet case, picked up his horn, blew the moisture out of the spit valve and yelled back at Mickey. "Don't wait on me, man, I'll fuggin' be there man, when the time comes, I'm fuggin' there, man."

Mickey, the former cowpoke, moseyed over to a box and removed a football helmet rigged with four copper tubes hooked to a Coleman lantern butane tank. When the lights went down, Mickey opened the valve and used a lighter to set off the flames on his head. Then the former Copperhead growled into the mike, "My Fucking Head's On Fire!" and the band broke into the song. "On Fire!" pronounced Fye-yuh "My Head is in Flames!" pronounced Fa-Lame-zah. Tommy's trumpet part was exactly three notes and he cracked the second one each time he tried to hit it. He looked down at me and smiled. It's sad watching a musician die like that, even if he is an asshole.

During the organ solo, Tommy lifted his chin toward the back of the room, indicating Reed was near the bar. I worked my way through a crowd of maniacs screaming, "Your Ass'll Flame! Your Ass'll Flame!" Halfway down the sidewall a woman pinched my seat.

"Hey, sugar britches," said Cricket, the Abyssinian bartender from The Apartment Club. She was with another black hooker I'd seen several times at the Coffee Cup. "What's a nice juice freak like you doing in a chemical plant?"

"Nothin' much, here on a little business, is all."

"Oh-h-h Biz-z-z-n-s-s-s, how romantic. Well, when y'all get ready for some real bid'ness, come see me, Sugah."

I smiled and continued to work my way down the wall. Reed was sitting on the last stool at the end of the bar, with a drink in one hand and a cigarette in the other. The diamond cuff links sparkled, serpentine bracelet strategically dangling, a red scarf billowed out of the pocket of a black double-breasted blazer with gold buttons. The paisley print tie was pumped up and snagged by a gold collar bar and diamond stickpin. He was talking to a beautiful brunette in her twenties wearing a tank top, mini skirt and sipping a Singapore Sling through a straw held between thumb and forefinger. Her Barbara Bach bangs and doe-eyed expression reminded me of a Herb Alpert album cover model. Fresh meat for the grill, I thought. Or the freezer, whichever comes first.

Reed's eyes were locked on her lips and I could see his gears grinding for this one. I wondered what Janet would think. I walked up behind the girl and nodded to Reed.

"Well, well, Josie." He said, taking a drag off his cigarette and exhaled in a smoke ring. "What brings you to this side of town?"

"You're a hard guy to keep up with." I said, totally ignoring the girl.

"Busy, busy, busy." He winked at the girl, took a sip of his drink, a drag off his cigarette and ran his finger slowly down the side of her face. "Every place I've been tonight people sayin' 'Josie's looking for you.'"

"You got a minute?" I said politely and smiled at the lovely victim.

"Sure, what's on your mind?"

"It's personal."

"No problem. Wicked Wanda here won't mind, will you baby?" He patted her on the leg about eight inches above her knee. She sat there grinning, straw held to mouth by thumb and forefinger and down she scoots off the barstool so her black skirt rides up high enough to show her white panties.

"You wanna talk," he said. "We talk right here, I may look like I'm socializing, but I've got a lot of balls in the air tonight, so make it fast."

"Wanda, there, is some kind of cute. Does Janet know about her?"

"Now that, Joseph, is none of your goddamn business." He took a drink, smacking his lips and thumping his cigarette on the ashtray. "I know you're not here checking up on my love life, but if you like Wanda, just say so, I'll see what I can do."

"I'm not here to talk about women. Let's talk about Bootsy Williams?"

"Bad subject to bring up at a party, Deacon," he shifted his weight. "Real buzz kill, if you catch my drift. Word all over town is the cops are watching everybody."

"No, they're not watching everybody, they're watching me," I said.

"That's bullshit, man. If they wanted you, they'd have you by now. You're still walking around free, still working, that ain't being looked at, man. Being looked at is sitting in a jail cell being fucking LOOKED-AT!"

"Maybe so," I said. "But I left your bag with Bootsy Williams."

"You oughta know better than to do favors for people you don't trust."

He was scanning the room.

"For somebody who doesn't know much, you sure seem to know a lot. This was a favor for you. You sent me on this gig, man. You saying I shouldn't trust you, of all people?"

"Of course you can trust me, you got paid a damn good piece of change for the gig, too, brother. Let's not forget that little crumb."

Wanda was whispering to a girl at the bar, she at least had sense enough to not pay attention.

"Well, my little crumb isn't the reason I'm here. I'm up to my eyebrows in alligators, and I need some help. From you." I was bearing down on him; he didn't like it.

"Me?" You need help from me? Now that's some funny shit right there, coming from you." He winked at Wanda. Sucking her straw, she scrunched her cute nose and gave him the thumb-and-forefinger-close-to-her-lips-pinch-the-straw-pucker-suck look hookers usually shoot from the other end of the bar. Reed tossed back his drink, signaled the bartender for another, crushed the butt and pulled out another pack. The handle of the .45 was visible under the jacket.

"I'm guessing here, Bill," I said, "but you know what my guess is?"

"Dying of curiosity here, Deacon. Just keeling over, you know what I mean?" He wasn't listening to me; he was enduring me, his gaze fixed on the dance floor, trying to discern some minute exchange in body language signaling changes in a relationship he needed to follow.

"My guess is, you aren't being straight with me, which makes me think I need to take protective measures, you know, like telling the cops about your buddy."

"Whoa, whoa, whoa, wait a minute, my friend. What buddy are you talking about?"

Like I said earlier, I had nothing to lose by throwing the first punch. Right or wrong, I'd at least started listening to my early warning system again, so I went with my gut and starting improvising.

"A man named Mark Ward paid me a visit today," I said.

"Who the fuck is Mark Ward? I don't know any Mark Ward." He took a drag.

"He's a new captain at the Naval Base. His wife is Kela Ward. You know her as Bobbie Storm, the girl singer in your house band, the one you told me stay away from." I watched his face for the reaction.

"Oh yeah, Bobbie Storm, sounded like a stage name. I didn't know she was married," he said. "And I never heard of her husband. Besides, there's no reason I'd know anybody associated with the Navy."

"Then you wouldn't know anything about this," I said, pulling one of the Sea Oat Corporation invoices out of my pocket. "These figures, and the ones on two other invoices I have, add up to exactly 20 grand, the exact total of fresh from the mint bills I gave to Williams."

"Where the hell'd you get that?" Reed sat straight up with his back arched. "Just because you're a little nervous is no reason to start talking fool, boy. My company business is none of your business. Has the pig really turned you suicidal? Is he really trying to nail you for this gig?"

"You and Captain Ward are defrauding the Navy by using fraudulent supply requisition CHITS to funnel money through your dummy corporation," I said. "I don't give a shit about that, I really don't care." Bill Reed looked at me like he had seen a ghost. "I need to be able to prove that I didn't do Williams. Because the cops are doing everything in their power to prove I did. They're on me like ugly on an ape. The Merch, my house, everywhere I go Bill, the fucking Navy is following me, they came to the club, hassling me, man. A Navy geek followed me into the men's room and watched me take a piss. He works for Ward, whose wife works for you. Do the fucking math, man!" I was getting so angry I could have strangled him.

"Hold your voice down, Deacon, they ain't on your piano playing sweetheart because she works for me."

I scanned his face.

"It's because you're tapping her behind her old man's back, now, ain't that right?"

"I haven't touched Kela Ward, but suppose I had, how'd you know we've seen each other off stage?"

I was shocked he'd held back his knowledge of my relationship with Kela, when a few minutes earlier he'd said he didn't even know she was married.

"Charleston is my town, now, in case you've forgotten. It's my business to know everything about everything making ripples in the pond." He took another nervous drag off the cigarette and threw a ten at the waiter who delivered his drink. "I own this fucking place."

"Screw you, man," I said, "you're not playing straight with me on this one, Bill. And the shit is getting old. Now somebody is going to come across with some information to clear me or I'm going to show this invoice to the State Law Enforcement Division."

"OK, OK, settle down, for the love of Christ. Give me a little time to put something together. I'll think of something. Don't start getting stupid and threatening me, man. God knows, I got little patience for that shit. You oughta know that by now. You only got this far because you're like family to me. I know you didn't mean to threaten me. 'Cause if I believed that, we'd have serious trouble here. I know you've got a problem. The pig is on you because he thinks you're about to crack. The Navy is on you because they think you're ballin' the boss's wife."

"Thigpen is ready to lock me up," I said. "He thinks I took Williams out and stole money he is convinced you gave me to drop. All he needs is a body and I'm toast. It's OK for you to play it cool because you're clean because there's no proof the money ever existed."

"Will you calm the fuck down and stop worrying for ten seconds? Ask yourself, when was the last time the cops hung up a white dude for doin' a spook?" He chuckled. "Fact is, white dudes don't do spooks. Except maybe up north. Down here, man, only cops and other spooks kill spooks. Lilies do lilies. Shit-fuck, they probably wanta give somebody a medal. Besides, if I was a cop, I'd be looking at Erlene Brown, that voodoo crap she's into got all the monkeys in the jungle runnin' for the trees. Her weird kid won't help, either. Besides, your story wouldn't sound any better, even if he was with you."

"So you know that, too? You know Rashad was with me, you know I was with Erlene Brown. Do you also know I saw your car pass mine on Maybank Highway, right after I left Williams alive and well? You know what I might think, Billy? I might think you punched Williams' card and stole the money and now you're trying to frame me. That's what I fucking think, Bill, except there's a problem. I saw him again Saturday night.

"Who? You saw who again?"

"Fucking Williams man, he was outside The Merch in the parking lot."

"You're shittin' me."

"And furthermore, I think I can prove you and Ward are not only working the Navy base angle and washing the money, but that Williams is trying to blend the black lottery into your Navy fraud scheme."

Open mouth, insert entire foot, and swallow. Three strikes and you're out. Fuck me I'd done it again. Reed put his hand on my shoulder.

"Listen kid, you're definitely out of your mind, the pressure is making you crazy. Let me send Wanda home with you tonight. You' forget all about your troubles. I'll send champagne to the Charleston Inn, come join us later, it's all on me."

The band took a break and the dance floor crowd merged with the furniture. The bar crowded up, arms all around us reaching for drinks.

"I don't want any more gifts or favors, I only want one thing," I said.

"Wanda will treat you right, give you a new lease on life." He knocked back his drink.

"Get me out of this mess you got me into. After that, I want nothing from you. We're out of business. It's too much trouble. I don't even know if I'm going to keep playing music."

I didn't believe I'd heard myself, it was like I was somebody else. Like I'd sneaked up behind myself. I knew I was going to quit as sure as I knew my name. I wanted out. I'd wanted out for over a year, but this was the first time I knew I'd do it.

"Put the Navy thing out of your mind, that's bullshit" he said. "But this cop thing and your girlfriend's old man, aren't the only tunes on your hit parade right now, you know?" Reed spit the remark out like a peanut shell.

"What do you mean?" I said.

"I mean you've got problems back at The Merch with old stiletto toes. Vincent don't cotton to the kind of attention you've been getting. You might get fired before you even get the chance to quit. Ask Sinclair or Montague, they know, the whole street knows, but you."

"Maybe I didn't make myself clear," I said "As soon as my name is cleared, I'm getting out of the business, forever."

He put his sleazy arm around my shoulder again. "Now, Deacon, Son, you came here asking a favor, you wanted my help on something that's out of control. And I'm more than happy to do what I can. And how do you ask? With threats and innuendo, how's that look? Now, what's in it for me? Why the fuck should I help, when you tell me now you won't come back to The Apartment Club after The Merch turns its back on you?"

At last, there we were, down to the downright rotten, low down dirty. He wasn't going to help me without some prearranged payback. His whole plan, from the start, included getting me and my band back over to his club so he could throw it up in everybody's face, just to feed his ego. I looked up at Tommy Bennett. He was sitting on a ladder chair off to one side of the stage, left hand cupped over the junkie's arm, nodding off, horn laying in his lap. That's me in two years I thought, if I don't get out.

"How can I say this," I said. "I'm in trouble because you strong-armed me into doing you one lousy favor I didn't wanna do in the first place. Now everybody's after me. I'm getting out of this, one fucking way or another. I'll walk away from it with or without your help, but I won't take a fall for you or anybody else. I'm warning you Bill, don't start me talking, or I swear to God, I'll tell everything I know. Everything, Billy, you understand me? I'll tell them about you, your club, your numbers operation, and I'll show them this," I waved the invoice in his face. "If I go down, you're going with me. So you've got two choices, kill me or help me."

"Josie, son, until you said that, I thought... thought, hell, maybe I, we, were, really believed we were friends. I understand now, I was wrong and it saddens me. I'll get you a story that'll stick and cover you for the whole night of the Williams gig. I hate to see you leave the business you've devoted so much of your life to, and are so damn good at, but at least if I can't have you, neither can anybody else. Hell, I might quit myself. I'm only trying to take care of some business, you understand."

"You'll go down with me, Billy, so don't bullshit me." I grinned my suicidal manic grin. "You let me down on this, you'll go straight to hell with me, I swear to God."

"You've got a ticket," he snapped. "Now, get out of here, or I'll send you to hell myself."

"That's cool, Bill, so long as we understand each other. I'm serious about this. All of it."

Reed looked disgusted, frustrated and furious. He spit on the spot in the floor where I'd been standing. When I walked back through the crowd toward the door, I thought about the time he told me he was a crazy man. Maybe so, maybe Bill Reed was also a dangerous man, a crazy dangerous man. But he was still afraid of dying. And that was the difference between us.

CHAPTER TWENTY-SIX

By six a.m., I was back at my apartment, watching the light grow brighter through the window. My body ached and my mind was numb from worrying about what the day would hold. I knew I needed sleep. Kela was on the sofa in the living room, curled up like a cat. I'd never seen the place so clean. Clean sheets on the bed, clean pillowcases, clean floors, she'd gone over the whole apartment.

When I got out of the shower, the smell of breakfast cooking floated on the air. My bathrobe was hanging on the back of the bathroom door; a clean T-shirt and jeans were lying on the bed. I got dressed, even though the need for sleep had never been more obvious.

I walked into the kitchen as she was sliding two fried eggs onto a plate with toast and bacon. A glass of orange juice sat next to a folded napkin. The shades were open; sunlight filled the room.

"You needed some light in here. This place is more like a cave than an apartment." She kissed my cheek. "Let's eat on the porch."

"The idea of facing every day at this hour doesn't seem half bad," I said.

"Change is good for the soul."

"What did you say?"

"I said, change is good for the soul."

"That's a phrase I've used. Last Friday, I told Jack 'Speculation is good for the soul.'"

"Great minds think alike."

The breeze coming up the river carried a cool saltwater tang, tingling my palate and making the eggs and bacon taste even better. My senses had never been so acute. Everything was amplified. Colors were brighter, food tasted better, street sounds were coming through in stereo. I could hear the feathers of sparrows and jays fluttering from branch to branch. A couple black Labs romped in the neighbor's backyard, barking, as squirrels with tiny claws scrambled up tree bark. Somewhere out in the river a small outboard purred. I could still feel the sting of last night in my eyes. My blood was churning from all the bourbon and I felt like I had a slight fever. The hot coffee burned the inside of my mouth, but it was a good hurt.

Off in the distance, I heard a siren and assumed it was either a fire truck or an ambulance. Sirens in the night usually signaled a police car racing to a shootout or knife fight.

"Rough night?" Kela said.

"More like insane." I looked at her. The bruises were almost gone; her eyes were back to normal, which I thought was odd. "You seem to be healing pretty fast. What's your secret? You got your own line of make-up?"

"Can I tell you something without you getting all bent out of shape?"

"We're still in the discovery process. After what I've been through, nothing you could say would surprise me," I said.

"Remember the old black man I mentioned, Abraham?"

"The guy in Alabama, the one you said Montague knew?"

"Yes, he's actually Montague's cousin. He was born here in Charleston, but the family moved to Alabama after World War II. Back to his family farm."

"Where are you going with this?"

"Here, give me your plate, I'll get you another cup of coffee, then I'll show you."

Inside the apartment Kela was putting the dishes in the sink. Seeing her bustling around the kitchen was the most comforting vision I'd witnessed in years. She wiped her hands on a dishtowel, poured two cups of coffee and came out on the deck. The scene would've been perfect if it hadn't been for all the baggage.

"Have you ever seen one of these?" She dropped a red flannel drawstring pouch on the table. I took a deep breath. "You have, haven't you? I can tell by the look on your face."

"A guy I was with had a similar one with him Friday night. It had some powder in it," I said.

"Then he must've had one of these as well." She set an old snuff tin beside the pouch.

"As a matter of fact, he did." I placed my fist next to the pouch; the three pink scars were visible, but only as three tiny lines. "These were open gashes at five o'clock Saturday morning."

"Well, now you know how I've managed to heal so quickly," she said.

"Did Abraham give you that?"

"He gave me the first one, and he taught me how to make my own."

Kela put her hand on mine and balled her fist. Three pink lines became visible on the back of her hand. I looked at her, she looked at me, and a warm glow descended over both of us.

The words "Our scars recognize each other," formed in my thoughts.

"So, this is real. All of it. It's all real," I said.

"Oh it's real, alright; you have no idea how real," she said.

"Are you a… "

"Bridge? Yes. And so are you."

"So I've been told."

A time comes in the life of all seekers when their true nature is revealed to them for the first time. Clarity arrives in a mind-expanding moment from which there is no return. Their character manifests like a religious experience. You just know. You understand like you've never understood before, your small, but extremely important role in a much bigger plan. Stone cold sober, no second guessing, no wondering, no excuses, and no external factors to blame, or chalk up to a transitory lapse of sanity. My moment had arrived. I realized beyond all doubt that I wanted to spend the rest of my life with Kela.

There was no lunging over the table in a mad embrace. No tearing each other's clothes off, falling into bed for mad passionate love making. We merely looked at each, understood each other, and realized simultaneously our spirits had known each other for thousands of years. There are no words to describe the feeling, but there are words to describe certain aspects. I felt like I'd been at war for way too many years and was finally at long last, home.

"This's all overwhelming," I said. "You sure you didn't spike the coffee?"

"No spikes in the coffee," she grinned.

"So you knew who I was, I mean I am, you recognized… "

"The moment I saw you in the Swamp Fox Room."

"And Montague?"

"He's suspected when you first sat in with the band as a teenager. He wasn't sure until you came back to Charleston."

"And the two of you have been discussing all this behind my back?"

"You weren't ready," she said. "You wouldn't be ready yet if Erlene hadn't pushed you into it. Normally, it takes years to get where you are now. It's a little like winning a lot of money and becoming a millioniare over night. Most people couldn't handle that much information, you know? Dumped on them all at once."

"Well, I don't know how to handle it; I thought I was losing my mind."

"You have lost your mind; your old mind, you're in the process of growing a new one."

"Where do we go from here?" I said.

"I have no idea."

"Do you know how it works?"

"All I know for sure is how it works for me. Apparently there is no one-size-fits-all."

"How many other people do you know who have …; I'm reluctant to call it a gift; so I'll say, who are aware of this particular aspect of nature?"

"There are no stupid questions, only stupid answers," she laughed. "Until I met you, I'd only known Abraham and his aunt. They told me, given time, I'd learn to recognize others. You met the initial criteria I'd been taught to look for, then I met Montague through you, so now I know three, other than myself. I'm pretty sure Erlene is one, though from what I've heard, she's customized her own Mojo, juju, hoodoo, whatever you wanna call it, into some homemade concoction only she understands."

"What is she, some sort of voodoo witch or hoodoo priestess?" I said.

"Not at all, those are archaic words from hundreds of years ago. They don't mean any more than words like sin, faith, pope, bishop, preacher, monk, devil, demon, or any other religious sounding words. They're subjective concepts people use to mean whatever they need them to mean, when they can't find a better term to explain what they don't understand."

"What about the voice?"

"What voice?" she said.

"I hear a voice, well I don't hear-hear like with my ears, more like an inner voice, a different voice than the one I think with."

"I don't have the inner voice, not yet anyway, I see things," she said.

"You mean like visions?"

"More like random day dreams." Kela stared into space for a solid minute. "You know how, when you're driving, you start thinking about something and before you realize it ten miles have gone by?"

"Happens to me all the time on Highway 61," I said.

"Your eyes are on the road, your hands are on the wheel, your foot is on the gas, and you've done it so many times it's like your brain is on cruise control. The next thing you know you're thinking about last night's gig, or some song you wanna learn, and before you know it your conscious mind is lost in thought, but your subconscious mind is driving the car," she said.

"I know exactly what you mean."

"Imagine you're standing in front of another person when suddenly you see him doing something, it could be anything, riding a bicycle, and the bicycle is a red Columbia bicycle and you see the guy fall and skin a knee. And you ask him 'how's your knee?' and it blows him away because they have on long pants and there is no way you could know he has a skinned knee." She looked at me and I was smiling. "What?"

"I'm serious. I know exactly what you're talking about. I've already had that happen to me," I said.

"Unsolicited daydreams are what I get, or pictures of things, like a wine bottle or a dog or a house, and sometimes I will see a word. I don't always act on it, unless I'm pushed."

"Pushed?" I said.

"Yes, the words pop out of my mouth without me even thinking about them, like they have a mind of their own."

"I'm getting exhausted thinking about it," I said.

"The only thing bothering me is I can't seem to gain any control over it."

"You can't summon it, in other words?" I said.

"No, I can't. Can you?"

"Hardly. Until we had this conversation, I thought I was going insane."

"Montague's been worried about you," she said.

"I know. I'm worried about me, and now I'm worried about how we're going to handle our current situation," I said.

"I'm going to take a shower," Kela said. "What are you going to do?"

"Trust me when I tell you, there's no place I'd rather be than with you in the shower, but there's something inside of me that won't let me."

"Why don't you take a walk, clear your head before the storm?" Kela set the morning paper on the table. "Here, read this." She pointed to the weather forecast. A new tropical depression had formed down in the Caribbean. The last one had blown up out in the Gulf, then bottomed out over the midlands causing flash floods. The latest one would cross the Florida panhandle, then track toward the Eastern Seaboard and Charleston.

"It's a weather report. I got it, it rains in September, goes with the territory."

"When this thing hits, the Ashley and the Cooper Rivers will crest to within inches of the lower bridges, within a few days. Downtown will be flooded worse than last Friday," she said. And she had a good point. "The Ashley Bridge and the one across the Stono at Buzzards Roost will probably become impassable. People will be hunkered down trying to ride it out. Charleston will be a mess."

"The upside is little or no traffic," I said. "The current will be picking up low-lying branches, adding to the debris the river already carries into the harbor. Swamps will be filling in the Upstate and detours will be set up to keep drivers from flooded areas."

"My guess?" Kela looked out over the porch rail toward the river. "This will be the perfect time for whoever is after you to make his move, while everyone's attention is focused on the weather."

"And you know this, how?" I said.

"I'm basically telling you what I saw," she said.

"OK then, in that case I'm going for a walk while I can still walk."

Reynolds's garden hammock seemed a worthy destination considering I'd had less than four hours sleep. I wrapped the napkin around the orange juice, then walked along the flagstone path. Off to the side, a wet spot had formed in the earth skirting the stones; moss and fungi grew in the mortar joints. Even the rocks around the drain culvert were sinking into the soggy ground. Some animal footprints, raccoons, squirrels, were filled with water. The moist air grew heavy.

The closer to the garden's edge I got, the more the sun's heat gave the humidity a life all its own. In the South, when the sun rises, the air heats up as quickly as a gas burner. Words like "stewing in your own juice" come to mind. All the scene needed was a good volcano and a brontosaur and I'd have been back millions of years in history, except for the houses, of course.

My eyes burned. The aches and pains of no sleep pushed me further down the road to total exhaustion. A sticky film of condensation formed on my skin. Within three minutes my T-shirt was soaked. I had the unshakable feeling the whole drama was coming to a head. I'd just settled into a chair by the birdbath when I heard Reynold's phone ringing. He looked at me through his kitchen window, told the caller to hold on; then he waved the receiver in my direction. I walked over and he handed me the phone through the open window.

The noise in the background sounded like a newsroom. A hand was moving back and forth over the mouthpiece on the other end and the caller was yelling at somebody in the background. Thigpen came on the line.

"What's up, Josie?" he chirped. ""Night like you had would make anybody's head bad. Slim said you put a hundred miles on your T-Bird last night. Slim is your night shadow, don't'cha know. That's how I know where you are right now. That dude with the cape who set his head on fire at the Coconut really freaked old Slim out. Slim grew up in Barnwell and swears the guy used to play country up at Dukes Barbecue in Ridgeville. Blew old Slim away with that Hell Fire routine. Slim said he didn't know dope could do that to a man."

"Whatever blows your skirt up, Thigpen," I said. "Surely you must've found Williams' body and the murder weapon, with my fingerprints on it, by now."

"Not unless you've got it on you," he joked. "You must be worn out to talk like that."

"What do you want from me, man? You know I didn't do this thing. Why're you all over me? I can't believe we're still having this conversation."

"To be honest with you, Chapman, I stayed up late last night myself, reading old news articles about your career. The papers followed you pretty close. If I didn't know better, I'd bet your buddies in the music business would have a hard time hiring a murder suspect, that's if you were ever planning on going back on the road. I did some background checking and found some interesting stuff. If any of this gets in the papers, you might even have a hard time getting a real job, after you leave the music business, I mean."

The man was unbelievable; he had me over a big barrel. Why didn't he just go ahead and arrest me? "Just out of curiosity, why didn't you ever say anything about Chapman not being your real name?" He paused. "Redding ain't such a bad name; I'm sure you wouldn't have to worry about people mixing you up with Otis. You don't hear much about rock musicians coming out of Dallas, North Carolina. You got kicked out of school in the fourth, fifth and sixth grades. Your uncle, cousin and father all did time in a North Carolina state penitentiary. Then, your father beats your mother and winds up dead six months later… about the same time you moved to Charleston. Your mother had both your names changed back to her maiden name of Chapman, and they never figured out who killed your father. Interesting life. Almost as interesting as the one you got going on here. Too bad about your old man."

"He's in hell where he belongs," I said.

"Still have a tender spot for his memory, do you?"

"My world has always been pretty unforgiving, Thigpen."

"Like I was trying to say, it's still nice knowing you're so forgiving."

"I've had to endure ignorant, arrogant, bullying assholes like you all my life. I told you I've had my ass kicked by meaner jerks than you, so get on with it. I'm ready for this to be over. What do you want?"

"You were living in the spotlight booth in the ceiling of the Folly Beach Pier, hitchhiking to school, playing in the bands at night to make money. Along comes rockin' Jerry Lee and a taste for the big time and off you go. In and out of college on music scholarships when you couldn't even read music. Faking it all the way. Thirty-five hours away from a BA degree, 3.0 GPA and high dollar gigs."

"What of it?" I said.

"You got busted in Hamilton, Alabama, for possession. A state trooper found synthetics and a hash pipe in your van. How'd you get out of that?"

"The van belonged to another roadie. He loaned to me. They let us go. The roadie never claimed the van, it was sold at auction. I wasn't charged."

"That's it? No phone call? No friends in high places? They just let you walk? You and your whole fucking band?"

"If you know so much about me, then you know I have a lot of friends, in a lot of places."

"You threatened a man's life yesterday in The Merch. Pulled a gun on him. He say something to piss you off?"

"I pointed my finger at him."

"Noon on the same day, you're in Hampton Park with a group of gunslingers from God knows where, eating peanuts and feeding ducks while discussing God knows what. You wouldn't happen to be mixed up with the mob, by any chance?"

If it hadn't been so pathetic it would have been funny. Thigpen was grabbing at straws big time. The idea that Ward's goons had been with the mob was a real hoot. Government security men mistaken for mob hit men. What a grocery store check-out headline that would make.

"Doesn't matter right now. Maybe you did a hit for the mob. All the trouble you've had in your life, with school, your old man, the dope dealing in Alabama and now this mafia thing pops up. And here I was thinking you were just another horn tooter. I should've recognized your hidden talents. I swear, Chapman, you're into something bigger than you're letting on. I'm betting you owe somebody money, or a big favor, now it's payback time, and you ain't got the goods. We need to have our overdue heart-to-heart this afternoon, maybe put you into protective custody."

"You've got an imagination straight out of Disneyland," I said.

"Maybe; maybe not. Anyway, that's my theory, and my Captain is buying it." He said. "We'll see you down here by two o'clock or I'm coming after you." He hung up on me.

The last time he came after me, I'd embarrassed him too much for his ego to stand. This time, he wanted pay back on his turf. Or maybe, I was just a source of entertainment for him.

My basic instinct was to get dressed, get in my car, and leave town. I could lay up with friends on the West Side of Manhattan and wait for the real killer to get caught. Instead, I sat in a chair by the birdbath and watched blue jays and mockingbirds splash and cuss each other in bird language. I tried to imagine what I'd do for a living without music. I dozed off, and started dreaming I'd been caught in a briar patch, when I heard Kela's footsteps.

I opened my eyes and tried to remember how I got where I was. Kela was wearing a pair of white shorts, a white tank top with sandals, and sunglasses pushed up on her head like a hair band. The black and blue marks on her neck, arms and thighs had completely disappeared. Those bruises had reminded me of what so much of this whole ordeal was all about. She sat on my lap and put her head down on my shoulder. It was obvious she'd been crying.

"How are you holding up? You look exhausted." She brushed my hair.

"My will to stay and fight is fading fast," I said. She sat up, pulled the rubber band from her hair and let it fall to her shoulders. We sat there watching the birds, feeling the breeze, letting the breath of the Lowcountry cool our skin. The strain was getting to her. The moment was solemn, being with her, smelling her scent, feeling her hair on my cheek, gave me a peace I'd never experienced. I was looking forward to telling her about my decision to get out of the business. I set my chin on her shoulder.

"You know what you said the other night about there being more to life than playing music?" I said it softly, twisting a strand of her hair with my finger. The swelling on her neck was gone. "You were right. I think I'll go back to school and…"

"Before you say anymore, I need to tell you something." She took my hand in both of hers and pulled my arms around her waist.

"What is it, Kela?"

"I don't want you to change just for me."

I thought it was an odd thing to say; since the whole change thing had been her idea. "What makes you think I'm going to change just for you?" I looked deep into her eyes, not sure what I was feeling. A fear knot formed in my chest.

"Josie," she whimpered. "I'm going back home, to Mark. I didn't want to tell you this morning, but he's flying to Paris for three weeks. He wants me to go with him. He wants us to try, one more time, to make it work between us. It will give you and me time to sort out our problems and put things into perspective. It's not what I want to do, but I don't have much of a choice."

My head fell on the back of the chair. I felt my heart start to slowly sink to my stomach. My soul was body slammed. The last thing I'd wanted, and what I'd run from all my life, was leaving myself open for a sucker punch by someone I let get too close. That old Murphy's Law, "the thing you take for granted is the one that will get you every time," had gotten me. I'd been completely set up. It all made perfect sense to get nailed to the wall like a coonskin on a boathouse, just when my walls were going down.

"What about everything we said not thirty minutes ago?"

"I'm not finished. Can you give me three weeks?"

"Are you going back to him today?" The wind had picked up, bringing a chill to my sweat soaked skin. "None of this makes any sense." The clouds rolled in, turning the sky the color of rippled slate. "When will I see you again?"

I tried to maintain a cool exterior, but I was dying inside. I saw the woman I loved not only slipping away, but plunging, head first, back into the belly of the beast.

"This is the hardest thing I've ever done," she said, eyes filling with tears until they finally broke into cascades down her cheeks. I handed her my napkin.

"I know what you mean," I said. The feeling of a dream state hits you when something unreal happens, your mind won't accept it as fact. "It's the right thing to do. We need to take it easy and let a few things work themselves out or our lives are going to blow up."

She eased off my lap and straightened her shirt and shorts. The rubber band she'd used to hold her hair in a ponytail was back in her teeth. She put it over the hair she'd twisted in her fingers. She was dropping into that fierce determination mode I'd seen before.

"I have a pet term I use for times like this."

She looped both her arms around one of mine.

"Tell me."

"I call what you're about to do flying straight into the mouth of oblivion."

"Will you promise to wait for me?" she asked quietly.

"I don't think you have to worry about me waiting. In jail all you do is wait."

"Mark and I have discussed that." She watched my eyes to see how this piece of information filtered through my consciousness.

"He knows some people. Some people he says can help you. He knows you didn't do it and he'll help prove it."

I should've told her about my meeting with her husband, how he'd had me followed that night, how he'd tried to use the information to buy me off.

"Tell him thanks, but no thanks," I said. "Time has its own way of working things out."

She was already in this thing too deep to suit me. If she went to Paris, I'd have one less problem. That didn't keep me from feeling like death warmed over while all this was being decided, though, especially not knowing if he would hit her again. I knew she loved me, that she wanted to be with me. It would be nice to leave the music business, settle down and have a daytime life. But the truth was clearer to me than it had ever been. I wanted out period. I wasn't wallowing in self-pity when I met Kela. And I was determined I wasn't going to wallow in it now. I kissed her as tenderly as I knew how.

"It will be alright," I said. "It can't get any worse."

And there I was, making the same old, stupid mistake, expecting different results. Taking it for granted that things couldn't get any worse, just when Murphy's Law was about to nail me again. Only, this time I knew who I was, what I was capable of, and I wasn't going to lie down so thugs could walk all over me. I decided to say goodbye and tell her I was going to the police.

CHAPTER TWENTY-SEVEN

I drove to the Charleston Police Department on the corner of Vanderhorst and St. Philips Street. A goofy-foot cleanup boy they called Fast Eddie, because he was so slow, led me back to the Officer of the Day desk where I was told I could wait in the lobby or in the back room. I chose the back room. Fast Eddie shuffled me back to a dingy yellow nicotine-coated cubical like Quasimodo going to the bell tower.

The wooden chairs, rust stained radiator and scarred old railroad desk were bathed in the sickening, blue-green neon lights with bad starters, buzzing in the ceiling. I was sure many a poor brother had sat in my seat. The seat of the wooden chair was so slick I had to grab the floor with my heels to keep from sliding onto the filthy tiles. The rank air clung to my skin like my sweat soaked T-shirt. I felt like I needed a bath simply from sitting in the room.

Through the door I could see into one of the cells. A concrete cot and floor drain were the only furnishings. There were no windows. Inside the cell three black males in various stages of undress were wadded up in three separate balls, one on the cot, the other two on the floor. All three had either been in a fight, or beaten by the cops, or both. They snored the deep-drunk, sleeping-it-off snore of 48 hour days in the street. The one on the concrete cot had a bandage over his left eye and a badly bruised, freshly-stitched cut on his forehead. The other two had bloody knuckles and scratched up faces. Whatever happened to them was rough enough to land them in the city jail, but from their appearance, they were better off in jail than in the street. I'd seen animals caged in Hampton Park with better living quarters. I remember thinking: This is the septic tank of Charleston's social structure, the bottom of the proverbial toilet bowl.

Thigpen took his time getting around to me. I tried not to get too jumpy waiting for the next shoe to drop. There was always the lobby, with the wall-eyed desk sergeant, if I wanted somebody to talk to. I decided to try breathing the outside air rather than lounging with the freaks. I sat by the window, listening.

Low laughter, snoring, metal objects banging against each other, a distant tug boat whistle, some woman crying and the ping of a bell were a few of the sounds floating in the air. Occasionally, a police radio clambered about a Two-Eleven or Code Blue or some other night noise rattled off in cop jargon.

Thigpen was taking his sweet time, I got up to pee. The restroom was surprisingly clean, if swirling a dirty mop soaked with pure bleach will make porcelain clean. At least, the urinal and toilet weren't littered with pubes and piss puddles. There was plenty of poetry on the walls. "Keep a tight asshole. Signed, Western Man." "Not all niggers is Driggers, but all Driggers is niggers." Scrawled over the urinal: "Look down, the joke is in your hand."

Back in my chair with my feet planted firmly on the floor, I watched the clock on the wall turn six-thirty. I heard a ruckus out front and looked back as three cops and a detective wrestled with a big guy with wild, red hair and matching beard. His face was burnt from long days in the sun. The red plaid shirt and blue jeans made him look like a farmer, but he wore the white rubber boots of a fisherman, shrimper maybe but, more likely, he worked a longline boat. It took all four cops to hold him down. He was all wide-eyed and slobbering, like he was foaming at the mouth. Fast Eddie looked up, yawned, and went back to moving dirt around with a broom. The guy was screaming about how his buddies would take care of the cops when they found out.

"The other guy started the whole thing," he raved. "Why the shit-fuckin'-fire hell ain't he down here, too? I'm going to sue all y'all cop sons-a-bitches, Charleston County, the State of South Carolina for all they're worth! I got rights, by God!"

After the four men brought him to his knees, they wasted no time taking him all the way down, until his cheek was on the dirty tile floor. Fast Eddie swept right past the guy's nose.

"Get outta here with that fuckin' broom!" One of the cops yelled.

Eddie jumped, flapping like a buzzard jumping back from a car passing a road kill raccoon. Finally, they broke the guy. He gave up the struggle, started sobbing, and the cops pulled him to his feet and dumped him in a cell. Eddie mopped up the sweat pool on the floor.

Humility is a hard pill to have shoved down your throat in front of an audience. Watching the police take the guy down affected the way I would look at everybody for the rest of my life. Seeing them break that big man's spirit reminded me of my own spiritual break down. That whole idea of being up against something bigger, stronger, and even more determined than you, can drain all the desire right out of you. When your final desperate lunge for freedom has failed, you feel like an animal trapped, hooked or shot, lying helpless at the mercy of the hunter. A buddy of mine, a guitar player, got shot in the leg fifteen minutes into his first firefight in Vietnam. Everybody in his unit died, but him. He said it felt like somebody hates you more than they ever had a right to. You come to realize no matter how big and bad you were in your world, in your time, when the system gets its claws into you, "dat is whey're," as Montague used to say, "de weepin' an'de wailin' an' de snatchin' out o' teeth will be."

I knew if I got sent to the state prison, I'd never live through it. I didn't know enough about street fighting, and I was too antisocial to fit in with a group of convicts. The first time they tried to rape me, I'd try to kill somebody. It would only be a matter of time before they killed me.

While staring blankly out the window, I replayed the events of the last few days. Once again, the thought of suicide worked its way into my consciousness as a viable option, hanging like a spider web over real time. I was thinking all this, when a wave of light reorganized the reflections in the glass. For a split second, I saw what appeared to be a pair of eyes staring at me from outside. I stared right into the illusion, for the first time thinking long and hard about what Montague had been trying to tell me about Strong Man. What if it was true? What if something super-natural was behind all the chaos and confusion? A cold chill washed over my skin.

Snapping back from the daydream, I looked around to see if anyone saw me shiver. No one else was in the room. I figured Thigpen must have forgotten what time he'd told me to be there. More likely, though, this was all part of the special revenge he had planned for me after Sinclair, Montague and the other black guys backed me up at The Merch. He was letting the city jail work its magic, hoping I'd become a little more cooperative. It would be interesting to see how long I could stall him while waiting for the lifeboat Reed was supposed to be sending me.

My car was parked out by the street. I told the OD I'd forgotten something then went outside, opened the trunk, opened my horn case and retrieved the little wooden crucifix. Back inside I went to the men's room and put the cross around my neck, next to my bare skin. I finished buttoning my shirt and was washing my hands when another cop came in.

"They're ready for you." He motioned me back to a room at the end of the hall.

Two other men in suits were going over some files on a table with six chairs around it. They glanced up when I walked in, then went straight back to the papers on the table. One of them, wearing wire rim glasses and a thin mustache, looked more like a CPA than a cop. For one thing, he wasn't wearing a gun. Instead, his right hand was flying over a calculator, while his eyes focused on a list of numbers. He stopped adding long enough to motion for me to sit at the table, while the rest of them continued to sort the different papers into separate piles. The scene reminded me more of an IRS audit than a murder investigation. Thigpen bustled in and hung his hat on the back of the door.

"Thigpen, you're late, where's the pizza?" Said the one with the glasses.

"I ate it, Shaft," he said. "That's my new nickname for you, Ross. Because I'm going to take your career and shove it up your ass."

Thigpen looked at me like I was a total stranger, then took a pizza box, turned edge up from under his jacket and spun it onto the table. The lid flew open, revealing three pieces of pizza piled in one corner of the box with tomato sauce slung all over the sides.

The one called Ross looked at Thigpen like he was some kind of joke. The guy next to him offered me a slice of pizza as Ross said, "Thigpen, if you thought about your job half as much as you think about your damn stomach, you might actually have a career."

I shook my head at the man with the pizza, indicating I didn't want any. Thigpen, then, turned his attention to me. "Well, how do you like our little love nest, Chapman? Got a nice homey touch to it, don't you think? Especially with these sweethearts."

"If you say so, Detective. I haven't had enough sleep to fully appreciate your crude attempts at humor," I said.

"Hey, if you can't run with the big dogs, stay on the porch."

He started laughing, quickly shutting up when the other three men stared at him like an imbecile. They started separating several different stacks of papers, making notes and matching sets of numbers from one page with those on another. Apparently they were trying to get everything in sequence all for my benefit.

"I think that's about it," the one with the mustache said. "Who wants to go first?" They all looked at Thigpen, who was looking at me. "You go first, Slick," he said to Ross.

A cockroach scooted along the baseboard, looking for a crack big enough to crawl into. I knew how the roach felt when it hit the corner and tried to push through the concrete and plaster, unable to get any further. After a few head butts, it caromed out of the corner, ran down the wall next to me, antennas waving like orangutan arms. This is about as low as I can go, I thought. If they were going to step on me, I was ready to get it over with. Desperation will do that to you.

Ross stood up, while the other two sat opposite me. Each had his personal paper stack, a legal pad and pen. Thigpen sat off to one side of the table, chair back leaning against the wall, his hands locked behind his head, all set to enjoy the show. All he needed was a box of popcorn and a Coke balanced on the prodigious belly hanging over his belt buckle. He was grinning.

The third guy was the oldest of the group. Until now, he hadn't even acknowledged my existence. If I had to guess, I would've guessed he was with the FBI. With gray hair, furrowed brow and bushy eyebrows, he wore a charcoal gray, chalk stripe suit, club tie and black wingtips. The all-business look of the other guys in the room was in stark contrast to the grinning, imbecilic slob leaning up against the wall on two chair legs. It was obvious the gray, striped suit was in charge, but he didn't say anything. They were all seated with their neat piles of paper in front of them. The guy in the middle, the one Thigpen called Ross stood up.

"Mr. Chapman, my name is David Ross; I work with the State Law Enforcement Division. This is Tom Walker with the Internal Revenue Service," indicating the man to his right, "And the gentleman on my left is Jim Stevens with the Naval Intelligence Service." Stevens acknowledged me for the first time. "Do you have any idea why Detective Thigpen has asked you to meet with us."

I shrugged. The game was on. Ross turned the top page of his stack of papers toward me.

"This is a list of people we suspect are involved in a large, citywide gambling operation, among other things, headquartered here in Charleston. Do you recognize any of these names?"

He slid the list across the table in front of me. I looked at the dozen or so names. Roy's name was there, along with Freddie May, Bill Reed, Rev. Gary W. Edwards, Erlene Brown and Krytorious "Bootsy" Williams. Out to the right of Edwards and Williams names respectively, were the words (The Preacher) and (The Farmer). As I continued down the list, I recognized every name but two. The name Abraham Williams was followed by (The Landlord) with a little stick figure snake drawn beside it and the word "Python?" Next to the name Albert Wigfall were the words (The Night Mayor) followed by "Strong Man?" I scanned the rest of the list.

"Obviously, you guys know I'm acquainted with most of them. I've heard the terms Strong Man and Python from Montague. Never heard of Abraham or Albert," I said.

Then suddenly, as if alive, the next name leaped from the page: Mark Ward. I swallowed hard, "What makes you think I know anything important about these people? I'm nobody, just a horn player in a nightclub band."

"Mr. Chapman, we can make this easy or difficult. We know you're acquainted with most of these people. We know you know who they are, where they are and what they do, as do we. But frankly, there are a few of them we don't know. We're asking you to fill in the blanks."

My throat was getting dry, eyes burning, slight chill running over my skin, the wooden cross on my chest felt warm. I looked out the window and wondered if this was what it felt like before your plane crash-landed in the middle of the ocean, during a storm.

"I'd like to help you gentlemen," I said. "But before I do, would you mind telling me what this is all about? Why are you showing me this list? Everybody in town knows these names. Roy Vincent and Bill Reed both own nightclubs, Reverend Edwards has his own radio show. I think maybe I need a lawyer, before this gets out of hand."

"You've been implicated, Chapman," Thigpen said.

"For what? By whom?" I looked directly into Ross' face.

"Williams' disappearance. Someone whose name is on the list," he said.

"Nobody, on that list, was with me the night of the murder. Thigpen knows this. He also knows I didn't kill Williams."

"Who said you did?" Thigpen said. "Any of you guys mention 'murder?'"

"Could be Detective Thigpen doesn't know a lot of things, but he does know one thing's for sure." Ross glared at me. "He knows, you know much more than you're telling. We can get it all now or later, it's up to you."

"You'll need a new suit for the courtroom," Thigpen picked at me. "I don't think bell bottom blue jeans will cut it with a jury, you know, patriotism being what it is and all."

"Don't talk to me about patriotism you son-of-a-bitch. You have not the first fucking clue what the word means." Thigpen stood up. "Sit the fuck down, motherfucker, before you step in a pile of shit so deep you'll never see the light of day." As God is my secret judge, I had no idea where those words came from.

Ross nodded toward Thigpen, who backed off.

"You people are amazing, you know I didn't do this, but you won't admit it," I said. "If you believed I was guilty, you'd have charged me by now. I don't know anything about a gambling ring. Because I don't fucking gamble. I wouldn't bet on whether or not the sun is going to come up tomorrow. And I have never seen any human on this list place a bet on anything, anywhere, except Reed. I saw him drop a five on a pool shot once. He made the shot and told the bettor to keep the money. I thought all the intrigue was about the Williams murder."

"Nobody's said a thing about Williams being dead," Thigpen said. Again.

"Mr. Chapman told you he didn't do it," Ross said, to Thigpen.

"If he didn't do it, he knows who did, and that's just as bad."

"However," Ross sighed and stacked his papers. "He doesn't strike me as the kind who could shoot a man, then go on with his life as if the investigation was merely a minor irritation in his somewhat complicated life."

Ross bent down, leaning on his knuckles in front of me, looking right into my eyes while talking about me in third person. "If he'd done it, he would've confessed, left town or be crazy by now. This man can dismiss a crime only if he's innocent. He couldn't care less about the details."

Thigpen's chair legs hit the floor with a thump, breaking the silence as he slapped his thighs getting up. Ross stood back up, rubbing the back of his neck and sighed again, ignoring Thigpen's existence. "Problem here is," he continued, "You're the only person all the evidence points to, and you don't have an alibi for the time of Williams' disappearance. Now I ask you, Mr. Chapman, what are we supposed to do with that?"

"You people really make me sick," I said.

All the little pieces were starting to fit together, except for one thing. They hadn't mentioned anything about Rashad being with me. Either they didn't know, or they were holding back for a reason. I figured they were grabbing thin air. "I guess the next thing you're going to do is beat me with a rubber hose until I confess?"

Thigpen had turned his back to the discussion and was looking out the window. He reached into his pocket, pulled something out of his shirt pocket and casually tossed it. The piece of scrap paper, shaped like the Star of David, with the scriptures on it floated to the table, with what appeared to be two bloodstains on it.

"Remember this?" Thigpen said. I looked at the paper. "We found it in the pocket of the coat we found in Williams' car." His voice was quiet now, almost sympathetic.

"I told you about this the last time we talked. You do remember the last time we talked?" I said. Ross picked up the conversation from there.

"That's your handwriting, isn't it?" I picked up the paper wondering if they'd looked up the scriptures. "Notice the blood stains around the edges? There're two blood types; yours and the type found on Williams jacket. Your tire tracks were at the scene, your footprints, and buttons from a shirt found in your apartment were in the floor of the car, you see our problem here?" Ross eyed me like the RCA Victor dog. "I don't believe you actually killed this man, Mr. Chapman, but somebody has gone to a great deal of trouble to make it appear you did. And we think that a person's name is on this list."

This all had to be a dream. By the time they laid the buttons on the table, I was ready to faint. I'd been so perfectly framed, it was unbelievable.

"There's nothing here I can't explain," I said.

"How about skin from your hand found on the front seat of the car?" Thigpen cracked. "Maybe you've got an explanation for that, a jury will believe."

"Williams never touched me, it is impossible for my skin to be in his car."

"Is that a fact?" Thigpen croaked. "The skin we found in the car matches skin we took from the razor in your bathroom. How do you explain that?"

"I can't."

Ross came back into the conversation. "And we know you well enough to know you don't have the stones to pull off a gig like this, even in the face of all the evidence. That's why you're here in this room with us instead of in there with them." He nodded toward the three black guys sleeping in the drunk tank.

"Well, with all this evidence," I sighed, "why don't you go ahead and charge me?"

"Oh, we're going to charge you," Thigpen snapped, "How long the list is going to be, though, depends on you."

"Why don't you just go after the real killer, if you don't think I did it? You obviously believe the killer's name is on this list." My ability to stall was collapsing.

Ross came around from behind the table and pulled his chair up beside me so our knees were almost touching. He put his hand on my arm.

"They've all got alibis, son. We've checked 'em all. That's what we've been trying to tell you. This is an orchestrated affair. Several people are involved in making it look like you killed Williams, hid the body and stole the money. Now, I'm going to go out on a limb here and share a little secret with you."

He reached down, took my hand and turned it over to look at the pink lines left over by the scratches. "She scratched you with one of these, right?" Ross pulled out the spurred talons of a gamecock and showed them to me. I nodded. Then he turned the talons over, revealing the underside of each curved claw, all three had been hollowed out and sharpened. Ross dragged the claw foot over the top of the pizza box, leaving three deep gashes, then turned them up and pulled the paper fibers out of the grooves. "That's where they got the skin to put in the car. We found this talon when we searched the St. James."

"So, you're saying somebody planned this whole thing from the beginning, and you guys have known this all along?" I looked at Thigpen.

"I didn't say we think you're an innocent bystander." Ross said, while the Navy guy watched for my reaction. "We do believe Bootsy Williams is dead. We know you were one of the last people to see him before he disappeared. As soon as the body turns up, you will be involved in a murder. That is a fact, Mr. Chapman. How deeply involved is what we're trying to determine here. Personally, I don't care for people like you, because I happen to have small children who are influenced by the kind of music you provide. I think white people who listen to black music or play it for that matter have a severe identity crisis, but I try not to let my personal prejudices interfere with my professionalism."

"Unlike your local associate." I said, looking at Thigpen.

"We all have our little short comings." Thigpen snickered.

"But, you made the drop," Ross continued to press me; "You came back to Charleston. After that I don't really know what happened, but there's much more going on here than meets the eye. Unfortunately, you're the only person implicated with motive and opportunity who doesn't have an alibi. Even if you're proven innocent, you will do time for withholding evidence if you don't help us find the person who committed this crime."

"It's called obstruction of justice," Thigpen chimed in.

"If I were you, I'd take another long look at the list," Ross said.

All of them were leaning in on me. Outside, the wind kicked up, whistling around the corner of the building, while the room filled with the smell of stale smoke hanging on heavy vibes from thousands of interrogations going back decades.

"I still don't understand what you want with me," I said. "You've got a list with the guilty person's name on it. Lean on it for a change."

Thigpen turned back toward the window and lit another cigarette. Speaking to me while looking out the window, he started pontificating again.

"What do you think we're doing, asshole? Your name is at the top of the list, and we're leaning on you. Satisfied? If it was up to me," he said, "I'd bust you right here, but these guys have their own agenda. Besides, you aren't going anywhere, anytime soon. Except, maybe, to look for a new job."

Ross continued, "Whoever hit Williams planned it well. They'll be watching you to see how much we get out of you. Then we can watch them watch you. But aside from the Williams issue, there's another little matter we haven't discussed that Mr. Stevens would like to touch on." I knew what was coming and tried to head it off.

"You know, I came off the road to settle down and lead a simple life, maybe someday buy my own club and retire. And right out of the chute, I get this crap." They were looking at me hard. "You've known all along I didn't kill anybody, but still you tried to make me crack. There may be more to this, as far as you're concerned, but, from my viewpoint, the only reason you guys aren't going after the real suspect is that you're afraid of stepping on somebody's toes. Somebody, who's name isn't on that list. I think there's somebody else you want or you two big guns from Naval Intelligence and the IRS wouldn't be down here trying to solve the murder of a black man few people ever heard of, much less give a shit about." I looked from one to the other and settled back looking toward Stevens who, so far, hadn't said a word.

Thigpen crushed his cigarette out in the ashtray, leaving a thin strand of residual smoke trailing in the air. "I think you ought to quit stalling while you're ahead, Chapman. To me, the choice is simple. Either help us now or we're going ahead with the evidence the way we see it."

I got up from my seat, as if to go.

"The way you see it is not the way these men see it, Thigpen. Anything else I can do for you, gentlemen?" I looked at the three of them.

"Aren't you interested in the other matter we haven't discussed?" Ross said.

Thigpen butted in. "Up till now, I've gone easy on you Chapman," he said. "But this is bigger than even a showboat like you can imagine. If I were you, I'd be making plans to cover my own ass. These men have offered you a chance to take care of yourself. You and your jive ass friends are going down harder and sooner, rather than softer and later." He stopped to let the thought sink in, then landed the final punch. "You're right. These guys don't give a shit about Williams. They're here because of Mark Ward. They think your piano-playing girlfriend's husband is behind a scheme to defraud the Navy. The scheme is so big it makes the numbers ring look like Stagger Lee's craps game on a street corner. They think he and Bill Reed are running a multi-million dollar operation using the blacks controlling the numbers game in all the hospitals, hotels and service areas in the city to launder the money. If you don't want her to get hurt in this thing, you'd better start cooperating with us. Are we clear? On that point at least?"

I looked at Thigpen with fire in my eyes, facing him full on, but talked only to the other men. I figured it was time for the rubber to meet the road.

"Officer Thigpen here took his badge off in my dressing room and threatened to do me bodily harm if I didn't confess to something I didn't do. I told him I made the drop. I even told him about the scrap of paper. Still, he threatened me at my place of business and hid behind his badge while doing it. How's that for starters in your investigation?" Ross looked at Thigpen. "Is what Mr. Chapman said true?"

Thigpen glared at me. "Chapman, that's bullshit and you know it," he said. "I was joking with you. What're you trying to do here, start off on another line of bullshit to confuse the issue?"

"Not really," I said. "Actually, it's more of a test, since you and I both know exactly what happened. I wanted to see if you would lie in front of these men to cover your ass, because, you see, that would prove to both of us what a dirty fucking cop you really are, Thigpen. It's my way of finding out exactly what I'm up against."

"Well, the next time, you and that pack of jungle-bunnies decide you want a piece of me, you'll all go down. I promise you that," he barked.

"Detective Thigpen, did you take off your badge and threaten Mr. Chapman?" Ross asked, as I smiled my best, put-up-or-shut-up grin, right in Thigpen's face.

"Yes. I did. But you gotta understand; me and this clown have a history. It was a joke."

"Thigpen, if you ever try to get physical with me again, badge on or off, be prepared to pay for it," I said.

"You're bordering on threatening a police officer, Chapman," he said.

"No, I'm warning an asshole."

"Listen, we're not interested in your personal history with Mr. Chapman or your sense of humor, Detective. We want to know what Mr. Chapman knows about the relationship between Bill Reed and Mark Ward. Now, Mr. Chapman…"

"Call me Josie," I said.

"Very well, Josie. Tell us about the relationship between Bill Reed and Mark Ward."

I thought long and hard about what to say. I picked up the Star of David with the scriptures on it and looked at the first one. The 23rd Psalm was the first scripture I'd ever memorized. It ran through my head, "Yea though I walk through the valley of the shadow of death, I will fear no evil…" I'm not a rat, but I'm not a martyr either, especially when it comes to protecting my enemies and whoever was framing me was definitely my enemy. I had to consider Kela. I couldn't figure out why they didn't know about Rashad. I thought about the actual cash in the bag, how it was all new money in bank wrapped straps, instead of wrinkled street cash usually associated with a numbers drop. I couldn't understand why Reed hadn't contacted somebody to get me a story that covered me during the time Williams' disappeared.

"Well, Josie? We're waiting." Ross said.

"Could I get a glass of water?" I said.

"Detective Thigpen, get Mr. Chap... I mean Josie, a cup of water," Ross said.

Thigpen snorted and sniffled, then dragged, his lead-weighted blubber belly out of the chair and ape-assed his way toward the door. As soon as he was out of the room, I turned to Ross and said, "I'll talk to you on one condition. Thigpen stays out of the room."

Ross got up and immediately locked the door. "Anything else?"

"You guys know why I came back to Charleston early, right?"

"Why don't you fill us in," Stevens said.

"Last chance. Tell me if you know. Otherwise, fuck it."

Ross took a deep breath, glanced at Stevens, then put his elbows on the table.

"We know you worked undercover for the Bureau of Narcotics and Dangerous Drugs," Ross said.

"Do you know why?" I said.

"Something to do with the SDS or the Weather Underground, war protests, civil rights."

"Fuck. No. I cut a deal with those guys to help them find some people pretending to be Weathermen. There were no real Weathermen. Only a couple of white supremacists posing as student radicals who were selling smack laced with strychnine to black soldiers who'd come home from Nam with heroin habits."

"What kind of deal did you cut with them?" Ross said.

"The same one I'm getting ready to cut with you," I said.

Ross nodded to Stevens. "Give us a second, will you?"

"Take all the time you need."

I knew what I was getting myself into. Making a deal with the government is second only to marrying the mob. Only this time, I wasn't going to make the same stupid mistake and expect different results. This time, I knew what to expect.

The two men came back to the table. "What do you want?" Ross said.

"A domestic version of Diplomatic Immunity."

"There's no such thing," Stevens said.

"Oh, yes the fuck there is," I said. "Maybe not by that name, but you guys can set up a variable of the Witness Protection Program, with a stipulation which says 'in the absence of any hard evidence' implicating me, I am not to be investigated, tailed, watched, harassed, called in for questioning, wiretapped, IRS audited, SLED investigated, none of the routine clandestine shit you pull on ordinary citizens. This is exactly like the arrangement I had in Columbia. Only this time I want it in writing. Doesn't have to go national, local will do fine." I leaned forward. "You put it in writing. I have Federal and State immunity protection from prosecution, no matter what I do. That's the deal." I sat back.

"You can't go on a crime spree in front of the whole city and not get looked at. That's crazy. No government agency would agree to anything so asinine."

"Do I look like a one man crime spree to you? Half the cops in the county are dirty. Thigpen out there is no more than a hoodlum with a badge. The County Sheriff shakes down half the clubs in the name of Democratic Party campaign contributions. A bag man makes a run to the Governor's office once a week. All I want is the freedom to live my life, and work, without the weight of whatever drama these guys bring down on themselves, or each other, or you guys either. I want the same protection you give the slob on the other side of that door. Only I want it without having to hide behind a badge."

"And what do we get in return?" Stevens said.

"A pair of eyes and ears in this city and state the likes of which you have never experienced."

"What if you decide to take somebody out?" Ross said. "We can't give you a 007 license to kill."

"You'll never have to worry about it. If I ever decide to hit somebody, not that I would, but if I did, nobody will ever know. What I want is to not get looked at. For anything. Somebody gets whacked, the first place you look and every place afterwards, is anywhere other than at me."

"And this is the deal you had in Columbia?" Stevens said.

"Yep, right up until the time I made the stupid mistake of trusting one of your best agents. He blew my cover. My drummer found out, freaked out, and I had to quit my band and leave town before I was ready. I'll never make that mistake again."

Ross said, "Anything you care to share with us, right now, as a show of good faith?"

"Yeah." I reached into my wallet for the folded up invoice I'd retrieved from the dumpster at The Apartment Club and threw it on the table. "Either one of you guys got a Bible?"

"Yes, as a matter of fact, I do," said Stevens.

Stevens snatched his briefcase from beside his seat, opened both latches simultaneously, produced a dog-eared King James Version and slid it across the table to me. I picked it up, immediately noticing all the notes in the margins; color-coded highlighted verses and various references. Finding the 23rd Psalm, I turned the Bible back around, pushed it respectfully toward Stevens and then laid the star-shaped scrap of paper on the opposite page from the scripture.

"Notice anything unusual?" I said.

Ross and Walker immediately hunkered down with the scrap of paper and started searching the scriptures. Stevens didn't take his eyes off me. When the other two men looked up with puzzled faces, Stevens said, simply, "There's no seventh verse in the 23rd Psalm."

"So?" asked Walker.

"The number 7 was the first number in last week's game," Stevens said. "Am I correct, Mr. Chapman?"

I nodded.

"And I believe, if you gentlemen look up the other scriptures written on the scrap of paper, you will find they all contain non-existent verses. The omitted numbers complete last week's winning sequence." Stevens eyes, still locked on my own, waited for confirmation. I nodded, again.

"But that's not all there is to it, is there, Mr. Chapman?" Stevens leaned down on his forearms, eyes bearing down on me.

"That's all I know, except the scriptures are broadcast over a gospel radio program by Reverend Edwards. He includes them in his devotional."

I felt like Judas.

"This invoice you gave us, Mr. Chapman," Stevens continued. "Have you looked at it?"

"I know it was for $7500," I said. "Two more in my car; one's $7500 and one's $5000."

Stevens was studying every twitch in my demeanor. He turned the Bible back around sliding it toward me, placing it opposite my right hand while placing the Star of David opposite my left, smoothed out the wrinkled invoice and slipped it in between the two so I could see all three objects at the same time.

"Tell me what you see, Mr. Chapman?" He said.

I looked back and forth over the three objects while all three of them watched. The wind outside had calmed and the room got quiet. I heard someone try to open the door. Thigpen had returned. Ross got up, opened the door and said something to Thigpen I couldn't understand. I looked back over my shoulder at the door, surprised Thigpen hadn't insisted on coming back in the room. Turning back around, I looked down at the invoice again. Then it hit me. The last four digits of the invoice number were P2367. The scripture on the Star of David was Psalm 23:6, 7.

"You didn't know, did you, Mr. Chapman?" Stevens said.

"Know what?" Ross said.

"What didn't he know?" said Walker.

I sat back in the chair, looking at Stevens, shaking my head, completely blown away. All I could think about was the danger Kela would be in if Mark Ward suspected I had something to do with the Navy figuring out the connection between his bogus CHITs, Bill Reed and the black organization running the numbers racket.

"Tell me about the money," Walker said.

"All new bills, bank wrapped hundreds, no dye marks," I said.

"Odd, using new money for a bag drop from a numbers operation?" Walker continued.

"Yes, I thought it was odd, but all I wanted to do was make the drop and leave. Besides, it had been a while since I bagged. I thought things might have changed," I said.

"You see what has happened, don't you Mr. Chapman?" Stevens said. "The money you transferred to Williams was obtained by cashing U.S. Navy checks issued to a dummy corporation owned by Bill Reed who produced the invoices, all of them for less than $10,000. Mark Ward issued the CHITs and the government computer spit out the check because all the numbers matched. The checks were deposited on different days in different banks and the money drawn out months later, in increments of varying amounts. All the major players had copies of the figures. There's a name for it:: Defrauding the United States Government. Disguising the whole affair as a numbers drop for a group of blacks insured that if anything went wrong, there'd be no way to trace the money back to Ward. The plan would have worked perfectly, as it has in the past, except this time somebody got greedy, killed Williams and stole the money, leaving you, Mr. Chapman, if you'll pardon the pun, holding the bag."

I wondered when they were going to lock me up. Wondered how I could warn Kela. Wondered why nobody from Reed's organization had attempted to contact me. In my entire life, I never felt more alone than I did sitting at that table with those three men staring at me.

"One more question, Mr. Chapman," said Stevens. "Then you're free to go. Were you alone the night you gave Williams the money?"

By default, I was in the gambling business. I did a quick mental inventory of how much I thought they knew. Nobody had mentioned Rashad. It was a coin toss – heads, I tell the truth; tails, I lie. I flipped the coin in my mind.

"Yes," I said.

Stevens slammed both fists on the table and stood up so pissed off he even scared me. For a second I thought he might pull out a gun and shoot me. Instead, he cursed me out.

"You lying little son-of-a-bitch!" he hissed. "What'd you think? You think because I carry a Bible in my briefcase, I'm some kind of motherfucking Sunday school teacher that doesn't know shit from Shinola about what's going on here? I make my living busting assholes who'd make you look like Bunny Rabbit on fucking Captain Kangaroo." He was seething and, obviously, not finished with me. "Let me tell you something, Mr. Chapman, I don't just carry a copy of the Bible with me." He reached into his briefcase pulling out another thick book and slammed it down on the table: The Complete Works of Shakespeare. "Everything, and I do mean every-fucking-thing, men can do wrong, is in one of these two books!" He paused while he dragged both hands through his hair, stretching his scalp. "One last chance to level with me before I feed you to the wolves that are waiting for you outside."

"What about our agreement?" I said.

"Tell us the truth and you'll have your agreement." Stevens adjusted his tie.

Call it what you like but I took no offense at his tone. Like I said before, you can't scare a man who's not afraid to die. And I'd had enough.

Agreement or no agreement, there was no way I was going to give up Rashad and ruin my back-up chance at clearing myself.

"I was alone," I said.

CHAPTER TWENTY-EIGHT

The trip back from the County Jail had been nerve-racking; I sat through two green lights and ran up on the curb at least three times because I couldn't take my eyes off the rear-view mirror. Instead of watching where I was going, I was watching where I'd been. My mind had played so many tricks on me I didn't trust my sense of judgment anymore. After waiting five minutes for the light to change at the corner of Broad Street, I turned left onto Savage. The gate to my driveway was open. I caught a glimpse of somebody jumping the fence behind my apartment. Or thought I did; until I saw several sets of muddy footprints on the stairs leading up to my door.

Again, out of my peripheral vision, I sensed a movement from the other side of the fence. A shimmer of blue-green flashed between the cracks in the wood pickets. Those colors weren't at all familiar and the hair on the back of my neck stood straight out of my skin. I should've jumped the fence and chased whoever it was, but the truth is, I was scared. Running up the steps, fighting to get my key in the door lock, I turned and looked down into the neighbor's backyard. A car door slammed on Colonial Street, an engine started, and then a blue-gray Ford sedan pulled out slowly from the curb and turned left on Tradd Street, heading away from the Battery. The driver wore sunglasses and a baseball cap and a shirt the same color blue-green I'd seen through the fence. He could've been a tourist who got lost wandering the Historic District or a contractor looking at a repair job. He didn't seem to be in any particular hurry, but I couldn't shake the feeling that I'd seen the shirt color before.

J. Reynolds stepped onto his front stoop. "The pest control man did a thorough inspection of the apartment. There were no fleas. I could've told him as much. Next time, would you be so kind as to inform me, in advance, when I need to let someone in."

"Sorry." I didn't tell J. Reynolds I hadn't ordered the inspection nor that I'd never found a flea in my apartment. "From now on, I'll make sure you're aware of anyone who might show up unexpectedly."

The rug on the living room floor had traces of mud matching tracks by the kitchen cabinets. I always took off my shoes at the door, so I knew the tracks weren't mine. The cops had ransacked the place. Cabinet doors left open, sofa cushions thrown in the floor. Even my toaster had been examined; there were crumbs all over the counter where someone turned it upside down.

The shoe prints faded at the door to my bedroom, so I figured whoever it was had gone in there, too. I took a mental inventory of the room: stereo, radio, TV, the bari, the tenor, the alto, the soprano, the flute, my albums, even the fifty dollars cash on my dresser were all still there. Since nothing was missing or stolen these things only proved someone had been in my home. What else could I have that anybody would want to steal? There was nothing left to take other than a bunch of records.

Every drawer was intact; there was nothing under the mattress. I pulled the mattress away from the wall and looked along the edge of the baseboard. My search was more thorough than any the cops had done. The only unusual thing I found was a yellow silk scarf wadded up under the fitted sheet. It belonged to Kela, it smelled like her. The odd thing was that I was sure she'd had it with her the last time I saw her, it was on the seat beside her in her car. I tried again to put her out of my mind. Getting involved with her had to rank at the top of my list of all time stupid mistakes.

Looking at it from her point of view, it was hard not to see how something like this could happen. Women really aren't as different from men, as most men think. Or maybe a better way to put it would be that some women aren't much different from some men. Some men have a way of categorizing women into groups. They're the ones you fantasize about, the ones you hang out with, the ones you sleep with, then there are the kind you marry and take home to mom. This last group is what moms call "acceptable." I also knew the same went for men. As for me, I was somewhere between group two and three, definitely "unacceptable." "Two different worlds" was where Kela and I came from. Given the prevailing social climate, she'd never fit into my world, and I damn sure couldn't fit into hers.

If the cops hadn't been all over me, I could've handled Kela's leaving the same way I would've handled any other woman I'd been with. In this business they come and go, unless you get married, nothing will change that. My big mistake was thinking, even believing, that I had a chance to live a normal life. That crushed dream was the most debilitating. I could rise above all the other mundane garbage, if there was even a ray of hope on the horizon. With Kela gone, I was almost helpless. I was worn out from fighting the system or, as Montague would say, "I'm weary from the struggle."

Self-pity was an unaccustomed, uncomfortable emotion. Running wasn't an option; I knew they'd come after me. It was inconceivable that I could prove my innocence on the run. I decided to do what I always did when I needed to escape. I put on "'Round Midnight" by Miles Davis, took down my bottle of Wild Turkey, found a joint I'd hidden in the freezer, then I laid down on the sofa drank some whiskey and got high.

Like I said earlier, whiskey is always a bad idea, and the weed wasn't much help, either. I tossed and turned on the sofa, wrestling fear from the grip of paranoia. My mind played out all the different scenarios. If the person behind the frame was going to tighten it enough to hang me for good, then he was probably under pressure to finish the job. I thought Ross might've orchestrated the break-in, but he worked for SLED, helping the Navy nail Ward. Why would he try to tie me to Ward's wife? It didn't make any sense. Whoever left the scarf wouldn't be stupid enough to think I'd lie down and take him planting evidence in my apartment. He also wouldn't be stupid enough to think he couldn't get caught if I came home early. He'd have to know where I was and how long I'd be gone. The gun, the money, and Bootsy Williams' body, supposedly, were still out there, somewhere. It didn't make any sense. Unless. I thought. Unless. The burglar was one of Thigpen's flunkies.

But that scenerio begged a few questions. Why would Thigpen want to tie me to Kela? Where did he get her scarf, and how did she fit into the legal scheme of things? If I were trying to put on a frame like this, I wouldn't consider her my weak spot. Just the opposite.

I poured another shot of Wild Turkey. The smart thing would be to plant the murder weapon someplace nobody, but me, would know about. They could stash it in my dressing room, but there are too many other people in and out of there. They could've put it somewhere in my apartment, but if they had, it wasn't there anymore. They could've buried it in the yard, if they could sneak it past Reynolds, or stick it into a cavity under the Thunderbird console, if they knew about it.

One thing for certain, whoever was out to get me wasn't sitting around getting wasted like some hippie. If I couldn't win this battle, I had to, at least, go down fighting. The right thing to do was not trying to run away from the situation, but to charge straight at it. They'd been counting on my fear to buy them the time they needed to lock up the frame.

A blue-gray Ford might sound like a common car, but in downtown Charleston, which is full of new Mercedes, BMW's and Volvos, a rag short like that would stick out like a fire truck. The bent bumper and the missing hubcap would be a dead giveaway the owner didn't blend. I walked out to the street, where my car was parked.

From the outside, the Thunderbird looked untouched, but that didn't mean anything. Muddy footprints aside, this guy wouldn't leave too many clues pointing to what he'd done, unless he wanted to plant a distraction. I'd left it unlocked. The sky-blue leather tuck and roll wrapped around the contours of the interior like a private booth in a fancy restaurant. The second hand on the dashboard clock clicked like a metronome. I put the key in the ignition and turned it to

ACC. The buttons on the radio still punched up the same stations. I checked the secret compartment in the depths of the console. When I checked the dash, the gas gauge showed empty. That couldn't have been right. I hadn't driven more than twenty-five miles since I filled it up the day before. I remembered the old saying "paranoia is just a heightened sense of awareness." When I leaned over to tap the gauge, my elbow accidentally hit the driver's side window button. The window closed.

Any other time, a loose connection jostled back together by a bump in the road or a loose wire under the dash wouldn't cause concern. But the wire I'd found dangling under the car, had been pulled out of the wiring harness. I should've never smoked that joint because weed will make you second guess yourself. When I was stoned, I expected my mind to play tricks on me. Otherwise, why bother? But I couldn't shake the certain chill that someone had been in my car.

The hood latch popped open easily, and I nosed around top of the engine. I stuck my fingers under the vacuum tubes, spark plug wires and exhaust manifold. Nothing was out of place. All the lines were right where I'd put them. The cowling shroud over the transmission housing was clear, besides it would have been impossible for a hand to reach far enough to wedge anything in there tight enough to keep it from falling out at the first pothole. I went back to the interior and checked the back seat. It was firmly in place. Then, back to the outside. I checked the fender skirts, hubcaps, the trunk, and tail light lenses. Nothing was under the spare tire, nothing inside the bumpers.

Ground clearance on a 1965 Thunderbird is six to seven inches depending on tire pressure. Not even a midget was small enough to crawl under my car; they would have had to use a jack. If they'd jacked the car up recently there would be a mark somewhere on the bumper or the frame. *"Unless they used a floor jack on the differential."* I was starting to get used to the third party thoughts popping into my head. I'd even considered talking back to them, but thought it one step away from carrying on a running conversation with thin air. And I wasn't quite ready for that next step.

Jennings Shell Station was right around the corner on East Bay Street. The owner, Roger, let me use his rack to change the oil right after I got back in town, so I decided to ask him if I could use the lift. I bit my lip, turned the ignition key and the car started without blowing up, which, all things considered, was a relief.

"Stoned Chapman here, yet again poking the bears of chaos." I said, without realizing I had, indeed, started talking to myself.

By the time I got to the station, I had a bad case of dry mouth. The lift bay was empty. I bought a Coke and Roger steered me into the lift then went back to his copy of Hot-Rod Magazine. I took a tire iron out of the trunk and put the car on the rack.

Ordinarily, I would've never given a white van parked across the street with two sailors in it a second thought. Those guys were like dozens of other runners out gathering supplies. They come into town, riding around, and pull over on a side street to sit, smoke and are not in a big hurry to get back to the base. But this situation wasn't ordinary. I'd already been followed by a white van, before. The pay phone was in the corner, I called Rigney to check in.

The phone rang three times. "Rigney residence, Reynolds speaking."

"Hi, Mr. Rigney, it's Josie, I'm checking in, have there been any calls for me? Anyone stop by, while I'm out?"

"I'm sorry," he said. "You must have the wrong number, this is a private residence. We don't sell flowers here." He hung up. Someone must've been standing near him. I figured I'd give him a few minutes, then try again.

With the T-Bird on the rack, I hung a drop light from the emergency brake cable and started looking for fresh scratches on the frame, the rear end and around the strut housing. Hot oil and road grit fell into my eyes as I checked the front end, chassis, cross members, and inside of the front bumpers. Stupid me, I remember thinking. I've got to get that oil leak fixed. All this shit going down, and I take time to worry about an oil leak.

"Sometimes I'm amazed at how stupid pot makes me." I must've said it louder than I thought.

"You say somethin'?" Roger yelled from the front counter.

"Cussing pot holes," I said.

"I hate hittin' 'em, too, but they're good for business."

I burnt my fingertips feeling around the pipes near the exhaust manifold. Coming down from the side of the engine, I skinned a knuckle on a sharp piece of steel by a shift rod on the transmission. I scraped the barb off the metal with a tire iron, working my way toward the rear of the chassis. A wispy image of the empty gas gauge floated before my eyes. I shook my head, the sending unit for the fuel gauge was broken off and the wire stripped bare as if it had been torn out from the bottom of the gas tank. Then, suddenly, I saw the unmistakable four prong teeth marks of a floor jack's lift plate embedded in the road dirt and gear grease caked around the differential. Somebody'd jacked up my car from behind since I got home. Otherwise, bottoming out in the muddy parking lot would've covered the marks, or at least splashed new mud on them.

A '65 Thunderbird has two sets of mufflers, four total. I moved the drop light back toward the resonators, which were smaller and located a few inches from either side of the back bumper. There was nothing there. I checked above the main muffler on the passenger's side, then crossed over to the one on the driver's side. As I ran my fingers along the top, I found a burnt wire lying on the hot muffler. The heat had melted the casing and shorted out the circuit. Someone had lifted the wire off the muffler, wrapped a piece of tape around it, and stuck it in a crack in the frame. That explained why my window didn't work before. The scary part was it also explained why the window worked now. Only I didn't fix it. Whoever jacked up the car must have fixed it.

As I worked my way further along the top of the muffler, my fingers traced the unmistakable rectangles and right angles of a .45 automatic. It was wedged between the top of the muffler and the bottom of the floorboard. I used the tire iron to release the pressure and the warm pistol slid off the muffler right into my hand.

It looked identical to the gun Rashad was carrying the night we made the drop. There was no way he could've planted it under my car. No Rastafaria could've jacked up a white man's car, in broad daylight, in downtown Charleston, and not have everybody on the street calling the cops.

Then it dawned on me. The problem with the white van was the civilian tags and a magnetic Allied Pest Control sign stuck on the door with two guys inside, wearing Navy dungaree shirts. They probably jacked up the car long enough for the blue-green shirt guy in the gray Chevy to slide under and plant the gun.

The clip had four bullets in it, which I thought was a dumb as fuck thing to put on top of a muffler, unless whoever planted it had intended for the bullets to explode. I was sure that when, and if, slugs were removed from Bootsy Williams' body, they would match a bullet fired from this gun. The frame was complete. The murder weapon, with my fingerprints on it, was now in my possession. If they'd been waiting for me to find it, this would be the perfect time to take me down. I looked out from under the car toward East Bay Street. There was nothing unusual going on. No other mysterious vehicles, no more shady characters, just the white van with the two sailors still yakking, smoking, eating sandwiches, to the casual observer just a normal day in the neighborhood. I wiped the .45 down with WD 40, and wrapped it in a mechanics towel.

Like I said earlier, I'd quit carrying a gun. I had no use for one because I didn't plan to kill anybody anytime in the near future. The way I figured it, the best place for the pistol was back in the hands of the last person who used it, which was probably Rashad, Reed or Ward. I put my money on Bill Reed.

I made another attempt at calling Rigney. The phone rang six times before he answered with a simple "Hello."

"Reynolds, it's me, again," I said.

"I'm sorry, you have the wrong number." The line went dead.

I took the car off the rack, put the towel wrapped pistol deep in the console and backed the T-Bird out of the bay, waving thanks to Roger. I drove back to Mosquito Beach and waited until thirty minutes after dark. No Rashad. Nobody else, either. The Fish Shack was deserted. I decided to try the St. James.

The time was 8:33 when I found Reed's black '66 Riviera, with the mag wheels and the California rake, parked at the St. James, way back in the dark shadow of the porch roof. Only the street light glinting off the shiny, mag wheels made it noticeable. A cat sat on the hood, licking its paws, while someone in the dilapidated, clapboard house next door splashed a bucket of water onto the concrete. I could see Reed through the window, off the back porch of the kitchen.

He'd cut the Riviera's front wheels hard to the right, like a pose in Car Craft Magazine. Several stray cats milled around, while the one big tabby, licking its paws, opted not to join the group, preferring the Riviera's hood.

"Cat's like warm car hoods." The thought came out of nowhere.

I looked around. Nobody was behind me, but I knew instantly both the origin and the reason. Reed hadn't been there long enough for the engine to cool. The cut wheels meant he'd pulled in fast, tried to hide his car in the shadows, then ducked quickly inside. He was in a hurry.

I circled the block and parked down the street on the opposite side, facing the back driveway of the St. James. With my driver's side mirror angled to watch the street behind me, I had a clear view of everything in front and back. Just before nine o'clock, Rashad came out and made a call from the corner pay phone, then walked behind and double-checked the Riviera's locked doors. He was dressed in a tie-dyed dashiki. Sunglasses sat tight against his face and the dread locks fell heavy on his shoulders. Striped bell-bottoms flared out over his black motorcycle boots. He checked his watch and then disappeared behind the hotel, only to emerge across the street in the parking lot of the Patio Drive-In. I had no idea how he pulled off the move without my seeing him.

Back in the kitchen, Reed had moved out of my line of sight. Only shadows flickered in the dim light behind the St. James. Stray dogs circled the garbage cans, looking for the cats while the cats stalked the rats scurrying around the storm drains. I wrapped the yellow scarf around the pistol, then the towel around both without letting my hands touch the metal, then stuck it in the waistband of my jeans and slipped out of my car. I left the keys in the ignition, in case I had to leave in a hurry.

Ducking the street light halo, I was trembling and had to force myself not to stop to pee. I knew if I was being watched by anyone, the moment I tried to plant the gun on Reed's car all hell would break loose. As I slid down the sidewalk closer and closer to the Riviera, I was sweating bullets, my heart pounding. I felt like I was carrying a time bomb set to go off any second. I should've taken the gun and the handkerchief to the police the second I found them. Survival instincts warred with fear of getting caught, as I moved in behind the Riviera.

My plan was to reach under the front bumper, jam the package into the hollow space behind the license plate mount and haul ass. But just as I reached under the bumper, the cat howled and jumped off the hood, which set the dogs barking. I crouched down by the wheel well. I should just go to the police, I thought; if I'd started running then, I could've made it before Reed realized I was there.

Walking around in the dark behind the St. James with a damn gun was insane. Or was I just plain scared, simply too chicken to do what I needed to do? The more I thought about it, the more pissed off I got. I stood up, walked to the front of the car, pulled the towel out of my waist band, then crouched down reaching my hand under the bumper.

At that moment, the all hell I was dreading did, in fact, break loose. A blue-gray Ford screeched into the driveway behind the Riviera and Mark Ward jumped out. I heard somebody running up behind me, spun around, and saw Rashad bearing down on me. The back door to the kitchen flew open and Reed came running down the steps, waving his fist in the air.

I figured everything out in a split second. Rashad's call must have been to Reed, letting him know I was outside the St. James. Reed then called Mark Ward to get his ass over here, at once. I knew how stupid my side of this would sound to the cops when I tried to explain how the missing pistol got into my pants. Even though I understood it all in an instant, my body froze with panic. I didn't know which way to turn. By the time the thought registered, Rashad had me by my arm, with one hand, and shoved something hard and gun barrel-like into my rib cage.

"Hey, take it easy," I said. "This is no way to handle the situation. Have you got a gun in my side? Man, get that fucking gun up off of me. Just don't do anything fucked up, Rashad. Seriously, man, you need to calm down, man…" I was running my mouth a mile a minute. "Let's just be cool about this."

Rashad didn't speak, as he kept dragging me back, away from the Riviera toward the Ford where Reed and Ward were waiting. They both looked scared and paranoid, constantly checking to see if anybody was watching us.

"So, you two guys do know each other after all," I said.

"Throw his ass in the car," Reed barked.

Rashad was strong, but he only had one free hand to hold me the other held his gun, which told me instantly the gun I had didn't belong to Rashad. There wasn't much he could do with my arm except try to hold on.

"Rashad, man, listen to me." I kept trying to get through to him. "This is stupid. Don't be a fool. Lose the gun, man, seriously, before somebody gets hurt. Do you really wanna shoot me?"

Rashad shot me a look. The words "play along" flashed in my mind. Reed grabbed my other arm and started dragging me toward the open car door. I jerked my arm out of his hand and kicked the shit out of his shinbone. He folded up and fell to his knee, ripping his pants leg in the process.

"You're a fucking idiot!" Ward cursed. "Grab the son-of-a-bitch!"

Rashad was still behind me, shoving me toward the open door of the Ford but failing to budge me more than a few inches at a time. It reminded me of the Three Stooges, very clown-like, totally absurd. Reed picked up a piece of 2x4 from off the pavement and tried to hit me with it, but missed and whacked Rashad's ankle instead. Rashad let go of me to grab the pain and Ward, who had been laying out of the fray, decided to finally jump in. He grabbed my shirt collar and tried, with one big jerk, to pull me head first into the back seat. The fabric ripped on my shirt and he sprawled backwards, careening off the rear fender of the passenger's side, into the trash cans. Up until now, I hadn't taken a swing at Rashad, since he hadn't tried to hit me.

He held on, tried to push me toward the open car door, but as long as I didn't try to hit him, he didn't try to hit me.

Ward and Reed, on the other hand, were clearly open and moving targets.

I got a couple licks in on each of them. Sloppy as it was, you'd think neither of them knew how to fight. Ward and Reed couldn't have been clumsier, if they were fighting on ice with one hand tied behind their back. I, on the other hand, wanted to get my hands on the 2x4. After a few minutes of this amateur scuffling, I finally ended up in the back seat, slid across and braced my back against the opposite door. When Ward stuck his head in the back seat, I kicked him right in the face with my heel. He fell back holding his nose, as the blood started to trickle from around his fingers.

"How do you like that, you wife-beating bastard?" The words came out of nowhere, as if somebody else had said them, and in a moment of total clarity, I knew I could kill him, I wanted to kill him and I'd decided to try.

When Ward fell back, he still had his hand inside the car door. I grabbed the door, slammed it shut on his hand, then opened it and hit him in the head with the leading edge. Reed was running around the car, banging on the glass, as I climbed over the front seat. The keys were still in the ignition so I started the car and raced the engine. By then, Rashad had managed to get hold of a shovel and started banging on the windshield with the bottom part of the spade. The other two knew, if they didn't get the situation under control, someone would call the police.

I kept putting the car in and out of drive and reverse rocking it back and forth in the driveway, squealing the tires. Rashad made one last attempt to bust the windshield, but the shovel handle broke and the spade careened into the fender of Reed's Riviera.

Reed screamed at Rashad, "Goddamit, you fucked up a four thousand dollar paint job, you Jamaican moron!"

The commotion stopped long enough for me to slam the car in reverse and fly backward out of the driveway into the street. The gun and handkerchief were still in my lap. I threw the whole package under the seat and bolted toward my own car. The whole scene was so chaotic, it was almost funny. In fact, once I'd gotten rid of the gun, I actually started laughing, while I was running. I was shocked. I'd thought two so-called bad asses like Ward and Reed would've been in better physical shape. I'd, at least, expected Ward, being a naval officer, to know some karate or something. What I hadn't expected from the two of them was their lack of coordination and just plain sloppy attempt at street fighting. I was extremely disappointed that two so-called "dangerous" men could be so utterly inept. Reed was sweating and holding his chest while Ward tried to hold his injured hand and nose at the same time. Both of them barely able to stand, they were so out of breath.

"Where the fuck did he go?" Reed yelled.

"He was right there in the street." Ward said.

I turned around. Even in low light, I could see them, but they couldn't see me.

CHAPTER TWENTY-NINE

By the time I got back to the T-Bird, I was walking instead of running. With my hands in my pockets, searching for my keys, I realized I'd left them in the ignition. I looked back over my shoulder at the two men standing in the street. Odd, I thought, that they didn't start walking toward the car until after I touched the door handle; like they couldn't see me until I touched a manmade object. I remembered what happened at Mosquito Beach, when everything behind me had disappeared except the natural elements. Rashad wasn't with them in the street because, when I opened the door he suddenly appeared in the passenger seat, dangling my keys between his fingers.

"Remember de hummingbird, mon," he said, slowly. "Time to face old Tom."

"Yeah," Reed wheezed. "We've got your little smart ass now."

"Shoot the motherfucker," Ward wheezed.

I didn't say anything. There was a moment, when the three of them stood silent panting and looking at me, Rashad beside me, Reed and Ward blocking the driver's side door, me in the middle.

"So, what the fuck are you trying to pull?" Reed gasped.

"Why'd you come here tonight?" Ward grabbed my shirt collar through the open window with his good hand, his swollen hand holding his busted nose.

"What am I doing here? What the fuck are you two doing here?" I continued. "This your idea of a sociology field trip?"

"We ask the questions, you answer them. That's how this deal works tonight," Reed growled. His custom made clothes were a mess, he'd lost one of his gambler's dice cuff links.

"So ask." I shrugged.

Neither of them said anything, they just looked at each other, then back at me. Rashad was motionless.

"We ought to haul his ass right to the cops," Reed suggested.

"How do you like that idea, Chapman?" Ward smacked me behind the head and grabbed another handful of shirt. I glared into his eyes and grinned.

"The cops know where to find me anytime they want. Now, get your fucking hands off me, you low-rent motherfucker, before I get suicidal and try to strangle your sorry ass right here. I can't think of a more noble way to die than trying to kill you."

Now that I was sure I could kick his ass even without a weapon, all I could think of was beating him to a bloody pulp for what he had done to Kela. I tried to jump out of the car, but Rashad threw his arm across my chest.

"You can't beat all three of us." Rashad held me back against the seat..

"You never said why you're sneaking around The Reed's car," Ward said.

"You know, for somebody who's supposed to be as important a member of Charleston's high society as you are, you sure hang with some low-rent pimps. What you are, Captain Ward, is about the dumbest asshole I've met lately. What the hell do you think I'm doing here? You think I'm going to let you two freaks frame me for murder?"

"You can't have a murder without a body." Reed tried to growl the words, but he was too out of breath to pull it off. "You killed Bootsy Williams. You know it, I know it, and the cops know it. Everybody knows it. What we want and what the cops want are two different things."

"Bill," I said, drumming my fingertips on the steering wheel, "who is this show for? Him?" I said, indicating Ward. "He knows damn well I was with this man right here, the night Bootsy Williams disappeared." I slapped Rashad on his chest. "Shell casings and slugs in a car seat, bloody clothes, even blood and skin samples don't mean shit if the body got up and walked away." I said. "And that's exactly what happened because I saw Bootsy Williams face-to-face twenty-four hours after he was supposedly killed. If he is dead, then he was killed sometime after 4 a.m. Sunday morning."

"You know what we want, and it ain't that nigger's body." Reed said. Rashad shifted in his seat and grunted. "That money bag had over a hundred grand in it, we think you know where it is."

"And you're a lying piece of shit." I looked at Ward. "Is that what he told you? That the money bag had a hundred thousand dollars in it?" Ward didn't move. "When Reed dropped the bag off to me, it contained two ten thousand dollar straps. That man right there," I pointed to Rashad, "looked into that bag himself and counted them both. If you gave him a hundred grand, then I will bet you my life, this lying piece of shit has stashed eighty of it somewhere in his house, his boat, his car or his club, because you can be damn sure, it's not in his corporate bank account. I didn't know jack shit about where the moneybag went. Because once I handed it off to Williams, I was done with the bag. It was Rashad here who decided we'd go into the poultry business." I turned toward Reed, "And your fucking Riviera, with the four thousand dollar paint job, passed me coming down Maybank Highway twenty minutes after I made the drop."

But that didn't stop Ward from thinking I still had the bag.

"Search his car," Ward ordered. "He might have a gun."

"Me? Have a gun?" I almost laughed. "There are the two motherfuckers with the guns," I said, pointing at Reed and Rashad.

Rashad took the keys and opened the trunk.

"And you get out of the car and spread 'em," Reed said.

They searched my pants pockets, checked my crotch and socks. I knew they weren't going to take me to the police. I also knew that they didn't know what exactly, they were going to do to me.

"You're goin to fry, you little bastard, you know that?" Reed nodded furiously. "When the body is recovered, it will have your name written all over it."

Rashad came back from the trunk and tossed the keys to Ward.

"Nothing," he said.

I was awestruck at how they kept up with the lies. Surely, they both knew the truth. They both had to know that I knew nothing about how Williams died, who shot him, how or when the body disappeared or where the moneybag went.

If the act hadn't been so pathetic, it would have been embarrassing. A prominent Naval officer and a Charleston businessmen, both running in the highest social circles, hobnobbing with the elite of the blue blood culture, now reduced to ragged, bleeding thugs fighting like alley cats, on a side street in an all-black neighborhood. And for what? Charity? Civil Rights? Injustice or trying to find a supposed killer of a black man? Of course not. They were after the same thing every crook that moved to Charleston was after: as much illegal money as possible, while still maintaining a high society image. What neither of them understood was native Charlestonians, be they black, white, or indifferent, don't care how much money you've got, money doesn't buy respect in Charleston.

When they were satisfied I didn't have what they wanted, Rashad gave me the keys. The three of them started walking back toward the St. James. When they were about thirty yards away, Ward stopped, walked back to the car and stuck his face down by the open driver's side window.

"Your time's coming, along with the bitch," he rasped, "I am going to kill you, but not before you have a chance to see what I'm going to do to my cute little wife for taking up with lowlife scum like you."

"Is that a threat or a promise?" I said. "Because, if it's only a threat, then I'm not bothered, but if it's a promise, well, I really might have to kill you, after all."

"I know you know where both the body and the money are," Ward said. "And sooner or later, both'll be found. If I don't get my money back soon, I'm going to take it out of both your asses, one dollar at a time."

He pulled his face back from the window as the steady electric hum of the now fixed window switch filled the hole with glass. Right before the window closed completely, I looked him right in the pupils and said, "Peace, motherfucker."

I started the engine, pulled away from the curb, leaving him standing in the streetlight's neon rainbow, shooting me the bird with his one good hand.

There were moments when I really questioned my sanity. Whatever was happening inside my mind and body as a result of becoming a 'Bridge' and the sink–or–swim world of Hoodoo root work, there was nothing I could do about it. Like it or not, I was all in, for better or worse, and there was no going back to the blissfully unaware naiveté of the straight-eyes-glazed-over world. Montague was right about my needing some education, especially when it came to the wisdom of my rule about not fighting over things that aren't worth killing over. I no longer viewed this as rule, but more of a guideline. Some things are worth fighting for simply because of the need to win. I was already starting to amend the rule to accommodate that need to simply cripple men like Mark Ward and Bill Reed. Men like them were actually too evil to deserve death.

Bill Reed needed to be pistol-whipped with his own gun, to use his own words, until he "couldn't walk, then beaten because he couldn't walk." Ward needed to be humiliated, lashed, and banished to a life of latrine duty in a public housing project. He needed punishment that kept his vanity, arrogance and prideful ego completely intact, long enough to raise his hope of recovery and then crush him like Sisyphus losing control of the rock. And have everybody know it, all the time. But that was wishful thinking on my part, my new eternity-based mindset stretching its wings.

A part of my old-self hated wishing harm on anybody. A part of my new-self was thrilled. I knew, in the long run, Charleston Karma would crush them both in ways I could never imagine. I'd have felt guilty cheating the city out of its chance to get even with two assholes "from off" who blow into town, throw money around and, in six months, start acting like they own the place. Charleston's ruling spirit doesn't abide outsiders trampling on the guest-host relationship. Even if I tried to follow through on what I wanted to do to either man, I knew intuitively nothing I could conjure up would be as bad as what would befall them. The God of Enough Rope would, eventually, take care of the Bill Reeds and the Mark Wards without any help from me. Thinking like that, trying to rationalize away the desire for revenge, lasted about five minutes, then I got over it. By the time I was back to my apartment, I wanted them both dead.

All things considered, I was happy with the way I'd handled the fuck-up fairies. I was even prouder of the way I'd gotten the gun and scarf into Ward's car. I thought I'd accomplished a respectable level of Hemingway's grace under pressure. I thought I'd maintained relative purity of the line through a maximum of exposure. For a split second, I almost felt cocky.

My false sense of security didn't last too long. I made another attempt to call my landlord.

When I finally got through to J. Reynolds Rigney, he said, "I haven't the slightest recollection of any phone calls from you."

"I called twice from a pay phone. Are there any messages for me?"

In a low voice that sounded like he had his hand cupped over the phone, he said "She called several times, but the police were all over the neighborhood looking for you. They found something in your apartment they're very excited about."

"If they found anything, they planted it, I give you my word"

"Whatever they found," he said, "is small enough to fit in a legal size manila envelope."

"Like I said, they planted whatever they found."

"Honestly, Joseph, I don't really care what they found, but it looks bad for the neighborhood, in general, and me, in particular. I am sorry, but I'm cancelling your lease. I want you out of the apartment as soon as possible…" He started to say something else, but the phone got jerked out of his hand.

Thigpen barked, "Where are you, Chapman?" I hung up.

I guess I should've gone back to the apartment and turned myself in, but the idea of doing time for a crime I didn't commit didn't sit very well on my new stomach. There were scores to settle; it would be too easy for the old me to go down without a fight while Reed and Ward walked. The fight was not over and I was determined to give as good as I got.

I called Montague at The Merch to see if he'd been able to find out anything about Reed and Ward. My heart sank as I heard Freddie's voice screaming angrily in the background.

"Gimme that goddamn phone!" Montague didn't have a chance to say anything before Freddie jerked the phone out of his hand.

"Chapman, you son-of-a-bitch, you were supposed to be here last night and you fuckin' blew it. Tommy had one of the biggest agents in the Southeast here to see what kind of entertainment we had for booking private parties and the leader of the fuckin' band is a goddamn NO SHOW!"

"Freddie, what can I say? I'm sorry, man. I'm going through a real rough time and…"

"Who gives a shit? You fuckin' blew it, Chapman!"

"Listen, I need to talk to Montague. Could you put him back on the phone?"

"Montague?" He barked. "Let me clue you in on something you may not be totally aware of, sweet cakes. Your gig here is fuckin' over, you dig? You don't work here anymore. You've been replaced. You like to think you're the only asshole in town that can handle this gig, but you're dead fuckin' wrong. Anybody can do what you do."

"All right. I've got it," I said. "I'm not only replaceable, but I've been replaced. Just let me talk to Montague for one minute. It's the least you can do."

"What're you, fuckin' deaf? You're gone man, you're history, you understand? I don't know you, I never knew you, nobody here knows you, none of the hired help knows you either. We never had this conversation. So, don't call back, if you know what's good for you!" He slammed the phone.

I stood there with the receiver in my hand, staring blankly at the three coin slots along the top of the pay phone. I was blown away, as the history that led up to that moment passed in front of my eyes. I thought of the hours I'd spent practicing my horn, listening to tapes, working out solos by ear, and even memorizing whole passages from John Coltrane albums. All this so I could be a working musician; someone respected in my field. At that moment, it all seemed like a total waste of time. I was no longer a working musician. I was wanted for murder. Even if the body had not been found, I was sure it soon would be. Running diminished sevenths from the top of the horn in the key of C# didn't mean anything. Owning my own club didn't mean anything. Why should I care if an agent had been stood up? The whole thing was crazy. My life was crazy. My faith in virtually everything that ever held any value in my life was spiraling down and out of my soul. Absolutely nothing I'd done with my life held any redeeming qualities. I'd finally hit bottom, and the system was about to bury me. One step away from a jail cell or worse, I could already see my name being changed to a number on a prison uniform. The realization settled into my neck and shoulders like an icy cramp, as the consequences of my actions hastened the collapse of the world around me. Nothing I'd done warranted this situation. The fact that it was happening now, just when I was on the verge of getting my life straightened out, should've made me want to scream. Instead, I shivered from exhilaration.

I dug down in my pocket for another dime trying to settle down before dialing Kela's number. I didn't want her to start worrying or feeling like she needed to help me. My last stab at nobility wasn't going to be very becoming and I knew it, but I needed to attempt something honorable, if for no other reason than to be able to look back at this whole situation with no regrets and feeling like a complete imbecile.

"You got my message," she said. "I was scared sick. Are you anywhere near your apartment?"

"Where I am right now is not important. Besides, it's better you don't know. I just wanted to say thank you and to tell you goodbye."

"Mr. Rigney told me the police found the murder weapon in your apartment," she said, hurriedly. "You can't go back there."

"I know. He told me, too."

"I can help you," she said. "Please let me help you. I can get some money together... find you a place to hide..."

"Stop worrying about me," I said. "It's important for me to know that you don't believe what they're saying. I haven't killed anybody. Yet."

"I know you didn't do it!" she cried. "I've always known you didn't."

Time stood still as I processed her voice.

"Kela, you're the only person in my life, other than Montague, who matters to me now."

"Have you talked to him?"

"Freddie wouldn't let him come to the phone."

"I have to see you," she whispered through her tears.

"Your husband and I ran into each other tonight, along with Bill Reed. They tried to beat the hell out of me, because I said I had no idea where the money was hidden."

"Dear God, are you hurt? Mark's a fifth-degree black belt. It's a wonder he didn't kill you."

"Yes, I'm fine. He's the bloody mess with a broken hand. I had help. Invisible help, if you know what I mean. This isn't the end though. Reed has screwed Mark big time, but Ward is so far up Reed's ass he can't see daylight. The best thing you can do right now is pack up and go home to your parents until this thing blows up or blows over."

"Stop doing this to me! I love you! You love me," she sobbed, "whether you'll admit it or not. You can't sacrifice our lives on the altar of nobility."

"The last thing your soon-to-be ex-husband said to me before we parted company was, let me see if I can get the words right..." and the words appeared overlaid onto the glass in the phone booth. "Your time's coming, along with the bitch. I am going to kill you, but not before you have a chance to see what I'm going to do to my cute little wife for taking up with lowlife scum like you." When I finished I could hear her choking back the tears. "Listen to me, Kela, you're the only person left in my life who is unspoiled by what is happening to me. I'm not going to drag you down with me. You have to allow me to say good-bye with my last shred of dignity intact."

"There is nothing dignified or noble or honorable about any of this. These men are evil and I'd rather die with you than live without you."

"May I remind you that your husband is one of the men trying to frame me? Not only does he want the money, there is something about Williams' body he wants. He never mentions one without mentioning the other." I let the words rest with her a few moments. "Is there any chance he knows who you really are, what you know, possibly anything about what you learned from old Abraham?"

"I'm not going to Europe," she insisted. "I told Mark that so he would help you. That's why I kept asking if you'd wait for me. But Mark lied to me. He never intended to help you. I'm divorcing him, regardless of what happens to us."

"Is this your idea of a joke?"

"If I'd told you that I was trying to get Mark to help you, you would never have let me go through with it. I didn't know anyone else who had the connections to help. I lied to help you, Josie."

The silence following her words was heavy as lead. Maybe she was telling me the truth, maybe not; it really didn't matter. The simple fact that she seemed to care enough to want to see me one last time was sufficient. So, dumb-as-fuck as I was back then, I dropped my guard again, and agreed to meet her one last time before the cops caught up with me or I caught up with Reed and Ward. And it didn't matter one way or another which came first.

"The old Davis farm on Johns Island," I said.

"I'm on the way." The line went dead.

CHAPTER THIRTY

The rain pelted Folly Road as a couple of police cars, coming from the opposite direction, whizzed by without seeing me. Thigpen would have sent out a description of my car with the license number, unless he didn't want to tip his hand so he could catch me himself. An ambulance crossed the bridge behind me, followed by three state troopers. So I turned down the street that runs through the center of the Westchester subdivision. There was an empty house with a For Sale sign, and I pulled into the driveway slow enough to see the flashing lights pass. What daylight I had left was fading fast. A boarded-up convenience store on the corner offered both shelter in the back and a pay phone out front. Sitting there alone in the dim twilight, I watched two more sets of flashing lights zoom past the intersection. Nothing worth worrying about, I thought, probably local cops chasing down unsuspecting beach road speeders to fill their ticket quotas. My car would've been easy to spot if it hadn't been dark blue. All they had to do was drive around behind the building. I wasn't surprised that neither of them doubled back.

The sun had completely set before I made my way to the pay phone. I called three cab companies before I found a service willing to send a taxi all the way out to Folly Road. I needed to know whose Hit Parade I was on, all of Charleston County, or Thigpen alone.

In the cab, I breathed easier knowing the cops were looking for my car in Charleston while I was in a taxi headed to John's Island. I kept my head down and avoided eye contact with the driver in his rear view mirror.

"Where to?" The driver said.

"Cherry Point Boat Landing," I said.

"Damn man, that's way out the other side o' the island. I ain't gonna pick up no fares way out there."

"Will this fix that?" I showed him a fifty dollar bill.

"Well, it's a start."

"What'll finish it?"

"Another twenty orta do it." He kept trying to find my face in his mirror.

If the driver was going to get a look at me, I wanted it to be on my terms. From the 7-11, we doubled back to the Wappoo Cut Bridge and hung a left on Maybank following the same route I'd driven the night of the drop. Past the golf course, Buzzard's Roost, at River Road, I said, "Pull into that tackle shop."

"You gonna pay me to wait? Meter's runnin', you know."

"You don't have a meter, you're a zone-to-zone driver."

"I mean the one in m'head."

"Here's a ten, dollar a minute should cover it."

"Dollar a minute's good."

The owner, a short, stubby, cigar-chewing character with a bald spot and a beer belly, had a police scanner running all the time. A box full of old lures sat under a hand written sign advertising collectibles. This was my chance to check the chatter. While looking through the boxes of lures, I heard one cop radio another that the suspect's blue Thunderbird had vanished. He requested his dispatcher notify the State Troopers to watch for it on the Interstate. I picked out a J&H Wig-Lit, opened the box and started turning it over in my hand, which immediately caught the owner's attention.

"That'un's a 1947. J&H closed up in '52, notice the treble hook in the tail. Can't find 'em like 'at anymore. All you see nowadays is the double hook weighted tail."

When Montague and I were fishing together, we always used live shrimp. I'd seen a few lures he kept in his tackle box in case we ran out of bait while the stripers were hitting.

"Got any Gamby's?" I said.

"All outta Gamby's, how 'bout a nice Floyd Roman, I got a couple nice Little Nikes, fresh and saltwater."

"I've got three Roman's. Besides, it's not for me, it's a birthday present for a buddy." Early in my music career I'd learned to follow two lines of audio input at the same time. What I called the up high and the down low, the music and the crowd noise. When a group of migrant workers came into the store to buy beer, a Charleston County officer followed them in. He was too busy watching them to pay attention to me or the scanner.

"Lemme take care of these customers." The owner made his way to the counter. So far, the diversion had worked.

"You see a dark blue Thunderbird come by here tonight?"

"Hardly ever notice the cars, unless they're haulin' ass through the intersection."

"Well you know we're looking for one, right?"

"Yeah, heard 'em talkin'. What'd he do?"

"Might'a killed a man." The cop said.

"I'll keep an eye out for 'im."

Between the conversation and the scanner, I'd heard everything I needed. One of the Mexicans elbowed another, mumbled something in Spanish, with the cop right behind them. The cop and the owner eye rolled each other. The Mexicans left without making eye contact with any of us. I picked out a Masterlure Snook Midget, then got in line behind the cop.

"Pack of Marlboro's," the cop said.

"You find one you like?" The owner said over the cop.

"I like this one," I said.

The cop turned around, gave me the once over, nodded. He didn't recognize me so they must not've circulated a physical description. He paid for his smokes.

"Not exactly a collector's item."

"It's a replacement for one he lost," I said.

The cop brushed by me on the way back to his cruiser.

"That'll be two-fifty, plus tax. Sorry, we don't gift wrap."

I paid him, then pocketed the box. The taxi driver was so engrossed in the "Lonely and Looking" section of the Hannahan News, he didn't know I'd come back until I got in the car.

"Where to now?" he said.

"Cherry Point," I told him. Again.

"Oh, yeah."

When we reached the landing, I gave the driver a fifty and a twenty.

"You gonna stay out here all by yourself?"

"My brother's on the way. Pull up under the street light. I'll wait for him there."

"You sure you want me to leave you out here alone. What if he don't show?"

"He'll show or he'll send somebody to get me. Here's another ten for your concern," I said, figuring he was waiting around to make one last run at more money. He pulled out, leaving me standing under the light. I watched the tail lights until they rounded the curve, then walked to the edge of the gravel to make sure he hadn't stopped and cut his lights.

The corrugated shed door was padlocked, but Montague kept a key hanging on a nail, under the dock. His little ten-foot Jon Boat, along with two others, was inside the shed. I dragged it into the water, then fired up the little 5 hp trolling motor.

It had been years since I'd been out on the river at night. Following the house lights dotting the waterfront landscape, I made my way to the mouth of Adams Creek. The tide was coming in so I didn't have to worry too much about sandbars. I passed an expensive home where a party was being thrown on the back deck. Dock lights danced on the water and the phosphorous sparkled in the foam of the boat wake. I'd fished Adams Creek first in my youth and later with Montague before going on the road. The ancient oak tree that hung out over the water behind the Sea Island Yacht Club was still there. Off in the distance, the clouds were breaking up and the full moon was rising over the ocean. I set the little outboard to idle and drifted with the tide, using a paddle to steer. For a few seconds, the timeless beauty of the creek, marsh and moonlight made time stand still and I remember thinking that if I ever got out of this mess, I was going to spend a lot more time on the water.

Stars peaked through the night sky haze. The air warmed up and felt good on my face and hands. I tried to soak up as much of the ancient southern environment as I could. Over the ocean, sheet lighting flashed, as the clouds moved inland. I don't know how long I sat there asking Heaven "Why me?" My skin moistened as dew formed on every surface. The laughing voices of the people from the deck of the party house were so clear I could hear ice clinking in their glasses. It's amazing how sound travels over the water. Every word they said bounced off the slick water, while they were totally unaware of my existence. Children laughing, dogs barking were beautiful night sounds, and I wondered how many years they'd floated over the waters of other Lowcountry evenings. The ripples clicking against the bottom of the Jon Boat reminded me of raindrops on a car roof at the beginning of a summer thunderstorm.

I'd have to goose the little outboard to go against the tide flowing out from the creek. And I was just before turning the handle when the little boat speeded up on its own. Boats don't drift upstream against an outgoing tide. Something was pulling it.

I looked for the rope attached to the carry handle, but it was lying in the bow. Phosphorus grew brighter as the boat made the turn into the mouth of the creek before slowing to a stop. The outgoing tide moved past, gathering speed as the Lowcountry wetlands drained to the sea. The glowing green gold specks formed a dazzling murmuration similar to a flock of starlings. Then, as suddenly as it appeared, the phosphorus disappeared, and a dead calm fell over the creek, the boat and me. The outboard went silent, the racing water smoothed to glass, reflecting a full moon in a cloudless sky. From beneath the hull came a sound like swarming bees, growing louder while filling the air, until I thought a squadron of WWII bombers was flying overhead. I felt the boat being lifted up and starting to spin, and I grabbed the sides to steady myself, as what can only be described as a liquid tornado with bright, glowing eyes rose from the water formed the head of a Python and spoke to me.

"I am Strong Man. I have chosen this vessel to bear witness to the children of Charles Towne. Neither God nor Devil am I, nor Demon nor Angel. I am spirit only, created from the fabric of mind and space and sustained by faith in the true nature of man and beast, fish and fowl, male and female, born to and inhabiting My Holy City of Charles Towne. My home is the flowing waters of harbor and history and heritage past, and present, and future. My sanctuary resides in the hearts of all who inhale Me in low-lying marshes, who breathe Me in through ocean air coursing through the moss-covered antiquity of ancient oaks and listen for My voice in the brackish water pools and creeks of forests, fields, and mudflats, in tide, streams and estuaries. Absorb Me through the oyster, ingest Me through fish, fowl, hoof, shrimp, crab, blossom, herb, root, and grain. I am filtered beneath beach, ship, and bridge; into the homes, houses, hearts and souls of all who love The Holy City. I float on the scents of tea olive, jasmine, and elixirs of salt marsh. As the fish flows through water, and water flows through the fish, Strong Man flows through the blood pulsing through the dual hearts of My children. As the bird flows through the air, and the air flows through the bird, Strong Man flows through the breath breathed by My children. From the days of the founding, I have traveled with your blood lines. As the root is anchored in the earth, and the earth is anchored in the root, Strong Man is anchored in the souls of My children. You are Me and I am you. You were called as My Bridge from the bloodlines of Barbados, Southampton and Ghana, to and across the divides of color and colorless, thought and process, belief and will, time and unforeseen occurrence, for the complete and full understanding of all My people, so they may gather together and know, absorb and ingest, live and breathe the Truth. We are All Spirits of the One True City. That Spirit is Charles Towne, My Holy City, Your Holy City, Our Holy City. You will stand in the gap for Me as I have stood for you, your ancestors, your brothers and your sisters against the machinations of the intruders, the alien interlocutors, the would be usurpers who would twist and bend the old words and ways of sky time, earth rhythm, water repose and blood line. Stand in the gap for Me. Tell them 'Love the Spirit of the City as you love Her streets, for Charles Towne and Strong Man and You are One.' Charles Towne mother, Strong Man father, You and Yours are our children. Tell them. And I *will protect you and yours in all your ways, this is My promise to all who have ears to listen, and eyes to see and hearts to discern the still inner voice of the City. I will guide you through Her streets by way of the still inner voice, whispered to each one who cherishes My Charles Towne. Tell them. 'This is all I require, that you love Me as you love My Holy City, for We are One.' As I am, you will be, I in you and you in Me, together in Our Holy City. Go now, bear witness to all those who would dishonor My children and pillage My Holy City. Tell them. 'You mind how you walk My streets, mind how you talk about My children, for Charles Towne and Strong Man are watching, listening, discerning your heart's every intention, your lust for our treasure and your longing for power.' Tell them. They will never prosper, they will never gain respect. They cannot buy power in Charles Towne, their riches mean nothing to the true children of The City. The lowest of the low who loves Me, is greater in the eyes of the Holy City, than the richest would-be usurper. They will be exiled in disgrace, heads hung low or be put to death by those of their own kind or by those who love Me. It matters not to Me which way they leave or which way they die. This is for My children to decide, but they will not remain to trample this sacred ground. My sacred ground. For I am Strong Man, I am Python, I am Charles Towne. I am in the City and the City is in Me. Go. Tell them. 'Despise My Holy City, disrespect My people, My children, dishonor Me and neither your treasure nor your God will be to able save you.' Go now, tell them, I am Strong Man, neither God nor Devil, neither Angel nor Demon, I am in You. You are in Me. The fish is of the water. The bird is of the air. The root is of the earth. All comingled. Your spirit, My spirit, comingled. Your spirit with My spirit becomes Our spirit. Together, your own greatest ally or your own worst enemy. Each must decide. For I am Strong Man and the Spirit of Charles Towne is of Me, My people, All of Us, together and alone. Go now. Tell them. Strong Man is with you."*

As quickly as this vision appeared, it disappeared. The motor started, the boat puttered upstream, and my mind was blown. The land and seascape glowed as warm water lapped the hull, sending soft salt spray into my face. I knew one of two things had happened. Either I'd completely and irrevocably lost every ounce of sanity I had left, or I was in touch with something so much larger than myself that everything else in my life paled in significance.

A cold chill rushed over my skin as I realized I'd done everything in my life for selfish reasons. I'd prostituted my talent; stepped on others to get where I wanted to go and never looked back until now. Having shared the spotlight with scores of world famous musicians, hearing the cheers of tens of thousands of people screaming for more, compared with the awesome power and beauty I'd witnessed in a boat, alone on the river in the Lowcountry, those moments of glory all looked vain and pathetic.

Then, from somewhere deep inside, I heard my thinking voice rise up all by itself. I felt my mouth open, and my speaking voice say to the sky, "If you get me out of this one last time, I promise, I'll never let anything like this happen again." I didn't know where the thought originated, but I knew I meant it.

"Born-again" is a term used by churchgoers to describe a particular religious experience. From what I'd heard, it meant the person was somehow transformed in heart, mind and value system. I simply decided I'd lost my mind, like being the only witness to a UFO landing, or coming face-to-face with a ghost. My problem, of course, was all the acid I'd taken when I was traveling. Hallucinations, though none as wild as what I'd just witnessed, were still pretty much a factor in my world view. Flashbacks were not uncommon even in people who hadn't dropped in several years. It would be easy to rationalize the whole experience away to the mental gymnastics of a drug-altered awareness. The potion on the chicken foot had probably contained some residual ingredient that triggered it, or at least part of it. Too many old friends wound up in the loony bin because they made the mental mistake of accepting hallucination as fact. And while I didn't feel crazy, neither was I afraid. I was calm, relaxed and determined to track down Reed and make sure he got what was coming to him. Once again, I started laughing.

"I might be crazy," I said to thin air, "But, by God, I'm not stupid."

As the moon rose higher over the marsh grass, an offshore breeze carried a few moisture laden clouds across the night sky. Light rain peppered the landscape as the outline of the Davis farm and the small floating dock came into view. I tied the Jon Boat off and made my way up the ramp to the thin strip of concrete walkway that led to the shore. Kela was waiting in her car, parked under the awning in back of the cabin. When she saw me coming up the walkway, she jumped out and ran to meet me with a towel. I'd never been so happy to see another person; never loved anyone so deeply.

"The car is packed and ready to go," she threw her arms around me. We kissed for what seemed like an eternity. Our only restraint was the packed back seat and the fact that time was quickly running out. When we finally came to our senses, the moon was high and bright over the water. The air had cooled, but the car was warm. For the moment, at least, we were safe and together.

"You see the haze of light off in the distance? Under that haze lies the city of Charleston and the end of my world, as I once knew it."

"I don't understand," she said.

"Like the lamp that burns brightest just before it goes out, I have tried to hang on to my dreams, and the feeling, the touch of your hand on my skin, makes me realize that at this most vulnerable of moments, I am more complete than I've ever been in my entire life."

"What's gotten into you?" she said. "It will be daylight in a few hours. We should've been moving hours ago."

"All I want, for the rest of my life, is to share every sunrise with you."

Maybe I'd finally given up hope and, like the drowning man who will grab anything, I was resigning myself to giving up my hold on the last thing I'd grabbed. There was no clear reason that came to mind for why I suddenly relaxed. All I know is that just as my decision to quit playing music for a living began to surface, so too, did my subconscious mind and body seem to be cooperating with each other, independently of any conscious rationale. Something else was making my decisions for me and had taken me, personally, out of the loop.

Kela had come to me because she believed in me as a person, alone and separate from what I did or what I could do for her. Nobody had ever accepted me on those terms. There was no way I was going to turn her away or allow anything to happen to her.

"Josie," she whispered. "Where do we go from here?"

"Well," I said. "I'd like to spend the next couple hours with you and then have you take me to my car so I can get out of town and head on up to New York."

I paused long enough to see tears start welling up in her eyes.

"Then, I'd want you to go on to Paris with your husband, think about all of this. In three weeks, I could be settled in Greenwich Village."

She shook her head back and forth. "Going back to Mark while you try to make a mad dash out of town in a marked car is not part of the bargain."

"We're in this together. Your car's packed; you've got plenty of cash, you could drive twenty-four hours straight through to New York yourself, and I'll meet you there."

"I have no desire to live one more minute without you," she cried.

"Kela, we're backed against the wall. We can't beat the system on the system's own turf."

"I'd rather go to jail in this life or to Hell in the next than go back to that demon Mark Ward."

"I'm telling you, the system, this system, the way it's setup, can't be beat."

"How about this – we can be together forever, I don't want to be apart even for a little while. There's no reason not to go for it," she said.

She was so insistent I almost gave in. Kela actually loved me enough to live on the run with me. "The chances of getting away with it are almost nonexistent. It'll take a miracle. If the cops catch you with me, you'll be charged as an accessory."

This whole thing was my fault. There was no way I was going to let her ruin her life because of my mistakes. If I let her put her own freedom at risk, just to be with me, I'd never be able to forgive myself.

"And if we get caught?" I said.

"Even if they put me in prison, I'll be safer than I am now or will be as long as Mark Ward is alive. Even if none of this stuff had happened, and I do mean none of it, Mark Ward is going to kill me, sooner or later, one way or another. Do you understand that?"

I said nothing. What could I say? She was right.

"OK. You've convinced me. He's going to kill you. I get it."

I made a cold decision. If this thing was going to blow up; if she wanted to wait for me; then I wanted her where she could visit me. Where we could start making plans for our lives after I got out of jail.

"Let me put it this way," she said, "I'm going with you either to jail or to New York. I'll tell the police I helped you escape. If we're going down, at least we'll be going down together."

"That's insane!"

"Maybe so, but no more insane than the life I'm living now." She crossed her arms. "I'm sick of my life, the way it is, and I'm prepared to take drastic measures to change it. If you don't take me with you, then I'll take matters into my own hands. You're in suicide mode and getting ready to make a big mistake. I'm not stupid. I know you aren't going to New York, unless I drive you there myself."

I sat there, astounded, as she continued. "You're going to go after Bill Reed and the others by yourself because you still believe, if you can catch them with the evidence, you can call the cops and everybody will make nice. Here are the facts: If Reed or Mark doesn't kill you, I'm sure the police will."

She was holding on to my arm with both hands, sobbing with streams of tears running down her cheeks. "You even told me yourself that the dumbest thing a single soldier can do is attack a fortified city."

Kela was about to fall apart. I had to calm her down, talk her into taking a course of action that would protect her from what was coming. I tried, again, to sell her on the story of my going to New York, while she was in Paris for three weeks. Let things cool down. Then, when she came back, we'd pick up right where we left off.

"We won't plan anything beyond that point," I said. "If we tried to leave town together, it would make it more difficult for me to cut and run. As soon as your husband realizes we're both gone, he'll have the entire Atlantic Fleet looking for us. As a Captain's wife, you'll be considered a definite national security risk. And I would, of course, be hung for kidnapping, treason and God only knows what else, provided I even got to trial."

Sitting there in the dark, listening as a light breeze rustled the leaves of the ancient oaks, I turned on the radio and tuned it to the Harry Abraham Show, broadcasting live from WABC out of New York. Thanks to the cloud bounce, the music was soft in the background. Harry was playing "Maiden Voyage" from Herbie Hancock's first album, then "Walking in Space" by Quincy Jones.

"My father abused my mother on a regular basis," she said. "He'd stay gone for days…" Her life story sounded like my own. The old man leaves for a week, maybe more, gets drunk, comes home looking for a fight he knows he can win. "It wasn't so much the beatings as the hate in his words. Nobody, no woman, no mother of a child, deserves to be hated with such intensity simply because she exists…" Word for word, images of my own childhood filled in the blanks of her narrative. The more she talked, the closer I felt to her. When she stopped, I picked up with my own story. We traded regrets back and forth for almost two hours. The wounds commiserating each other, confirming the damage, scar for scar, in the cold light of the full moon. When the last of the purging was out, we laid in each other's arms absorbing our mutual grief. I ran my fingertips across her cheek, then gently kissed her forehead.

"How will you get out of town driving your own car?" she said. "Everyone knows it."

"That is a problem," I said, "but I don't have much choice."

She stared out the windshield for a moment, then reached behind the back seat and pulled a shopping bag up from the floor. In it was a wig, along with a baseball cap and a pair of sunglasses.

"You'll wear this, drive my car and I'll drive yours," she said, handing me the cap.

To her way of thinking, I'd be well across state lines before the cops figured out I was gone. As soon as I got settled in New York, and she was back in Charleston, I'd send for her. We decided to leave it like that.

"You better be in New York," she said. "I'll track you to the ends of the earth, if I have too."

She'd turned her back on every support system available in her life to be with me. How does a person do something like that? I really felt that if I didn't give her something to hang on to, she might do herself bodily harm. It would have been like dying and going to heaven to just run away with her. I could start a new life in another state. But unless they found the real killer soon, or at least a body; unless that happened, our relationship was doomed. I knew that for a fact. And I got the distinct impression she was finally realizing it, too. She put her arms around my neck and kissed me again.

"I've got to get going," I said. "The sun will be up in the next couple hours, and you've got to hang in there with me, if we're going to pull this off.

OK.'" She started the car. "Three weeks is nothing in the grand scheme of things. By the time I get back, you'll be set up and they'll have the real killer. All this'll be history."

I patted her on the leg, as we started down the dirt road that led off the Davis property.

The streets were still wet after the light drizzle that had fallen. Very few cars on the road. As we pulled out onto the highway, I thought about all she was willing to endure just to be with me. I felt guilty about not telling her my true intentions, but I knew that if I did tell her, I'd have to waste valuable time justifying my decision.

We drove in silence back to where I'd parked my car behind the vacant 7-11. Streaks of black clouds racing in from the sea crossed the face of the moon. I got out of the car and opened Kela's door. When she stood up, she threw her arms around my neck and kissed me like she might never see me again.

I hated lying to her, but for her own protection, I had to convince her to let me go. The business at hand couldn't accommodate a love affair.

"Just drop my car off in the parking lot of The Merch," I said.

"Please let me come with you," she pleaded.

"They will rip us apart like a slave family in the 1800s. This way we can gain our freedom and never be taken away from each other."

I put her behind the driver's seat. I leaned in, put the key in the ignition and started the engine. Then I lowered the driver's side window and shut the door. I kissed her again and made my way back to her car. I watched the T-Bird pull onto Folly Road and accepted the very real possibility that I was seeing Kela; my life and my car; my sanctuary, for the last time.

CHAPTER THIRTY-ONE

Once I was alone in Kela's car, I started formulating my plan to get back into Charleston unnoticed. As I drove down Folly Road, I looked for cop cars in the parking lots of Hardees, the boiled peanut stand, a couple of used car lots and The Reef. I remembered the last gig I played there, when it was the only 24 hour bar between Charleston and the beach with a live band playing until 4 a.m. Renken Boats and the new James Island Shopping Center came up on the left. The light was red at the intersection of Camp Road. It was a lot like time travel because every address had a string of memories attached to it. Even some of the new buildings were built on lots where we rode our Honda motorcycles or played sand lot ballgames.

The streetlights and stoplights reflected in the wet asphalt and gave the whole scene an eerie dreamlike quality. As I rounded the curve past the intersection of Harbor View Road, I saw the new Citizens and Southern Bank sitting on the corner of Maybank and Folly. Up ahead was the Wappoo Cut Bridge and on the other side of it was a downhill descent into West Ashley and a straight shot across the Ashley River Bridge into Charleston. From the top of the bridge, I could see the lights of the city glowing on the skyline. I figured this must be what Hell looks like from about three miles out.

I felt weak from lack of sleep. My shoulders ached and the knot in my stomach was making me nauseous; I needed to eat something, but my mind kept pushing my body forward. Once I crossed the Ashley River, I pulled in to the side parking lot of the Elks' Club. Kela's car would be safe there and I could walk to the St. James in less than three minutes. Finally, being back on foot and away from her car, I felt stronger than I'd felt all night.

Working my way through the shadows of buildings and dimly lit side streets gave me a sense of safety absent in something as bulky as a car. I worked my way past the Patio Drive-In and ducked into the walled-in trash bin. Through the cracks in the wood slats, I could see the front of the St. James. Reed's Buick was nowhere in sight.

A couple of cop cars cruised down Spring Street, and a drunk was huddled up on the sidewalk, but aside from him, the drizzling rain had emptied the street. A cream colored Lincoln Mark IV was parked on the opposite side of the street, but there was no sign of Reed. I knew he was somewhere in the area. I could feel him in the air. I wasn't scared, shaking or nervous. I'd never felt more businesslike. Nothing was going to stop me.

A large cloud covered the moon, and the temperature was dropping. Fog forming on the river began drifting into the street. The mercury vapor lights projected their wet halos and the neon buzzing of the St. James sign sputtered twice before going totally dark. I could see in the kitchen window. I was sure Reed was nowhere on the premises, but as soon as I made this assumption, I heard a car coming up Hagood Avenue out of the fog.

Reed's Riviera pulled up alongside the curb. He closed his eyes, scrunched up his face and smiled like he was exhaling a good hit of reefer. Cricket's head popped up from his lap. When he gave her a bump from his coke spoon, she started giggling and counting money. I could see him lighting a cigarette. Then she got out, wearing a tight leather miniskirt and a fur jacket, leaned in his window and gave him a big kiss. Reed pulled away from the curb and she did the cutesy "hooker running on tip-toes in spike heels" trot across the street and dropped in behind the wheel of the Mark IV. The Buick turned the corner and headed over to the Charleston Inn. The Lincoln followed. Both cars disappeared behind the motel.

I sprinted across the street to where the Lincoln had been parked and got up against the wall in the shadows. As I was getting ready to run back across the street to the Patio, I saw another set of headlights coming up Hagood, out of the fog. Racing the oncoming beams, I managed to get inside a doorway as Janet Collins, driving her Mustang and accompanied by Freddie May and Thigpen, came to the corner, stopped and traced the same route Reed had taken. She followed his course around back of the Charleston Inn. It didn't take much to put two and two together and figure out Janet was following Bill. Why she had company was a question I couldn't answer.

After about thirty seconds, when I knew I wouldn't be seen, I ran across the Patio parking lot, jumped the median and cut through the breezeway to the back of the hotel. The Riviera and the Lincoln were both empty, but Janet was standing beside her Mustang with a pair of binoculars scanning the windows of the third floor. She apparently didn't see what she was looking for, but both men got out of the car, opened the trunk and pulled out shotguns, loaded them, and started walking toward the breezeway.

The flagstone sidewalk was slippery and I skidded racing back to the front of the building. Handrails, dripping wet, were hard to hang on to and I slid around the corner heading toward the front desk. The dampness everywhere only seemed to enhance the swamp-like atmosphere.

A two-lane drive-through with a gable roof was right in front of double French doors leading into the lobby. Through the glass front door, I could see the stuffed chairs, antebellum sofas and Charleston reproduction furniture of the lobby proper. A distinguished black man with silver hair and moustache was working behind the counter. I was on my way to tell him what was going on when I heard my name called from the hallway leading to the restaurant.

"Josie Fucking Chapman! What the Hell are you doing here?" Bill Reed was standing by the Pepsi machine with an ice bucket under his arm. He had on his pants, a t-shirt, slippers and a bathrobe. The robe was hanging open, and I could see the handle of his .45 sticking out of the waistband. I stopped cold in my tracks and stared at him.

"Boy, the whole town is looking for you. Where you been hidin', son?" His voice was calm enough, but his eyes were wild.

For some stupid reason, I almost warned him about Janet, but as soon as I opened my mouth an invisible hand wrapped around my face. Looking back, I believe that was the moment I truly crossed the line. Knowing that two men with shotguns were waiting for him and not telling him about it was, in my estimation, a serious character flaw which I later learned to cherish. Sometimes you have to let the God of Enough Rope do His thing. Maybe, if I'd said something, the situation would've turned out different, but I didn't because I couldn't, because as luck would have it, Bill Reed decided to play his tough guy role right up to the last minute and something inside of me refused to let me speak, even if I'd wanted to.

The cops would probably say this makes me an accessory to what happened next, but I don't think so. In fact, I know it doesn't because when Reed came over and grabbed me by the shirt, I was actually thinking of grabbing his gun and shooting him myself. I'd reached the end of my own rope, so I made a conscious decision to let him hang himself right there. The truth is, I knew in that instant that life, as I'd known it, was over for me. All that really mattered was that I stayed alive. Pretty basic, stay alive. Like I said before, I'd proven I had a talent for flying into the mouth of oblivion.

We stood by the ice machine, glaring at each other. I could hear the desk clerk dialing the phone. I figured three minutes and the place would be crawling with cops. My head was pounding from the fatigue and the choking sensation of Reed's hand tightening my collar. I jerked loose from his hand.

The desk clerk disappeared, and Reed grabbed at me again. I batted his hand away and he pulled the pistol out of his pants.

"You got brass balls, boy, you know that?" He spat the words at me, literally as drops of saliva spewed from his mouth. "Either that or you're the stupidest motherfucker ever walked the planet." He cocked his head to one side. "I'm going with the latter."

There was a pause as he adjusted his robe, then he stepped back and flashed the pistol like a knife. It was the first time I'd seen the look on his face that I'd heard others talk about. The look he had right before he smacked his victim across the face with his gun and then preceded to pistol whip them into a coma. His eyes blazed, his forehead wrinkled up like a washboard, and his teeth glowed behind an open mouth. It lasted long enough for me to notice the hand with the pistol as it lashed out like a snake's tongue and caught me on the upper left corner of my forehead.

"What's-a-matter, Josie, cat gotcha tongue? I asked you a question!"

He tried faking to the left and right throwing the pistol from hand to hand, shaking it in my face with each toss. His bathrobe was open and his tee shirt rode up his belly showing the black hair on the white skin. Little red spots like ant bites were scattered about his torso.

"You're the one with all the nerve, Bill." I backed down the hallway toward the restaurant and lounge. "When are you going to stop staying in sleazy joints like this and find a real home in the St. James?"

I opened the door to the lounge and took a quick look around. The Xanadu Lounge reminded me of club in New York called The Loft. The room sported its own light show, a mirror ball hanging from the ceiling. Every wall was covered with framed movie posters and red crushed velvet roll-and-pleat armchairs snuggled between faux zebra skin sofas. There were three art deco lamps with stained glass shades, featuring the outline of dragonflies whose eyes lit up when the bulb was on. Everything was cheap, plastic and designed to take spilled drinks. Through the window I saw Janet, Freddie and Thigpen. I swatted the light switch, but hit the rheostat by mistake, this fired up the spots and turned on the light show. Perfect, I thought, "death by disco." It was a term I'd picked up at The Loft.

Reed stepped into the room, closing the door behind him, his eyes searching the room as the dots of light circled the walls.

"I'm asking you, again. Why are you here?" he said.

"I wanta know why you're doing this to me and when you plan to stop?"

"I don't know what you're talking about." He dropped the clip from the gun, checked it and popped it back into the grip. "But I'm getting sick of you fucking up my business. It ain't an easy business, as it is. You know?"

He backed me up to the bar, pressing his face in on me. My arms spread out on the bar, my fingers found one of those red table candles with the white plastic netting around it. I grabbed it and swung it like a baseball right at his face. It hit him between the eyes, and he grabbed his head with his free hand.

"Gawddamit, you little shit," he screamed. "I oughta put a damn clip in you right here, right now."

"Why me? Bill, just answer me that. Why not one of those stupid junkies who work for you,? Why'd you pick me, Bill?"

"You're way out of your league." He glared at me through his fingers, blood starting to trickle down his face. "If I didn't know the net was about to drop around your nigger-lovin', lily-white ass, I'd do you myself right here."

"What're you talking about? Me not being a racist pig like you doesn't make me Abraham Lincoln."

"Even the street niggers hate you, and the Toms you hang with. That's why we picked you, asshole. You and your kind are bad for business. Did you really think we were going to sit by and let a pussy like you take over the hottest club in town?" He raised the edge of his robe to wipe the blood from his face. When he did, I kicked the gun out of his hand and rushed past him.

Once outside, I raced around to the back of the building, up the stairs to the second floor. The janitor's closet was open, so I ducked behind a stack of toilet paper boxes. I heard Reed huffing up the stairs, running from one end of the balcony to the other. A door slammed to the room right next to me.

I stood up and peeked out of the closet. The slight drizzle was turning into real rain, soaking the walkway. Lightning flashed out over the harbor as peals of thunder rumbled hard enough to rattle plate-glass. The curtain in Bill's room wasn't pulled tight. I could see him standing in front of the dresser, patting his forehead with a washcloth. Cricket was sitting on the edge of the bed wearing a pink lace teddy. She moved when he reached under the bed for a small satchel, looked inside, and then almost stuffed it back under the bed. I say almost because I could see the corner sticking out from under the dust ruffle.

For some reason I didn't fully understand, this really got to me. Again, I'm guessing because I was crazy. It was OK for Reed to call me a nigger lover and use it as an excuse to frame me for the murder of Bootsy Williams, while he slept with black hookers. That's when it dawned on me – even though these corrupt blacks and lowlife whites were all racists themselves, their dislike for each other didn't stop them from working together when it came to large sums of money. What both sides hated, more than they hated each other, was anyone, black or white screwing around with their business of fleecing the public. The racism was real, but it was nothing compared to the greed driving the whole machine. Something moved in the hallway and I ducked around the corner. I heard Janet's voice whispering.

"Hello, Josie." And I felt cold steel on my neck. "Just step right over to the door, and you won't get hurt. Much." She snickered.

"Charlie, you on the left and Freddie May, you take the right, I'm going up the middle." Then she knocked on the door.

"What!?" Reed barked. Janet nodded for me to answer him.

"It's me, Josie." I said. Janet nudged me with the pistol. "I wanna try to work this out, peacefully."

"You're one stupid prick, son-of-a bitch. You come here thinking you can just fuck with me in my town…" Reed's voice grew louder as he came closer to the door. Janet pushed me aside. She wanted to be the first person he saw when he opened the door. "…I'm the one person who's always trying to help you, and all you do is take my money and cause me grief." I heard the chain lock being removed from the inside of the door. "I thought I could trust you, man, and here you're biting the hand that feeds you."

As the door opened, Janet and her two men burst into the room. I was left on the balcony watching the whole scene from the handrail.

"Well, well…" she said, calmly. "Talk about trust and biting the hand that feeds you. Who's your little Brown Sugar friend, Billy? Aren't you going to introduce us?"

"What's it to you," he sneered. "You and I are finished, anyway."

"Don't you think you should've let me in on that little piece of information?" I mean, really, Billy. Around here, when a gentleman breaks up with his lady, there's usually a considerable sum of money involved, especially as much money as you owe me." Her two escorts racked their shotguns.

"You might try asking your musician friend about that. He's the one who had the bag last," Reed pointed his pistol at me. Janet didn't even look back. She kept her eyes and her gun trained on Reed.

"Billy, who do you think you're talking to about money? I know you killed Williams, and you took the money. I also know what you did with the money, and I know you still have it. I didn't ask you for money. I said, you owe me money."

"How much?" I said, almost under my breath, stepping back into the room. "Just a ballpark figure, since I'm the one who's getting blamed for all this." They all just looked at me.

"I'll tell you." Janet turned sideways so she could watch us both, the hatred seething under the surface of her model face. "It was exactly fifty-thousand, Josie. And this slime ball blew the whole wad paying off one of his own lame ass, gambling debts."

"Fifty thousand was your cut? Or fifty thousand was in the bag?"

"My cut. Fifty percent," she said.

"So, how much was in the bag? Or, supposed to be in the bag?" I said.

"One hundred thousand dollars." Janet rattled the number off like a carnival barker.

"Well, when I got the bag it only had twenty thousand in it." I said, "Not that it makes any difference right here, right now."

"You're a lying piece of shit, Chapman."

"If you know all this, then you don't need me, right?"

She grinned over her shoulders, looking first at me, then at Reed, as if she was trying to decide which of us to shoot first. "Ward found the gun you left in his car," Reed said. "Had his driver take it right back to your apartment and told your SLED buddy Ross right where to find it. There's all the evidence they need right there; the murder weapon right there in your house. Like I said, you're in way over your head, man. Besides, as you can see, I got my own problems."

He picked up a pack of cigarettes off the nightstand, lit up and took a deep drag, like he'd polished off an important piece of business. He was waiting for something, watching Janet and her two friends. I had a sinking feeling in my stomach; I knew the desk clerk had already called the police.

Janet said, "Take him outside. We'll deal with him later."

Freddie nudged me in the ribs with his shotgun. "You heard the lady. Let's go Elvis."

As I moved toward the door, she turned her pistol around, holding it by the barrel. It was obvious she was going to hit Reed in the face with the butt of the gun. She held it up like a starter's flag, then turned it slowly making it obvious what she planned to do.

"You're pretty brave when you have one of these in your hand," she said softly. "I think you ought to know what it feels like to be on the recieving end of a pistol whipping."

"Can I just ask one question?" I said. "Why me?"

"Because you're a stupid little fuck with his head up his ass. You and your crazy ideas about buying The Merch. Did you really think we were going to let that happen? Not on your life." She paused and then said, rather calmly for the moment, "I always thought you were smart, but you have no idea how Charleston operates. You thought you were selling music and a night out on the town to those assholes…" I was listening, but I was also watching everybody else in the room. "…This town is about money. Getting it, and keeping it, anyway you can." There was one lamp on the dresser and one beside the bed where the corner of the satchel was sticking out. I could reach the one on the dresser and it was a straight shot across the bed to other lamp. "Do you really not understand that?" Janet still had the pistol high up over her head. Freddie poked the shotgun in my back and shoved me toward the door.

"She's right. This town ain't about fun and games," Reed scoffed. "It's all about money. I make money; we all make money. I go down, we're all going down. I got no more use for this bullshit." He focused his attention squarely on Janet. "And you, bitch, are you going to use that thing or just hold it over your head like you're the Statue of Fuckin' Liberty or something…"

I grabbed the lamp off the dresser and threw it across the room at the other lamp, both exploded on the floor. The room was suddenly dark, except for the parking lot lights coming through the door. I wasn't prepared for the butt of the shotgun to come down across the side of my head. I saw nothing but black; blood was running into my eyes as soon as my head hit the floor. I rolled over and grabbed the satchel from under the bed. Reed was trying to wrestle the pistol out of Janet's hand, while Freddie and Thigpen hammered him like they were trying to break down a wall. They continued to lay into him while I, now almost blind in one eye from the blood running down my forehead; tried to sit up.

"You son-of-a-whore-hopper!" Janet screamed at Reed. "You take my money to cover your ass, then cheat on me with that black bitch!"

She brought her knee up into his groin; he doubled over. Thigpen brought the barrel of his shotgun up hard under Reed's chin, knocking him back on the bed. I heard his sickening moan as his skull smacked the headboard driving it into the wall. A chair scraped behind me. Cricket was on her hands and knees, crawling out the door. Janet was trying to get her left foot untangled from the lamp cord, kicking violently, still waving the gun in the air. She backed up to the edge of the bed with the pistol pointed right at Reed's head; her other hand pulling her hair out of her face, her skirt riding high up her leg. For a moment the room stood as still as a crypt. The only sound was heavy breathing pulsing in sync with the rain hitting the walkway.

I struggled to my knees, grabbing the dresser chair with my free hand. It turned over, sending me crashing to the floor again. A moment later I heard the click-clack of an automatic racking a round into the chamber. I made another attempt to get up, again losing my footing on the wet carpet. Janet was panting like a rabid dog and motioning with her pistol toward Freddie who was behind me. I turned to look up at him, then kicked him straight in the kneecap with the tip of my shoe. The butt of his shotgun came hurling down so hard, when I raised my arm to protect myself, the stock of the gun cracked the bone with such force it hit me right between the eyes.

I was semi-conscious. I heard a pistol fire several times. Something hit the floor next to my head with a dull thud. I was being dragged out of the room feet first. The satchel was jerked out of my hand and in the distance, I could hear sirens wailing. This is where things get foggy. I know I was outside, lying next to the handrail. I tried to struggle to my feet, but when I put my weight on my arm, the pain shot through me and I slipped on the wet concrete. Half hanging, half leaning on a rail. Janet crouched beside me, her skirt so high up her legs, I could see her underwear, her blouse open and exposing the deep cleavage of her heaving breasts. Her hair spilled over her face; she grabbed my own face; turning it back and forth. She huffed as she rolled me over. My broken arm was turning numb. I made one last attempt to grab her leg and pull her to the floor, but the weight of her knee on my back pinned me down. Something hit me in the back of the head and everything went black. Just before I lost total consciousness, I heard the door slam and shuffling footsteps as people trundled down the walkway.

I could hear police radios and sirens screaming up Lockwood Boulevard, followed by the crunch of tires sliding to a stop on the wet asphalt, and car doors slamming. A few moments later, the room was a blaze of lights and voices. Pulsating blue light was pouring through the door. I remember lying flat on the side of my face, looking at what seemed to be dozens of pairs of feet stepping all over and around me. My arm was totally numb and someone was trying to check my pulse. The cold rain was blowing through the open door and dripping off the raincoats of the paramedics. Someone said something about taking the gun out of my hand and making sure to get a good set of prints. I could feel their hands on my hand, but I couldn't see them. My head and arm felt like they were on fire. Before I finally lost consciousness, I remember being picked up and put on a stretcher. An oxygen mask was fitted over my face, and I watched the top of the door-casing pass over head as they wheeled be down the walkway. I was vaguely aware of the tilt of the stairs, and the last thing I heard was the guy on the radio calling the trauma unit of the County Emergency Room.

"Have a room and table ready in three minutes, this one's lost a lot of blood, severe trauma to the head and arm, he's fading fast," the driver said.

That was the last thing I remembered.

CHAPTER THIRTY-TWO

Light-trimmed parallels of shadow bend across a dull facade of beige, each line forming rungs in a ladder, cascading beyond vision. Consciousness rising from darkness reveals the corner of a room; right angles basked in the low glow of sunlight filtering through undulating venetian blinds. A realization sparks strains of understanding, something inside is aware it is aware. Paper noises, pages turning, the scrape of soft shoe soles on polished tile, seat shifting, knowledge creeps in, recognizes the sounds firing, converting them to images – newspaper, shoe, floor, isolating direction. A muscle twitches, the mind arcs, peripheral alertness turns toward the sound seeking the source, the head follows, processing, until gradually alertness dawns. Sheet, bed, arms, head, this now, awareness is here.

A woman sits next to you reading a paper. A nurse enters, checks the IV and adjusts the traction on your right arm. In the mirror, you see a body in bandages tries to speak and your jaw hurts. Claustrophobia tightens neck muscles invoking recalled images of late night black and white horror films. You know the horror film. The victim is buried alive, then suddenly, as if seized by a new thought, you realize the awareness is you.

The woman leans over the bed. "Hello Sunshine." In her melodic whisper I hear a song. "Don't you hear your lady love a' softly calling … callin' you back …I thought you … didn't love me no more…. You've been gone an awfully long time…" Her eyes search my eyes, her finger tips trace my eyebrows, shoo shoo bop shoo bop … my lover … oooo."

You think you know this song, you think you know her face, you're sure you know her voice, her soft, low-hanging demeanor comforts you like a concerned relative. Your eyes flutter, then you regain full consciousness, find your face wrapped in bandages, your arm in traction. The awareness which flowed into you becomes me. That was how I came out of the coma.

"Don't try to talk and don't move your head; you have a fractured jaw."

She touched my good arm. I am tired, so very tired, I thought, trying to form words and push them through my teeth, but she laid her fingertip on my lips. The throbbing pressure in my temples required most of my concentration simply to maintain a sense of the present. Sitting on the edge of the bed, she studied my eyes. "*Can you hear my thoughts? The worst is over.*"

For a moment, she looked like a total stranger. I kept thinking this was another bad dream. That I'd soon wake up. She was talking between thoughts; "We have a future now. . . *a fresh start with days full of sunlight* . . . You're safe now *the bridge is almost complete.*"

I lay terrified, staring at her angelic face. I remember thinking I was either dead or dying. She was holding my good hand, which had fallen, limp fingers dangling off the edge of the bed. My stomach cramped, sending a metallic bile of acid reflux rising into the back of my throat.

She sat beside me and closed her eyes. I thought about the vision on the creek, how real it had seemed, and thought this woman was a hallucination, too. Then I saw a change in her chest as she inhaled a deep, gasp of air. Her breasts rose up, she placed her free hand palm down on my chest. Suddenly she tightened her fist, inclined her chin, her unfocused eyes stared into mine, then she whispered, "Deliver him." She closed her eyes, let go of my hand, then removed her fist from my chest. As consciousness once again started fading to black, I recognized Kela.

I reached for her with my good hand; my fingers hit the cold steel of the bed rail. A belt of some kind held my arm and I could feel the grain of the weave on my skin. I wondered what sort of industrial evolution led to the design of restraining belts and how many men had broken free before the invention of straps that could not be broken. Kela watched me test the strength of my restraints. As the weariness of struggle gave way to despair, once again she touched my arm.

"There, there, Josie, you need to relax. If you understand me, blink twice for yes."

I blinked. Twice.

"Good. Do you know who I am?"

Blink. Blink.

"Do you know where you are?"

Twice more, then once.

I took a measure of comfort and a sense of relief knowing Kela was with me. The bruises on her face had disappeared, her hair was shorter and the little bald patch on her scalp was covered. She looked rested, calmer than I remembered. But even looking at her in this new light didn't make me any less concerned about our fate. An enormous black funk was sitting on my soul, as more memories came into focus. All I could see in my mind's eye were future images of policemen, court trials and a life spent in a cell.

After processing the initial shock of my condition, an odd combination of emotions worked through me. I tried to recall the sequence of events that put me in a hospital bed. A policeman came in to check on me and folded his paper when he realized I was conscious. He checked his watch, and I felt him start moving toward the door. I tried to motion Kela to come close to me, but the cop was obviously getting ready to tell her she had to leave.

Kela said something to him, and he walked out.

"Reed is dead?" I whispered.

"Very dead. They found what was left of his body floating in the marsh two days ago."

"Two days ago? How long have I been out?"

"You've been in and out for almost a week."

"They think I killed Reed. I remember having a gun in my hand."

"It was planted on you by the real killer," she said. "After the killer wiped it down, he or she, put it in your right hand, which didn't work because your arm was broken."

"He or she?"

"We're not sure who pulled the trigger; Freddie, Thigpen or Janet."

"The police have the weapon used to kill Williams, too, and Reed was the only person who could prove I didn't."

"You're not going to go to jail for something you didn't do. I won't let it happen." She said. "Besides, they haven't found Williams' body."

"They'll find it. Eventually. They'll find it."

"Do you remember the night Williams disappeared? Where you went? Where you spent the night?" she said.

"I went home. Slept in my own bed."

"That may be true, but I'm going to say you were with me, from the time you got back until after sunrise when I went home." She leaned in closer. "I don't care what happens."

"How can you say that?"

"I can say anything I want. I've got credibility." Her smile lit up her face.

"You're only making it harder."

"I'll tell them we talked all night," she insisted, "about music and the business and Charleston. I'll say it was after eight in the morning when I left your apartment. And you lied to protect me."

"That's obstruction of justice."

"It's only obstruction if they can prove it's not true, which they can't."

"What about your husband? Won't Mark say you were home that night?"

"Mark didn't get back until Saturday night, remember the bruises?"

"This is insane."

"What is it Sinclair says? 'if it ain't true it oughta be.' Or something like that. It's closer to the truth than any hard evidence they have against you." She touched a spot of bare skin on my forehead.

"I can't let you do this."

"I can and I will," she said. "I'm meeting with the FBI agent later today, to discuss Mark's involvement. He's AWOL, by the way. I've already found Cricket. She told me Janet, Freddie and Thigpen were in the room. She saw Janet shoot Reed. I don't know if Freddie or Thigpen hit you with a shotgun. I'll admit coming over to your apartment when Mark beat me. Mr. Rigney will confirm my story about being with you all night, after you got back from John's Island."

"What about Rashad?' I said. "This would all be so simple if he'd come forward and confirm I was with him during the bag drop. Even Erlene told me she knew Reed killed Williams."

"Who is Rashad?" Kela said.

"He's Erlene's son, I told you about him when we were talking on the deck, he rode with me the entire trip out to John's Island." I said. "He had a red flannel pouch, and the snuff tin, like yours."

"You said you were with a guy. You've never mentioned his name before," Kela said. "You never told me about anyone named Rashad. The police haven't asked about him, Erlene doesn't have any children; I talked to her. There is no one named Rashad involved in this whole ordeal."

My head was pounding. I couldn't think clearly, but I could've sworn somebody other than me had been in contact with Rashad. Reed and Ward knew who he was. He'd helped them hold me down when we fought in the street. I was too weak to do much more mental backtracking.

"What about Williams?" I mumbled. "The cops still think I killed him. Thigpen will never let it rest."

"You're almost right. Thigpen wouldn't let the Williams thing rest; he's responsible for your still being held in protective custody. But Thigpen is nowhere to be found. And nobody else believes you had anything to do with Williams' disappearance. As far as the FBI, SLED, the IRS are concerned, Bootsy Williams is a missing person. No body, no murder. In fact, Ross thinks Williams' staged his own death and took off with the money. The Navy never cared about him. They just wanted Mark. You don't need to worry about anything except getting well, so you can go back to work."

There was a knock on the door and a different nurse, a black nurse came in to check the IV and change my bandages. For the first time, she loosened the straps holding me to the bed. I heard the rustle of the policeman's leather holster and boots against the cloth of his uniform as he slowly walked to the door.

"They sure didn't want you tossing and turning, did they?" The nurse smiled.

"The way you were fighting when they brought you in here, you would've broken your other arm, if we hadn't restrained you."

Kela stepped back out of the way, leaving the nurse to take care of my wounds. The roar in my head slowly subsided as the painkiller flowed into my bloodstream. The hum of the air conditioner slid back into my mind as I drifted back to semi-consciousness. Soft hands started removing the bandages from around my face.

"Oh my, ain't you something." The nurse said. "I don't think you'll scar too bad."

"Scars give the old Charleston houses their character," I said.

"Character? Sounds to me like you been running with a whole slew of characters. Maybe you should try hanging around with some normal people for a change." "In Charleston?" I whispered. "There are no normal people in Charleston."

I'm going to step out for a minute," Kela said.

"You go ahead on, Missy; I'll take care of this boy." The cool air made my skin tingle as the nurse rewrapped the bandages. "This might sting a little bit," she traced her fingers along my face.

"Feels like you're painting me with clown makeup."

"Some'thin like it." She had a gentle touch, which reminded me of my mother. I relaxed, giving into the velvet strokes as she smoothed the salve across my face. "That's right, you lay on back, rest easy, jest keep rockin' in th' bosom of Abraham." A light went on in my head, but I kept my eyes closed. "Hummuh, now you startin' t' see." My breathing relaxed, my heart rate slowed. "We can't have our pretty, little thin-lipped white boy, all stitched up, a cast aside Raggedy Ann."

"Erlene?"

"That's right, boy, Sista E's got you. Don't you worry one bit. You one of we people now."

"A Bridge."

"Hummuh." She smiled. "I knew you had a lot of soul for a white boy. Might'a pushed you a little hard, but old Erlene knows who is and who ain't in this life, well as the next. You see 'em?"

"Who?"

"You know who I'm talkin' about. He show hisself?"

I didn't answer.

"Ain't nobody in here but us, you can tell me."

"Yes."

"That's good, that's real good. He talk to you? Put chu on yo' path?"

I swallowed hard. "Yes."

"And he let chu go through the fire, too, all in th' same night. Ain't many gets it all in one dose."

"Get what?"

"Gets to see Old Scrong Man, get put on they pathway, an' get tested right after."

"I think I'm losing my mind," I said.

"Is he talkin' to you regular, yet?"

"Talking regular?"

"In yo' mind, son, in yo' mind. The still inner voice."

"I think so. I hear a voice, like a thought. And I see things."

"Like what?"

"Things about people. Things I have no way of knowing."

"Oh, you jus' be gettin' started, boy. How you think I knew you was a Bridge? You think thas luck, think I was jest guessin'? An' Rashad, an' old Montague, an' even old Boots, thinkin' I pushed you too soon. Sha' bowyee! Scrong Man called you. Not me. I jest did my little part." She put away the salve and rewrapped the bandages. "Now, I'm going to put something right here in your broke arm hand, and I want you to try to hold on to it." A few seconds later I felt a soft bag, with a drawstring, being nudged between the bandages wrapped around my palm. "Squeeze 'til 'e hurts, an' keep squeezing 'til 'e stops hurting."

I did what she told me to do. The pain, at first, was excruciating, like fire running from my fingers to my shoulder, then, by degrees, it subsided until the pain vanished. After about 20 minutes, she finished, and stood up. "I'm going now, but I'll keep check on you. You rest, let the magic work. You gone be fine. And you ain't losin' your mind. To the contrary," she gently touched my face, "you just now coming into your own true self."

Kela came back into my line of sight, sat down and put her hand on my bandaged arm. She was watching my eyes from the bedside.

"He gone be alright, Missy, needn't worry your pretty head 'bout a thing."

"Thanks, Erlene," Kela said.

"You two know each other?"

The two of them looked at each other.

"There is one other thing you should know," Kela whispered. "I didn't want to tell you until you were better, but we talked it over with Montague, and decided you should know."

"Mr. Roy passed night before last." Erlene put her hand on mine.

I don't know why I wasn't surprised. Roy had said he didn't think he'd last much longer, but I didn't expect to never see him again.

"His attorney, Mr. Goldman, wants to meet with you. You're in Roy's will."

"Did Goldman say anything about why I'd be mentioned in Roy's will?" I managed. "He wouldn't give me all the details. He did say Roy had signed the lease for The Merch over to you and it's paid up for the next five years."

"Who is the lease with?" I said.

"He wouldn't tell me anything other than The Merch was yours for the next five years."

I laid there for what seemed like a very long time. While I was thinking through the jumble of chaos rolling around in my mind, the doctor came in.

"Well, Mr. Chapman, sounds like you lead quite the interesting life. Let's have a look into those banged up eyes of yours."

The doctor pulled out his little doctor flashlight and pulled my eyelids apart. "You're very fortunate. If you'd been hit any harder, I don't think you'd be here. Under the circumstances, though, I think you'll be up and about in a day or so, but I'm afraid it's going to be a while before you play the saxophone again."

After the doctor left, the cop who was guarding me came back and told Kela she'd have to leave. I don't know why it didn't bother me. Kela leaned over and pecked me on the forehead.

"Where is Freddie? And Thigpen, where's he?" I whispered. "Who's running The Merch?"

"Montague and Sinclair have everything under control." Kela said.

"Call Montague, tell him to fire Freddie May. Tell him he's the new boss."

"Freddie is gone. You won't be seeing him again."

"Thigpen? He's a cop, he can't..."

"Was a cop. Now, he's on the run. He and Janet Collins are the suspects in Reed's murder."

———

I was able to leave the hospital a few days later. The bandages were off. My arm was still sore, but the break had mended perfectly, and my face had healed so quickly the doctor called it nothing short of miraculous. Kela drove me to meet with Goldman. Charleston's slowest elevator took us to the third floor of his Broad Street office. His receptionist guided us into the conference room, pulled out our chairs and shut the door.

I sat down opposite a sharply dressed older black gentleman, who was looking over several documents. He looked at me and smiled. I immediately noticed his gold tooth. Kela walked around the table and hugged him.

"Hello, Abraham," she said, then kissed him on the forehead.

"Hello Miss Kela, what's it been? Ten years? Feels like a hundred."

"Josie, this is Abraham Williams. Abraham, this is Joseph Chapman."

You could've knocked me over with a feather if I'd been standing up.

"Mr. Chapman," Goldman said, "Mr. Williams owns the property where The Merchant Seaman's Club is located." He slid a copy of the lease greement toward me. "Along with several other properties in and around Charleston, I might add."

"You're the Landlord? But I thought…"

"Only for the duration of this lease," Goldman said. "At the end of this agreement, the property will be sold and the proceeds given to The Anointed Bateau Mission."

"Why them?" I said.

"Reverend Jeremiah LaRoche was a friend of mine." Williams said. "He started the mission back in 1914, playing organ for prisoners. Reverend Green followed in his footsteps. You remember Reverend Green, I'm sure."

"I used to listen to his radio show. He dedicated songs to the prisoners kept down on the county farm," I said.

"Well, on behalf of those fine brothers, I'm liquidating several holdings in Charleston," Williams said, "the city is on the verge of a major renovation, many changes on the horizon. Real estate values will skyrocket in the coming years. I don't care for the attention which will surely be visited upon me. When the locals, along with the rest of the world, discover an old black man from Alabama holds title to some of the most notoriously segregated property in South Carolina, well, you can see how much more difficult it will be for me to maintain the low profile of which I've grown so fond."

"Did you know about this?" I asked Kela.

"I'm on a learning curve, just like you."

"Well, you kids can discuss all this later. Let's get these papers signed, shall we?" Goldman said.

We left the conference room together. Waiting for the elevator, Kela and Abraham Williams exchanged pleasantries like long-lost cousins at a family reunion.

"Do you mind if I ask you a question?" I said to Williams.

"You can ask me anything, Joseph." I started to tell him to just call me Josie, but decided instead to keep things businesslike. Kela stopped smiling, took a deep breath and looked at me.

"Do you know a man named Bootsy Williams?

"Ah, Alfonso Krytorious, the literal black sheep of the family. He's my brother, why do you ask?"

"You seem to know everything about everything and everybody, including me, Kela, Roy. Montague is a personal friend of yours, right? You two have a history. I'm sure you know why I'm asking?"

"Josie ...," Kela put her hand on my arm.

"It's OK, Missy. The man has a right to know, especially after what he's been through."

The elevator light came on with a ding-ding. The doors crawled apart and the three of us stepped inside the car. A full minute passed in silence before the doors edged back together.

"My brother is, for the present, no longer a factor in this ... situation," Williams said.

"I gathered that," I said.

"He won't be interfering with your plans over the coming years."

"You don't, by any chance, know where he is?"

"I'm not at liberty to say. I can tell you he won't be roaming these streets anytime soon."

"Josie, let it go," Kela said. Williams touched her arm.

"I know who you are, son, I know what you've seen. As the saying goes, 'you've got some edgy'cation comin.' My advice to you, if I could be so bold, is to always remember to never look back, keep your eyes on the future, not on the past. Cut your losses, count your blessings, and move on."

"The cops, among others, think I killed him."

"The truth is whatever you believe it is. If you know your own truth, your mind is free. Can we leave it at that?" Williams said.

The elevator bumped to a stop; we stepped out on the marble foyer floor.

"Joseph, it's been my pleasure," Williams offered his hand and we shook.

"Miss Kela, always a blessing, my dear." They hugged. "I have a gift for you. Something we talked about many years ago." He pulled a red flannel drawstring bag from his pocket, larger than the ones I'd seen and gave it to her. Kela opened it. A beautiful snakeskin box slid into her hand. She looked at him like a schoolgirl.

"Go ahead, open it," he said.

Inside the box was a silver, bone-handled teaspoon. "Is this what I think it is," Kela gasped. Williams nodded. I had no clue what was going on. "This is the same one…? The one…"

"That belonged to Aunt Bertie; yes, it's the same one. She wanted you to have it."

"What is it?" I said.

"A family heirloom," Williams said, "Kela used to play with it when she was a child. Before Aunt Bertie passed, she willed it to my mother with a stipulation. She asked my mother to make sure Missy was next in line." Kela had tears in her eyes and once more stood on tiptoes to wrap her arms around the neck of Abraham Williams. "Well, I have places to go and people to see, and as the saying goes, if I don't see you sooner, I'll see you later, so sooner or later I'll see you. Take care of each other. I bid you farewell."

Mr. Abraham Williams stepped through the front door of the Goldman Law Firm, took a left on Meeting Street and disappeared. We drove to The Merch for my first staff meeting. Montague, Sinclair and the rest of the guys were waiting for me, along with the core members of The Magnificent Seven, Monk, Gary, Wayne and Jack, and of all things, a coconut cake. Right in the middle of the cake sat a highball glass with Wild Turkey on ice, which Kela immediately snatched up.

"Ah, Missy," said Sinclair, "Let de' boy have a little fun, after all he been through."

Kela lifted the glass to toast the men. "Here's to perseverance," she said, taking a sip of the drink, then handing it to me. I lifted the glass.

"What's the word?"

"Thunderbird!" They all shouted.

"What's the price?"

"Thirty twice!"

"What's the reason?"

"Grapes in season!"

And we all threw back our shots.

"Well, we bes' be getting busy," Montague said. "Sinclair, git de candles lit, and the tables set so folks can see where t'sit when they git heah."

"Bowye!" Sinclair barked, "Don't say too much to me. You say too much t' me, I'm gone box yo' upside the head `til yo' tongue slap yo' brains out."

As I walked around the club, I had a hard time believing everything that had happened. We hired a crazy sax player named Wesley to take my place while my jaw mended. He was only booked for a month, but he was so good we kept him as a permanent member of the band. The Magnificent Seven with Kela singing lead never sounded better, and Montague's special T-bone steak was the talk of the town.

Six weeks later, my arm was out of the cast, The Merch was rocking along and life couldn't have been better. Barry's blackjack game was still the only honest one in town, but we stopped allowing the prostitutes to work out of the club. This actually worked out better for them. Secrets are hard to keep and when word finally got out about Charleston, a higher class of crooks who wanted to keep low profiles found their way to the city. The hookers started dressing in business suits, blouses and slacks, carrying briefcases, high end hand bags; looking more like fashion models making house calls; or supplying room service to well-heeled clients staying in the better hotels. So, it worked out better for everybody.

Then one Saturday night after the staff, including Kela, had gone home, Montague came into my office. He sat down across from Roy's old desk and poured himself a shot from the bottle of J&B Scotch we kept on the desk as a memento. I knew he had something weighing heavy on his mind, because he wasn't smiling or frowning. He just looked tired.

"There's something you needs to know, Cap'n," he said.

"You're not going to quit, are you, Montague?" I said.

"Not ezackly, but after you heah what I got to say, you might not wanna be keepin' me around much longer." He threw back the shot of Scotch, then carefully placed the glass on the desk. "I ain't quittin', but I do have to go 'way for a bit." He watched me carefully, choosing his words with great caution. "Yo' see, I got'a sister who's got'a boy down Louisiana way needs help."

"I didn't know you had family in the bayou. Of course, you can go visit your sister," I said. "We can handle the club, until you get back."

"Well, dat's de problem, you see, I don't ezackly know when I'm gonna get back," he said, reaching for the Scotch bottle again.

I grabbed the bottle, "Let me get that for you. Say when." This was the first time I'd ever actually seen Montague drink or had the privilege of pouring him one. He showed two fingers.

"Whatever it is, take all the time you need. Do you need money?" I said. Montague laughed like I'd told him a joke. "No Cap'n. I don't need no money, my sista, she got plenty o' money. Money ain't never a problem."

He tossed back the second shot.

"Well, then, what's the problem?" I said.

Montague stood up and walked out of the office, motioning for me to follow him out past the empty tables and chairs, toward the middle of the dance floor, where he stood in front of the B3. Surveying the room as if he was looking at it for the last time, he started swaying to some rhythm only he could hear. Then he started dancing a soft shoe shuffle. He glided over by the restroom, grabbed a broom and used it as a cane. After floating all the way around the edge of the dance floor, he ended on one knee right in the center, with both palms out, Jolson style and while I softly applauded, he dropped a chicken claw on the floor between us.

My hands froze in midair and I stared down at the talon. It was exactly like the ones Erlene Brown had used on my hand. I picked it up, turned it over, and saw the grooves hollowed out under the claws. I looked into Montague's piercing eyes. Gone was the Jolson smile. His face, hair and clothing began to morph until he became the vision of an African Chieftain. I heard the back door open, people coming into the room, a priestess, and a prince in full West African regalia. Their beautiful, flawless skin so black it appeared purple, hair, eyes, faces painted, each carrying a white candle, making their way to the center of the room, they stood on each side of Montague stepping into the light, the three of them facing me. Montague, Erlene, Rashad.

Rashad spoke. "It's the unpredictable, the freak storm that'll always get you. It's never the one you can see coming." He turned his candle revealing my name carved into the wax then set it at his feet.

Erlene spoke next. "May all good things come to you. May nothing whatsoever harm you. May your heart be light. May your travels be safe. May your health be good. May your mind be sound. May your friendships sustain you." She turned her candle revealing my name. "Bridge Joseph, may you be blessed in every way." She set the candle at her feet. The three chanted in unison:

> "Caress the sill and caress the wall. Only true blessings here befall.
> Bless this candle who's no longer alone. Bless his work, and bless his home.
> Bless the pillow for his head. Bless the blanket and the light by his bed.
> Let those who linger in this place, know a fivefold blessing full of grace.
> Calm for the weary – safety from fright. Faith in each morning, noon and
> night. Friends who gather, let them hear..."

Kela came in, picking up the chant,

> "...The music of blessing of laughter, hope and cheer.
> Roof and floor, lintel and wall, only blessings and goodness, this place befall."

The room fell silent as Erlene, Rashad and Kela drifted back through the kitchen door, leaving Montague and me alone. His countenance returned to that of the man I'd come to love more than I'd loved Roy, as much as I ever dared dream of loving any revered father figure in my life.

Stepping out of the light, Montague backed up revealing the spot previously covered by his shadow. With a sweeping gesture, he indicated the floor directly under his feet. A section, four feet by six feet, whose tiles appeared to glow a shade lighter than the rest of the floor. The rectangle was outlined by a thin rectangular line not wider than a finishing saw blade. Montage spoke to me with perfect diction. "Strong Man has given you five years to make your money and get out of this place. Then forty more years to plan for the storm that's coming. Strong Man took a liking to you, boy, even though he knows you were reluctant to become one of his own. You have blood down your bloodline, an intercessory ancestry, people who stood in the gap for the Royal Prince of Barbados, Englishmen who aided the brothers of Python, and their blessing is now bequeathed unto you." He smiled the loving smile of a wise grandfather and winked. "So you bes' mind how you walk and mind how yo' talk 'bout Scrong Man. 'Cause you're a Bridge now, between his world and this one and he's watchin' you. An' if you ain't walkin' scraight, an' standin', an' true, an' bridging the gap, he'll withdraw from you. He'll never turn against you. But shirk yo' callin' and you'll be on your own." He arched his eyebrows and I nodded. "Stay true to your calling and Strong Man will stay true to you. Cross Him like this one here," he stooped down and shadow traced a circle on the outlined section on the floor, "an' you'll be the one gets buried."

With that, Montague stood up, walked toward me and pulled out a knife. Slipped it under the top two buttons of my shirt and cut them loose. He reached in, pulled out the wooden cross, and popped the strand of leather. Then he cut his palm with the knife. "Give me your hand," he said.

I held out my palm. The tip of the blade opened a thin red line. He placed the cross between our two hands, then squeezed until the blood dripped, then he reversed the cross and repeated the squeeze.

"Your white blood, my black blood, and the blood of the slaves of this world, black and white are now commingled. The Bridge is complete." And Montague Bonneau removed a handkerchief from his pocket, wiped my hand and his, with his blood and mine, he stained the thin line of saw marks outlining a four by six rectangular section of the dance floor, until the marks blended in with the parquet tiles.

PART THREE

"It is said the warrior's is the twofold Way of pen and sword, and he should have a taste for both Ways. Even if a man has no natural ability, he can be a warrior by sticking assiduously to both divisions of the Way."

— *Miyamoto Musashi, The Book of Five Rings*

CHAPTER THIRTY-THREE

Present Day

Some might argue preemptive self-defense by proxy is a fancy way of saying anticipatory self-defense. Roy's streetwise version of the concept, "when conflict is inevitable, there's no dishonor in throwing the first punch," would have worked in this case had I been the only person in danger. If it were only my life in the cross hairs, I'd go with 'strike before you're struck,' in and out, one and done or some other cliché. But others are involved, friends of mine, people who still live in this Holiest of Cities, and Kela, my wife, of course. That's where the by proxy part comes in. I'm not only covering my own ass, I'm covering theirs as well, especially hers. Which is still, even after forty-four years, a very nice ass indeed.

I was staring at the previous paragraph, thinking it was a pretty nice paragraph for a guy who'd never written a book before. A catchy topic sentence, a nice body explaining the topic in more detail, then ending with a couple concluding remarks, and grinning because the image conjured up in my last remark made me smile. And I was thinking to myself, which was redundant because who else are you going to think to? Unless, of course, you're with a woman who can read your mind, and you can read hers. And then maybe you could think to each other, which happens all the time now, especially between Kela and I, and sometimes with other people, depending on the circumstances, and whether or not we allow it. She's much better at it than I am. But that's another book. For the moment though I was alone, thinking to myself it was a good paragraph and how much I missed my wife and her ass, when the doorbell rang.

"Hey man," Jack said. "Skinny and I are here to get those chairs."

"Come on in," I said. "You guys want a drink? Half a bottle left."

"Where's the other half?" Sinclair said.

"I drank it."

"What you celebratin'?"

"Nothing. I'm working. I like a little scotch when I'm working." I fixed a pair of crystal highball glasses. "Water, soda, or straight up?"

"Water," Jack said.

"You got any milk?" Sinclair said. Jack rolled his eyes. "What? You never heard of scotch and milk? I bet Josie's heard of it, ain't you man?"

"I knew a cornet player once who drank it," I said. "Said he had ulcers; the milk kept the stomach acid from lighting them up."

"The Beatles drank scotch and coke," Jack said. "I tried it once. Almost gagged."

"Prolly drank himself to death didn't 'e? "

"Yes, I think he did."

I went to the kitchen for milk. When I came back, Sinclair was fingering the legal pads on my desk.

"What's all this?" He'd picked up two.

"A little project I'm working on."

"Looks like you writin' a book. You writin' a book? What kind of book you writin'? Hey Crack, look at this, Josie's writin' a book."

"What's the book about?" Jack said.

"Well, it's none of your damn business, but if you must know, it's the story of how Kela and I met."

"Bullshit." Sinclair poured milk in his scotch.

"Yeah, bullshit," Jack said. "Am I in it?"

"Yes. You are."

"How 'bout me?" Sinclair said. "You make me out th' cool motherfucker I am, or just another step-'n-fetch-it shine?"

I took a drink, then refilled my glass, added some ice. "Let me taste that," I said.

Sinclair took a drink, ran his lips all the way around the rim of the glass, and handed it to me. I drained the glass.

"You can hardly taste the scotch," I said. "Here, try this." I poured in an ounce of milk giving the scotch the pale brown color of unbleached linen. Then ran my lips around the rim of the glass and handed it to Sinclair. He emptied it.

"What's going on between you two?" Jack said.

"You wanna tell him? Or you want me to?" I looked at Sinclair.

"I don't know what the fuck you're talking about."

I looked at Jack.

"Me either," he said.

The scotch bottle was almost empty. I got another one and freshened three glasses, including one with milk. The room was half lit with the long orange glow of the setting sun filtering through the windows.

"Have a seat," I said.

"Man, I'd like to," Jack said, "but I have to get back. Susan needs the car."

"Yeah, and I'm ridin' with him, so. . . What's this all about anyway?"

I pushed my glasses up and rubbed my eyes. "Let me… how should I say this… give me a second." I held up my hand. "I want to make sure I say this right, so there's no misunderstanding. How about this? Sit the fuck down, or walk through that door, and never come back."

Jack and Sinclair looked at each other.

"How's that? Clear enough?" I said.

Across the room by the fireplace were two chairs and a sofa. We each took a seat. I took a small sip of my drink, sitting the glass on the coffee table. Sinclair and Jack followed suit.

"All three of us know what the coroner's office carried out of The Merch. Now one of two things is true here. Either you both knew, but you decided together not to tell me, or you each knew individually, but you didn't know about each other." Jack was looking down at the floor, Sinclair's eyes searched the ceiling. "I'm not angry. I am hurt, and I'm humiliated to learn my two closest friends, other than my wife, of course, chose to remain silent, about a matter which will ultimately pose the biggest threat to my life and my family."

"If I may," Jack said, "and I think I can speak for both of us…" Sinclair nodded, "… we thought you knew there was a body buried under the floor."

"To quote both you geniuses, 'Bullshit.' Of course I knew. What I didn't know, was that you two knew."

"Code of silence, you know, outta sight, outta mind," Sinclair said.

"How'd you know we knew?" Jack said.

I walked to my desk, picked up a legal pad and flipped through the pages. "What did you mean by 'Well the monkey's out of the sack?"

"Did I say that? When did I say that?"

"You said it in the car when them cats started yellin'," Sinclair said.

"Funny, I don't remember saying that. You sure it was me?"

I looked at Sinclair. "How'd you know the body was buried in the middle of the dance floor? Why'd you keep insisting there was an A/C vent centered over the floor, making excuses for the cold spot, when there'd been a wheel light there for years and a disco ball after that?"

"Listen brother, I'm gonna be straight up with you. I'm gonna stand this shit up right now." Sinclair leaned forward, his elbows on his knees. "You're right, I should've told you I knew, but everything was happenin' so fast, I figured you'd figured it out and we were doin' that plausibly deniable thing, you know, like Nixon and shit, less said the better. Besides, I had to cover my own ass too you know? Don't need the fuckin' Man tryin' to accessorize my black ass after the fuckin' fact. You dig?"

"What difference does it make now?" Jack said. "We didn't say anything for your own good."

"So, not telling me you knew; that was your way of trying to protect me?"

"Yeah, I guess, and myself too, all of us, if you wanna know the low down dirty truth," Jack said.

"Plausibly deniable, Brother, 'ats all it was. Like Nixon and shit. Dig?"

"There's so many ways this thing could've gone south over the last forty-four years. The way the city's constantly digging up shit around here, this whole fucking thing could've unraveled a dozen ways, a dozen times," I said.

"But it didn't, man. And it ain't unravelin' now if we all keep our mouths shut about what we knew and when we knew it," Sinclair said.

"That's easy for you to say Skinny. It's not your ass they'll fry for the murder of Bootsy Williams. There's no statute of limitations for murder. Once his body is identified, they'll reopen the cold case with my name all over it and put the pieces together. Life as I know it will be toast. Just tell me how you found out about the grave? So I can figure out who else might know the body was buried there while I owned The Merch. That's all I want right now. Did Montague tell you? Because if he did, he lied to me when he led me to believe he and I were the only two people who understood what that patch of parquet tile floor signified."

"That's all you worried about ain't it? Coverin' your ass." Sinclair said. "You don't care 'bout a damn thing long as your own ass is covered."

"Excuse me. But what part of, 'they got all the circumstantial evidence they need to crucify me, but the murder victim's body,' did you not understand?"

"You really want to know? You sure you want to know? Because once you know a thing there ain't no goin' back to not knowin' it. So make sure you can handle this before I go off on it, because if you really want to know motherfucker I'm gon' fuckin' tell you. You think he really wants to know Cracker-Jack?"

Jack had his head in his hands. "I can't believe this shit," he said.

"You wanta tell 'em, or you want me to, 'cause I'm going to tell his fuckin' ass, I'm gonna stand this shit straight up, then I'm done."

Jack shook his head.

"You ready?" Sinclair said.

I nodded.

"The way me and your boy Jack here knew about the grave was, we dug the motherfucker."

"What?!"

"You heard me. Montague wanted Jack and me to help him. Said it was a little maintenance project, something about a drain line. So, Jack brought a fine blade skill saw from his cabinet shop, and we went over that Sunday night after everybody was gone. Jack cut out a nice, neat rectangle right along the tile lines; then Montague and I helped him get the wood up in one piece. It took all three of us to set it aside because the tiles were glued to 3/4 plywood nailed to 5/4 heart pine which was nailed to the floor joist. Must've weighed two hundred pounds. Montague said he'd tell us when to help him put it back."

"I didn't know it was going to be a grave, I swear to God on a stack of Bibles," Jack said. "And I didn't get called to help them replace the wood."

"What did you think Montague was going to do?" I said.

"I didn't know and I didn't want to. Montague said something about needing access to the sewer drain line in case the toilets started backing up with all the rain." Jack sat with his arms across his chest.

"Did you see a drain line after you cut the piece out? Something to tap into?"

"No." Jack said. "And that sort of bothered me. I didn't find out until…"

"… I told him," Sinclair said. "In case he needed to know to get his alibi straight if the question ever came up."

"So you helped Montague replace the floor?"

"I didn't say that. You just assumin' I helped him."

Jack stood up. "I'm leaving, my wife needs the car. I'll grab two chairs off the truck." He looked at Sinclair. "You stayin' or you coming?"

"Go ahead, put my two in the trunk for me. I'm right behind you."Sinclair put his hand on my shoulder. "You know I love you, don't you? And I know you love me too. I also know you're a Bridge." I looked at him. "It's cool, it's cool, Montague told me, and I know your wife is a Bridge. Charleston needs people like you two to stand in the gap. So I want you to listen carefully to what I'm gettin' ready to tell you." Sinclair shut the front door. "This thing ain't over. In fact, dependin' on how you handle what's comin', it may never be over. That'll be up to you."

"But wha…"

"Don't ask me any more questions. I've said all I'm gonna say. What happens from here on out is all on you. Me and old Cracker Jack have a deal. We don't know nothin' about nothin'. I suggest you join us in our endeavor."

"I don't know whether to laugh or cry or put my fist through the wall."

"Well, brother man, I can't help you there except to say you ain't gonna put your fist through any o' these walls 'cause that's 5/4 pecky cypress, and you'll break your fuckin' hand." He slapped me on the back. "Remember what Montague used to say, 'In the absent of cold hard fact, the truth is whatever you believe it is.' I suggest you find yourself a truth and start believin' it."

"Yeah, but just because you believe something don't make it true."

"Ezackly. But if you do believe it, it'll be true for you. Ultimately, when you think about it, and I mean really think about it; your own personal truth is the only truth that matters."

CHAPTER THIRTY-FOUR

The next morning I got two phone calls back to back. The first one, from Kela, came to my cell phone.

"Hey there Sunshine, you still in bed?" she said.

"No, I'm up. You?"

"I'm actually in the car about to pass John's Island airport. You want a biscuit?"

"You don't have to stop for me; I'm not really hungry," I said.

"What's wrong?"

"I really don't want to talk over the phone. You never know who's listening."

"Well, I'm going by Dunkin' Donuts and get myself one of those greasy smoked sausage biscuits. Are you sure you don't want a croissant?"

"Sure, a croissant will be good."

"See you in few."

The second call was the house phone. It was from Jack.

"You get the morning paper?" he said.

"Yeah, why?"

"Read it." He hung up.

I walked onto the front porch, but there was no paper. Nothing on the sidewalk either. I found it inside the fence by the bird fountain. The plastic moisture bag was off, and the paper was soaked. I managed to open it enough to make out part of the headline. Body of missin ...discove ... under... lub.

The pages were like wet paper Mache, I was trying to lay them out the porch floor when a dark blue SUV with heavily tinted glass pulled up across the street. Two suits in sunglasses got out, looking up and down the street. One was big with a crew cut, he was in charge, checking his watch, squaring his shoulders, the boxer side to side neck stretch. The other leaned more toward the account type. Glasses, slight built, briefcase. I went back inside and watched them through the window. They were checking house numbers against a list, finally settling on mine. After a minute or two the doorbell rang. The bigger one shielded his eyes against the decorative glass in the door, trying to see inside, while the other looked over the wet paper.

I answered the door. "Can I help you?"

"Mr. Chapman?" said the big one.

"Yes."

"Mr. Joseph Chapman?"

"I'm Joseph Chapman. What's this all about?"

"Mr. Chapman, I'm Special Agent Michael Malandrino. This is Special Agent Eric Flint. We're with the Naval Criminal Investigative Service. We'd like to come in and talk with you for a few minutes, if you don't mind."

"What if I do mind?"

"We'd rather you didn't, Sir. If it's all the same to you," Flint said. "We're all grownups here, let's play nice."

"We're not here to make trouble or embarrass you Mr. Chapman. We only want to talk to you. This won't take long I can assure you."

"OK, come on in, make yourselves at home. Coffee? Tea?"

"No thanks, we're fine," said Malandrino.

"Actually, a cup of tea would be nice," said Flint.

"Good, well, as you can see I'm still in my robe and slippers. I'll put on a kettle and change, then I'll be right back. Make yourselves at home."

"Is Mrs. Chapman at home by chance?" Flint said.

"Not at the moment. She's been overseeing a few repairs at our beach home. But she's due back sometime later this morning."

My cell phone was in my bathrobe pocket. As I made busy work out of putting on a pot of water, I managed to mute the ringer volume in time to feel it vibrate. At the top of the stairs, I checked the text from Kela; a single question mark. In the bedroom I replied with an anchor emoticon and a snapshot of the SUV parked across the street. She replied with a thumbs up, a peace sign, and 2mn. I put on a pair of khakis, a golf shirt and docksiders, then went to the kitchen for tea.

"Here you go agent." I set the tray on the coffee table. "Milk? Sugar?"

"No thank you, this is fine," Flint sipped his tea.

"Mr. Chapman…"

"Please call me Josie, everybody calls me Josie."

"Certainly, Josie, Agent Malandrino would like to…"

"Michael, right?" I said. "And you're Eric. So Michael and Eric."

"Mr. Chapman, Josie, we don't want to waste our time or yours, so if you don't mind, we'd like to get straight to the reason for our visit."

A flash of mirror reflected light signaled Kela turning into the driveway. I pretended not to notice.

"Of course, go ahead. I'm listening."

"Josie, do you know anything about…"

I heard Kela come up the back steps, through the door, and her keys hit the countertop. "Hold that thought," I said. "My wife is home. I'm sure she'd like to hear whatever you have to say."

"Hello, everyone. Hello Josie." She kissed me on the cheek. "Did I miss anything?"

"Gentlemen, this is my wife. Kela," I said. "These men are from NCIS. This is Agent Malandrino, first name Michael, and this is Eric, otherwise known as Agent Flint."

Kela beamed and said, "Love the show, it's one of our favorites, let me guess, you want to use the house for an episode set in Charleston. Army Wives is such a hit, it was only a matter of time."

"Actually Mrs. Chapman we're not from the TV show," said Malandrino.

"You're not? What a shame, I was looking so forward to meeting Mark Harmon."

"They're the real NCIS dear," I said.

"Really? Then why on earth are you here?"

"Please Mrs. Chapman, I think you both know why we're here," said Flint. "Your husband's body was found buried under the floor of a nightclub formerly owned by you, Mr. Chapman."

"You're referring to my former husband, Mark Ward. Why, that's impossible. Mark Ward went AWOL forty-four years ago. He was embezzling money from the Navy, the FBI investigated; even the CIA was after him. He wiped out our bank account, took all my jewelry and left the country. At least that's what they led me to believe at the time."

"Yes, ma'am, we're aware of all that, but we're certain it's Captain Ward's body," said Flint.

"Josie, I don't know what to make of this," Kela said.

I didn't know what these guys were up to but I wasn't going to let it go on any further.

"I don't know where you got your information, but the body they found wasn't Mark Ward. It's a black farmer from Johns Island, named Krytorious Williams. Went by the nickname Bootsy." The two agents looked at each other, then back at me. "If you'd done all your homework you would've found a whole file on this case going back to 1970. The Charleston County Police tried everything to pen Williams' death of on me. One detective, Charlie Thigpen, disappeared along with Mark Ward and a guy named Freddie May. They were all in it together with another guy named Bill Reed. When they realized Reed was stealing from all of them, they killed him, threw his body in the marsh, then disappeared."

"Who buried the body under the floor?" Malandrino said.

"I have no idea, and that's the God's honest truth. I do know it was there before I signed the lease and took ownership of the club. So you can't hang that wrap on me."

"When did you realize a murder victim might be buried under the floor?" Flint said.

"Same time as everybody else. What was it, two days ago? Until then, all I knew was Montague, the cook who worked for Roy Vincent forty-four years ago, had added a sewer tap to a drain line in case the water started backing up from all the rain."

Flint sipped his tea carefully, pursing his lips, relishing every drop, never taking his eyes off me, "Fantastic tea," he said.

"It's locally grown by The Charleston Tea Company," I said.

"What makes you so sure the body belongs to Mark Ward?" Kela said. "Have you run DNA tests?"

"We have a partial match on his dental records."

"Partial?"

"Yes, ma'am. We found a tooth, an incisor, which matches an incisor on Ward's dental records."

"You have a tooth, as in one tooth?"

"Yes, ma'am. All the other teeth were missing," Malandrino said. "There were other, shall we say, abnormalities; associated with the body as well."

"Yeah, yeah, yeah," I said. "I know all about the one gold tooth, and the chicken claw foot, there was probably some amulet bag with the body, looked like a voodoo ritual murder."

"How do you know about those things?" Flint said.

"Because I was there when the body was discovered, I walked through the place, one last look before the walls came tumbling down. "I've even got three chairs in the back of my pickup."

"Sir, did you actually see the body those workers discovered?" Flint said.

"Well, no, but I heard the men yelling; heard them describing what they'd found."

Flint opened his briefcase and pulled out an envelope full of photographs. He shuffled through them and picked out three in particular.

"Take a look at these. Tell me if you notice anything unusual, I mean, over and above what you've already described." Flint turned the photos.

There were the toothless skull, the rooster talons, and the gold tooth.

"What are we looking for?" Kela said.

"Look at the close up of the skull itself." Flint said.

"I see a bunch of little, what are they, teeth marks, and indentions like rats gnawed it." I said.

"Yes, that's what we thought too, until we found these." Malandrino pulled out a plastic bag with two rotted and worn shims of leather about the size and shape of a sweet potato skins. "Notice the brad marks near the tips, see those holes?"

"Yes, so?"

"Those holes held these…" Flint retrieved another smaller bag, with two steel isosceles triangles, each with four holes punched along the baseline. "…These two pieces of leather, Mr. Chapman, are boot soles, and when you line up the holes in these triangles, with the holes in the tip of the soles, they're a perfect match." I looked at Kela, she looked at me. "You recognize these items don't you Mr. Chapman?" I didn't say anything. "Please don't worry about this Mr. Chapman, we aren't here to arrest you, and quite frankly we couldn't if we wanted to, because you're a civilian, and well, we're not. We're simply trying to make sense of all these puzzle pieces. We were hoping you could shed some light on this little mystery, so we, and you and your lovely wife, can get on with our lives."

I was speechless; didn't know what to tell them.

"Could you do that for us Mr. Chapman?" Flint said.

"I'll tell you what happened," Kela said. "Because I know this is why you came here, so here's the truth. Those boots belonged to Freddie May, he wore them to intimidate unruly customers. Freddie and Mark worked as a team; nobody but Freddie and Thigpen knew Reed was the middle man. I know because I was married to Ward, and he set me up to work for Reed so I could keep an eye on him. Only Reed didn't know, at first, that I was married to Mark. When he found out, he went ape, told Freddie that Mark was cheating them out of money, so Freddie went to Mark demanding his cut, and when Mark told him he was crazy, Freddie did one of his fancy kicks to Mark's head and killed him. After he killed him, he kicked out all his teeth, but one, put a gold cap on it, then hung a chicken foot around Mark's neck so it would look like a hoodoo ritual killing. Freddie hauled the body to The Merch, took up the floor, disposed of the body, along with the murder weapon. How am I doing so far?"

The three of us were literally mesmerized by Kela's account of the events. I felt like I was watching her on a stage, her slash and burn take no prisoners energy from forty-four years ago, on full display. I never felt more in love with the woman in my entire life.

"I don't know about you guys, but that was fuckin' awesome," I said.

"I thought you'd like it," Kela said, and kissed me again. "Well?"

"All very impressive, Mrs. Chapman, but how do we know that you didn't do everything you just described?" Flint said.

"Good question. I need a drink. Either of you gentlemen like a drink?"

"No, ma'am," Malandrino said. "We're on duty."

"What are you having?" Flint said.

"Double scotch on the rocks," said Kela.

"I'll have the same."

"Josie?"

"I've got you covered, Babe. Excuse me, gentlemen."

Sometimes you get lucky just showing up. Kela blew me away the first time I laid eyes on her, and forty-four years later she was still blowing me away. I fixed a tray of scotches and came back to find her working the magic.

"…So the drunk goes into the bathroom, right? And a few minutes later the bartender hears him screaming. 'God help me! Something's got me!' The bartender bangs on the door yellin' 'You alright? What's wrong in there?!' And the drunk says, 'I don't know man, I sat down here, did my business, and every time I try to flush this thing something grabs me by the balls!' And the bartender says, 'Did you turn the light on like I told you?'"

I sat the scotches down. Flint and Malandrino both grabbed one and within seconds were shaking their glasses at me for a refill.

"What happened next, what happened next?" Malandrino said.

"The door to the bathroom is locked, right? So the bartender gets his keys." Kela drained her glass. "He comes back, unlocks the door and says 'it's dark as Hell in here? I told you to turn on the lights.' 'I know man,' says the drunk, 'but this thing's got me by the balls. I can't get up.' So the bartender flips on the light and says, 'No wonder fool, you're sittin' on a mop bucket.'"

Let me tell you something, they fell out. Flint was crying he was laughing so hard, and Malandrino, I thought he was going to puke. I sat there holding my head in my hands, and peeped out just in time to see Kela wink at me.

"You still didn't answer the question," Flint said, wiping the tears from his eyes.

"What question?" Kela said.

"How do we know you didn't do it?" Malandrino sobbed for a refill.

"Oh yeah, that. Well, here's the thing." Kela said, "I really did do it. And I killed Freddie and Thigpen both. Shot both the bastards from about a hundred yards with a scoped out 30.06."

"I love this woman," Malandrino said.

"Me too, she's a trip," Flint said. "So, how'd you kill your husband?"

"What was I Josie, back then I mean? 110, 115 pounds?"

"I think you were pushing 120, give or take a few."

"We'll split the difference, OK?"

"OK." I said.

"I was 117 pounds and what Josie? 39-21-40 shape? Y'all know that song?"

Flint and Malandrino shook their heads.

"I think closer to 36-22-36, same as Marilyn Monroe but with dark hair."

"I love this man, can y'all tell? Anyway, my husband at the time, Mark Ward, a Captain at the Charleston Naval Shipyard, and the biggest son-of-bitch who ever walked the earth, what was he Josie? 6'2"-200 pounds?"

"More like 6' 3", and 225," I said.

"That size fit with the body you found?" Kela said.

"Pretty close," said Flint.

"Anyway, my husband, let's call him The Asshole, that work for everybody?"

We all three nodded.

"Well, The Asshole, decides one night he's going to beat the shit out of me, a third time, mind you. But this time I was ready for him. Roy Vincent, the guy who'd owned The Merch before Josie, gave me a .45 automatic with a threaded barrel. Y'all know about threaded barrels?"

"Yeah, we know," said Malandrino

"Anyway, I got a .45 with a threaded barrel, and Montague secured a threaded barrel adapter. Y'all know about threaded barrel adapters? 1/2 X 28 on the female part? 3/4 X 16 on the male end?"

"Yeah, we know about adapters," said Flint.

"Good, because you're both going to love this part. I went to West Ashley Auto Parts and bought a Wix oil filter with the same thread pattern as the male end of the adapter and hooked that sucker up with a couple of flat rubber washers to stop the blow back, then when The Asshole, the sorry motherfucker, Captain Mark Ward came at me, I unloaded a fifteen round mag of JHPs right in his chest. He was dead as a hammer when he hit the floor. Then I put on Freddie's boots and kicked his head until all but one of his teeth fell out, dragged his body to The Merch, capped the one tooth, and put all that voodoo shot around him so people would think he'd been murdered by a bunch of black people."

"Did you say fifteen rounds?" Malandrino said.

"Yes, why? How many bullets did you find?" Kela said.

"Seven, actually," said Flint.

"Only seven? I could've sworn I used a high capacity magazine. You know, like the ones they use on NCIS." Kela looked up, counting her fingers.

"Fifteen round magazines for handguns didn't exist in 1970," said Malandrino.

"Well, I must've lost count after the first three or four rounds. If you hear one loud bang you've heard them all. But trust me, if I'd had fifteen rounds, I would've shot him fifteen times."

"I have no doubt," said Malandrino.

"How'd you come by Freddie's boots?" Flint sipped his drink.

"Took them after I shot him, just before he became crab bait," Kela said.

They stared at her like they'd just seen Janis Joplin's closing number before the encore.

"So cuff me," Kela extended her wrists. "I'm ready to pay my debt to society."

"And Thigpen? What'd you say about him?" Malandrino looked at Flint.

"One to the head with the 30.06. I left him in the marsh where he fell. Went back while Josie was in the hospital. What the buzzards didn't get, the raccoons, possums, and crabs did."

"And you did all this by yourself?" Flint said. "Nobody helped you?"

"Well …, I did have help… But no other 'person' as in 'human being' helped me."

Both men put their drinks on the coffee table.

"Can y'all keep a secret? If I tell you the truth will you promise you won't let our neighbors find out? People around here talk enough as it is, and the last thing we need are the neighbors thinking I'm crazy. There's a gracious plenty of crazy people in Charleston as it is, without adding Josie and me to the list."

Flint elbowed Malandrino, they turned to me, I shrugged my shoulders. Flint said, "You have our word. We won't say anything to your neighbors."

Kela looked out the window, then leaned toward them and whispered like there might be somebody else in the room eves dropping. "Even though I'm not what you'd call a big girl, I have supernatural powers." The two men were motionless. "When I'm invisible, I have superhuman strength. That's how, at 5'6" and 117 pounds, give or take, I was able to kill all three men, dispose of their bodies, in three different locations, and within a thirty mile radius of Charleston, all in one night, by myself with no outside help." Kela sat back with her hands in her lap. "And I'm ready to put it all in writing, swear to it in court, and testify to the Navy high command. Who knows, NCIS the TV show might want to buy the story and I'd finally get to meet Mark Harmon." Kela winked, then patted me a couple good slaps on the knee. "You don't mind my having a crush on Mark Harmon, do you Babe?"

"Nnn-oope," I said.

"So how are we going to do this? Do I write it all down, or do you record it, then I sign off on a transcription. I'm ready to make a full confession. Pay my debt to society and move on with my life." Kela patted my knee again. "You'll wait for me, won't you Babe?"

"I don't know about you, but I'm worn out," Malandrino said to Flint.

"Yeah," said Flint, "pretty much settles it for me."

Kela, smiling, "Good, then it's settled," once again offering her wrists.

Both Flint and Malandrino drained their glasses, rubbed their faces with their hands, laughing, uncontrollably.

"What's so funny?" Kela smiled. "Y'all think I'm joking, you think I made all this up?"

"Please, I'm begging you, Mrs. Chapman, let us out of here before we lose ..." Flint was struggling.

"What? Your jobs? Here you have a golden opportunity to solve three murders at once and y'all aren't going to cuff me and take me to jail?"

"Lose our jobs? Yes ma'am. among other things," said Malandrino.

"Like our sanity," said Flint. He and Malandrino stood up.

"Guess I'm not going to meet Mark Harmon after all," Kela said.

"I'm afraid not, ma'am," said Flint.

"Well, have it your way, then," Kela hugged them, giving each man a kiss on the cheek. "But you can't say I didn't level with you."

"No, ma'am, we can't say that," said Malandrino. "What would you like for us to do with your late husband's remains?"

"You mean The Asshole's bones?" Kela said.

"We have to ask," said Flint.

Kela motioned for me to splash a bit of scotch in the four glasses.

"Would you two fine gentlemen mind doing me one last favor before we conclude this matter?"

The two men threw a questioning glance toward me; I winked at them.

"Josie, put a glass in each of their hands," she said. I passed them the drinks. She picked up hers, I picked up mine. "Now, I want you two sterling representatives of The United States Navy to ask me again, but this time instead of saying 'my late husband's remains' I want you to throw back your shots and say, 'The Asshole's bones.' Would you do that for me? In unison."

Flint's tears ran down his cheeks. "You aren't recording this are you?"

"Of course not," Kela said. "What good would it do? I'm making a memory." She put her hand over her heart. "Trying to get some closure."

Malandrino almost choked, then stared at the floor shaking his head. "Let's do this."

The two men stood erect, tossed back the scotch, and as if they'd rehearsed beforehand and repeated in unison, "Mrs. Chapman, on behalf of the United States Navy, what would you like us to do with The Asshole's bones?"

Kela smiled, threw back her drink. "Bag 'em up, dump 'em in the river, see if any float."

The two men leaned on each other for support. I patted both on the back.

"Can I fix you fellas a traveler?" I said. Apparently they were unfamiliar with the term.

"That's Charlestonian lingo. It means 'one for the road?'" Kela said.

"No, no, please, let us get to our van, and we'll be on our way," said Flint.

I walked them to the SUV with a measure of relief few men know.

"You are one lucky man," Flint said.

"Luck's got nothing to do with it. She and I were born to be together."

"Here, I almost forgot," said Malandrino. He reached back into the briefcase and gave me a little snack sized zip lock bag with a piece of polished white bone in it.

"What's this?" I said.

"Just something we found during our investigation of the crime scene."

"You mean you found it at The Merch? Specifically?" I said.

"Yes, you know, the area around where the body was discovered."

"I ask, because the entire city of Charleston is all one big crime scene."

"He means this particular crime scene," Flint giggled.

"Are you two OK to drive?" I said.

"It was lying beside the body. Forensics said it was feline metacarpal," Malandrino said.

"Yeah, we're fine," Flint flexed his neck muscles.

"We figured a cat must've gotten trapped under the building sometime over the years and died next to the corpse." This time Malandrino started giggling. "What the rats didn't get, ants and roaches probably did."

Flint, picking up on Malandrino's giggle fit, wiped his eyes. "We couldn't figure out why a decomposing body didn't stink. You didn't smell anything while you were there?"

"Nothing more than spilled beer, never one complaint from a customer."

"Forensics even said the bones appeared to have been bleached, or boiled, but there was no chlorine and the skeleton was completely intact." Malandrino applied a handkerchief to his eyes.

"Which couldn't have happened because of the position of the body," said Flint.

"Gentlemen, your guess is as good as mine."

"Thanks for all your help Mr. Chapman," Flint said.

"Well, thanks, I'll keep this as a memento. There was a time, you know?"

"I'm sure there was, Mr. Chapman, I just have one more question," said Flint. "When your wife suggested throwing," Flint elbowed Malandrino, "The Asshole's bones in the river and see if any of them float, do you have any idea what she was referring to?"

"No idea," I said.

"You and your wife have a wonderful day, sir," Malandrino said.

I put the plastic bag in my pants pocket as the SUV pulled out of sight.

———

Back in the house, my beautiful house, I found my wife, my beautiful wife, making a grit bowl. A grit bowl is a bowl of grits with a handful of crushed bacon stirred in, topped with a couple scrambled eggs. I came up behind her and wrapped my arms around her waist. I kissed her on the back of the neck and felt the chill go through her.

Now listen to me carefully, I'm giving you another one for free: Never, ever underestimate the power of a kiss on the back of a woman's neck.

"You were amazing," I said, warping my arms around her waist while kissing her neck.

"I thought you'd like it. I can still work a room you know?"

"You really had those two going."

"Before I cook breakfast, will you do me a favor?" Kela whispered.

"Anything."

"Will you take me to bed?"

"It will be an honor."

"Just like old times?"

"Absolutely."

I got undressed while Kela slipped into a black see-through teddy. It'd been a week since we'd made love, and even though we were both in our sixties the passion of our youth had never left us. We crawled under the sheets and did what married couples have done for centuries, and judging from the internet, we did it as well as any couple a third our age. Lying in bed, in the warm afterglow, her head on my shoulder, I thought how truly blessed we were to have each other and share such an extraordinary life.

"You hungry?" She nuzzled my neck.

"I just ate."

Kela purred, "Well, so did I, but now I want bacon, eggs and grits."

She slipped into her robe, then padded down stairs. I put on my pants, my watch, and was slipping my wallet in my front pocket, when my fingers touched the baggy containing the bone. I set it on the dresser and opened Kela's jewelry box where I kept my wedding band. The silver teaspoon with the bone handle, the one Abraham had given Kela all those years ago lay in an indented section molded for a spoon exactly that size. When I compared the two bones, they were identical.

A whiff of frying bacon floated up from the kitchen. Kela was scrambling the eggs as I pulled up a chair at the bar. I laid the bag on the counter like it was the morning mail.

"One egg or two?" she said.

"One is fine."

"No morning paper?"

"It got wet, landed in the bird bath."

Kela set the bowls on a white wicker tray along with coffee cups, toast and tossed a couple sprigs of parsley over sliced strawberries and orange wedges. She placed the tray directly in front of me, inches from the bone.

"Let's eat in the sun room," she said. "You carry this, I'll bring the coffee."

The sunroom was warm, the plants were green, and as she set the table her robe opened revealing her body delicately shaded by the black lace teddy. Morning sex, hot grits, and a black teddy, breakfast doesn't get any better.

"I never cease to be amazed at how good you look," I said.

"You mean for a woman my age?"

"I didn't say that."

"But you were thinking it."

"How do you know what I was thinking? I didn't invite you in?"

"You let your shields down, Sunshine, and I looked right through you."

"If I can't trust you then I might as well hang it up," I said.

"Good point. Now, are you going to ask me before breakfast or after?"

"Ask you what?"

"If I brutally murdered The Asshole?"

"Did you?"

"What do you think?" She sipped her coffee, "you've got your shields up, so I can't see."

"You've had your shields up since you got home."

"Would it make any difference, one way or another?"

"I guess not."

"You guess? You don't know?" She chased a spoon full of grits with coffee.

"How should I say this ... ?"

"Make it romantic, just for me." She steepled her fingers.

I ate about half of what was on my plate, thinking about how I was going to satisfy my curiosity without blowing up a beautiful day. I folded my napkin, freshened my coffee, and leaned back in the chair.

"Considering that you, my darling, embody the essence of every delicate, feminine sensibility a man could want. I find it difficult to visualize you carrying out the deed the way you described it to those agents."

"You like the first one better, with Freddie's doing him?"

"Well, that version explains the boot toe blades."

"You're right, I hadn't thought of that," she said.

"It makes more sense than your personalized version."

"Yes, it does, because if you believe I acted alone, you'd also have to assume I killed Freddie, stole his boots, and dumped his body, before I killed Mark and buried him under The Merch. Unless Freddie had two pairs of boots and I somehow managed to steal one."

"You left out Thigpen."

"Right, I would've had to kill him, too."

"And ditch the bodies."

"Yes, there's that."

"That's a hell of a gig even for someone as tough as you were back then."

"What you mean back then?" Her bare toes climbed my pant leg. "I'm still pretty tough."

"You're definitely still pretty, I'll give you that; tough I'm not so sure."

"I'm tough enough for you."

"Yes, you are," I said. "Which reminds me, and I don't know why, but have you ever heard the name Albert Wigfall?"

"I knew an Alberta Wigfall. She was Abraham Williams' grandmother. She's been dead for years. We called her Little Bertie. Why do you ask?"

"The name came up when the Feds were interrogating me. I'd forgotten all about it until I started writing. No big deal. I have to pee," I said. "I'll be right back."

It would take a level of mental gymnastics way above my pay grade to imagine this woman I'd loved and trusted with my life, for forty-four years, brutally murdering three ruthless gangsters twice her size, and walking away without a scratch. Unless, she'd had help.

A vision of Freddie's boots flashed in my mind. The two blades, F.M. scrolled into the leather right above the ankle were the last images I'd seen before he tried to crush my skull. He'd worn those every night at The Merch. If Freddie had had a second pair he would've showed them off. He also wouldn't have buried such a piece of self-incriminating evidence, along with the body. Freddie might not've been God's gift to the gene pool of intelligence, but he wasn't stupid.

Back upstairs, I grabbed my iPad, went in the bathroom and shut the door. I Googled Black Cat Bone + Hoodoo + Properties. Wikipedia was the first search result: "It is thought to insure etc…romantic success." The word "invisibility" leaped off the screen. So that's why Mark Ward was so interested in the location of Williams' body. He must've thought Bootsy had a black cat bone just like Kela's. It also explained why Ward was afraid of his wife; why he'd beaten her. He wanted that damn bone. The one I'd just left on the counter. A cold chill ran down my spine.

Back downstairs, I turned the corner, Kela didn't see me come into the kitchen. She didn't know I saw her slip the baggy into the pocket of her robe. I waited for her to turn around.

"I didn't hear you come in," she said. "How long have you been there?"

"Long enough," I said. "I know you did it. And I know how you did it?"

"Then you also know why I did it."

I pulled her close, she held her breasts against my chest, her arms around my neck, for longer than I can remember, until she whispered, "What are we going to do?"

I held her face in my hands, stared into her eyes, and kissed her until all her shields were down. When she relaxed completely, I searched her mind as she searched mine. I pulled the little black cat bone from the pocket of her robe, turned it over in my hand, studying every facet of the surface. I put my lips close to her ear until our breathing became as one, and whispered, "Improvise."

EPILOGUE

Six Months Later

You think you know somebody. You think you understand a person. Your life-long friends, your coworkers, even your family. Truth is the only person you have a real chance of knowing is yourself. Because your "self" is who you spend most of your time with. A lot of people don't even know themselves as well as they think they do. So, how can they think they know anyone else? And if you only live in your own mind, then just remember, you're living behind enemy lines. That's why I believe there's a lot to be said for the institution of marriage; having a soul mate to bounce ideas off. I love knowing who I'm going to spend the rest of my life with.

But, in the light of these recent revelations, I'd be lying if I said I didn't have a few unanswered questions. Coming to grips with what Kela had done to Mark all those years ago didn't change my feelings for her. If anything I loved her even more. Which honestly, I didn't think was possible. But I didn't know her as well as I thought I did; still don't, even after all these years.

I certainly don't blame her for killing him. God knows, I should've killed him myself. Because if ever there was a man who needed killing it was Mark Ward and the more brutal the better as far as I was concerned. No women should have to suffer physical abuse from a man; I don't give a damn how important his job is to society. But until Ward's remains were discovered, I actually believed he'd left the country and Kela had nothing to do with his disappearance. I'm proud of her for standing up for her "self" after I'd refused to get involved in her personal relationship with Mark. Especially since not once did she ever hint she wanted my help in dealing directly with her husband.

Out of respect for me she even went along with the two of us not sleeping together during the year it took for her divorce on the grounds of abandonment.

She was probably laughing inside the whole time. Because when I think about how naïve and stupid I was back then, before my "edgy'cation" was complete, it is kinda of funny. We were married the same day her divorce was finalized. And I've cherished every minute of our time together.

Still, Kela never did come right out and tell me the straight up details. She was employing that great trick all women know: Just be vague and let them come to their own conclusions. There was the whole 'whatever really happened to Freddie May' issue. How did Freddie's boots end up next to Ward's battered skull? Did she kill Thigpen, too? Or did someone else kill him? Did she have help? Where did Janet Collins run off to? I sure as hell didn't know Kela knew how to silence a .45 using an oil filter. She's her own person and some of the things that go on in that pretty head of hers I'm sure I'll never understand.

If she brings up the subject we'll discuss it. Until she does, I'm not going to push her. As the song goes, "If you haven't found it yet, I guess some things are better left alone."

To be clear, then, it's not what she did to her husband, or any of the other players, but how she managed to pull it off. That's what I was having the most trouble getting my mind around. I simply couldn't accept that she acted alone. She was half her husband's size and at least eight inches shorter. I figured she must have had help and the only person I could think of was Montague Bonneau. Initially, the thought my two closest soul travelers being involved in three brutal murders, didn't piss me off so much as hurt my feelings. An issue like this required some thinking through, and I'd been thinking through it for months without saying anything.

And I was still thinking about it while driving to Haddrell's Point in Mt. Pleasant when I looked around and I realized a car show was in town. I had no idea where the event was being held, but the old cars were everywhere and I was impressed by the vanity plates. Vanity plates only allow seven letters. Some of the owners had gotten very creative since most of the more obvious names were taken. For instance, one 1964 Pontiac GTO had this plate: 1964GTO, while another

GTO had 64-GOAT. Some owners name their cars the way people might name a pet, or a piece of art. A '49 Mercury painted Caspian Blue caught my attention because it was the color of my '65 Thunderbird. The vanity plate read BLUEBOY.

The day was bright, crisp and clean. I'd pulled up behind a '75 Coupe Deville named SLORIDE at East Bay and Columbus. The car was sitting beside an Anointed Bateau Mission, stake body truck, just like the one used to haul the furniture from The Merch. An immaculate, perfectly restored, black 1968 Buick Electra 225 pulled up behind the truck, which, of course, put it right next to me. There were two older black men sporting Fedoras sitting up front with the Philly lean down cold. They were talking in low tones and smiling, which got me to thinking about how the old Charleston is still here. Hard bopping down the sidewalks. You just have to look for it. Also, it helps if you know what you're looking for. The men must've realized I was staring at them, because the one in the passenger seat turned toward me and smiled, revealing a gold capped tooth. My heart stopped when I realized I was staring into the face of Abraham Williams. He nodded toward me, the driver leaned forward and winked. "Bootsy?" The light changed, the cars pulled forward, both men raised an index finger, almost, but not quite, touching their brims. The Buick eased through the light followed by a taxi. I tried to change lanes. I wanted to follow them, but I'd already committed to the on ramp over the Ravenel Bridge and the traffic was unforgiving. SLORIDE was living up to its name. Within half a block of following the black car, the Buick's turn signal lit up. They were taking a left on Cooper heading toward America where a topographical hump runs north and south along Drake Street one block down.

The hump is subtle enough so you don't notice the change in elevation, but you can't see down any of those streets. Cars taking a left off East Bay go up the small elevation, down the other side, then disappear. So I slowed, hoping for one last look, when a third passenger in the back seat turned, smiled, and waved. The passenger was Montague.

As the tail end of the car lifted up at the hump, he pointed toward the trunk, indicating he wanted me to look down. I only had a second before they disappeared, but a second was long enough. The Electra had a vanity plate, and what the letters spelled was this: NTMAYOR.

Even so, even after all the drama, I'm still not sure how I feel about Kela's killing her husband and keeping it a secret from me all these years. I don't know why she felt she couldn't tell me. The fact is, when you stand the truth straight up; it's really none of my business. Because, regardless of what the neighbors might say, a secret shared between a man and his wife is nobody's business but their own. But after spending forty-four years married to Kela, and putting into practice so many of the things I've learned from her, there are a few things I am damn sure about: The truth is whatever you believe it is. We are all drawn out and enticed by our own desires. The only meaning anything has is the meaning we give it. And last but certainly not least, if it's not worth dying for, it's not worth fighting over.

However, when confrontation is inevitable, there's no dishonor in striking before you're struck. Just make sure you never ever draw the sword without drawing somebody's blood, even if you have to cut yourself before you sheath it. Then maybe, next time, you won't forget.

ABOUT THE AUTHOR

Born in 1947 J. Nelson Eldridge has been telling stories since he learned to talk. As a toddler, he had an imaginary friend named Richard, who told him stories until Jimmy became fully self-aware somewhere around the second grade, when he started making up his own stories to entertain his playmates, classmates and teachers. Known to family and friends by his stage name, Jimmy Hager, from the age of fourteen to age twenty-seven; he played rock and roll saxophone in various South Carolina bands. During this time Jimmy's groups opened for Jerry Lee Lewis, Janis Joplin, Chicago, The Allman Brothers, Poco, and virtually every major soul and rock act touring America from 1963 until 1972. When his friend Duane Allman died tragically, Jimmy quit touring, moved back to Charleston and got married. He became a public speaker, got his degree in English from The College of Charleston, all while becoming a self-taught Faux Finish Artist. Specializing in high-end interior painted finishes in the historic district of Charleston, SC, his expertise lead to authoring a book on the craft, *The Faux Finish Artist: Professional Decorative Painting Secrets*, which is available on Amazon. Divorced in 1998, Jimmy decided to give acting a go and after his first audition was cast as Atticus Finch in the Charleston Stage Production of *To Kill A Mockingbird* at the historic Dock Street Theater. During his acting career, he appeared in dozens of stage plays, over one hundred television commercials and twenty films. Working with film legends such as Gale Anne Hurd, Julia Ormond, Jim Caviezel, Sam Shepard, Joe Anderson, Danielle Panabaker, Michael Landon, Jr. and Brian Bird. He lives in Columbia, SC with his wife Joanne and their spoiled rotten English Cocker Spaniel Berkeley. *The Merch* is his first novel and first creative work under his birth name J. Nelson "Jimmy" Eldridge.

CPSIA information can be obtained
at www.ICGtesting.com
Printed in the USA
LVHW040400130820
663046LV00004B/1308